PRAISE FOR *TO CHASE THE GLOWING HOURS*

"Kirkpatrick tells the grandest archaeological story: the discovery of King Tutankhamun's tomb. She perfectly conveys the thrill of the chase and its tumultuous aftermath while immersing us in Egypt's rich and mysterious culture."

—John Van Auken, author of *Ancient Egyptian Visions of Our Soul Life* and Director of Archaeological Research at the Association for Research and Enlightenment (A.R.E.)

"Lady Eve of Highclere Castle is a plucky Jazz Age heroine whose real-life adventures lead her through geopolitical intrigue, romantic entanglements, and the dazzling mysteries of the Valley of the Kings. Drawing on deep historical research and scandalous newly discovered letters, *To Chase the Glowing Hours* evokes the excitement of *Raiders of the Lost Ark* and the glamour of *Downton Abbey*, with a dash of Agatha Christie's suspense. It's a thrilling read!"

—Debby Applegate, Pulitzer Prize-winning author of *Madam: The Biography of Polly Adler, Icon of the Jazz Age*

"An archaeological romance full of Roaring Twenties glamor and grit, made all the more fascinating for being based in truth. Kirkpatrick brings the discovery of King Tutankhamun's tomb to life through the sharp and wondering eyes of the youthful ingenue Lady Evelyn Herbert, in a tribute to treasure."

—Elizabeth Wein, author of the *New York Times* bestseller *Code Name Verity*

"A compelling love story set in 1922 and based on the history of the daughter of an earl who falls in love with both the 3000-year-old Egyptian tomb of King Tut and the handsome, brooding archaeologist who discovered it. All of Egypt springs to life in the pages of this book: the decimating heat, the poverty, the riots, and the magical treasures found in the earth. I read until the early hours of the morning, unable to put it down. A joy to read. Highest recommendation."

—Stephanie Cowell, author of *The Boy in the Rain, The Man in the Stone Cottage: A Novel of the Brontë Sisters,* and *Claude & Camille*

"*To Chase the Glowing Hours* brings to vivid life the remarkable 1922 discovery of King Tutankhamun's tomb in Egypt's Valley of the Kings... A romantic, beguiling story steeped in historical truth and Jazz Age hopes and dreams."

—Gioia Diliberto, author of *Coco at the Ritz*

"Katherine Kirkpatrick delivers a meticulously researched, unabashedly romantic story. Told from the point of view of the plucky, privileged, and beautiful Lady Evelyn, daughter of the Fifth Earl of Carnarvon and Lord of Highclere Castle (familiar to us as the setting for *Downton Abbey*), *To Chase the Glowing Hours* lets readers experience the thrill of the biggest, most dazzling archaeological discovery of the 20th century... [A] made-for-a-miniseries slice of history."

—Barbara Quick, author of *Vivaldi's Virgins* and *What Disappears*

"Evoking Lady Evelyn's memories of the most fantastic archaeological find of all time, *To Chase the Glowing Hours* captures the excitement of discovery in 1920s Egypt during the opening of King Tutankhamun's tomb. Katherine Kirkpatrick doesn't shy away from exploring complex issues surrounding competing national loyalties and colonial attitudes. A rich and immersive reading experience, glowing with adventure and personal reflection, that will transport the reader to a bygone era whose echoes are as relevant as ever today."

—Mitchell James Kaplan, author of *By Fire, By Water, Into the Unbounded Night,* and *Rhapsody*

"[A] stunning achievement. Kirkpatrick has created a captivating love story and exciting adventure saga rooted in the facts of one of the world's most dazzling archaeological discoveries."

—Barbara Weisberg, author of *Strong Passions: A Scandalous Divorce in Old New York*

"Imagine being the first to set eyes on the treasures of King Tut's tomb. Katherine Kirkpatrick brings that moment to life in *To Chase the Glowing Hours*. Through Lady Eve, the twenty-one-year-old daughter of eccentric, amateur Egyptologist Lord Carnarvon, and the brilliant and temperamental archaeologist Howard Carter, the novel explores the heady days of discovery, and the complications of privilege, nationalism, and love. Richly drawn and well-researched, this glimpse into the historic discovery and its complicated consequences will thrill readers and archaeology buffs alike."

—Judith Lindbergh, author of *Akmaral*

"A work of meticulous research, combined with the novelist's attention to people and places, makes this book not only a huge contribution to educational enlightenment but an entertaining account of one of the great archeological discoveries of our century."

—Andrea Simon, author of *Bashert: A Granddaughter's Holocaust Quest, Esfir Is Alive*, and *Floating in the Neversink*

"[Lady Eve] is spunky and unforgettable, and her times marked the beginning of significant change in women's roles. *To Chase the Golden Hours* is impressively researched and told with confidence and great energy."

—Kathleen Novak, author of *Come Back, I Love You [A Ghost Story]*, and *Steel*

To Chase the Glowing Hours

A Novel of Highclere and Egypt

Katherine Kirkpatrick

Regal House Publishing

Published by
Regal House Publishing, LLC
Raleigh, NC 27605
All rights reserved

ISBN -13 (paperback): 9781646036271
ISBN -13 (epub): 9781646036288
Library of Congress Control Number: 2024950446

Cover images and design by © studiochi.art

Printed in the United States of America

Regal House Publishing, LLC
https://regalhousepublishing.com

Lovingly dedicated to my sister and brother:
Jennifer Alice Kirkpatrick
and
Sidney Dale Kirkpatrick III

On with the dance! let joy be unconfined;
No sleep till morn, when youth and pleasure meet
To chase the glowing hours with flying feet.

—Lord Byron

PROLOGUE

The fifty-year-old telegram, browned to the color of a mummy's skin, flutters out of her hand as she takes it from her father's Egyptian cigar box. As if the brittle scrap of paper has a life of its own, it loops before it glides to the floor.

Lady Evelyn bends to reach for the paper. She reads:

6 November 1922
To Lord Carnarvon, Highclere Castle
At last have made wonderful discovery in Valley; a magnificent tomb with seals intact. Re-covered same for your arrival; congratulations.
Carter

Half a century later, Eve feels the blood rushing through her veins as if she hears the news for the first time.

She sorts through the photographs in the box and finds the one she is looking for, taken the afternoon she arrived in Cairo. How young she was—twenty-one. Beautiful, and she knew it; her smile shows it. She was lanky then, almost flat-chested, with her dark hair in a stylish bob. That day she wore a white, dropped-waist dress, all the rage, with a wide-brimmed hat. Heels, silk, pointed. Frightfully impractical (where did she think she was going in *those* shoes?). She carried pink roses. Roses in Egypt, yes, by God. For her, an earl's daughter, anything was done. Occasionally, she appreciated the efforts.

There was her father, Lord Carnarvon, cane in hand, striped jacket, too-big trousers belted in to compensate for the weight he'd lost. For someone so ill and frail, it was astonishing how energetic he was. Always the charmer, he curled his mustache up at the ends.

Her gaze turns to the man standing on her left. Howard Carter looked so hopeful. Indeed, he was on the brink of a great discovery, which was why he'd summoned her father to Egypt. There they were, the three of them, so eager to solve the ancient riddle; they had no idea of the price they'd pay.

How handsome Carter looked then. Muscular. Filling out his white linen suit. So strong, he could have moved a stone sphinx. Tanned. A full mustache. He had thick, straight black hair. This was the day she first took notice of him as anything other than an adored uncle of sorts, who worked for her father. Carter was over twenty years her senior. Working-class. Driven. Volatile at times. Talented and brilliant. He was quite simply the most extraordinary person she had ever met. There was no one in the world more knowledgeable about Egyptology. More than that, the man was magical, so in tune with the ancients that in his company she could occasionally glimpse the Middle Kingdom.

She drops the old telegram again and watches it twirl across the room. She pauses before picking it up, distracted by her thoughts. On this day of days, the grand exhibition opens at the British Museum. She feels the magic stirring. Today, as she remembers those long-ago times with Howard Carter, the air is luminous with possibility. Today, the sky shimmers with gold.

1

She presses her eyes into field glasses. Dozens of small craft dot a sea the color of turquoise. Their triangular sails, arching in the wind, glow white in the bright sunlight of the early morning. Enormous flocks of gulls circle the sky with riotous calls. The P&O *Sobroan* cuts through the surf with low, steady throbs; under her feet, she feels the vibration of the steamer's engines and the swelling of the waves. Just ahead, the mosaic of pink and yellow squares transforms into a city. Small homes tucked into green hills. Whitewashed hotels. Mosques. Colonnaded public buildings. Alexandria.

With a deep inhalation, Eve enjoys the warmth of the sunlight and the cool, fresh air, and she takes in all that is ancient and all that is very new. At long last, she's arrived in Egypt. This view makes the maddening slowness of the vessel and those tedious evenings of cards and parlor games with elderly passengers worthwhile.

The engines silence, there's quiet for one blessed minute, then the ship's horn blasts with a sound that could wake the city's patriarchs in their tombs of cold marble. Eve stuffs the field glasses into their leather case and pushes them into her satchel. She wheels around just in time to see her father, Lord Carnarvon, leaning far over the ship's balustrade with his box camera. It is a lovely modern thing, that camera, red Spanish mahogany with brass fittings, with bellows that expand and contract like an accordion. Her father's so taken up with photographing that he forgets himself. Beside him hovers his loyal valet, Fearnside, one hand on the shiny bronze rail and the other gripping the arm of his master.

Eve rushes toward them. "Father!" she calls. "Hold on to the rail! Hand me that camera!"

Carnarvon turns. Eve sees the shocked look on his blotchy face at the moment when the horn sounds again. With a great jolt, the steamer drifts into the pilings. Too late. Her father falls backward onto the deck. Before Eve can get to him, Fearnside helps Carnarvon to his feet and into a deck chair. Eve retrieves Carnarvon's rumpled canvas hat and the camera, which, like her father, are worse for wear but remarkably intact.

"You've had a rough landing, Father," Eve says.

Carnarvon gasps for air, but soon he's himself again, his breath even, his blue eyes lively. He gives Eve one of the mischievous grins she loves so well. His smile is ever so slightly askew, since his jaws were reset after an automobile accident that nearly killed him when she was an infant. Since then, he's smashed up four other sports cars. "I'm perfectly all right, my dear. A bit of a tumble."

Eve and the valet exchange glances. She sighs, loudly, a bit too dramatically, as her mother would do. She doesn't blame Fearnside for the fall; he would have kept her father safely ensconced on a cushioned bench if he could have. Carnarvon heeds no one. Even though she and Fearnside constantly watch out for him, her father has frequent mishaps. And they still have ahead of them a four-hour train trip to Cairo, another tedious day's journey by train to Luxor, a passage across the Nile, and on top of all that, a miserable, slow donkey ride across the desert.

Eve, Carnarvon, and Fearnside manage to find a coach that will take them to the train station. No detours to Eve's favorite childhood sites: the Roman amphitheater and the pink granite sphinx. Her father's hired archaeologist, Howard Carter, waits in Cairo to accompany them to Luxor and on to the Valley of the Kings. If there's any chance at all that Carter has found a royal tomb, they had best be there before thieves try to take its contents or the Egyptian government becomes involved.

En route to Cairo, Eve feels drained by the heat and closes her eyes while Carnarvon dozes. The back-and-forth shimmy of the train and the hypnotic moving view of the too-bright sky over the green fields of sugarcane put Eve to sleep.

It isn't long before Fearnside shakes her awake. "We're almost there, Lady Eve."

In the train's washroom, she brushes her glossy brunette hair, recently cut into a smart bob. She pinches her cheeks and smooths her wrinkled white linen frock, which ends fashionably just below the knees in a row of pleats.

The train stops, and a porter swings open the door. Together, Eve and Fearnside help Carnarvon down the steps of the train. On even ground, he clutches his cane. "Carter!" he calls out.

Eve scans the platform of dark-skinned, robed people and sees, right before her, Carter's deeply tanned face. He is just as she recalls him: fit, stocky, muscular, wearing a wrinkled white linen suit and a bowler hat. His mustache is trimmed. His piercing dark eyes show his intense and mercurial disposition. She has idolized him for the many years her father has been funding his digs and has tried to follow in his footsteps—to the extent her upbringing allows. She has studied *First Steps in Egyptian Hieroglyphics* by Sir Ernest Alfred Thompson Wallis Budge, frequently visited the British Museum, and sketched the artifacts in her father's collection at Highclere. She treasures every gift Carter has ever brought her on his visits, especially a bright blue pottery statuette of a hippopotamus.

Carter's outward appearance hasn't changed. But this morning, the archaeologist glows with a joyous pride that makes him more striking than Eve remembers. He seems more youthful, too, like a man in his thirties, not approaching fifty.

"Carnarvon! You're here at last," he says to her father. To Eve he says, "Lady Eve, so glad you've come."

She wonders if this is true. The man doesn't like distractions from his work. "A delight to see you, Mr. Carter."

From a leather bag, he takes out a bouquet of pink roses and settles them into her arms. Remarkably, the flowers have not yet wilted in the heat.

"Thank you!" She beams. Of course, the gift of flowers for a lady arriving at her destination is customary. Yet she has always thought the archaeologist to be oblivious of anything other than his scholarship.

"Darling, I must photograph you with those roses," Carnarvon tells Eve. "Where the devil did you get them, Carter?"

Carter gives him a playful look.

A Nubian porter wearing flowing white robes moves the group's suitcases from the train onto a low wagon. From a padded bag, Fearnside takes out the camera and unfolds it.

Eve is eager to leave the station, but she will comply with her father's wishes—she almost always does. "Father, for once, you must be in the picture with me," Eve says, knowing this means he'll have to allow Fearnside to handle his camera.

"All right. Jolly good," he says. "Carter, you, too." Carnarvon instructs his valet how to operate the levers that set the shutter speed and allow the lens to drop into place. Carnarvon and Carter position themselves on either side of Eve. Fearnside grins as he holds the camera at waist level and peers through the viewfinder. With a clink and a thump, the day is recorded for posterity.

The group follows the porter out of the station into the heat and dazzling sun of a crowded plaza overlooking a canal. Speaking fluent Arabic, Carter arranges for two carriages, called *hantoors*, to take their party to the Grand Continental Hotel. Fearnside will depart first with the bags and roses. Eve observes how Carter deals with the robed Egyptian coachmen in case she ever needs to hire one on her own. The draft horses, sepia brown with brown manes, look gaunt to her. At the same time, because she's a Carnarvon and her family owns the famous Highclere Stud, Eve knows that some breeds of working horses are not heavyset. Egypt's native Baladi lack elegance and well-defined bloodlines, though their coats come in a wide variety of attractive colors.

In the *hantoor*, Eve and Carnarvon share a seat facing the archaeologist. A black collapsible leather hood stretches over their heads. The driver pulls back on the reins, and the carriage jolts forward onto the main avenue, Sharia Nubar Pasha.

All around them, Cairo flaunts its exotic splendor—domes, towers, medieval mosques. It is so very different from London. The *hantoor* presses past donkey carts and an automobile, its top down, driven by an English gentleman in a top hat. How oddly formal he looks. Everywhere are crowds of robed men and boys, with only an occasional veiled woman or girl. It's awful, Eve thinks, for women to be kept mostly at home, and to be robed from head to toe in this heat if they ever appear in public.

The driver detours onto narrow streets flanked by two-story orange tenements. A horrid odor of urine rises. Roosters scratch in a heap of trash. Under the shade of a tamarind tree, several robed men sleep on the ground. It is this sort of poverty that keeps Eve's mother from returning to Egypt. In England, her mother founded a hospital. Here, what can be done? Not one blessed thing.

Carter speaks to the driver, then explains. "We've gone 'round due to the crowds."

Stalled behind donkey carts, the carriage slows. Carnarvon wipes sweat from his forehead with his handkerchief. Eve turns to the archaeologist. "Tell us, Mr. Carter, how you made the discovery."

Carter relates how, several weeks earlier, he dismantled the stone foundations of ancient huts near the tomb of Ramesses VI. He instructed his team to dig below the place where the huts had been. A water boy, clearing rubble for a place to set his water jar, found the top step of a limestone stairway. Carter dug out many more steps. To his astonishment, he uncovered the uppermost section of a walled-off doorway. Smoothed over with plaster, the partition is imprinted with large clay stamps—seals with hieroglyphs on them.

"The seals indicate a *royal necropolis?*" Carnarvon asks.

Carter says, "Yes, I feel almost sure."

"I'm more thrilled than I can say, Mr. Carter," Eve gushes. The archaeologist's discovery is the most exciting thing she's experienced in her whole life. She's not sorry to be missing the London season's balls because of it. "Thank you for waiting for us before excavating further."

"I told myself, Carnarvon needs to share this adventure, so I stopped," Carter says.

Eve knows he is grateful for her father's funding, which, if not for this discovery, would be ending in a few months. After fifteen years of support, Carter has found very little of marketable value. Eve's mother, and her brother, Lord Porchester (Porchey), continually chide Carnarvon over the fortune he has spent on his Egyptian digs. Carnarvon nearly cut off Carter last spring, then decided to give him one last chance to excavate.

The *hantoor* turns onto Sharia Kamel Pasha Street, lined with spreading lebbek trees, and into a fine neighborhood of four-and five-story white houses with balconies. On their bottom level are shops and eateries shaded by awnings. Enticing aromas of onion, garlic, and curry waft out from the open windows and doors. Eve sees the walls of a restaurant decorated, incongruously, with posters of Charlie Chaplin and other film stars. The palms and the tall, pod-laden lebbek trees make this area of the city feel cooler, a most welcome change.

Before long, the view opens up to El Opera Square. The statue of General Ibrahim Pasha, one of Viceroy Muhammad Ali's sons, straddling a horse, looms in the distance. At the sound of shouting, Eve tenses. Men in white robes crowd around the statue and the adjacent fountain. A man with a long beard, speaking from the base of the statue, appears to lead the others. Something about him terrifies her to the bone. It is the force of his manner, the way he punches his fists into the air. Palpable anger. She can feel it even at a distance. Carter and the driver talk again. Eve recognizes the word *Ingliz* and feels her heart race. Do these native people hate everyone who is English? Even her and her father?

The archaeologist explains that the rally involves the government party called the Wafd, made up of the country's poorest. The party has turned against their sultan, King Fouad I, whom they regard as a puppet of the British. Six months earlier, the Crown nominally dissolved Egypt's protectorate, yet Britain continues to use Egypt as a military base. The Egyptians still suffer from unemployment and high prices for goods, while Britain profits from the sales of cotton and other Egyptian commodities. The Wafd party pushes for parliamentary democracy and the removal of British troops.

"They want independence," Carnarvon says, "but they also want our trains, roads, dams, and canals. If not for Britain, this country would be in chaos."

"Perhaps," Carter says, "but little wonder they resent us. Who wants a foreign military camping in your city?"

Maybe, Eve thinks, the Egyptian people are justified in feeling angry over the martial rule. But seeing such a large crowd makes her limbs and bowels feel shaky. How many of these men carry guns? She is the only Englishwoman among the hundreds of people here. What would these men do to her if they saw her?

"We need to get inside," she says, "I need to use the—"

"The hotel's just ahead, at the far end of El Opera Square," Carter says. "The crowd must be blocking the street. Let's walk."

Carnarvon says he'll stay with the carriage. Eve wonders if it is denial or bravery that makes her father so unflappable.

She takes Carter's arm. They dash along a promenade of lebbek trees that runs parallel to the street. Her toes pinch in her pointed shoes.

British soldiers in khaki uniforms, carrying rifles, march double time into the square from the road between the great opera building and the Ezbekiyah Gardens. Eve thinks of wartime images, of men shot to death on the ground. It has only been a few years since all of Europe was at war and her own home was temporarily converted into a hospital. "What will they do, Mr. Carter?"

"They'll break up the rally," Carter says.

She turns to look behind her. "What about Father?"

"He'll reach the hotel safely. Let's move along."

Out of breath, Eve stumbles, then pulls herself up again. They trek the length of El Opera Square, and the Grand Continental Hotel comes into view at last. The hotel is an elegant, European-style four-story building with balconies shaded by awnings: the embodiment to Eve of comfort and safety. It looks like it was transplanted from London or Paris with Egyptian touches added. The red flags of Egypt flap from its upper stories. Twin stone stairways, each forming half a circle, curve upward onto a veranda full of empty rattan chairs and tables. Two native doormen in white robes, red sashes, and red tarbooshes stand under the hotel's shaded walkway.

One doorman greets Eve, but in her haste, she pushes forward, ignoring him. Carter whisks her up the steps and through heavy bronze doors. Eve thinks of the crowd and prickles with terror. Dear God, her mother was right to try to stop her from going to Egypt. But the chance to discover a lost pharaoh's tomb is worth the danger.

2

Carnarvon yawns, but Eve is surprised to see him awake so early, after traveling four hundred miles by train the previous day. Truly, he's a marvel. They take their morning tea, toast, and Duerr's English marmalade while looking out at the Nile from their balcony at the Luxor Winter Palace Hotel. They're now in the city that the ancients knew as Thebes. Songbirds chirp and flit about in nearby date palms. Doves hoot. Potted jasmines exude sweet aromas. The river appears lime green against a cloudless sky. Felucca with their triangular sails circle and sweep by each other, nearly colliding; these are the reckless, early-morning escapades of young men enjoying themselves when they have no tourists in tow.

Eve opens the gold case of her pendant watch to glance at the time. Soon they will journey to Howard Carter's house, to refresh themselves before traveling on to the Valley of the Kings. After packing a satchel and pulling on her heavy, long-sleeved overdress to cover her blouse and skirt, Eve joins Carnarvon, Fearnside, and Carter in the lobby. Admiring the archaeologist, who looks so energetic and strong he could conquer the world, Eve ties on her scarf, puts on her wide-brimmed white canvas hat, and slips on her long gloves.

They step out into the blistering sun. Just across the street and down a short flight of steps, they board the hotel's ferry to cross the Nile. A porter brings their bags.

The vessel will do nicely, Eve thinks. It looks like a proper little ship. Its open-air cabin is the width of its flat-bottomed hull, and its upper deck is covered by a blue-and-white-striped awning. A little farther upriver, several houseboats bob low in the water. Their proprietors wait for tourists to hire them. Not many will. The houseboats' cushions and blankets are known to contain fleas.

Propelled by an oily-smelling motor, the ferry makes the short crossing. Soon after arriving on the west bank, they mount hired donkeys. Eve's donkey has very dirty gray fur but seems reliable and eager for exercise. Carter takes the lead, followed by Carnarvon, Eve, then Fearnside. Native handlers walk beside them, whips in hand. Donkeys carrying their luggage bring up the rear.

The donkeys follow a plain made lush and green by the Nile. Egrets, stalking the swampy periphery alongside the road, take flight. Eve catches a whiff of something decaying in the mud and swats away flies. They pass sugarcane fields, the green crop waist high, and a group of boys herding black-headed goats. Two of the donkeys, including Eve's, veer off the trail to chase after the goats. Eve's donkey brays when a handler flogs it back into line. "Stop!" Eve cries. The man does not stop until Carter, roused from his silence, speaks to him in Arabic.

The landscape gives way to desert hills, sand, and boulders in a wide expanse extending to high brown cliffs. Here there are no trees, no plants. Despite the wrap over her face, Eve breathes in dust. If only those donkeys could quicken their pace! She misses the speed and agility of her horse, Lady Grey.

Ahead of her, Carnarvon drinks often from his canteen. He coughs a great deal, and Eve fears he'll pass out during the remaining miles to Carter's house.

They ride along the road through acrid dung and swarms of stinging flies. Eve sees the outlines of buildings. It is the dusty village of Qurna. Beyond the village and a cemetery, against the hills, Carter's irregularly shaped house, capped by a dome, comes into sight. Closer up, Eve can see a single acacia tree spreading its limbs over one corner of the house.

Eve dismounts, and the drivers leave for the village with their animals. Carter ushers the group inside. "Welcome to Castle Carter," he says.

"Castle Carter" is the name she gave the house when she visited it as a child. Eve is touched that he remembers. Situated on Qurna's edge, the house is more like a villa than a castle. It is built of yellow-white bricks taken from an estate her father once owned in England. A ladder on one side leads to the roof, where Carter says his manservant, Abd el-Aal Ahmed, sleeps. On very hot nights, Carter makes a bed on another portion of the roof. Eve finds Carter's lifestyle, like the house itself, to be quirky and rough, but at the same time fascinating. Somehow in this remote place he has indoor plumbing, a flush toilet, and a few electric lights.

Ahmed, a robed man with a slightly curved back and long dark beard, seems aged, though his face indicates he is no older than thirty. Eve follows him and Carter from the small entranceway, through the domed hall, and into the sole spare bedroom that will be hers whenever they visit. On those occasions, her father will take Carter's bedroom, Carter will sleep on the sofa in his sitting room, and Fearnside, if not at the hotel in Luxor, will claim the sofa in an alcove.

Once alone, Eve slips off her overdress. On the walls, handsome watercolors of ancient ruins bear the signature "H. Carter." Eve knows some of the archaeologist's personal history. As a fifteen-year-old boy in Swaffham, Norfolk, the son of an artist and artistically talented himself, Carter was hired by a gentleman, Baron William Tyssen-Amherst, to copy papyrus scrolls at his country estate. When Carter was seventeen, Lord Amherst took him to Egypt to participate in an archaeological survey for which an artist was needed. Carter stayed on and worked as a draftsman, eventually being trained as an archaeologist by the famous Sir Flinders Petrie. Carter once held a series of important positions in Egypt's Antiquities Service. He left the Service, Eve recalls, due to a scandal involving tourists vandalizing a tomb. His supervisors felt that Carter had handled the incident inappropriately. She wishes she knew the full story.

A curious chirping leads Eve down the hallway to the open door of Carter's study. In a cage, a bright yellow canary fills the room with song. It flutters its wings when it sees her. "How handsome you are!" she says.

Bent over his cluttered desk, already at work though he's just arrived home, Carter turns to her. "I see you've found Sir Golden." He opens the cage and holds out a finger for the bird to hop onto. When he puts his hand next to Eve's, the bird steps to her finger.

"I bought him a few weeks before I found the tomb," Carter tells her. "Ahmed believes it was the canary who brought me luck. He calls the site the Tomb of the Golden Bird. He told me, 'The tomb will be filled with gold.'"

"I hope it will be," Eve says.

Carter looks at her with his dark eyes. "The canary's yours when you visit."

She smiles. Without making eye contact with Carter, Eve watches the bird, who still grips her thumb. The canary feels surprisingly heavy. She talks softly to him. Putting her hand out, grazing Carter's calloused fingers, she transfers the bird. Their shoulders and arms touch. The intimacy of the moment startles her. Feeling herself redden, Eve hastens to the washroom to freshen up.

Carnarvon wakes from a nap, and they share a meal of tinned goods.

Then Carter and Fearnside pack Carter's donkeys with canteens, water bags, and equipment, and they also tie on a wooden chair. Eve readies herself in her now-soiled desert attire. Grinning, Carnarvon hoists himself onto a donkey. "Onward," he says.

On the dirt road that will bring them to the distant cliffs, Eve grips the donkey with her legs and listens to the sounds of its hooves clattering along on the hot earth. A warm wind blows sand into her face. She coughs, then rubs her eyes with her scarf. The road turns, they swing around a hill, and they move through a high passageway of rock. Suddenly the landscape opens to a panorama of high red-brown cliffs against a wide blue sky. Rugged slopes and fissures, viewed as a single mass, resemble a god's round head and hunched shoulders. A giant Egyptian hieroglyph, Eve thinks, blinking at the sight of the Valley of the Kings.

When the route forks, they veer east toward the main branch of the Valley, where the majority of the royal tombs are located. The cliffs rise from the bedrock, one above the other, in a series of abrupt shelves. One pyramid-shaped cliff stands higher than the rest, the peak of el-Qurn. The Valley was carved out of the plateau by floods millions of years ago. With a bit of imagination, Eve can envision ancient waterfalls tumbling down the cliff faces.

Gullies and caves pocket the crags, and dark squares indicate the entrances to tombs that were cut into solid rock. Desperate ventures have taken place here. Grave robbers, both ancient and modern, have met at night, bribed guards, and burrowed into the burial chambers to steal gold. Now these former caverns of riches look pathetically poor and humble—a wasteland. Yet a sense of mystery hangs in the air.

The donkeys labor on, panting, sweating, resisting the climb. The group stops briefly so that Carter can point out a rectangle of gray about halfway down one of the cliffs. "That's the tomb of Ramesses VI," he says. "Use it as a landmark. Our site lies just below it, a bit to the right." Far ahead, Eve can see several more passages cut into the cliff at various angles. Each of these cavities represents a pharaoh's tomb that can be accessed by a path that zigzags upward.

Modern mud-brick buildings, two of which are marked "WC," indicate the official entranceway. It is not yet tourist season, so there are no vendors or ticket sellers; the only signs of life are two donkeys, comfortably chewing hay in the shade of a thatch-covered stall.

Eve rides past one empty tomb, then another. She remembers, as a child, discovering colorful murals in some of those cavernous spaces. Now she finds the brown landscape jarring. Everywhere, sand and piles of loose stones lie in untidy heaps, debris carelessly left by excavators, mostly British and French, who've been digging, piling, and repiling the dry soil for over a century.

While still low down on the slopes, Eve rounds a bend and encounters the sounds of loud, melodious voices and iron hoes striking rock. They have arrived. Eve draws in the reins and brings the donkey to a halt. There, in an irregularly shaped cavity surrounded by hills, about fifty robed Egyptian men and boys labor in the hot sun.

Three pathways intersect on this level plot of ground. The area contains no fewer than ten tombs that jut out from surrounding hillocks. The largest tomb, twice the size of any of the others, belongs to Ramesses VI—the tomb she saw from afar. Its cave-like foyer is so wide that the ancients could have easily danced inside it. Carter's crew of workers congregates in front of this entrance, concealing the place where the newly found stairway must be.

Among the rubble piles, a five-sided blue-and-white-striped tent rises on poles driven into the sand. A balding, portly Englishman of about forty stands in the shade of the tent, engrossed in sanding the edges of a wooden door on sawhorses. At his feet lies a pile of electrical wires. Crates and boxes form a wall in back of him.

Eve dismounts along with the others. Laborers lead the donkeys back down the road. Under the tent, Carter introduces Arthur Callender, known as Pecky, the engineer he's recently hired to help with the excavation. His white suit is snug on his stout frame. His scarlet bow tie and red, clean-shaven face make Eve think, incongruously, of a comic character on a stage.

"Welcome! 'Tis not every day a lordy and lady come to see us," Callender says. Eve likes him instantly for his lack of pretense.

Callender continues to talk while Carter disappears into the crowd of workers. Soon after the laborers cleared the stairway, the engineer says, Carter ordered it to be refilled again as a precaution against thieves. Then, only yesterday, upon hearing of Carnarvon's arrival, the workers began to clear the stairway a second time. Meanwhile, Callender has almost finished making a door for the tomb.

"I'll have it hung the minute we need it, and I have a lock only an ancient magician could break. Eventually, we can order a steel door."

"Excellent." Carnarvon wipes his brow with his handkerchief. "Already a step ahead!"

"More than a *step* ahead—follow? Ah, pardon the pun! And with those cables, I can run lines down the stairway for lights."

Eve follows Callender's gaze to the triangular entrance of a tomb, higher up on the cliff, belonging to a different Ramesses king. An electrical generator, used during the tourist seasons, is located there, he says. Carter has arranged with the Antiquities Service to borrow it.

"I'll put in a string of lights before the inspector arrives," Callender says. "He'll be here soon." He pauses. "No one's permitted to enter the tomb without him, you know."

"Yes." Eve frowns. She is aware, from overhearing her father's conversations with Carter, that they dislike having inspectors supervise their archaeological digs. Neither Carter nor her father likes being told what to do. But curiously, Carter seems to believe the Antiquities Service would like to take over the dig and claim everything that is found. Eve wonders if there is any basis for his fear.

Carter returns and leads Eve, Carnarvon, and Fearnside through the crowd of workers toward the Ramesses VI tomb. Slightly to the right of the gigantic tomb's entrance, a tiny passage, like the entrance of a mine, disappears into the ground. Four men in the pit labor with shovels. Other men and boys carry baskets of rock out from the stairway, passing them hand to hand until the material is heaved onto waist-high piles.

Carter speaks to the workers in Arabic, and one by one, they climb the stairway and stand back from the excavation area. The archaeologist smiles at Eve as he points to the dark cavity. "Here we are!"

"Oh." Eve's heart sinks. Before her is an empty hole. Why did Carter write in his telegram "magnificent tomb"?

She looks at Carter, then at her father, who silently twirls one end of his mustache.

"Show us everything, Carter," Carnarvon says, as cheerfully as ever.

The archaeologist goes down the steps first, creating shadows with a kerosene lamp. Eve, Carnarvon, and Fearnside follow.

Precisely hewn limestone steps descend into the ground at a steep pitch. Each step shines pearly white, in contrast to the surrounding reddish-brown rock. Eve counts the steps—sixteen in all. They dead-end into a rectangular doorway that has been plastered over.

At the top of the partition, where the outer surface has flaked off, there's a heavy-looking wooden beam—the lintel. Oval red globs dot the crumbling white surface. "These ovals of red clay are a priest's seals," Carter says, pointing carefully with his spade. "If you look closely, you'll see hieroglyphs." The seals are made of mud mixed with oil, he explains. Some seals are stamped vertically, some at angles. Each is about the size of Eve's hand.

On closer inspection, the seals hold a subtle though detailed impression of an oval cartouche, and inside that, figures. "It's a jackal," Eve says, pleased to show her knowledge. "Anubis!"

"Yes, that's it," Carter says.

"Anubis above nine captives tied with ropes," Carter continues. "You see? That image is stamped into the plaster again and again."

Carnarvon prepares his camera. "So curious. What does it say, Carter?"

"It isn't a name or a word. It must be an emblem," Carter answers. "Priests in the necropolis stamped their insignia before sealing a tomb."

While Carter holds a lamp over her, Eve squints to make out details on more seals. The images of squatting captives are meant, she supposes, to scare away thieves.

"Now, we'll have to crouch to see the rest." Carter's eyes are aglow. At the base of the partition, he does careful work with a spade and tiny brush on another seal of ancient red-brown mud. He moves aside so Eve can take his place.

The imprint is shallow. Yet, sure enough, she recognizes the wavy lines, the ankh, the chick, the flail, and other hieroglyphs in the cartouche. She mouths aloud. "Aaaa. AM-mun. That's king."

Carter crouches beside her, and Eve feels a tingling sensation as their elbows touch. "Go on," he says.

"Too Ahh-k." Eve's heart races. "Amun-tut-ankh. King Tutankhamun! My God." She squeezes herself out of the tight spot next to Carter and stands on a higher step. Carnarvon moves into the space where she has been but falls backward when he squats to take a photograph.

Carter helps Carnarvon to his feet and leads him, panting, back up the stairway. He protests, but Eve insists. She seats him under the shade of the tent in their one chair; all others sit on boxes. The dried dirt on Carnarvon's face cracks as he gulps down water.

Eve looks out at the rocky hills and high cliffs, yellow in the afternoon light. Low voices pulse from a distance, the sound of the workers saying their afternoon prayers. Beyond a pile of diggings, Carter says, they spread their prayer mats. While Eve, Carnarvon, and Fearnside rest, Callender connects a wire to the generator and plugs in two electric torches for use on the stairway. Then he mounts the door at the stairway's base.

By and by, the inspector assigned to the excavation arrives at the site. He's a middle-aged Egyptian wearing a white suit and red hat that is shaped like a cone but flat on top, with black tassels—a tarboosh.

"Lord Carnarvon and Lady Evelyn," Carter says, "may I introduce Inspector Ibrahim El Mofty Effendi. He's from the Antiquities Service."

The official raises his right arm upward, touches his chest above his heart, taps his forehead with his fingers, then sweeps his arm out in a traditional greeting.

"We are grateful for your assistance," Carnarvon says, his voice flat.

Carter leads El Mofty down the steps to inspect the partition. As before, Eve, her father, and Fearnside press in close. The inspector examines the seals with a magnifying glass.

Carter aims his torch at a browned half circle on the doorway's plaster. "This electric light shows me things I've not seen before." He points at a stained area several feet wide.

El Mofty passes his hand over his mustache. "What are you thinking, Mr. Carter?"

"Tomb robbers have been here," Carter says, his voice growing loud.

The inspector leans forward, squinting. "And yet the seals of Anubis are stamped all over the area. And there's Tutankhamun's seal at the bottom, which you showed me earlier. A pity about the thieves!"

Carter frowns. "So they broke in long ago, possibly soon after the burial. And afterward, someone, a priest or guard, carefully sealed the entrance again." He lowers his torch to illuminate the base of the doorway. "Here, too, I suspect there was another break-in."

Eve looks closely along the plaster where the light plays. Her father asks the unanswerable. "How much of the tomb is likely to be complete?"

"I have no answer for that," El Mofty says. He feels the plaster with his hand. "This entranceway seems too small for a tomb. It could be a storeroom. Or a crypt where mummies were placed after their graves were ransacked."

"Or it's an unpillaged royal tomb," Carnarvon says. "Perhaps the thieves were caught before they had a chance to remove any of the treasures. The guards slit their throats."

Eve laughs out of nervousness. "Father, you have such a way of saying things!"

Carter tells everyone except the inspector to vacate the stairway while he cuts the seals out of the plaster. One by one he and the inspector carry the seals up to the tent. Eve and Carnarvon do not go below again until Carter has his pickaxe ready to demolish the partition. The stairway is more crowded than ever, because Callender joins them.

Carter takes a firm grip on a pickaxe and faces the center of the wall. The inspector shines a torch. Carnarvon positions himself with his camera. Eve bites down on a smile. What lies beyond? Desolation? Splendor?

With a mighty swing and a loud whack, Carter strikes the plaster. Dust flies into everyone's face. Clouds of it rise as Carter swings again and again. Carnarvon coughs. The pick's blade strikes with a *clang*.

Puzzled, Eve waits for Carter to explain. "That's not plaster," he says. "I believe the pick broke through to a wall of rock."

Rock. Eve feels doubts and fears circling in the stale air. There's no way they can enter today, that is clear.

The inspector hunches his shoulders. "This is a disappointment."

"What next?" Carnarvon says. His face is red and dripping with sweat.

Carter takes a drink from his canteen, then goes back to striking the wall. After several hits, a cascade of shiny black chips pours out with a hiss, like a great eruption of rain. "Beyond the plaster and rocks, it seems there is a tunnel. But it's blocked with debris!" He puts down the axe and scoops up a handful of chips. He and the inspector analyze them with their torches.

"Odd. These are black limestone," the inspector says. "The tunnel seems partly filled in with limestone pieces, and the rest of the filling is light brown rock."

Eve and her father exchange glances. "The very deuce!" Carnarvon says. "Just as it appeared we were getting somewhere."

Callender's laughter breaks up the tension. "Patience. We're closer than we were before."

"The change in rock corresponds to where the stain was on the doorway," El Mofty says.

When Carter puts down the pickaxe, Eve comes forward and shines his torch into the shallow depression he has carved out. As he said, one area appears darker than the rest. "Why the two kinds of stones?"

"The tunnel was already filled when the thieves dug out a crawl space," Carter says. "It looks like officials filled it again later."

"Did the thieves get in and steal the treasures?"

"Perhaps. We won't know until we remove the rubble," Carter says.

Ever optimistic, at least to outward appearances, Carnarvon says, "Carry on, Carter."

Carter picks up one of the black shards and tosses it back and forth between his hands. His expression seems almost violent.

"We're going to succeed," Eve says, as much to herself as to the archaeologist. She likes hearing herself say the word "we."

His voice softens. "I hope so."

3

Stone by stone, bucket by bucket, the laborers cart debris up the ancient stairway. Another day goes by. The tunnel contains more than chips of shiny black limestone. Every time the workers discover something unusual, like a decorated pottery shard, a piece of a leather drinking vessel, or part of a wooden box, they bring it to Carter. Eve hovers about the archaeologist, inspecting every new find. "Might I help you?" she says.

At first, he merely gives her a sidelong glance, as if he doesn't take her seriously. Eventually, he allows her to record where the artifacts have been discovered. At the table under the tent, she carefully removes silt from the objects with a small brush and paints tiny numbers on the backs.

Eve sees the archaeologist at his most capable that week. She thinks he would have made a fine professor if he'd had the opportunity to attend university. Carter can differentiate between man-hewn flakes and natural bits of rock, and determine the approximate age of every pile. Each pebble, or change in the soil, reveals secrets to him. And she, an eager student, listens to the sound of the men shoveling up the rock as she tries to remain patient. Egypt's brown-red dirt cakes the buckles of her leather shoes. Stains dot her skirts. No matter. She senses they are on the brink of discovering something phenomenal, and she is right there in the midst of it, by Carter's side.

As the tunnel empties, three new waist-high hills of debris rise upward. Carnarvon delights in photographing the artifacts that fill the table, and he chats with Inspector El Mofty Effendi, who visits in the morning. Eve and Carnarvon sleep at Carter's house. Fearnside remains at their suite at the Luxor Winter Palace Hotel, where he oversees the washing, ironing, and mending and keeps incidentals, such as Carnarvon's cigarettes, cigars, and lemon cough drops, in ready supply.

On the third day, Eve and Carnarvon arrive at the excavation to find the workers sprawled out on their mats in the shade of a cliff as Callender, seated under the tent, makes calculations on a pad of paper. "Carter's on his own today," the engineer says, shifting his eyes to the stairway. Dust clings to his hair and the top of his balding head. "El

Mofty's gone. Carter told him it would take a few more days to clear out that rubble." He adds, with a wink, "But 'tis almost done!"

Interest lights up Carnarvon's face. "Is that so?" he says. Eve and her father exchange gleeful glances. No pesky interference from the official today. After she and her father gulp down glasses of warm, metallic-tasting water, they head to the stairway. She takes Carnarvon's camera bag so he can concentrate on his balance. At the bottom, she swings open the heavy wooden door. Light bulbs, strung along the top of the tunnel, reveal the bare shaft that slants underground.

The air grows hotter and staler as they creep downward. The shaft is so narrow, they walk single file. Just ahead, Carter's stooped figure casts shadows where the tunnel dead-ends. He stops his task of excavating a seal with a small knife and brush, and he turns. He wipes his brow in the sweltering air. "We've come up against another partition. Here are more seals of Tutankhamun. But"—he points to two semicircular areas with his electric torch—"look at these stains, in the upper left. They're in the same positions as the first wall."

"So the doorway was breached," Eve says, feeling cross. "Thieves again!"

"There's still hope of treasures," Carter says. "The seals show no one's been here since ancient times."

Carnarvon grins. "There's no inspector here. So why don't we go ahead? Carve out a small section. Take just a peek. No harm in that."

"You mean poke a small hole, and who's to know?" Eve says, keeping a straight face. Her urge to go on is monstrous.

In the dim light, Carter looks at Carnarvon evenly. "I follow you, Carnarvon. It's not likely El Mofty will return here today." He glances at his pocket watch. "Still, I don't know. The inspectors are looking for an excuse to get rid of us."

Carnarvon rubs the back of his neck and says nothing.

"Supposing we're found out?" Eve asks. "Could they make us leave Egypt?"

"It's possible," Carter says. "The Egyptian government is becoming increasingly hostile toward foreigners."

Carnarvon clutches his cane. "We'll simply plaster up the hole," he says, as if the request were nothing.

"Well, if we do proceed on our own, we can't do it with the workers here." Carter taps his knuckles against the plaster. "Mind, I haven't agreed to anything." But Eve sees that something in him has turned like an electrical switch. Temptation is a powerful force.

By and by, the laborers file out of the Valley to Qurna following the rocky and lifeless trail that zigzags around the tombs and then drops to the main road at the base of the cliffs. Eve watches the long line of robed men and boys and wonders if any suspect why Carter has released them earlier than usual. Will one of them think to warn the authorities?

When the workers are out of sight, Eve, her father, Callender, and Carter meet at the stairway. Thanks to Callender's ingenuity, they have two electric torches to share. With Carter in the lead and Eve next, they descend, their shadows creating ghostlike moving forms. The area around the partition is so small that only two at a time can stand there.

"Let's hope there's not another tunnel beyond this, also filled with rocks," Eve says.

"I hope there *is*," Callender teases. "I love rocks, don't you?" Jokes cannot ease the tension. Eve and Callender hold up their electric torches toward Carter, whose bent-over form glows orange in the darkness. She listens to the sound of her father's labored breathing and tastes the dust in the stale air.

Of the two stained areas on the upper left of the partition, Carter chooses one at about his eye level and uses a steel rod to shove through the plaster. With a circling motion, he widens the opening until the hole is about the size of his fist. "I need to test the air." He lights a candle from his toolbox and slides it through the opening. The flame flickers but keeps burning. "Good so far," Carter says.

Silence falls over the group like a net.

"Can you see anything?" Eve asks.

Carter presses his face to the hole for what seems to Eve a very long time. She crowds in closer, toward him.

"Yes," Carter replies, his voice soft. "Wonderful things."

Carnarvon pushes ahead next. He looks in and cries, "Wonderful, wonderful!"

Then it is Eve's turn. When her eyes grow accustomed to the dim space, she sees fantastic gilded forms; strange, elongated animals with curling tails, emerging from a tangled mass of objects. A gigantic gilded cow with horns. A shimmering lion. Chests, boxes, baskets, vases, giant wheels. Life-size statues, piled in jumbled confusion. The flame flickers in the hot air. Shadows shift. More and more faces appear, of both humans and animals. She listens to the sound of her breathing. She cannot utter a word. Here is a king's treasure; it can be nothing else. Everywhere, gold gleams, lit by the candle's halo.

Carter enlarges the hole a few feet from the ground, and nobody tries to stop him. He chisels out the plaster until he can hoist his leg up and squeeze through. "What's there?" Carnarvon calls to him, passing the electric torches through the opening before Callender hoists him into the interior. Then in climbs Callender, slowly because he is so portly. Without waiting another second, Eve hauls herself up, grabs Callender's outstretched hands, and plunges headfirst through the opening. The drop isn't steep, but she loses her bearings and lands on her backside on the stone floor.

Two bright torches come toward her face. She closes her eyes for a moment against the brightness. As she pushes herself into a sitting position, she touches a small object with her shoe. It tips over. A captivating smell wafts out into the warm air, a sweet perfume with just a hint of spice. Frankincense. She breathes in the rich aroma.

Carter hands her a torch. He holds the little jar near his face and then puts back the lid. "Still fragrant—astonishing!"

Eve turns her light in a steady arc. She is in a forest of gold-and-cream-colored plants. Their slender branches divide as they curve upward. She reaches toward one of the branches. She feels cool, smooth stone on her hand and realizes the lovely, twining things are not plants but vessels made from alabaster. And the perfume or oil that they hold is every bit as fresh as if they were left a day ago.

As Eve takes in the heady fragrance near her, she rises to her feet and casts the light of the torch to find she's in a small, cluttered chamber. All around her are objects haphazardly stacked against the walls: furniture, parts from dismantled chariots, and sculptures. Those heads of animals she saw a moment earlier now emerge as goddesses: the lioness Sekhmet, the cow Hathor, and the hippopotamus Taweret with a gaping mouth that seems to be laughing.

On the floor lie dried reeds and flowers, baskets, curious egg-shaped cases, and many more alabaster containers. To order her senses, she fixes on the room's middle, which offers a space where the four of them can stand and observe.

"My God!" Carter says softly.

"That scent…" Callender's voice trails off. "Exquisite."

Eve moves between Carter and her father. Carnarvon wipes away a tear. Carter is in rapture. So is Eve. The atmosphere seems so set apart, so holy, that it leaves her, for a while, unable to speak. "Mr. Carter," she says at last, "there's such peace in this place."

"Yes," Carter replies. "The peace of three thousand years."

She shines her torch about the room. The haphazard movement of the torches casts mysterious shadows. Animal heads lengthen and twist. "Father, did you see something move?"

"By God, I thought those beasts were alive," he says.

Carter's voice, abruptly stern, brings her back to reality. "Nothing must be disturbed. Remember the inspectors! And I will need to know the exact placement of the objects. My recordings will one day be invaluable. This is the greatest find of our century."

How pompous the archaeologist sounds, but Eve knows he is speaking the truth. She watches her father reach toward a statue. "Carnarvon, hold back," Carter snaps at him.

Eve shines her torch toward her father to see his expression. He looks both entranced and defiantly disappointed. He gently lifts his hand away and nods.

Are they leaving footprints or fingerprints? There seems to be surprisingly little dust, Eve thinks. Then again, it is difficult to tell in the dim light. The beam of her torch now illuminates Callender's face. He looks around with wonder, then worry. "The way these things are stacked invites an avalanche. One hasty move, and—"

"You're right," Eve says. "We'd better be careful."

Eve finds an open egg-shaped box that is empty. Clearly the work of thieves. Near her, Callender studies a golden wheel. "Chariots," he says. "The tomb officials took them apart to get 'em in here. And I don't know how we're going to get 'em out."

Eve feels the smoothness of an alabaster vase. She enters into a dreamlike euphoria. Every sense is magnified. Intense heat. Colors appear in the darkness. Sweet aromas.

Carter squats, inspecting smaller treasures stored under the furniture. "Unique in Egyptian art. So much vitality," he says, over and over. "Here's the Tell el-Amarna style, at its very best. Better than I've ever seen. Or the world has seen."

Eve wipes her brow with the palm of her hand. Despite the heat, she shivers. She shines her torch on an overturned tiny mummy-shaped figure. Its glass eyes, like a cat's, glow back at her. All about her, pairs of eyes peer out from shadows as if coming alive.

Against a whitewashed plaster wall, two black, life-size statues of young men face each other. Each seems about to step forward in his golden sandals.

"Ka figures," Carter explains. "They represent the king's double, a part of him that stays alive after death." They wear gold kilts and gold armbands, and each holds a gold staff. Their glass eyes are rimmed with gold. Mounted on their headdresses are tiny cobras, flexed, heads high—ready to strike.

Carter points out that these images show the king as a young man. "I think he may have died young," he says.

How sad, Eve thinks.

Carter shines his torch on a decorated wooden chest on the floor near the figures. Eve and Carter kneel in front of it. The chest's painted battle scene depicts an archer, a chariot, and two plumed horses in a flying gallop. "It's the young king trampling his enemies," Carter says. The king, painted much larger than the other figures, shoots arrows that pierce falling warriors.

"Yes," Eve breathes, filled with happiness to be sharing this moment with him.

Casting her torch about, Eve sees bands of red, blue, and yellow in a rainbow shape. Carefully folded in a basket nearby lies a beaded collar. The stripes of color alternate with golden rosettes. Without thinking, she reaches to pick up the jewelry.

"No, don't touch it. It's very fragile," Carter says.

Feeling rebuked, she holds back. Carter is right: the collar's cloth backing might have turned to dust, showering the beads and rosettes onto the floor.

Next, a majestic throne, radiant gold and detailed with many other colors, appears in the beam of her torch. The chair glows. Her heart leaps, and she feels transported into a state of timeless joy once again. She steps over smaller objects to reach the throne. Carter follows. "*This* is surely one of the most beautiful things ever found in Egypt," Eve says.

Carter breaks into a smile. "It could well be."

Eve carries her torch around it carefully. Each arm of the throne is capped with a golden lion's head. On gilt wooden panels that form the arms, feathered goddesses spread their wings. An illustration on the back shows the young queen bending toward the pharaoh and holding a cup. "She's putting perfumed ointment on him," Eve says.

The king and queen look at each other gently, out of almond-shaped eyes. The pair wear colorful beaded collars. The queen's transparent linen garment exposes the shape of her small breasts and legs. Perhaps she's about Eve's age.

"Look what's above him," Carter says. "It's Aten, the disk of the sun. The Amarna style, to be sure. I can hardly believe it! And yet this room is filled with earlier Egyptian gods, too." He clenches his fists, grinning. "It is a mystery. One that I plan to solve."

Eve studies the sun disk with its beams of light reaching to the pharaoh. Tutankhamun's father, or some say grandfather, Akhenaten, decreed the only god to be worshipped was Aten. It is unclear why the artwork of one religion should coexist alongside another. But the figures of the royal couple interest her more. "What was the queen's name?"

"Ankhesenamum," Carter reads.

"They were young and in love," Eve says.

"It seems that way. This picture shows great feeling. The whole scene is exquisite." His voice is soft. They stand together, shoulders touching. "Lady Eve, this is the best day of my life."

"Just Eve. And it certainly is *my* best day," she says. Her torch held in the crook of her arm, she presses her hand on the top edge of the golden throne. Carter does not try to stop her this time. How long they shine their torches on the throne, staring at it, she does not know. The magical world dissolves into the present reality again when Callender approaches.

"Where do you think the sarcophagus might be?" he asks Carter.

"That's a good question." Eve feels Carter's attention pull away from her, though they continue to stand close together.

Carter and Callender discuss the tomb of Ramesses VI, which was constructed in the style of many other rock-cut tombs in the Valley. Its straight tunnel with side chambers leads to a great hall framed by pillars. "This looks like we're in a storeroom, not a tomb," Carter says. "Unless there's another portal."

In her excitement, it hasn't occurred to Eve to think about a sarcophagus. The room is so small and crowded, she does not see how anything so massive could be in there.

Carter enlists the group to help him search for doors. It is crowded work for four, so they separate. Eve finds something at her feet. It is a bouquet of dried flowers, so well preserved it looks new. Astonishing! She pictures the grieving queen leaving the bouquet for her husband.

"An opening, here!" Carter calls from across the room. On the long plaster wall, crowded with chariots and animal-headed beds, Carter traces a small, low, arched doorway leading to another chamber. The great animal beds have partly hidden it from view. Single file, helping each other with care through the precarious jumble of artifacts, they pass into the chamber. It is smaller than the one they've left and even more crowded. Tables and chairs are piled in odd positions, as if thrown over each other. Vessels lie on their sides, overturned.

"Look at this havoc. The thieves!" Carnarvon says.

"Evidently officials tried to set things right in the other room. Here, it seems, they gave up," Carter says.

As in the first chamber, there are beds shaped like animals. This room contains golden bows, arrows, and shields. Why didn't the thieves take them?

Carter finds a blackened lamp that someone left, perhaps the thieves. He inspects the walls. "Still no sarcophagus, no mummy," he says.

Carter and Callender crouch back into the first room to inspect the walls again. Eve and her father are looking at game boards inlaid with checkerboard squares when Carter calls, "Carnarvon. I've found the entrance!"

Carter soon shows the group the outlines of a plastered-over doorway directly between the two ka figures facing each other. "Why did I not realize it before? They're sentinels." Carter lowers his voice. "They're guarding the king."

"The burial chamber?" Eve asks.

He nods. "I think so."

Carnarvon clears his throat. "We're close—I feel it!"

On his knees, Carter shines his torch along the bottom of the wall. "When I moved aside these baskets, I found this dark stain. More evidence of replastering."

"So the plunderers got in here, too," Eve says. "What a shame." But she knows that if the tomb is not intact, it is to their benefit.

A crack about an inch high runs the length of the plaster. She crouches down on the stone floor and shines her torch into it. She cannot see anything.

"This crack might be made wider," Carnarvon observes.

Carter glances at Carnarvon. Then he trails his fingers along the fissure.

"But the inspectors," Eve says. "Do we dare?"

"Of course," Carnarvon answers for all of them. Eve thinks Carter is too focused on the task at hand to reply.

Eve feels a great rush of excitement. There is no real question about it. They have already gone too far. Now there is no holding back.

4

A mere foot of chalky plaster separates them from what Eve hopes is the burial chamber. She and Carter test the hardness of the plaster by chiseling away at the gap at the bottom of the wall with pocket knives, and limestone dust swirls in the air like an ancient incantation.

Carnarvon breaks into a hacking cough. This time he doesn't stop until Carter thumps him on the back. "Father, let's go above ground," Eve says. "I can't have you choking to death."

Carnarvon's voice is hoarse. "My dear, I'm perfectly—" he says, then coughs again.

Carter announces that any explorations will have to wait. They all need air, water, and dinner, not just Carnarvon. It is a momentous task to get her father to leave the dazzling beauty of this realm. And Eve, too, wills herself, step-by-step, away from the treasures. When Carter locks the stout wooden door at the base of the stairway, she feels, oddly, a pang of despair. She asks herself if she can ever recapture the state of wonder she felt in the tomb. The experience has changed her forever.

As they ascend the stairway, Eve notices her father's bulging jacket pocket. Anger boils up in her. Well, confronting him now will not do, she decides.

Callender stays to guard the tomb while the rest of them quit the Valley. At Carter's house, Eve notices that Ahmed, good servant that he is, does not ask questions. But surely, by the way Carnarvon whoops during the meal, Ahmed must suspect they've found something extraordinary. Eve worries that he'll talk to his friends in Qurna, who might talk to the inspectors. She also wonders what her father did with the stolen goods in his pocket.

Over cigarettes and brandy, and after Ahmed has retired for the evening, Carter says, "All right, we go back tonight. But we won't let on about this to anyone. Ever."

Carnarvon leans in. "Agreed."

"You have my word," Eve says, wondering if she should put a stop to it.

Carnarvon lifts his glass, and Carter clinks it with his.

By now, darkness has fallen like a shroud. Eve, Carter, and Carnarvon return to the Valley under cover of the moonless night. Callender unlocks the door to the tomb, and they climb into the cluttered subterranean room they explored several hours earlier. Carter names it the Antechamber.

The two ka figures of the pharaoh hold their graceful poses as they have for several thousand years: one foot forward, each gripping a staff and mace. Going against his own rule that nothing in the tomb be disturbed until it has been charted, Carter moves baskets, reeds, boxes, and a chest. Once again, Eve stops herself from speaking up. She is as eager as the rest of them to see what lies beyond.

With a mallet, Carter knocks at the bottom portion of the wall between the figures. Ancient replastering has caused a round stain; this will be a good place for them to enter, because it will be easy to conceal. On the floor sits a pot of plaster, which Callender has freshly mixed, to cover the first doorway they've breached and the wall after they've seen what is behind it.

"It's late for me to speak up, Carter, but we should not be doing this," Callender says.

Eve feels an odd stirring in her chest. "I agree with Mr. Callender. Shouldn't we be following the laws of Egypt? Think of the consequences."

Carter, hands on hips, lowers his voice. "I want to know for sure that we've found a royal tomb before the inspectors show up and make their demands."

"I'm willing to take any risk," Carnarvon says, as though they all didn't know it already.

Carter swings again. More plaster falls to the floor. He opens a hole just large enough for someone to get through. He puts his torch into the hole. "I'm going in," he says. With considerable effort, he slides into the tight space on his back, feet first.

Eve listens intently but hears only silence.

Carnarvon calls after him, "Are you all right? What's in there?"

"God Almighty. I'm kneeling before a solid wall of gold," Carter says.

Eve clenches her fists. The gold is more than a clue that they've found a burial chamber. But another wall? She can't think why the ancients would use their precious gold for a wall.

She passes in her torch to Carter, wriggles on her back through the hole, slides downward, and drops about a foot with a bump. She coughs in the stifling air. It smells scorched, rotten, and dry, all at once. For a moment, she fears she might suffocate. Sitting up, she sees a shimmering wall. Gilt designs on wood stand out against a blue background. Only two feet separate the gold wall from the plaster one they've just entered. It's little more than airspace.

"A tight spot," Carter says.

Eve maneuvers around him and manages to stand, bumping her head on the way.

Next, Carnarvon slides his feet through the hole. Eve draws him inside bit by bit to ease his landing. "Made it," Carnarvon says, "but it's so hot I can hardly breathe. I hope we won't all suffocate."

Next come Callender's big feet and legs. Carter cannot move him very far. "I'm stuck," Callender says. "I'm too bloody fat."

On another occasion, Eve might have laughed.

"I'll go back. Chisel the opening bigger," Callender says.

"Don't do it," Carter says. "The smaller the hole we make, the better."

"Right." Callender withdraws his legs and passes in another torch.

Eve clasps her father's hand and helps him to his feet, then shines her torch on the dazzling wall. In the hot air, its surface appears to ripple.

"It's not a wall after all," Carter announces after a brief examination. "It's the great tomb where the pharaoh's mummy was placed—the burial shrine. Magnificent."

The realization takes a moment to sink in. Eve raises her hand and touches the wood lightly. If it has been left undisturbed, this find changes the history of archaeology. The only royal Egyptian sarcophagus found intact. Heat rises to her face. So Carter has done what no man has done before. He's brilliant. He's a genius! She only wishes she can see his expression at that moment.

Her voice sinks a notch lower. "Tutankhamun's tomb. This is it."

Beside her, Carnarvon says, "Ah! I knew he was here." He cheers as if he's at the racetrack.

With a finger, Eve traces the pattern of repeating amuletic symbols on the shrine, the alternating columns and ankhs, and translates "Endurance and life."

Edging sideways with her back to the plaster, she follows Carter along one side of the golden shrine. She arches her back and stares upward to the structure's roof, decorated with cornices. The walls of this chamber, unlike the other walls in this tomb that she has seen, are painted with colorful hieroglyphs and pictures. In the dim light, she can't make out details.

Callender's muffled voice comes through the opening. He sounds farther and farther away. "What are you seeing? Tell me."

"It's a great burial shrine of gilded wood, and every bit of it is decorated," Carter calls. "It rises high above our heads and nearly fills this room. The sarcophagus is surely in there."

"It's beautiful, so beautiful," Eve says, her voice catching in her throat. To think, no living person has entered this place in more than three thousand years.

She edges around a corner to meet Carter at the front of the shrine. Squeezed in together, their arms touching, they face double doors. At the center of the shrine's doors are two loops of rope that could be handles. Above and below the loops, dark bolts hold the doors closed.

Carter, peering up and down, says, "Something appears to be missing. These loops on the middle of the door are meant to hold a rope, or perhaps another bolt. And I don't see any seals." He frowns intently.

Carnarvon presses closer. "What are you waiting for? If you don't open these doors, I will."

"Patience, Carnarvon." Carter shoots him one of his intense looks. He crouches, studying the bolts from a new angle. Then he rises to his feet and reaches toward the door.

The air is heavy, and there is almost no room to move. Eve hardly cares. Her father chuckles with excitement. Sweat pours off Carter's face. There's the smell of perspiration mixed with stale dust and a hint of ancient perfume.

Eve leans forward as Carter slides the upper bolt. It moves smoothly and almost as soundlessly as if it has been oiled the day before. Then he slides the lower bolt. With both hands, he grasps the handles of the double doors. "Here we go," he says.

The doors do not budge.

Still gently, but with more force, Carter pulls again.

Creaking loudly, enough to make Eve jump, the portals suddenly yield and swing open.

There, attached to a wooden frame, hangs a red gossamer curtain. Transparent, it is studded with golden coin-sized rosettes. Just beyond it lies a second golden, cabinet-like shrine almost as large as the first. Between the shrines, the enormous, lightweight curtain sways in the gentle breeze created by opening the doors. Several rosettes from the curtain fall to the floor, sparkling in the torchlight. Carter bends and puts them in the pocket of his trousers. In his excitement, Eve notices, he seems to forget his own warnings.

She waits, breathless. Carter draws back the veil. Behind it, the second shrine is also closed with double doors. These are even more richly decorated than the first, with illustrated panels of the young pharaoh and other figures etched into the gilt surface. Fastening these doors is a neatly coiled rope. A clay seal is plastered into the center of the rope. On the seal is an image she has seen many times by now: a jackal over nine bound prisoners.

"He's in there." Carnarvon's voice rises. "Congratulations, Carter!" Carter swallows as if holding back tears. Both he and her father look happier than she has ever seen them. Eve feels ready to shout for joy. To think, her father planned to stop the archaeologist's funding!

"We won't break the seal now," Carter says. "There may be more shrines. We must dismantle all this at the proper time, in the proper way. And with the officials here, of course."

Eve sighs, though she knows it is for the best that they not break the seal. She runs her hand near the design of the left door. It shows the young, crowned pharaoh between a mummy-like male figure who also wears a high crown and a beautiful woman in a sheathlike robe. The goddess Isis presents the pharaoh to Osiris, the lord of the Underworld.

Her heart goes out to the pharaoh. Here lies a person, and they are intruders. Their entry, with their electric torches, marks the beginning of profound changes for his shrines. Her mind jumps ahead to curators, restorations, and museums. She longs to be part of that process—and yet, a part of her thinks they should leave the mummy alone.

Neatly tucked on the floor between the outer and second shrine doors stand several gilt staffs and canes, set in place for the pharaoh to use again, along with carved boxes and containers of dried-up oils. The scent Eve smelled earlier must have permeated the shrine's wood. The lid of one small alabaster jar is capped by a figurine of a lion. With its extended pink tongue, it looks lifelike, panting in the heat.

Carnarvon picks up the jar. "This is exquisite. I must have it."

Carter shakes his head. "Carnarvon," he says sternly, "everyone would know precisely where it came from." He points to a cartouche on the jar. "There. The hieroglyphs of Tutankhamun."

Frowning, Carnarvon sets down the lion-headed container. "In due time, then."

Between the outer and inner shrines, Eve's gaze rests on a tiny gold box inlaid with jewels. When she stoops toward it, Carter doesn't stop her. Curiosity is getting the better of them all. The box, shaped like an M, fits neatly into her hand. On its lid, two mirror profiles of the pharaoh as a boy face each other. Each image wears what looks like a lock of real hair.

"How curious," she says. She opens the box, and though it seems empty, a rich, smoky scent wafts out.

Taking the box from her, Carter slips it into the pocket of his jacket. "I want to study it," he says.

"Mr. Carter," Eve says, "I thought you said not to—"

He cuts her off with an even, clear voice. "I will bring it back here later."

"Should any of us be taking things?" Eve returns. She wouldn't mind so much if he hadn't forbidden her father to do the same.

"It's fine, Lady Eve," Carter snaps. "After the official opening, every single item in this tomb will be cataloged, and all will be accounted for. I borrow these objects for study."

"All right, then," she says, "but I do not like it."

Carter examines the paintings on the plaster walls while Eve and Carnarvon explore the narrow aisles between the walls and the burial shrine. Eve leads the way around a corner. From a shallow depression in the wall, a tiny mummy-shaped form peers out with glowing eyes. Startled, Eve drops her torch.

The torch lands in such a way that its beam shines down the corridor. Now she can see oars that an ancient tomb official ceremoniously placed in a pattern like footprints. Left, right, left, right, all the way down the aisle. How fantastic! Perhaps the pharaoh was meant to follow their movement to the river barge that will take him to the afterworld.

Carter aims his torch high on the wall above him, revealing a motif of blue baboons, each shown, in profile, in its own square. He comments that the artistic quality isn't what they've seen elsewhere in the tomb. They were hastily painted, he says. It is a clue that the pharaoh died suddenly, before the tomb was completed.

Carnarvon pushes past Eve and carefully steps over the oars. From farther down the back wall, he calls out, "I've found another room!"

Eve follows her father's voice around the corner of the shrine to find an open rectangular doorway leading to another room. Rising from the floor to above their heads, and nearly filling the portal, is a jet-black figure of a jackal, the god Anubis, seated on a chest of gilded wood. The figure holds up his slender head watchfully. A mantle of shimmering lightweight material hangs from his golden neck. The god's ears, lined with gold as revealed in Eve's torch beam, point upward, listening keenly. His painted golden eyes seem to gaze back at her as if taking in her every move.

"I'm stunned," Carter says, running his hand through his hair. "This Anubis is the most lifelike I've ever seen in any dynasty."

"He's majestic," Eve says.

"Exactly," Carter says. "Majestic. See how Anubis is on carrying poles? That's how the tomb officials got him here. While the mummification coffin was transported by a giant sledge probably pulled by oxen, the jackal was carried. He would have led the procession."

In her mind's eye, Eve imagines the funeral parade. After going up the Nile by barge, the corpse, in his wooden mummification coffin, displayed under a canopy with his royal riches, was heaved across the desert. Following behind came the laborers, carrying the pharaoh's everyday possessions, and mourners shrieking and wailing.

Eve lifts her arm to touch Anubis's nose. Then she, Carter, and Carnarvon slip by the jackal into a square room beyond. Eve's torch lights a sight so spectacular that she stands transfixed. Here is another tall, golden shrine. At each corner stands a radiant golden statue of a young goddess. The goddesses hold their graceful arms out as if protecting the sacred contents of the cabinet. Their expressions are so sweet, so compassionate, Eve cannot stop gazing at them.

Carnarvon walks toward her, his torch blinding her for a moment. He stands beside her. Neither of them speaks for a long time.

"Father," Eve says. "Father." In an easy, unconscious gesture, she takes his hand. He squeezes her fingers in return.

Carnarvon breathes, "Simply marvelous! All of it."

Carter, who has been pacing, shining his torch at different angles, crowds between Carnarvon and Eve. He studies the figures with a look of rapture. "The four goddesses of the dead. The most exquisite faces I've ever seen."

Two of the shrine goddesses gaze at the side of the cabinet, while two others peer over their shoulders toward the portal to watch for anything approaching. The goddesses seem to say, *Do not take another step. We're here to protect the chest.*

After a long pause, Carter says in a low voice, as if to himself, "Always, it's the eyes that make a face come to life." The archaeologist is on the verge of tears. "Of all the marvels we've seen in this tomb, this shrine is the most spectacular."

He examines hieroglyphs up close. "The shrine surely contains canopic jars, vessels holding the pharaoh's organs," he says. "The spells written on the shrine are needed for the organs to be joined to the pharaoh in the afterlife." Carter draws back again and spreads his arms wide, as in adoration.

"So beautiful," Carter chokes out. "Beyond imagining."

"I've never seen anything more gorgeous in my life," Eve agrees.

"Smashing!" Carnarvon says.

"I'm going to call this room the Treasury," Carter says. "It holds the finest treasures in the world."

The ancient Egyptians believed their temples and their tombs were living entities to unite them with eternity. Eve begins to understand why they might think so. She feels heady, electrified, her sensations magnified. All sense of time and place leaves her. For a moment, all she can see is a light of luminous gold. A phrase from one of Lord Byron's poems about the nighttime revelry of a group of young soldiers incongruously pops into her head: to chase the glowing hours. Glowing hours, golden hours. These are they. Here in the depth of her spirit there is no sadness or growing old or war, only pleasure and youth and supreme beauty. She wants to linger, to stay in the feeling of euphoria. Experiencing the splendor with her father and Carter is part of that joy.

What if the inspectors find out we were here? The worrisome thought brings her back to the semidark, crowded room, and the spell is broken. "Father, it is time we return to Carter's house before someone looks for us," Eve whispers. She motions for her father to leave with her. Carter follows.

Eve knows that entering Tutankhamun's tomb will be the most significant event of her life. She has reached the apex of a great wheel that will turn from top to bottom and up again, many times, with both joys and sorrows. Already, as she watches Carter fill fresh plaster into the hole leading out of the tiny crypt, and as she sees him conceal the area with a lid from a gigantic round basket, she feels herself turning downward. She's involved in a grand deceit. Nothing good can come from dishonesty. And yet, what splendors she has seen!

5

The next morning, back at the excavation site and waiting for the Antiquities Service official, Eve closes her eyes after a sleepless night but cannot rest. She imagines that the laborers, who are clearing the tunnel of further debris, whisper to each other. Carnarvon, his legs outstretched, happily snores away. Carter, fueled by his nerves, tidies areas under the tent that to Eve seem perfectly orderly. He folds and stacks his Arabic newspapers, collects empty tins and wine bottles, and rearranges his mountain of boxes that help to block the sun.

Eve snaps to full awareness when she hears Carter calling her name. "Lady Eve! Carnarvon!" Carter, cradling an object under his arm, approaches. The object is wrapped in a clean undershirt that he keeps at the excavation.

Carnarvon wakes with a start when Carter shakes him. "What now, Carter?"

"A statue," Carter says, and places it on Carnarvon's lap. "One of the workers found it near the end of the tunnel. Perhaps the robbers left it there in their hurry."

"Let me see." Eve unwraps the bundle to find a wooden, nearly life-size bust of the young pharaoh. His head emerges from a lotus flower. His skin is painted the color of Nile mud. Dots suggest hair, and his large ears have holes for earrings.

"How enchanting," Eve says. "This shows him, I'd think, at ten or eleven."

"Exquisite workmanship," Carnarvon says, taking up the head.

"Yes, isn't it?" Carter looks wistful. "I believe this is one of the tomb's most interesting pieces. It's so simple, so personal."

Eve loves the youthful expression in the young king's eyes, with his full lips closed in an almost-smile, as if he's just enjoyed a game or sport.

"We should hide this away before the inspector comes," Carnarvon says.

"Shouldn't you declare it?" Eve asks.

Carter strokes his mustache, as he often does when he thinks things over. "Too late. We'll be in real trouble if they find we have it here above ground. And I'd like time to study it."

Carnarvon covers the bust with the shirt. Carter rummages through boxes and retrieves an empty Fortnum & Mason crate that once held four wine bottles. "Look, Carnarvon, a perfect fit," he says, slipping the wrapped bust inside and closing the lid.

"Oh." Eve frowns. "Must you?"

Carter and Carnarvon nod toward each other as if a bond between them has now been sealed. Eve looks about for Callender, a voice of reason, then remembers he'd gone to Carter's house to sleep after his all-night watch.

The archaeologist hides the crate among the food supplies. He lights a cigarette and begins to pace. As watchful and attentive as the falcon god Horus, he circles from the tent to the tunnel to the switchback in the road leading up from the Valley.

"What do you think Mr. Carter intends to do with that bust?" Eve asks Carnarvon.

"I'll have him ship it to Highclere," Carnarvon says.

"Father! You'll do nothing of the sort." She recalls the previous day when she noticed his pocket bulging. What else has he taken?

Just then, a figure rides toward them on a donkey. The man wears a Western-style suit jacket over his native robes, and on his head is a red tarboosh. Eve bites her lip. It is El Mofty.

After she and her father and Carter greet the inspector, Eve busies herself serving water and dried apricots. Carnarvon, calm and secretive as the desert hills, chats about the dig while El Mofty rests. By and by, Carter orders the workers out of the tunnel. This time he places a guard at the entrance, a stout, gray-bearded man named Reis Ahmed Gerigar, his foreman.

The inspector removes the jacket he wears over his galabiya. Carter and the inspector bring a pickaxe and mallets down into the tunnel. Eve and Carnarvon join them. Soon after, Carter bashes through the partition leading to the Antechamber with energetic swings of his mallet. Eve is relieved to see that he strikes the newly covered area first. Then he works from top to bottom, plaster dust flying, and the enchanted realm of the golden treasures emerges.

For a moment there is silence. "How spectacular!" Carter shouts.

"It's all wonderful, wonderful!" Carnarvon says.

"Who could have imagined?" Eve says.

El Mofty, his eyes bright, turns to Carter. "The sight of this gold is enough to dazzle a blind man."

Carter puffs up like a proud father. "These are the finest treasures in all of Egypt."

Carter and El Mofty weave through the Antechamber, Eve following. By the electric torch light, Carnarvon takes photos. Captivated by the royal scene before them, it is a long time before anyone talks. Eve does not know if minutes have passed or half an hour. Once again she feels lost in a timeless spell.

"Who could have imagined?" Carnarvon says to the inspector. "Bows. Slings. Arrows. Look at it all."

"Chariots, at least several of them," Eve says.

"Lord Carnarvon, Lady Evelyn," says El Mofty, "you seem very familiar with what's here."

Eve feels herself flush. "No, inspector." She locks eyes with him.

After a long minute, the inspector continues to explore the pile of furniture and chariot parts. He looks up and down, pivots, and stoops onto his hands and knees. He is wiry and has no trouble moving about without knocking things over. His curly hair, damp with sweat, clings to his neck.

When he rises again, El Mofty approaches and admires the black-and-gold pharaoh statues for some time. Then, after moving his torch over the horizontal plastered area between them, he says, "Ah! Behind here is another chamber."

On the floor, the large basket lid and a bundle of reeds conceal the hole leading into the burial room. All El Mofty needs to do is brush aside the basket lid, and he will see damp plaster.

A knot forms in Eve's stomach. She tries not to picture herself in an Egyptian courtroom being interrogated by lawyers.

Standing between El Mofty and the wall, she brushes dust off her skirt. Her voice rises higher than usual. "Inspector, do you think this passage could lead to a storeroom?"

"Not flanked by two such statues," he says. "Other chambers must exist. I'm led to think that this one is momentous."

"I would like to knock down that wall," Carter says. "But as you know, I would need to clear this room first to keep from damaging these artifacts."

The inspector steps closer to Eve, pauses, then runs his hand along the wall on either side of her head. Biting her lip, she waits for the inspector to ask her to move.

Carter runs his hand over his mustache.

At that moment, Carnarvon begins one of his fits of coughing. Though timely, it is involuntary. He clears his throat and composes himself. "How long do you think it would take to clear the room, Carter?"

"I don't know." He points his torch at four dismembered chariot wheels lying in a heap. His beam of light slowly moves to the body of the chariot and beyond it to a mass of gilded wooden parts.

"Two weeks?" the inspector asks. "Three?"

"Much more than that, El Mofty, Effendi," Carter replies. "Months." He says he will need to conserve anything fragile in situ before it's exposed to the outside air. And each artifact needs to be documented before being carefully packed and crated by experts. Only then can the artifacts go to the Egyptian Museum in Cairo, where any distributions will be made.

"The staff of the Egyptian Museum will help you," says the inspector, "and as you know, Pierre Lacau, the director-general of our Antiquities Service, has his office there. He will personally supervise the workers."

"The museum does not have anyone trained in conservation," Carter snaps. "The contents of this tomb will be as good as ruined if we get those amateurs involved."

The inspector scowls. "Mr. Carter, you are insulting my fellow Egyptians."

Eve shoots her father an imploring look.

"I know that I'm required to move the contents of this tomb to the Egyptian Museum," Carter says, "but already the museum is overcrowded. It's utterly chaotic. It has no security. Antiquities are lost or broken or stolen there all the time—"

Eve interrupts. "Should you talk about the future now, with so much to do first?"

"Eve has a point," Carnarvon says. "We can wait, and cooperate on any plans needed for the museum."

Still, Carter's diatribe hangs in the air just like a curse.

"El Mofty, Effendi," Eve says, "everyone wants the same thing. We have only the greatest respect for your heritage. We want these antiquities to be treated with the utmost care."

"Inspector," Carnarvon says, "Carter and I will work with you in whatever manner is needed."

"I hope so. I would not want to give you sanctions. Or report your lack of cooperation to our director-general," the inspector says. He finds his tarboosh, which he's rested on the floor, and bows to Carter, Eve, and her father.

Moments later, the tunnel echoes with footsteps running toward them. One of the younger workers bursts into the Antechamber. Behind him races Gerigar, the foreman. He grabs the young man by the waist and yanks him backward. But it is too late. The worker has seen the Antechamber. *"Dhahab!"* he says.

The worker breaks away from Gerigar and scrambles back along the tunnel. Gerigar chases him, followed by Carter and the inspector, both shouting in Arabic.

Eve bolts after them, her father hobbling behind her. He is breathing so deeply that he starts to wheeze.

Carter, the inspector, and Gerigar punch and shove back three workers who are trying to force their way inside the tomb.

"Carnarvon, Lady Eve. Stand behind us and block off the steps," Carter says.

Eve pushes hard against Carter's back to try to stop the fight. Carnarvon spreads his arms across the stairway.

Carter yanks out a pistol. Eve had no idea he owns such a thing. She stands gripping the wall, waiting for an explosion. Perhaps a death. Shouting in Arabic, Carter points the weapon at a worker whose eyes are narrow and piercing. A boy darts between the man's legs and comes out directly in front of Carter. For a moment, everyone freezes.

The boy speaks to the other workers. Carter creeps forward. Two older workers turn and dash up the stairway. The youth, with the pistol at his shoulders, climbs up reluctantly, head tipped back.

El Mofty follows Carter up the steps behind them.

Eve wants to go above ground with her father, too. Escape from this wretchedly hot cave where they might be shot by accident. Or attacked. Some disgruntled worker could come at her with a sharpened blade. But the sound of shouting indicates agitated workers have crowded around the entranceway to the stairs. Eve takes a deep breath. One option seems as risky as another. She can occasionally make out the word *dhahab*.

Carnarvon, clutching his cane as if he wants to join the fight, follows the others up the stairway. Eve creeps close behind. She and Carnarvon emerge into a cloud of acrid, choking dust that has been churned up by the crowd. Carnarvon coughs so hard, she thinks he may vomit. Eve coughs as well.

The dirty cloud lifts enough for her to see Gerigar, the inspector, and Carter standing shoulder to shoulder against the workers. El Mofty takes a pistol from his jacket and points it at one of the men. Several laborers call out and leap forward to join El Mofty to hold the blockade. The crowd of Egyptians argue and shove one another. Milling in the dust, the group of men shrinks into a smaller, yet still crazed, band that threatens to break through.

"Lady Eve. Get back into the tunnel," Carter warns.

Eve clutches Carnarvon's hand as he wheezes and spits. God help us, she thinks. With her father's weak lungs, he could suffocate right here and now. She must guide him to safety, back into the tomb, but there the air is no better. And the heat is worse. Three young men break through the crowd and race toward them, clearly intent on stealing from the tomb. A laborer Eve recognizes by his perpetual scowl pushes past Carnarvon and attempts to get by her. Elbows out, she tries to block the way. Carnarvon swings his cane at the man, loses his balance, and falls over backward.

Gritty dust engulfs them. Hot sand seems to fill Eve's lungs. She cannot see through the dust but can hear her father coughing violently. As the dust begins to clear again, she sees her father crouched beside her, his hands over his head. From somewhere in the confusion, Carter comes toward them. He scolds the crowd in Arabic, then grips the pistol with his two hands and stretches his arms above him. Standing with his feet wide apart, he presses the trigger.

The explosion pierces the air. It rings in her ears. Eve goes rigid. Carter yanks his arms up into the air again and fires another shot. Eve helps Carnarvon to his feet and embraces him.

Carter and El Mofty fire more shots into the air. Finally, slowly, the workers, still arguing, begin to disperse toward the road that leads out of the Valley. Taking her father's hand, Eve moves him to the shade of the tent and settles him into a chair.

Carter and El Mofty eventually come to the tent after talking to groups of workers, both continuing to hold their revolvers as they converse in Arabic.

"Was anyone hurt?" Eve asks.

"No. The pistols stopped them." He explains how his first shot gave them enough control that the inspector could talk to them. El Mofty has reminded the men of the futility of stealing—even if they got away for a time, they are known and risk a great deal. They could have a hand cut off. Or worse.

Eve wipes sweat from her forehead with her palm. Her heartbeat is slowing.

El Mofty's grip tightens on his pistol. Eve fears it will somehow go off and kill one of them by accident. His brow crinkles as he looks at Carnarvon. "I will bring in some professional guards. Even that will pose a risk. We have to find people who are trustworthy."

Carter strokes his chin with his revolver and says nothing. Eve flinches. My God, he seems casual with that weapon!

"I have confidence in you, El Mofty," Carnarvon says hoarsely. He clears his throat. His breath is short. The events of the day have certainly left him exhausted, she thinks, but he doesn't seem as shaken as she. "Those scoundrels!" he says. "We were jolly lucky."

Eve addresses Carter, though she could have just as easily spoken to El Mofty. "What is that word they keep saying? *Dhahab*?"

"Gold," Carter replies.

Gold. Of course. The workers who got inside the tomb were dazzled by it. Now it will take armed guards to keep these men away. Considering the riches in the tomb, and the poverty outside it, it's not surprising that a few of Carter's laborers would turn against him, even risking their lives, to pilfer a statuette or amulet.

The enchanted world doesn't just belong to her and her father and Carter anymore. The secret is out.

6

That night, Eve feeds Sir Golden seeds before putting him back in his cage on the table near the window of her room at Castle Carter. It is quite a spacious cage, but bent here and there, and as soon as she latches the door, it pops open again. Finally, Eve is able to fasten it. Before she goes to bed, she leaves the window ajar. The dry climate of the Valley, unlike that of Luxor, keeps mosquitoes away. Refreshed by the cool air, she drops off to sleep. The day of terror has exhausted her as if she's hiked for miles.

She awakes to fluttering sounds and a high-pitched cry. Trembling, she rolls out of bed and flicks on the overhead light. There, in Sir Golden's cage, is a hideous black snake.

She presses herself against the wall and screams.

The snake holds up its flattened head and spreads wide its mouth, revealing fangs. Its jaw expands to engulf the bird.

Eve grabs a book from a nearby table and hurls it.

The snake slides out of the open door of the cage and down a table leg. On the floor, it unfurls to a length of about three feet. Mesmerized, Eve watches. Pale yellow cross-bands extend down its body. Below its mouth is a bulge. Ahmed dashes into the room just as the snake slides out the window and disappears.

"A cobra," says Ahmed.

"I should have kept the window closed," Eve says.

"You couldn't have known, lady." He frowns. "Cobras are not common here. It's been years since I've seen one."

He opens the window wider and peers out. "Gone," he says. Eve looks, too. There is nothing to see but darkness. He shuts the window. Almost immediately, Carter is there.

Eve points to the empty cage. Three yellow feathers lie on the bottom. "A cobra!" She gasps. "Sir Golden..."

He understands at once.

"The door to the cage," Eve says, her voice throbbing, "must not have fastened properly, and...I left the window open. I..."

"Shhh, it's all right," he says, enfolding her in his strong arms. "It's not your fault." He hugs her with both strength and tenderness.

Despite her sorrow over the bird's death, she relaxes into his embrace and presses against him. He is still for a moment, then gently drops his arms. Feeling embarrassed, she cannot look at him. Has she gone too far? Her mother would think so.

The next morning, Eve has no appetite for breakfast. She feels pinched and full of tension and wishes she could take a bath at the hotel. She tells her father that she wants to return to Luxor for a day or two. Carnarvon readily agrees. First, they will accompany Carter to the excavation site to make sure no one had broken into the tomb during the night. Then, in Luxor, Carnarvon and Eve will plan an event for local dignitaries. The tomb must have an official opening, Carnarvon says, so they can let the world know of their discovery. And in order to receive support in safeguarding the tomb, they must notify Egyptian government officials as soon as possible.

At the site, Carter's laborers, following his orders, block up the entrance to the tomb with rocks and sand as a temporary security measure. Callender coils up the electrical extension cords he has just removed, and three native guards patrol the area around the stairway. The older and heavier of the robed guards, his hands on his hips, puffs out his chest. In addition to the pistol he wears, two knives dangle in leather sheaves from his belt, one on each side of his torso. The larger knife, slightly curved and a foot long, could easily sever a limb, Eve thinks. These weapons are not for show. What is she doing in the desert with these rough, dangerous people?

Eve confers with Carnarvon; Carter instructs two laborers to bring up their donkeys to the tent. But just then, Eve sees that most of the workers have put down their shovels and baskets. Near the entrance to the stairway, a short man with a gray beard, wearing robes and a turban, talks animatedly.

Eve's mouth feels dry. "Who is that man?" she asks Carter.

"His name's Abuar. He's one of the workers—and he's the uncle of my manservant, Ahmed. I've never known him to be trouble before." Carter reaches into his satchel and takes out the pistol. He strides toward the group.

Abuar waves his arms. His voice carries. From the crowd comes an undercurrent of murmurs. Eyes wide, the foreman raises his hands. Then he strikes the air. Good God, what's next? Eve thinks.

Carter pushes his way through the crowd. He takes a whistle from his pocket and blows it with such a piercing sound, some of the men jump. In a stream of Arabic, he reprimands both Abuar for stirring up the workers and Gerigar, his foreman, for allowing the commotion.

Gerigar stops speaking and bows, then takes up his station near the wall of boxes, his post for awaiting instructions. The laborers, all but nine of them, go back to hauling debris to fill the stairway. Those nine, Abuar included, roll up their rugs and set out on the track to the village.

Eve pushes past the laborers to Carter's side. "What's the matter?" she asks.

"Go join your father," he says, his expression stern. "I'll talk to you there."

When Carter has finished conferring with Gerigar, he comes to the tent. Callender offers him a cigarette and lights it for him. "My foreman is someone I greatly esteem," Carter says. "He's a hard worker. He can control a crowd. But even my most trusted man has turned out to be a superstitious fool."

"What the devil is happening, Carter?" Carnarvon asks.

"Ahmed was gossiping in the village this morning. Then his uncle Abuar told the workers that the death of the bird means bad luck. Some talk of it as a curse: 'The pharaoh is angry for being disturbed from his sleep of death.'"

"That's silly," Eve says.

"Yes. A lot of rot," Carnarvon says, as if giving the last word on the subject. Yet Eve thinks he looks less than convinced.

"It is rot," Callender chimes in.

"Why don't you go after the men who've left?" Eve says. "Is there any way to reason with them? Get them back?"

Carter frowns. "It won't do any good. Abuar said to the workers, 'Before the winter is out, someone will die.' They're taking the curse very seriously."

"Who is he to be announcing curses?" Carnarvon says. "The others, meantime, follow his every breath."

"Yes, even Gerigar." Carter's forgotten to inhale, it seems; he blows the smoke out of his mouth. "There is an irony, I must admit," he says, his expression reflective. "In life, the pharaohs wore the flexed cobra on their crowns, representing royalty and a goddess of protection."

"Still a bit of nonsense," Callender says.

Carter shrugs. "I don't care about their superstitions," he says. "What matters is if a few men, disgruntled for whatever reason, stir up a crowd."

"But how can you avoid that?" Eve asks.

"Starting today, after the stairway is filled in, I'll let most of my workers go," he says. "I no longer need them. I'll only keep on twenty. That should be sufficient to ready the tomb for its official opening."

The reminder of the official opening gives Eve a lift. A tour of the tomb could be combined with a party. "Tell me a date, Mr. Carter, and I'll start sending invitations."

Carter twists his neck toward the line of workers passing baskets of rocks, relay fashion. Eve senses he'd distracted and understandably so.

"Let's say December 2," Carnarvon puts in.

Carter nods toward Carnarvon. "All right," he says, his voice flat.

"Then Eve and I shall leave Luxor the day after the opening," Carnarvon announces. His tone is cheerful. "Then we can still be home for Christmas."

Christmas! Eve's hand flies to her chest. "Father, I can hardly believe I forgot all about the holiday!" To Eve's surprise, she feels a division within herself, like the two banks of the Nile. Of course she wants to go home, to her mother, to her horse, to her castle and its cool, wet green grounds. And yet she wants to be in Egypt at the same time, to share in the making of history with Howard Carter.

"Carnarvon, Lady Eve, go on to Luxor," Carter says. "I'll see you at the hotel tomorrow."

"Be in time for dinner," Carnarvon says. "Perhaps I can arrange for Arthur Merton to join us."

"Good idea, Father!" Eve says. She knows that Merton is head of the *Times* bureau in Egypt and has read many of his articles.

Carter huffs in disapproval. "Do what you must, Carnarvon. I don't care for reporters, but Merton writes more accurately than the rest of them."

Eve looks away from Carter's frowning face. "Let's go, Father."

The donkeys, crowded into the scarce shade of the cliff's overhang, await Eve and Carnarvon. Carter helps Carnarvon mount his donkey.

Then, standing alone with Eve under the tent, Carter places his hand on her shoulder. As comforting as the feeling is, she pulls away in case her father is watching. He isn't.

"I'm sorry for all you've gone through," he says.

"I'm fine," she says. "I would go through it again. The crowd. The gunshots. I've seen splendors I could never imagine. All because of you."

Her words are daring, she knows.

He nods and gives her a warm smile. She senses he is not used to praise. "Come now. Your father is waiting for you."

After the amazing but tumultuous events in the desert, Eve and Carnarvon cross the Nile into the more familiar comforts and opulence of the Luxor Winter Palace Hotel. The hotel's red-carpeted stairway spirals upward, shell-like, to a series of balconies. The botanical garden, so green and lush, seems like the paradise of the gods after the heat and dust of the Valley. The songbirds, the date palms, the gurgling fountain. The aroma of the jasmine that she loves so much. She and Carnarvon sit on the grand balcony of the hotel and sip from glasses of sweetened, rose-colored hibiscus tea while looking out at the Nile.

Eve takes notes as her father tells her the names of the important British and Egyptian government officials they will invite to the tomb. Following a tour, the guests will be served a meal at the excavation site. How important she feels to be in charge of the reception! Eve accepts the exciting responsibility of sending invitations; recording acceptances and regrets; planning the menu; ordering foods, wines, tables, chairs, tablecloths, silver, and glassware; and making sure the supplies will be delivered by donkey to the Valley in good time. She'll see to it that the newspapers in London will cover it. What a fabulous event it will be!

The sky turns bloodred in the sunset and then, with remarkable speed, turns orchid purple, then sapphire blue. Eve closes her eyes to savor the experience.

The following morning, Eve confers with the chef at the hotel, while Carnarvon places calls on the hotel's phone. Together Eve and her father write letters and draft telegrams to friends, family, scholars, and British dignitaries. Carnarvon addresses his first telegram to Lady Carnarvon:

29 November 1922

To Lady Almina Carnarvon, Highclere Castle

My darling, Carter has discovered the most spectacular find in the history of Egyptian archaeology. A treasure trove of splendid artifacts. Simply breathtaking. Eve and I will come home for the holidays.

Love, regards, George and Eve

Eve goes to the Luxor telegraph office near the hotel to place her father's telegrams. Then, that afternoon, she returns to the office to pick up any responses that might have come in. Carter is at the sending window, dictating a message. She sucks in a breath and her lips part.

"Mr. Carter," she says, stepping toward him. "You didn't send word you were coming."

He turns and smiles. "I was about to look for you."

The operator, a young British woman, takes down Carter's words on a transmitting device that resembles a postal scale but is as big as a sewing machine. Pressing the sixteen black and white keys, the typist causes the machine to tip amusingly from side to side. Eve hears him dictate:

29 November 1922

To Mr. A. M. Lythgoe, Metropolitan Museum, New York

Discovery colossal and need every assistance.

Carter

"Time's up, Mr. Carter," the operator says. "I must help other customers. Please come back later, sir, if you want to send more."

Eve and Carter move to the message-receiving area, where a machine nearly the size of a piano turns a large wheel of paper tape. This is where the words of incoming telegrams roll out.

"The Metropolitan Museum in New York has the most exceptional staff of Egyptologists anywhere," Carter says. "Their men will know how to properly handle and document the artifacts."

"Even better than the experts at the British Museum?"

"Many of them *used* to be at the British Museum. The Americans offered them good salaries. Among other great talents, the Metropolitan now has Harry Burton, a British photographer who lives mostly in Italy. He does ripping good work. It's my dream for him to assist me."

"But if Mr. Burton comes," Eve says, her voice light, "Father will have to move over as chief photographer. What a blow to his ego!"

Carter laughs. "He'll get over it." The archaeologist reports that her father's efforts and his own photography lab in Castle Carter have produced only murky images of the tomb's interior. "I suspect he's already taken to his new post as director of publicity."

"Yes, rather," Eve says. "Soon he'll be on to selling cinema rights. He's made a list of film directors. He's even blocked out a scene reenacting the pharaoh's burial. You should hear him. He has dancing girls with floral collars covering their bare breasts."

"That's Carnarvon!" Carter says.

A lock of thick black hair falls across Carter's eyes. Eve stifles the urge to reach out and push it back.

"Speaking of publicity," Eve says, "if I dare suggest, it might be a good time for a hair trim. If you like, I could make an appointment with the hotel barber today."

"There isn't time." His voice is gentle. Surprisingly, he doesn't rebuff her as she imagined he would.

"Um," Eve says, tendering her finger toward his chest, "I see something there."

Carter glances down at his shirt pocket, where his fountain pen has left an inky black stain. "What a nuisance."

"Shall I have one of Father's shirts pressed for you?"

"All right. You're kind. I'll borrow a shirt, then."

She gives a quick nod, pleased that Carter is allowing her to take care of such intimate details as his clothing. She's just crossed a line of her mother's and of society at large and doesn't care the least little bit. Maybe she should have several shirts pressed. Carter will feel grateful to her, she thinks, when he looks his best for the dinner with the journalist tonight and the opening of the tomb the day after tomorrow.

A bell rings on the telegraph-receiving machine, and its wheel begins to turn. The clerk puts the message into an envelope. Eve hastens to the clerk's desk and discovers it's a message for her father. All excitement, she signs for it, rips open the envelope, then peers at the words on the tape.

It is a note from her mother.

29 November 1922

To Lord Carnarvon, Luxor Winter Palace Hotel.

Darling, have received your good news about the tomb. Look forward to seeing you for Christmas. Porchey is off to India after the holiday.

Yours, lovingly, Almina

Eve sighs. Does her mother have any idea of the importance of the Tutankhamun find? She will never understand her mother's lack of interest in Egyptology.

She shows Carter the message. Her thoughts tumble out. She wants to see her brother before he leaves England for his new army post. But if she travels home for Christmas, she probably won't return to Egypt before February. "I don't want to miss anything important. When are you going to open the burial chamber? I must see what's inside that shrine."

"I won't open the burial chamber without you and Carnarvon." His wistful eyes look at her and then at the telegraph machine. "When you're away, I'll gather the best experts. That will take some weeks. It could be a month before we start clearing the Antechamber."

Carter must sense her mood. "Look at me," he says. He reaches to tilt up her chin. "You won't miss much here. I've closed the tomb. Nine-tenths of the time, archaeology is about waiting—in the heat. Go and enjoy yourself."

"I'd rather be at the tomb," she says.

"You will be. When you return."

She nods, but she cannot help but feel that she's a player on an athletic field who has just been taken out of the game. She wants to be central, not peripheral. And she wants to feel again, even just one more time, that blaze of glory, when she and Carter and her father stood together in the golden light.

7

The sun beats down on the desert, and still the crowds come. On foot and on donkeys, they fill the road from Carter's house to the Valley. To Eve, traveling by donkey with her father and Fearnside, it is a vexing sight, this buzz of tourists and natives. One never knows what a crowd will do. How did so many people hear about the opening of the tomb? But ah, those *ghaffirs*, those Egyptian policemen in princely white uniforms with red sashes and tall red tarbooshes, do look very fine. They stand guard at intervals along the way. A jubilant Carnarvon gives them his Royal Army salute.

At the hut where tickets are usually sold, just before the road angles and opens wider to the excavation area and its surrounding Ramesses tombs, four *ghaffirs* turn away anyone not on Eve's guest list. The twenty esteemed visitors (not including attendants) are due to arrive at midday. Thank heavens, the police have cordoned off the road where it intersects with the Ramesses' tombs. This measure keeps tourists away from most of the tombs in the eastern section of the Valley. It belongs to her and her father and their guests today.

At the excavation site, the hot air carries the scent of roasted lamb and garlic. Eve's detailed instructions have been followed. A dozen folding tables and many chairs stand under two white canvas shelters at the center of the triangular excavation site. The striped tent and wall of boxes now lie off to one side. An awning, attached by ropes from the Ramesses VI tomb to poles on either side of the stairway, covers the entrance to the tomb. Relieved to be away from the crowds, Eve slips on low-heeled pink shoes. Carnarvon and Fearnside, who carries the cameras as always, join Carter and Callender in the chambers below. Egyptian servers from the Luxor Winter Palace Hotel spread white linen tablecloths and arrange the linen napkins, silverware, and crystal glasses.

Eve picks up a glass pitcher of lemonade and repositions it to the exact center of a table. She moves bowls of dates and cashews to make room for the next course. List in hand, Eve checks to see whether all the other foods have been prepared: pita and barley bread, crackers, caviar, stuffed peppers, lentil salad, and her favorite, almond cake. Three Egyptian boys, looking hot and listless, stand by with fabric paddle fans that resemble badminton rackets.

The local dignitaries, both English and Egyptian, will be impressed, Eve thinks proudly. All will recognize Carter and Carnarvon as expert caretakers of the most exquisite treasures Egypt has ever known.

Callender appears above ground. "Everything smells wonderful, Lady Eve," he says. "And you look so pretty: glamorous, like a starlet!"

She beams at him. In her pink pleated-silk frock, she feels restored to her most elegant self. "Everything is set here. I'll help inside the tomb now."

"It's better you stay out, m'lady. You know how Carter acts when he's nervous. Besides, we want to surprise you." He pours himself some lemonade and gulps it down.

"What have the three of you been doing? I notice you have a lot more electrical cables."

"You'll see," he says, all red bow tie and cheerfulness.

Callender grabs a handful of cashews and strides away. Eve glances at a neat pile of rocks and an idea comes to her. With permission from Callender, she takes out supplies from the tent and, careful not to let any India ink drip on her dress, paints the Carnarvon family emblem on a triangular stone. The design features mirror images of a capital *C*, one frontward and one facing it, interlocking.

Voila! Feeling satisfied, she places the rock near the top of the stairway so that those going down to the tomb will pass it.

Carnarvon emerges from the tomb, cane in hand. He dabs his forehead with a handkerchief. Eve brings him a fresh shirt. Gesturing to the tables, he says, "What a perfect job you've done! You have your mother's artistic and organizational talents." She kisses him on the cheek. When he turns and notices her rock, his smile widens.

The first Egyptian dignitaries arrive on donkeys and camels. Eve wishes they had brought their wives; apparently that is not their custom. As their servants help them dismount, Eve greets each guest with a curtsy and the practiced pronunciation of their names.

More guests arrive, and finally a woman among them. She's a graceful, middle-aged lady, clothed in a long dress of red plaid silk: Lady Adelaide Allenby, wife of Viscount Edmund Allenby, the British high commissioner for Egypt. But where is her husband? "I'm afraid Lord

Allenby cannot be with us today," she says. "More trouble in Cairo with the Wafdists."

Lady Allenby relates the news of the previous night, which Eve has not yet heard. There was a protest near the Armory, and at least one British tourist was trampled to death.

"How awful!" Eve says, her voice breaking. She feels prickling heat move up to her head. Images come to her, first of the rally she saw in El Opera Square and then of the workers pushing their way into the Antechamber. Arthur Merton, the *Times* of London reporter, ushers Lady Allenby to the tent for a private conversation, and Eve takes a moment to compose herself before greeting more guests.

"Gentlemen, feel free to take off your jackets," Carnarvon says, but few do.

Before long, Carter emerges from the tomb and struts toward the group. Eve's eyes open wide in surprise. He's freshly shaved and wearing a new shirt. What's more, he acts with a graciousness she's never seen in him before. Making introductions. Smiling as he shakes hands. Who would have thought he could play the politician? His gaze rests on Eve, just for a moment, with a tender expression.

Before Eve has time to further consider the small number of policemen on hand in comparison to the size of the crowd, Carter leads the first guests down the stairway to the tomb. Carnarvon, bubbling over with enthusiasm, acts as a second tour guide. As each group emerges, dabbing their brows and necks with handkerchiefs, it takes them a few moments to overcome their awe and break their silence. Eve and Fearnside offer them chairs and invite them to partake of the buffet, and an Egyptian waiter serves them glasses of lemonade. The surprised, joyous expressions on their faces show how deeply moved they are by the sight of the ancient trove. Eve feels as proud as she does when she gives guests tours of Highclere.

After she eats, and after all the dignitaries have gone through, Eve finally has her chance to see the tomb again. Carter asks her to join him for a private tour. He shuts the massive door behind them. Since the tunnel is so well lit, it comes as a shock to her when she and Carter enter into the blackness of the Antechamber. Then Carter switches on the electric power, the Antechamber glows with golden light, and the enchanted realm comes to life. The artifacts now stand out in full relief and surprisingly bright color. Oh, so marvelous!

Hiding the electric bulbs without moving the treasures, Carter has planted lights behind the most spectacular pieces. The forest of alabaster vessels radiates a soft yellow. Splashes of blues, blacks, and reds punctuate the great gilded animal couches. The lighting shows clearly the curves of their upright tails and the odd shapes of their gaping mouths. Today the black faces of the guardian statues, backlit, shine hauntingly, their striding forms glistening.

The gold surprises her in its variations: on some gilt surfaces, there are purplish or reddish tints; on others, the gold, in its purest form, appears bright yellow. The gold throne, simply dazzling, now shows the figures of the king and queen to have red-brown skin, blue wigs, and blue-and-gold collars. The wings of the vultures that decorate the throne's arms are made of blue glass inlays, Eve sees. How they sparkle!

Everywhere, precious stones gleam. Even the chariots are studded with them. Eve notices other objects for the first time. On the floor, half visible behind boxes and vessels, sits a small, gilded wooden casket decorated with blue-violet faience. The motifs feature alternating cartouches and images of gold cobras, all under a row of golden sun disks. Another snake ripples its body along the edge of the casket's lid. Kneeling figures, mirror images of each other, decorate the panel at the end of the box. Even the knob of this casket is beautiful—it is blue faience and inscribed with white hieroglyphs.

"Mr. Carter, this is magical. Your lighting brings out the true beauty here," she says.

"Can you envision how these treasures would have looked in the bright Egyptian sunlight? Even more striking."

"I can't imagine beauty greater than this," she says.

"Nor can I."

Above ground, the party continues. Her father has probably become so engrossed in his conversations that he isn't missing her, Eve thinks. She will give herself just a little longer to enjoy the peaceful chamber, its beauty, and the rare time alone with Carter.

Eve realizes that it isn't just the new electrical bulbs that give her the ability to see colors and details. In Carter's presence, the beauty magnifies as if she sees it through his eyes: the varied colors of gold, the scarabs of lapis lazuli. She notices more details when he stands beside her. It seems they hardly need to use words anymore, for anything he might tell her she already knows. They are at one with the vast and diverse beauty around them. Is this what love feels like?

The room grows hotter. Eve takes in a whiff of sweet frankincense. She can almost feel the cool alabaster vessels warming, the caskets' lapis lazuli panels loosening, and the motionless statues beginning to stir. It is as if the chamber, startled by the intense feelings of the people within it, wakes up.

Eve daringly rests her head against Carter's chest, and he puts his arms around her waist. The gesture feels right, their faces illuminated by the glow of the golden treasures. Oh, the supreme joy and comfort of being in his arms. To connect physically, as they have already merged, powerfully, in the nonphysical realm. Surely he shares that awareness?

Minutes pass before Carter finally speaks. His face is partly in shadow, his tone gentle. "Lady Eve, we shouldn't be together like this. I must not betray your father's trust in me. What would he—"

"Shush, don't speak," Eve says.

Then, in the midst of this intensity of emotion, comes a shattering. A breaking of the spell. A voice calls.

"Carter! Are you there?" It is Callender. "Someone has passed through the blockade."

The transition back to reality could not be more sudden. Out again in the bright sunlight, she sees a stranger standing over her father at the head of the table. He is an Englishman, from the looks of him, about thirty, clean-shaven, with a leather portfolio slung over his shoulder. How has he slipped past the sentries? Meanwhile, the servers pour hibiscus tea into china cups and set out cakes for the guests.

"Carter," the stranger says as Carter and Eve come near.

"Weigall." Carter frowns, and his eyes glint with a steely edge. "What are you doing here?"

"And you must be Lady Evelyn Herbert, Lord Carnarvon's daughter," the man says.

"Sir," she says, and extends her hand.

"Arthur Weigall here, chief Cairo correspondent for the *Daily Mail.*" He tips his broad hat, revealing a head of blond curls. "Your father and I dined from time to time when he was excavating Queen Hatshepsut's valley tomb."

"How do you do," she says, aware that all her guests are watching her. How can she defuse the tension? Should she ask the reporter to sit down and have some cake?

Weigall leans toward Carnarvon with his hand on the table. "I'm sure you remember me. We talked for some time after you and Mr. Carter found Hatshepsut's sarcophagus—the abandoned one," the reporter says. "You'll recall I was an inspector for the Antiquities Service."

Oh? Eve senses a story here.

"Sir, at the moment I'm engaged," Carnarvon says. "You may contact me, if you wish, at the Winter Palace Hotel." He smiles briefly, then nods toward Carter, who is listening closely with his hands clenched. Carnarvon's subtle expression seems to say, *Please conduct this man out of here.*

Weigall presses on. "I'm from the *Daily Mail*," he repeats. He displays his identification. "I'd like to tour the tomb."

"You're not welcome here," Carter says. The archaeologist steps toward Weigall like a striking cobra. His voice is controlled but hardened. "Mr. Weigall, I must ask that you leave. Now."

The journalist scowls. Eve looks helplessly toward the cordoned-off area where the main pathway intersects with the clearing of the Ramesses tombs. Just out of sight, not one but four *ghaffirs* stand guard, she knows. It is maddening that not one of them is at hand.

Weigall scans the luncheon party. "I see Merton's here. May I ask, Lord Carnarvon, why you've invited a reporter from the *Times* of London and not any other paper? The Egyptian journalists should all be here."

A frozen silence falls over the party. Eve feels a thickness in her throat. She is mortified that everyone hears the strangled exchange.

"Listen, Carter." Weigall's tone changes abruptly. "You've no right to ban me from the tomb."

Carter's face is set tight. The guests wait, motionless—except for a tall Egyptian official of middle years, who walks up to the reporter with the stride of a man of authority. "Mohammed Bey Fahmy," he says. "I am the chief of police of this district. Is there some difficulty?"

At any moment, it seems, Bey Fahmy might grab the reporter by the neck. Or Carter might do it himself, Eve thinks.

Weigall straightens. "Never mind—I'll be on my way." He gives Carnarvon a business card. "Here are telephone numbers for our offices in Cairo and Luxor, and a private number."

Carnarvon receives the card. Without smiling, he shakes Weigall's hand. Weigall, instead of heading away, eyes Carter, then all the guests one after another as if taking a mental note of each one. "Pierre Lacau is absent," he says. "It looks like no one from the Antiquities Service is here. Weren't they invited, Lord Carnarvon?"

Carnarvon says only, with a tad of irritation, "Good day, sir."

Despite having declared that he is on his way, the reporter makes no motion to leave. Carter says, "*Sir.* Please go."

Weigall steps back a few paces. He brings out a small box camera from his shoulder bag and, before anyone can stop him, snaps a photo of Eve, Carnarvon, and Carter, surrounded by their party. Then he strides across the clearing of the Ramesses tombs and onto the main pathway toward the blockade of guards. Bey Fahmy takes a seat, as does a glowering Carter.

To smile at this moment would seem forced. So Eve turns to her guests and says, "Well! We met a former antiquities inspector turned reporter, a most fascinating man who was passing this way. Would anyone like more almond cake?"

"I should!" says Carnarvon.

Eve asks the server to pour her father and Lady Allenby more hibiscus tea.

"I do recall dining, *exactly once*, with the gentleman who was just here," Carnarvon says. "It was several years ago, at the close of the war, when Carter and I discovered the sarcophagus of Queen Hatshepsut. As most of you know, this queen holds a unique position in history as the only female pharaoh. Nonetheless, she wore the ceremonial beard…"

Carnarvon talks on, telling the story Eve knows well, about the empty sarcophagus, an unused burial chamber bearing Hatshepsut's name, and Carter's encounter with bandits in a remote cliff cave. Her father, ever the conversationalist, manages to ease the discomfort among the guests that the reporter created. But she feels a headache coming on as Weigall's questions to her father sear in her mind. Why *didn't* they invite Pierre Lacau, the director-general of the Antiquities Service, to their gathering? And was it right to exclude the Egyptian press?

When she and her father went over the guest list, he said that he'd extended Lacau a separate invitation. But she never noticed a reply come in. Eve allowed him to dodge the question. An inspector from the Service is required to be present when anyone enters the tomb, as Carnarvon, Carter, and Eve all well knew. Eve begins to realize, at that moment, that the marvelous party she worked so hard to orchestrate has been a colossal mistake.

8

The next day, Eve, her father, and Carter, seated within a circle of armed guards outside the tomb, thumb through newspapers while awaiting the arrival of Pierre Lacau. Eve is thrilled to see her photo appear in the *Times* of London. But there she is again in Weigall's paper, as well. The caption reads, "The Carnarvons host private affair at the tomb. Antiquities Service excluded."

What fools we were, she thinks, to antagonize the Egyptians now, when they are massing to further break from Britain's influence. She cannot undo the party. All she can do is try her best to charm the top-level government administrator who will ultimately decide on the disposition of the Tutankhamun treasures. She is about to get her opportunity.

A donkey train passes through the crowd of clamoring tourists and into the circle of armed guards posted around the entrance to the tomb. Carnarvon points to a tall man with snow-white hair and a neatly trimmed beard and mustache, and says, to Eve's surprise, "That's Pierre Lacau. I've heard that he's a Jesuit, but maybe that's a rumor. He's hardly dressed like a monk or priest." The gentleman wears a top hat and an elegant suit of buff-colored silk. How distinguished he looks, how kind. Eve can hardly believe that Carnarvon and Carter consider him their adversary.

Carnarvon introduces himself and Carter, and then Eve.

"Lady Evelyn, it is a pleasure to make your acquaintance," Lacau says. He bows low and kisses her hand. She looks into the Frenchman's sparkling blue eyes and sees a calmness there. She loves his elegant French accent.

"And it is a pleasure to meet you, Director-General," she says.

"Lady Evelyn, you are even more lovely than in your photograph in the papers," Lacau says. Eve holds her breath for a moment. So the Frenchman has seen the article about the luncheon, as of course he would. Yet by the tone of his voice and the kind way he meets Eve's eyes, he doesn't act slighted at not having been invited. Perhaps he is above those kinds of feelings.

Eve and Lacau chat in French, which she speaks fluently; in the years before her French grandmother died, she made many trips to see her in Paris, and private tutors taught her well.

Carter escorts Lacau to the tomb's entrance. He allows only Eve, Carter, and Carnarvon to accompany him today. Fearnside, Lacau's guard, and an attendant will wait under the tent; and the ten laborers on the site will refill the stairway after Lacau's visit.

Carter unlocks the door at the base of the steps, and Eve follows the Frenchman along the tunnel. Carter switches on the special lights in the Antechamber. As before, the dazzling spectacle springs forth from the surrounding darkness like a fairy tale. A lemony light shines from the artifacts.

Eve eyes the Frenchman as he looks about, taking in the golden inlaid chariot parts, the gold chairs and beds. He draws near the glistening golden throne and falls to his knees. "*Magnifique!*" he says, tears in the corners of his eyes.

Eve is glad that Lacau appreciates what he sees. How could he not? The tomb is the most fantastic place to be on earth—well, aside from the heat. The tomb is even hotter than usual. So far, her father seems to be handling the heat. For the first time, though, Eve isn't sure she can.

As the men talk, she looks from one ka figure to the other and grows lightheaded. She tries to hold steady, to direct the meeting. But she daydreams of Highclere. How handsome the guardian figures will look there, framing the grand fireplace in the saloon, where the Carnarvons entertain their guests. Eve is only vaguely aware of her father and the eloquent official moving in and out of the Antechamber, or crawling between the great legs of the hippo couch into the smaller room Carter has named the Annexe. Sweat soaks her cotton frock.

She is near fainting when Carter startles her out of her trance by brushing his hand against hers. A jolt of energy radiates through her body as he clasps her hand lightly. Carter leads her out through the still, hot air of the tunnel and into the shade of the tent. He pulls out a chair for her. Fearnside pours her some water.

"Are you feeling better?" Carter asks.

"Better, just very hot," she says. "I shouldn't have stood in one place for so long."

Lacau and Carnarvon, engrossed in intense conversation, join them under the tent. Fearnside and Lacau's attendant and guard listen in silence. Carter pours Eve another glass of water and stands over her protectively. Carnarvon looks her way every now and again.

"I've had many inquiries from the press. The Egyptian journalists want entry," Lacau says. "I will leave them to you, Lord Carnarvon."

Carnarvon nods. "I can handle the press."

Can he? They have already made mistakes, Eve thinks.

"As you say, the sealed-off area between the ka figures could be a burial chamber," Lacau says. "So let me ask, when will you dismantle the partition?"

Eve pats the sweat off her face and neck and takes a drink of water. The tension is stronger than the heat. At any moment, her father or Carter may slip up by saying the wrong thing. Or is it clearly written on her own guilty face that she has already gone into the burial chamber?

"When my daughter and I come back after the holidays. Early February," Carnarvon says.

"Very well." The Frenchman strokes his white beard. "I shall look forward to it." Maintaining his pleasant but serious tone, he adds, "If it is an intact tomb, every item here will belong to the Egyptian government—as you know."

Eve starts, suddenly coming to full attention.

"We shall see," Carnarvon replies. "Certainly you acknowledge there has been a break-in?"

"Yes, but this is the most complete tomb I've ever seen. If there is a mummy, I will say it's intact. Regardless, you will still be compensated for your recovery efforts, Lord Carnarvon. I know you've spent a great deal and put in years of time and effort digging in the Valley. I will make sure you receive fair recompense." Lacau rises from his chair. "Shall we shake hands on it?"

"Shake hands on...on what?" Carnarvon is clearly caught off guard.

"On our mutual goodwill. On acting responsibly when we make our agreements for the tomb." Lacau assesses her father with keen eyes, and Eve prickles. Does Lacau regard her father as untrustworthy? She tells herself that her father is a man of his word—but is he? Will he attempt to bribe officials over Lacau if the Frenchman doesn't give him what he wants? Eve holds in her heart the wild hope that Lacau will allow her father to take half the treasures, and that they will not have to butt heads over the matter.

Carnarvon stands. His clenched teeth make his grin seem even more angular than usual. He shakes the priest's hand and says, "To fair agreements."

Lacau turns to Eve and bows low. "This has been a most glorious visit, and I shall remember it for the rest of my life," he says.

"I'm so glad you could come today," she returns.

With the sun still scorching down on them like the rays of the sun god, Lacau and his men leave on their donkeys, and their donkey train disappears into the Valley.

Carter takes the chair vacated by the Frenchman. "He's got nerve, Carnarvon," he says. "Forcing you to shake hands without the actual agreement spelled out."

"Yes, I could see his ploy, but what could I do?" Carnarvon replies. "A pity that the French still insist on running the Antiquities Service when every other governing post in this country belongs to Great Britain."

It is true. Napoleon's army left Egypt more than a century ago, but that has little to do with the matter at hand. "Well," Eve says, "I'm sure you're right, Father. But let me also say that I think Mr. Lacau was a perfect gentleman."

Carter snorts. "You think so?"

"Yes, I do."

"Odd chap, that Lacau," Carnarvon says. "Singular, religious. Doesn't drink or smoke. Eve's right: He's a gentleman. I wouldn't mind dealing with him if he didn't ascribe to the absurd notion that the Egyptians should own everything found in Egypt." Eve thinks that the way her father gazes over the Valley is the same way he likes to survey Highclere and their surrounding lands from a hilltop. "I'll see to it that Lacau gives me half of the artifacts and treasures, fair and square, if it means exerting all the political pressure I can muster."

Carter says, "Well, Carnarvon, if anyone's up to the task, it's you." He takes a cigarette from his case. "But I'm more than a little worried." He sighs.

"I can handle the director-general," Eve says. "Leave him to me."

Carnarvon pulls at one of his whiskers.

Eve cannot stop herself from voicing her thoughts. "If I'd followed my instinct, instead of listening to you, Mr. Lacau would have come to the official opening and—"

"Forget about it, darling." Carnarvon strokes his throat.

Eve drums her fingers on the arm of the chair. Clearly, her father does not want her involved in the politics of the tomb. Neither does Carter. But she will not hold still; moving forward, she will insist on being present at all meetings involving Lacau. She will not allow those two stubborn men to ruin their relations with the Antiquities Service.

Eve, Carter, Carnarvon, and Fearnside travel to Cairo, leaving the entrance to the tomb not only filled with rocky debris but secured by both Callender and El Mofty's guards. Unlike the Carnarvon party, who will travel on to Alexandria to board a ship, Carter comes to the city to purchase supplies—enough, as it turns out, to fill a newly rented storeroom. While the men shop for electrical paraphernalia, light bulbs, and equipment for a new darkroom, they send Eve to find soft wrapping so the treasures can be safely taken out of the tomb. She buys enough linen and bandages to fill her mother's London hospital. Carter orders a steel door to replace Callender's wooden one.

Shepheard's Hotel, chic and fashionable, is *the* place to be in Cairo if you are a young British woman of twenty-one. So, despite Carnarvon's dislike of the hotel's late-night bands and the long wait for drinks at the bar, Eve insists they and Carter stay there. The hotel is a palatial white stone building that rises to five stories in its center wing; inside, it is a veritable Aladdin's cave of exotic furnishings, art, and Persian carpets. The lotus-topped columns and friezes, based on the ancient temple at Karnak, together with the Moorish arches, transport Eve into a dream world.

On their final night in Cairo, Eve is disappointed when Carnarvon, ill with a cold and slight fever, remains in his suite under the supervision of a nurse. She was looking forward to attending the hotel's dance. Over dinner in the hotel's dining room, she asks Carter, "Please, accompany me."

He twitches his mustache. "I don't have the right clothes."

"The shop at the hotel can rent you a tuxedo," she says.

He gives a nervous laugh.

"Please," Eve says, leaning closer. Dancing is the only thing she misses about the society functions she'd be attending at home.

Carter's cheeks flush. "I'm considering it."

During their long wait for food, Carter pulls out a little leather book from his blazer pocket and makes pencil sketches of Eve. She finds it

unnerving, in a way, to have him scrutinize her, yet she loves the attention. She casts her eyes down, then up again, wondering how to pose.

"Let me see." She leans across the table.

Her lips half open, and a lock of hair playfully coiling over one
cheek, she appears alluring. So he finds me attractive, Eve thinks with
satisfaction. She laughs with pleasure.

Later, with the band in full swing in the Shepheard's ballroom, Carter
takes Eve's arm and leads her out onto the dance floor. The silk crêpe
of her yellow-and-black overdress, worn over black silk chiffon and
designed to look like a butterfly, rises and falls like real wings on her
back. She feels the easy pressure of his hand at her waist. As she rests
a hand on his shoulder, her other hand clasps his while the band music
guides them through a waltz. Eve feels joyous, light as air. What does it
matter if Carter's dancing skills are not refined? It is his gaze, so caring
and admiring, that counts. Can this truly be the scholarly archaeologist
who has up to now spent evenings alone with his work?

"You look simply ravishing tonight," he says.

"Thank you," Eve replies. "And you are very handsome." She imagines this may be one of the few times he has worn a tuxedo. This one
looks dapper with a black silk jacket, gray waistcoat, and gray silk tie.
His strong figure fills it out nicely.

Eve loves being a butterfly. Her shiny black bodice, cut into a low
V and embroidered with swirls of black and emerald beads, draws in
her waist. The loose crêpe of her overdress flutters as she moves. They
dance around and around, one-two-three, one-two-three. Only occasionally does she take her eyes from Carter's suntanned face to glance at
the other couples on the floor, mostly British, a few decked in military
honors.

"Do you think the ancient Egyptian kings and queens would have
enjoyed a ball like this?" Eve asks. "Certainly, they'd have been interested in our clothing. They dressed lavishly."

He returns her gaze. "I can't picture them out dancing like this,"
he says. "They went to bed after dark. They ordered their lives by the
sunrises and sunsets."

Eve laughs. "You make the royal Egyptians sound so practical. I
think they must have been a people of great excesses. Otherwise why
did their craftsmen put so much effort and artistry into small boxes or
oil containers?"

"What the vessels held was usually precious or sacred. But you have a point," he says.

All too soon the waltz ends, and the orchestra strikes up a foxtrot. "I'm sorry, Lady Eve, I don't know how to dance this one," Carter says.

But the foxtrot is ridiculously simple, she thinks. "I can teach—" she starts to say, then stops when she sees his expression change. She must not offend his pride. She takes his hand, and they scurry off to the side of the room that has a row of windows. "Perhaps we could go for a walk?" she asks.

Double doors lead out to a balcony overlooking lush botanical gardens. A stairway connects the balcony to the garden pathway below. By some stroke of extraordinary luck, they have the grounds to themselves. Eve and Carter walk arm in arm in the darkness, along the promenade of lanterns and palm trees. They come to a secluded kiosk near one of the fountains and sit down. The seat is cold. Eve shivers slightly and moves in close to Carter.

That she is leaving for Alexandria the next morning gives her the courage to speak. "Howard...may I call you that? What will happen after the dig is over? I mean...with you and me?"

Carter's eyes widen as he looks from Eve to the fountain and its cascading waterfall. For a long time, he sits, as if frozen. Finally, he turns back and presses her hand between his own. "You speak as if we're not from different social circles, Lady Eve." His eyebrows draw in as he frowns. "Your parents would never approve."

"They might, in time," she says, knowing full well her mother is immovable on the subject of Eve marrying a titled gentleman. Her father? Honestly, she isn't sure.

"Carnarvon loves all kinds of people, of all classes. I know he's fond of me, but what he wants for his daughter is a different matter."

Carter pauses, lets go of her hand, and rises to his feet. He paces about, then returns to the stone bench, where he stands over her. "Lady Eve, you don't understand. It's my lot, as it was my father's, to serve the aristocracy. I was taught to enjoy their art, to read their books, and not to desire what I am forever barred from having. I'd better myself in every possible way—if I thought there were a chance—but I know about aristocratic fathers and daughters."

Eve can feel his anguish. She stands and puts her hand on his back. How can she make him understand that she doesn't care about his humble upbringing? It has made what he's accomplished all the more remarkable. She coaxes him to turn to her. "Howard, you're as great an archaeologist as any who ever lived. Better than those with degrees from Oxford or Cambridge. And I know Father thinks so." She places her hands on his shoulders. "Finding the lost tomb of King Tutankhamun was thought to be impossible. All the other archaeologists gave up on it. Yet you persisted. *You* found it."

He meets her eyes. "Thank you. Your encouragement means a great deal to me." They sit on the bench again. She gazes up at him and then lifts her lips toward his. He hesitates. Then he kisses her eyelids and cheeks, and finally her lips. They kiss for a long time, passionately, hungrily. His face is warm, and she can sense the heat of his body. She plants kisses on his dark eyes, his nose, his mustache, and his chin. He touches the small of her back and runs his hands lightly over the silk crêpe of her overdress. How far will she allow herself to go?

As Eve becomes lost in the sensation of his embrace, so close that she can hear his heartbeat, she hears his muffled voice say, "If only we *could* be together."

The thrilling image comes to her of standing as a bride in her family's church, St. Margaret's Church, Westminster Abbey, with Carter by her side. "We can!" she whispers. "Why not?"

"A hundred reasons. Most of all, I'd need a steady position."

"You'll have one." Then she says the words that she's sure will galvanize him the most. "Your fame is growing. The greatest scholars in the world will acknowledge you."

He inclines his head and smiles. Something in him has shifted; he now looks at her with hope. He edges himself toward the side of the bench, underneath the lantern. "Lady Eve—Eve, come closer to the light," he says. "I have something for you. A gift."

From his pocket, he takes out a handkerchief that is tied in a knot and hands it to her. She unwraps it and cries out in surprise when a small gold ring falls into her lap. It is flat on one side, like a man's ring, but very tiny. As she examines it closely, she sees that the flat side holds a miniature falcon's head, the emblem of Horus.

"A child's ring," she says. "From the tomb?"

"It must have been the pharaoh's when he was very young."

She gazes at it for a long time. "Howard, you told Father and me not to touch anything," she says, though gently.

He looks as if stung by a scorpion. "There were a number of rings in one box, and they mostly looked the same. Carnarvon *is* entitled to all duplicates. This ring won't be missed."

She says nothing while she holds the ring in the center of her palm, considering whether to hand it back to him or not. Rings are symbolic, but Carter is not promising marriage to her. And very clearly, he should not have taken it from the tomb. "It's beautiful," she says finally, making an effort to keep her voice from rising. She waits for him to say more.

He smiles under his mustache, an expression at once sweet, shy, and awkward. "Just a small token of my affection," he says. "Keep it as a remembrance of what we've experienced together."

Eve hesitates, then slips the ring onto her little finger. The diminutive gold ring feels light, comfortable. It fits perfectly, if only on her smallest finger.

And she wonders: will Howard Carter give me another ring someday?

Not wanting the night to end, she says, "Let's go inside and have a drink." He nods, stands, and takes her arm in a protective way that makes her feel as if she is floating on air.

9

They squeeze their way through the crowded ballroom, then pass through the outer, striped arches into the Moorish Hall. Guests sit at elaborately carved tables, sipping their after-dinner drinks. An Egyptian waiter clad in a white jacket moves about the Persian carpets serving sherry and cordials. Eve scans the area to find a place to sit.

Then her body goes rigid. She pulls her arm away from Carter's. On one of the divans sits her father—who is supposed to be ill in bed—with his arm around his young blond nurse, still in uniform.

She marches over to him. "Father," she says under her breath. "What in God's name are you doing?"

Surprise creeps over his face, replaced by a guilty, crooked grimace. The young woman flushes and fixes her gaze on the floor. For heaven's sake, she is nearly Eve's own age!

"I was just giving my account of the discovery of the tomb," Carnarvon says, sliding away from the nurse. "Would you care to join us, Eve?"

"Certainly not," Eve says, "and you are supposed to be resting in bed so you will be well enough to go to Alexandria in the morning."

Carnarvon takes a gulp from his glass of wine and coughs.

Eve and Carter exchange glances. Carter's face flushes.

A childhood memory comes to Eve: the sudden disappearance of her governess. The governess was a very pretty blond woman, not unlike this nurse. "I sent her away" was all her mother would say. Later, Eve heard that she'd been posing for her father's photographs, in his studio in the castle basement.

Obviously, neither her father's age nor his ill health has changed his ways. What transpired in the hotel room between the nurse and her father when Eve was having her hair styled, buying clothes, and dancing at the ball?

"Your services are no longer needed," Eve tells the nurse. "Please take your things and meet me in the lobby in ten minutes."

Oh, how she glares, that trollop! The nurse exits the loggia. Good riddance, Eve thinks. No wonder the maids her mother hires at Highclere tend to be plain.

Carter crosses his arms and knits his thick eyebrows. "Carnarvon, we have business to talk about before you leave."

Carnarvon uses one hand to make a pretended adjustment to his cufflink. "Sit down and order some sherry," he tells Carter.

"We need to talk in private," Carter says.

"Oh?" Eve says, wondering what is on Carter's mind. "May I join you?"

Carter nods gravely. "I think that would be a good idea."

While Carter and Carnarvon take the elevator to the Carnarvons' suite, Eve waits for the nurse at the bottom of the hotel's grand staircase. On either side of the landing is a life-size bronze female statue, in pharaonic headdress and holding an electric lamp. Bare breasted. A little risqué for a hotel.

In the lobby, Eve arranges for a carriage and pays the nurse's wages. Then she takes the stairs up to the third-floor suite that she shares with her father. She settles down beside him in the sitting room, on the couch. Carter, smoking a cigarette, faces them on the settee. She can hear distant polka music from another room; that will be Fearnside, listening to a radio while whittling figurines out of meerschaum. No doubt her father has given him the evening off.

"Carnarvon, you are leaving tomorrow, so I have to ask this now," Carter says. "If by chance you've taken anything out of the tomb, I need to know. Before you board the ship, the customs agents in Alexandria will go through everything quite thoroughly, I'm afraid."

Carnarvon gives his all-too-familiar crooked grin.

"He's right, Father. You must let us know," Eve says, her voice shaky. She's a hypocrite for keeping the gold ring, which she will continue to hide inside one of her gloves. But that's not so bad, is it? It's tiny and a duplicate. No one could ever trace its origin. She feels relieved Carter is finally putting into words a subject that has concerned her for some time. She wonders why Carter hasn't approached her father earlier. What in heaven's name has he removed from the tomb, and what does he intend to do with it?

"All right," Carnarvon says. "I'll show you."

Eve follows him and Carter into the adjoining bedroom, where her father fumbles through one of his suitcases. "Careful—hold it with two hands," Carnarvon says as he passes to Eve an object, heavy as a rock, wrapped in an undershirt. It seems about a foot and a half high and almost as wide. Whatever it is, he should not have taken it.

Eve sits on the corner of her father's bed and unwraps an alabaster chalice. "It's beautiful!" she says.

The stemmed cup is shaped like an opened lotus flower. Its two handles are lotus flowers with buds. On top of the buds are baskets that support kneeling figures in striped headdresses. The figures hold palm branches bearing the ankh symbols of eternal life.

Focused on the chalice, Eve is transported back through the millennia. She pictures the young king and queen drinking from it in turn, as part of a ceremony. She runs her fingers along the rim, where a band of hieroglyphs is etched and painted over in dark blue. What do the words say? She would need her hieroglyphics text to help her translate them. Then new thoughts break the chalice's spell. She wonders when her father walked off with it, and how he managed to bring out something so large without anyone seeing him. It seems he has no fear of being caught. Eve tenses. How easily their lives can be brought down by her father's carelessness.

"My God, Carnarvon, this is far, far worse than I'd imagined," Carter says, his face clouded in a frown. "Let me see it, Lady Eve."

He sits beside her, and she gently hands him the chalice. He accepts it with reverence. Carnarvon, hunched and gripping his cane, stands over them. Carter puts a finger on the square panel of hieroglyphs on the chalice's side. Eve can immediately see that below the band, there are two cartouches, and at least one is Tutankhamun's name.

Carter points to the oval. "You see here, Carnarvon: 'Tutankhamun.' If you try to bring this chalice to England, you'll be found out. What in the world were you thinking?"

"I wanted it as a present for my wife." Carnarvon's tone is sheepish.

"The chalice must go back to the tomb," Carter says. "In the exact spot where it belongs. Where did you find it?"

"On the floor of the Antechamber. Near the entrance to the tunnel."

Eve faces Carnarvon. "You should be following the laws of Egypt." Then she turns to Carter. "You as well, Mr. Carter." The tiny ring she wears burns on her pinky finger. It's proof of his guilt. Who is a worse liar—Carter or her father? Panic rushes through her now as she remembers the wooden bust of the young boy king.

"Mr. Carter, what about the carved head in the Fortnum & Mason wine bottle box?"

"I'm going to put it back in the tomb," he says—a bit too defensively, she thinks.

Carter looks hard at Carnarvon. "Listen to me, Carnarvon. You must show me everything you have taken, no matter how small."

From various pockets in his suitcases, Carnarvon produces three other treasures: a bronze-and-gilt puppy with its head turned ("for my son, Porchey"); a graceful ivory gazelle missing its horns ("for Eve"); and a chestnut-colored leaping horse of painted ivory ("for myself"). The puppy and gazelle are small enough to fit in the palm of Eve's hand, and the horse is just a bit larger. She loves each one; though, once again, the idea of being caught makes her feel ill.

"That's all," Carnarvon says.

Frowning, Carter inspects them. He grips the horse. "It was probably a handle for a whip," he says.

"Or a riding crop?" Eve asks.

"Maybe. How lifelike this little horse is," Carter marvels. "Masterful carving."

"There's exquisite carving on this gazelle, too," Eve says. The figure stands on graceful legs, as if ready to step forward in her hand. A painted block, etched with foliage, supports the tiny animal. "It's so well formed—it's stunning."

His thick eyebrows knit, Carter quizzes Carnarvon as to where in the tomb he found each object. Most were taken from the Annexe.

"You *opened boxes*?" Eve says. "Mr. Carter told us not to touch the artifacts."

"I was careful not to break anything," Carnarvon says.

Eve feels palpable tension in the room. She is sure her father and Carter will argue. To her surprise, Carter says, "What's done is done. Keep these small figures. If the customs agents ask, say they're from another tomb—a plundered one—and that you bought them from a dealer. I'll write a letter of provenance for you to have while you travel."

Eve says, "Mr. Carter, I would prefer if you take those artifacts back and place them in the tomb. Even if you have to dig out the stairway again."

Carter ignores her, preoccupied with the horse statuette. He holds it up close to his face. Eve clenches the tiny gazelle. She feels almost as if an inspector is looking over her shoulder.

"You're frowning, Eve," Carnarvon says. "Do not worry."

"How can I not worry about your concession being taken from you? You could be thrown in prison!" she says. "What if we're stopped by—"

"Don't give the customs agents another thought," Carnarvon says with a dismissive air. "They will accept bribes."

So her father has bribed officials before.

"Father, I don't know how you can always be so sure of yourself," Eve says. "Or you, Mr. Carter." She eyes him. "I expected more integrity and caution from both of you."

Carnarvon remains aloof, casual. Carter looks at Eve questioningly, his dark eyes slightly downcast. "These small objects are a very small part of the vast collection," he says. "Thousands of artifacts, and remember, half of them belong to your father."

She sets her jaw, wishing he weren't dishonest.

When Eve doesn't reply, Carter adds, "If somehow we're denied the treasures, Carnarvon will at least come away with some handsome, if tiny, artworks."

"So you admit something could go wrong," Eve says. "You believe our position with the Egyptian government isn't strong. You think the director-general would prosecute us?"

"Stop," Carter says, his voice sharp.

Eve tries to push away thoughts of Egyptian prison or deportation. Is Carter thinking the same? After a long silence, he hands Carnarvon the little horse, then says, "Eve, Carnarvon. We all need to rest."

"Go along, Eve. Fearnside will take over," Carnarvon says. He pushes the servant's buzzer that connects to the valet's room in their suite. Eve feels defeated.

"Carnarvon, good night," Carter says abruptly. Then he leans over toward Eve, an uneasy smile on his lips. "I'm sorry, Lady Eve, that the evening did not turn out as we'd hoped. I'll be up early to see you off." He pauses, then says in a low voice. "I'll write to you to let you know how things go at the tomb. You'll write me back?"

Eve gives him a nod and sighs. It is time to hang up her pretty butterfly dress and sleep. Before she sets out for her own chamber, she says, "Father, do you think you can behave yourself from now on?" She sounds like her mother, but she cannot help it. Her nostrils flare.

She sees the hurt in his eyes. Frowning, Carnarvon gives Eve the salute that he learned in the British Royal Army. It is the sign he always gives Lady Carnarvon when he follows her instructions.

10

It is Eve who handles the customs officials at every international crossing point. Fortunately, no one questions Carter's letter that the artifacts they carry come from an antiquities dealer. And no one finds the little gold ring, hidden in her white silk glove. She relaxes when she steps onto British soil in Dover, though she misses Carter so much she can hardly stand to be away from him. She relives his kisses in her mind and wonders how the night at Shepheard's might have turned out differently if they hadn't encountered her father that night.

Back at Highclere, she savors her breakfasts of clotted cream and guava jelly on toast. She rides her beloved Lady Grey, her sweet-tempered and frisky gray mare, across the sweeping parkland. In her favorite parlor, the Egyptian room, she arranges the gazelle, horse, and puppy in one of the glass display cases and visits them on her way to meals. She keeps her little ring hidden in the glove in the bottom drawer of her linen chest, away from the prying eyes of her inquisitive sixteen-year-old maid, Marcelle.

Eve looks forward to her forthcoming trip to London, where she and her parents will meet Porchey and his new wife, Catherine. Carnarvon will visit King George V in Buckingham Palace to tell him of the Tutankhamun discovery. Then the whole family will return to Highclere for Christmas. But all the time she is enjoying Highclere, a part of her recalls the moment of discovery of the tomb.

The fact of the discovery merely annoys her mother. One morning, as Eve and Carnarvon sit at his desk in the terra-cotta-colored smoking room, checking the *Times* of London for articles about the tomb, Lady Carnarvon storms in. She throws down an armful of papers and envelopes onto the desk. Then, before taking a seat on the leather sofa in front of the fireplace, she moves Susie, the family's three-legged fox terrier, from the sofa onto the floor.

"George, in the weeks you've been gone, I've been pestered by our accountant with more and more bills," Lady Carnarvon says. "Now you show up, and you're busy seeing visitors, writing letters, concocting business schemes—always spending more money. What used to be *my* money. A telephone for Mr. Carter! Now an *automobile*! Delivered to Luxor!"

This news takes Eve by surprise. "Father, you've ordered a telephone for Mr. Carter and an automobile? Wonderful!"

Eve breathes in the sweet smell of Carnarvon's Egyptian cigar smoke lingering in the air from the night before. She looks from him to her mother, tiny and slender in blue silk that makes her eyes even bluer, staring fiercely at her father.

Eve keeps her voice calm. "Mother, please understand. With an automobile, Father and I will no longer have to ride on donkeys. It will save us so much time."

"What I'd like to know is who is going to pay for it?" Lady Carnarvon says. She waves an envelope in her hand for emphasis.

"Darling, there will be so much cash rolling in because of the treasures, you won't believe it," Carnarvon says. "All the museums of the world will want a share. And they'll pay to the skies. Besides, there will be book and cinema rights."

"All that Father has spent will be covered many times over," Eve says. Carnarvon, taking Susie onto his lap, nods emphatically.

Lady Carnarvon does not return Carnarvon's smile. "There's a very large hole waiting for any money, when and if it ever comes in," she says.

Of course, her mother has a point. But whenever Eve listens to her, the life force in her drains away, replaced by worries. And the experience of being in love has helped Eve to distance herself from her mother's problems.

"George," Lady Carnarvon continues, "I've had expenses for my hospital. My priorities are for the people who are living. We got by for many years on my father's generosity. Then we spent my inheritance. Now we must pay our own debts."

How much debt is she referring to? Eve wonders if it is the right time to ask. Her mother is in exactly the sort of mood when she is most likely to treat Eve as if she were a child, with no right to ask questions. Just then, someone knocks at the door. Streatfield, Highclere's distinguished elderly steward, quietly enters and announces, "Lord Carnarvon—Sir Alan Gardiner."

From trips to Egypt as a child, Eve remembers her father's friend Sir Alan, an expert in deciphering hieroglyphics. He was a friendly, middle-aged man wearing round glasses and a safari hat, always holding an ancient Egyptian papyrus.

"Excellent. Please see him in. I'll meet him here in the smoking room," Carnarvon says. He turns to Eve. "I've invited Sir Alan to become part of Carter's archaeological team, and he's accepted the appointment."

"That is good news. Everyone on the dig will enjoy his company," Eve says.

Lady Carnarvon speaks to Streatfield. "We need ten minutes. Lord Carnarvon has business to settle."

The steward leaves, and Lady Carnarvon says to Carnarvon, "Please look at ten pieces of mail. It's a small favor I ask. I just want to see you get a start on it."

Carnarvon sighs. "Almina, please try not to be so difficult." He sets down the dog.

Lady Carnarvon looks on as her husband flips through several opened bills. "We can ignore these for now," he says.

Frowning, Eve eyes Lady Carnarvon. How humiliating that her mother treats her father as a child, just as she does Eve!

Long before ten minutes pass, there comes another knock. Streatfield enters, looking apologetic. "A second gentleman to see you, Lord Carnarvon. Mr. Geoffrey Dawson, editor of the *Times*."

"He doesn't have an appointment," Carnarvon says. "Ask him to make one for another time. Please give him my apologies."

When Streatfield leaves, Carnarvon cuts open a sealed envelope with his silver-plated letter opener. Eve sees it has the return address of Count Louis le Warner Hamon.

"It's Cheiro," Lord Carnarvon says with a chuckle. "Let's see what he has to say."

Lady Carnarvon groans. "If it's the fortune teller I'm thinking of, don't bother with his letter now. Better throw it out."

Carnarvon's involvement with the London Spiritual Alliance is another point of disagreement between Eve's parents. Several years earlier her mother, thankfully, banned séances at Highclere. Eve has always found occult dealings to be unsettling.

Carnarvon takes the letter from the envelope. His face falls. Standing and looking over his shoulder, Eve reads the short message.

Lord Carnarvon,

The spirits have told me: The pharaoh is angered that you have disturbed his sleep. You must abandon the excavation. Above all, do not remove any relics from the tomb, or you will contract a sickness from which you will not recover, and death shall claim you in Egypt. Heed my warning.

Cheiro

"Complete rubbish," Eve says. She pushes away memories of Sir Golden and the cobra, and the workers' reactions to that disaster.

Lady Carnarvon's eyes look fierce. "How irresponsible of the man."

"Not to worry, my dear," Lord Carnarvon says. "You know I never allow messages from the spiritualists to override my common sense. Furthermore, if at this moment all the mummies in Egypt were to come to life to warn me to stay away from the tomb, I would go ahead with my plans just the same."

At times of crisis, Lady Carnarvon mutters to herself in French, her native language, and she does so now. Streatfield the steward knocks again and enters with the bald, portly, bespectacled Sir Alan. Eve smiles. "Excuse me, Lord Carnarvon," Streatfield says in a low voice. "Mr. Dawson of the *Times* said to tell you he'll wait all day to have a word with you."

"Tell that damned fellow he can't show up unannounced," Carnarvon says to Streatfield.

The steward nods and leaves the room. After greetings are exchanged, Carnarvon says to Sir Alan, "Ever since I've arrived in England, the man's been hounding me with messages. He wants exclusive coverage of the tomb."

"Good heavens, Carnarvon! Dawson is the chief editor. You must bring him in at once," says Sir Alan. "An exclusive with the *Times* is exactly what you want."

"Do you really think so?" Carnarvon pauses. "Very well. Let's have him in, and we'll hear what he has to say."

Before her father can ring for Streatfield, Eve dashes from the smoking room to give the message. She feels buoyant. Carter will be relieved that from now on he will only need to talk to one reporter. And judging from Sir Alan's enthusiasm, her father is about to have a lucky financial break. The *Times* will help him pay his bills by giving the tomb world publicity. At least she hopes so.

Relations between her parents are still chilly when the family moves several days later to their London house, Seymour Place. There Eve writes to Carter.

22 December 1922
Howard, dear,
I know you are in contact with Father through cables. Let me extend my own congratulations and, I will add, my relief, that Father is signing a contract for exclusive media coverage with the *Times* of London. Soon the reporters from all the other papers will have to leave you in peace.

Father is this very day calling on none other than His Majesty George V at Buckingham Palace.

Everywhere there is talk of King Tutankhamun's tomb. All the world now thinks of you. By now you are world-renowned, and your name, dear, will be added to the famous men in the annals of history. It is wonderful, and I wish you could have flown to England if only for a few hours, for the genuine, universal interest and excitement that your discovery has created would have thrilled you with pleasure.

Highclere has been full of visitors, Seymour Place, too, and it has quite tired us out. Father seems about to collapse in exhaustion. However, he revels in it all. When he's weary, he calls me in to talk to him again about our night together in the Holy of Holies, and he brightens up as if he's had a glass of champagne.

How can I ever thank you for letting me be part of the phenomenal discovery? It was and always will be the Great Moment of my life. More I cannot say, except that with my entire being, I'm eager to return to you and to be in your arms again, my darling.
Your loving,
Eve

That afternoon, as Carnarvon visits the king, Lady Carnarvon holds a tea. Her guests are Porchey, Catherine, and Eve's favorite friend from her debutante days, Anne James, along with Anne's mother and toddler daughter. In the music room, listening to her mother playing Mozart's Sonata Number 11 on the pianoforte, Eve wonders if Carter might already have written to her, as promised.

Roberts, the Seymour Place butler, collects the incoming letters on a silver tray that the family keeps in the alcove on the credenza near the front door. Eve anticipates the afternoon post and slips away from her company. On top of the pile—joy, oh joy—she sees an envelope with Carter's neat script addressed to her.

She snatches up the letter. Caution warns her not to look at it immediately; she had best return to her company. Just as she lifts the letter from the tray, she feels a tap on her shoulder and spins around. Anne looks at her with her ever-inquiring eyes. Her hair, worn up in a twist and two side curls, is nearly as light as her creamy skin. "Is the letter from Brograve?"

"Him? No!" Eve danced and flirted with Sir Brograve Beauchamp, her brother's friend, at a ball and again at Porchey's wedding six months earlier. Unlike other aristocrats, he has an actual job, at the Bank of London, and knows about what working people say and do; this intrigued her. But she hasn't thought about him since before her trip to Egypt—months that feel like eons.

"Oh," Anne says, recognition in her eyes. "It's from that archaeologist in Egypt, isn't it? The one you keep talking about."

Eve beams. Of all the people in the world, she can trust Anne with her secret.

"Are you in love with him?" Anne whispers.

"Yes," Eve says, "and he's in love with me."

"How do you know?"

"He said he wished he could marry me," Eve says, exaggerating the truth. "Think what a risk he's taking by pursuing me while he works for Father." She tells Anne about their kisses at Shepheard's.

Anne twirls her hair with a finger and then says in a low voice, "Your mother would kill you if she found out."

"She'd be upset," Eve admits.

"Eve, you have lost your senses," Anne says, though her tone is sympathetic. "He's lowborn. Where can your romance lead?"

"Well," Eve says, "to marriage, I hope. Why not? Mr. Carter may not be considered a gentleman now, but soon he'll be famous. No doubt he'll be presented to King George and knighted."

It is possible, Eve thinks. Her father is, at this very moment, enjoying the king's company.

Anne purses her lips. "Where would you live? Not in Egypt."

"We'd winter in Luxor. The rest of the time we'd spend in London. Mr. Carter has a home in Collington Gardens, not far from yours." Eve does not say it's an apartment shared with his brother. And that they probably rent a single floor.

Eve pauses for a moment, listening to the lively Mozart tune. "I'd help him with his excavations. I'm learning all about archaeology, Anne. I've become good at deciphering hieroglyphs. I'd translate his academic papers into French, and I'd act as his chief publicist."

"Oh, Eve." Anne touches her arm. "I don't know what to say. I hope you aren't building up false hopes."

Eve flinches. "I don't think I am," she says, though Anne's pointed concern makes her feel off-balance. She wishes that she had not confided in her.

"I need to read my letter," Eve says. "Tell the others I'll be there in a few minutes."

Anne turns, her skirts swishing, and Eve holds the envelope to her chest. Then she dashes into a nearby guest bedroom, locks the door, and sits on the bed.

With trembling hands, Eve opens the envelope and unfolds the letter in her lap. She spreads it out and strokes the white stationery that Carter's own hand has touched.

8 December 1922

Dear Lady Eve,

It has only been four nights since I left Cairo and saw you and your father off, though it seems much longer. I returned to the Valley to find that several of my new team of scholars, a mix of Americans and "Brits"—as the Americans call us—had already arrived from elsewhere in Egypt and moved with their families into a large house east of Deir al Bahari. They've named it "Metropolitan House" for the museum in New York where they are employed.

Callender has installed the new steel door at the tomb's entrance. We're forming a systematic plan for removing the treasures in the Antechamber, a task that will begin after Christmas. I've kept on thirty-five Egyptian workers who will help with the packing and transporting.

The Antiquities Service has lent us the tomb of Ramesses XI in which to store our supplies. Before their transport to Cairo, the treasures will go to the tomb of Sethos II while they are being conserved. You will remember this tomb—a gigantic, empty cave cut into the bedrock and located about a quarter of a mile from our site. Mr. Harry Burton, our photographer, has already claimed one room in Sethos II as his photographic studio and will use Tomb 55, just across the path from us, for his darkroom.

Though it may not always be possible to acknowledge your considerable contributions in public, know that I value them highly. You alone were responsible for making our official opening of the tomb such a success, and no doubt you will do the same when we show the world the burial chamber. I regard you with the greatest esteem. Whenever we are surrounded by company, and I raise my glass before I speak, you will know I am acknowledging and thanking you. Let it be our own secret signal. And now, in private, I raise my glass to you.

I eagerly await your return.

Yours,

Howard Carter

Eve slips the letter back into its envelope and presses it to her chest. She loves what he said about raising a glass to her. But heavens, why is he still calling her "Lady Eve"? She wishes he would let go of that pointless convention. She recalls Anne's words "lowborn" and "false hopes" and feels the sudden urge to cry.

11

The following evening, the Carnarvons sit in their Grand Tier box at the Royal Opera House, waiting for the towering red curtain to rise for Verdi's *Don Carlo*. Carnarvon has been detained. In the past two days, he's met with King George, a reporter from the *Times* of London, a film director, and possibly others Eve has not heard about yet.

Her brother and Catherine make an odd couple, Eve thinks. She, blond and leggy. Brash, like so many Americans. Stunning, and more than a head taller than Porchey. He, short (though the army has taught him to hold himself very straight) and a bit paunchy. He has jet-black hair and a broad face with prominent features. Somehow, he attracts beautiful women easily.

"Operas are so romantic," Catherine says. The diamonds of the Carnarvon family tiara sparkle in her hair.

"Yes." Eve stares up at the great gilt dome. Inside it, the coffering on the ceiling forms a star. She loves this place, yet being in the company of the newlyweds makes her feel lonely.

Porchey, pressing so close to Catherine that their heads touch, surveys the seating area below them with opera glasses. "I mentioned to Brograve that we'd be here. I thought I told him to come to our box, but maybe your Romeo is wandering about in the crowd."

"You didn't ask him! You're joking," Eve says.

Sparing Eve from further teasing, a woman in a leopard coat bursts into their box. Eve recognizes this middle-aged woman with straight, bleached platinum-blond hair as Mrs. Dennistoun, one of her mother's many social friends. Lady Carnarvon gasps as if startled by a gunshot.

"Dorothy," Lady Carnarvon says, standing to greet her. Eve guesses by the flatness of her mother's voice that she is not pleased to see Mrs. Dennistoun.

"Almina, at last, here you are. Why, without any warning, did you stop answering my letters?"

"It's the holidays, and my children are home," Lady Carnarvon snaps. Eve sniffs the woman's horrid perfume. Both Eve and her mother wrinkle their noses.

Her mother has kept a seat empty beside her in case her husband should show up. Mrs. Dennistoun promptly takes it and leans toward Lady Carnarvon. If the woman thinks that she and her mother are having a private conversation, she is mistaken. Their box is so small that Eve can hear every word.

"How's Tiger?" Mrs. Dennistoun asks.

"He's recovering," Lady Carnarvon says. "He's not so thin as he was before, poor soul. At least he's better fed and has coal now for heat."

Eve assumes that "Tiger" is a patient in the London hospital her mother founded. But as they talk, Eve realizes that he is a man in France. She thought that her mother traveled to Paris only for shopping and museums. Does she have hospital charity work there, too? Why hasn't Eve heard of it? The house lights flick off, then on, signaling five minutes until the performance.

"The overture will be starting," says Mrs. Dennistoun. "May I stay here, Almina?"

"I'm afraid not, Dorothy," Lady Carnarvon replies. "George will come at any moment, and Porchey expects friends."

"Chaps from Eton," Porchey says, helping their mother along.

Mrs. Dennistoun takes the hint, leaving the stinking scent of her perfume behind.

At that moment a tall form steps into their box. It is Brograve, dark and charming, with a newspaper in his hand. He looks a bit like Carter, only much taller, less muscular, and quite a bit younger.

"So sorry to be late," he says, all enthusiasm.

Eve swallows, wishing she had never flirted with the man. Is he still interested in her? Her family must think so, for there is a shifting of positions. In another minute, Brograve sits beside her while her mother moves to the row behind them.

First Brograve drops his red tartan wool scarf, then his keys. He's comic in his clumsiness. Eve tries not to laugh.

The red-velvet curtain rises and the grand opera unfolds. Brograve mouths the words of the arias, a rather eccentric thing to do, Eve thinks, though she's impressed that he seems to know the libretto by heart. Once, when Brograve's program slips to the floor, she picks it up for him. Their eyes meet and he keeps on with his pretend singing, as if singing to her. How silly!

Her mind wanders from Brograve to Carter. The Grand Inquisitor onstage reminds her of the inspectors and reporters who constantly keep her father and Carter in their sights. She knows the opera's story ends in a tomb. Soon she gives up following the drama of *Don Carlo* and simply lets the passionate arias wash over her.

Still thinking of Carter, she feels herself redden during the lovers' duet. Despite herself, she turns toward Brograve. She wants to see if he is singing along. He is!

At last, the curtain drops for intermission, the enormous glass chandeliers of the hall shine brightly, and Eve scurries out of the opera box while Brograve chats with Porchey. After she freshens up in the ladies' lounge, she meets her family and Brograve in the bar on the main level. Porchey finds them a table and pours a glass of red wine for her. Then he reads aloud from Brograve's newly printed evening edition of the *Times*.

"Lord Carnarvon said, 'I feel certain that a burial shrine exists behind the sealed door. Probably the shrine will be gilt wood. It may be a series of compartments, nested inside each other. Inside the sarcophagus, there will be a coffin, perhaps more than one. A pharaoh's mummy will be adorned for a male-deity, perhaps with a gold mask—who knows? It could be a surprise for the ages.'"

Eve swallows hard. Oh, dear. Her father should not talk to the world as if he's already visited the burial chamber. Doesn't he realize Lacau will read the papers?

As if on cue, Carnarvon, in his tails and top hat, joins the group. By his side is a bald man in a tweed suit holding a red beret. It's typical of her father to bring along odd companions to their family gatherings; Eve wishes that he wouldn't.

Eve rises and gives her father a peck on the cheek, and he returns the kiss. Brograve finds chairs for Carnarvon and his friend.

"Father, Porchey's reading what you blabbed to the king and to the whole world," Eve scolds. "You shouldn't have told King George about the burial shrine. People might think you entered the burial chamber *before* its official opening."

"I was merely making some logical guesses," Carnarvon replies. "Any specialist in Egyptology would do the same." He turns to his companion. "The gold mask came from a vision of my friend's. Everyone, meet Vladimir Velma. He is a talented seer. We wanted to continue a most interesting conversation, so I invited him along tonight."

"Pleased to meet you all," says the seer. His accent is foreign. Is he

Russian? Eve wonders how she can tolerate any more surprises in one day.

Lady Carnarvon's eyes turn cold. "Hello, Mr. Velma."

"Call me Velma, please."

Carnarvon, Velma, and Brograve visit the bar to bring back another bottle of wine and more glasses. Eve takes a seat near Catherine, avoiding the empty one near Brograve. When Catherine whispers to Porchey, Eve has no trouble hearing his answer. His voice, too loud as always, is helped along by the wine. "My father has many odd acquaintances, including fortune tellers," Porchey tells Catherine. "There's something I must explain to you, my dear, about my family and about British aristocrats in general. An aristocrat is someone who thinks he must try everything on earth that there is to try."

"I'll make an effort to understand, then," Catherine says. To Eve's irritation, Porchey gives her a quick kiss on the lips.

Carnarvon tells everyone at the table about his visit with King George the day before. "The king said he greatly enjoyed our talk and invited me to come again to Buckingham Palace—anytime."

Surely this is an exaggeration, Eve thinks. She suspects the king wants her father's share of the Tutankhamun finds to go to the British Museum. Meanwhile, she knows the Metropolitan Museum is staking its own claim by providing Carter with several of their expert staff members free of charge. Knowing her father, he will not address the conflict if he can help it.

The conversation turns toward clairvoyance. "Velma has a message for Catherine," Carnarvon says. "He says she'll give birth to a child in the near future."

Catherine gives a breathy giggle. "That's good news. A boy or a girl?"

Velma addresses her from across the table. "A boy, I think."

Porchey breaks into a grin. "A Carnarvon heir. Tell us when to expect this happy event."

"I can only see the shape of the future in a general way," says Velma. "I couldn't say when unless we made an appointment for a full reading."

Porchey laughs. "In other words, you'll tell me if I come to your office with payment in hand."

Velma frowns. "You misunderstand me, Lord Porchester. When a client asks a question in which timing is involved, I draw up astrological charts. In astrology, we can look at specific dates. Counsel from the higher sources tends to be more general."

"Spirits?" Porchey says, eyebrows raised.

"Lord Porchester," Velma says, "I'll give you the same warning I gave your father earlier today. Your too-casual manner may carry into all areas of life. It may cause you grief."

"What do you mean?" Porchey asks.

"Don't be overconfident. And spend within your means, or you'll be sorry. Don't gamble on horses."

Touché! Eve suppresses a laugh, and Porchey's smug smile fades.

Lady Carnarvon glowers at Velma. "I think we've heard quite enough."

"I'm sorry to have upset you, Lady Carnarvon," Velma says. "But first, let me give you a personal message from the spirits. You are a woman of great compassion, but right now, you're not being honest with yourself or others."

Lady Carnarvon, her eyes wide, frowns. Eve wonders if that odd message has something to do with the man she calls Tiger.

Carnarvon gives the seer a grave look. "Thank you, Velma. You'd better stop there."

Her mother is right to distrust clairvoyants, Eve thinks, and yet Eve cannot help herself from listening to the man. "But you haven't told my fortune, Mr. Velma," she pipes up. "Do the spirits have a message for me?"

Velma closes his eyes for a moment, hums, then opens them again. "You are a dear soul, a tad self-centered, but with a great capacity to love. You and your father are very close, aren't you? He often talks to me about you, and over the years we've reviewed your charts. You've had a great life-changing experience, haven't you?"

"Go on," she says, pursing her lips. Is he referring to the opening of the tomb? Her romance with Carter? Both?

"Take heed, Lady Evelyn. You're about to experience some of the most momentous events of your lifetime."

"What do you mean?" Despite herself, she quivers as she speaks.

"I don't want Eve to hear any more of this," Lady Carnarvon says. She walks to Eve, grasps her hand, and pulls her out of her chair.

"The intermission must be nearly over," Porchey says, standing.

Brograve, who seems lost in thought, turns sharply when Velma addresses him. "The spirits say you are a man who lives according to your principles and values. This is why you can make crystal-clear decisions, and why life comes easily to you. Something has recently changed for you. I see a pink light in your aura that complements Lady Evelyn's."

"You've gone too far, sir," Eve says, not knowing if she is more angry or embarrassed. Without looking at Brograve, she takes her mother by the arm and they march toward the stairs that lead to their box. How right her mother was to ban spiritualists from Highclere!

The evening continues to simmer like a teakettle. Eve does her best to ignore Brograve. After the performance, while standing at the back of the portico with their coats on, she and Brograve look at each other awkwardly.

"Will I see you again this season?" he asks.

"I'll be returning to Egypt and will miss the rest of the winter events," Eve says.

His smile drops. She has clearly disappointed him. "Well, I hope to see you back in England in the spring."

"Yes, probably in the spring," she says.

They shake hands. He winds his tartan scarf around his neck. Then he walks slowly down the wide marble steps and turns right onto Bow Street, toward Covent Garden. Eve stands in the portico and watches him with a regret she does not understand.

Highclere is decorated for Christmas when the family returns. Lady Carnarvon has left detailed instructions for the maids and housekeeper about the placement of garlands and ornaments for the immense Christmas tree in the saloon. Eve goes to her room to wrap the gifts she purchased in London. Her maid, Marcelle, tiptoes about the room, putting away freshly ironed and laundered silk stockings and dresses. "You're awfully quiet today," Eve says.

Marcelle turns her slim back on Eve, swishing her long auburn braids.

"What is it?" Eve says.

"Unless you're needing anything, I'll be off now, miss," the girl says, her voice soft and nervous.

"Marcelle." Eve points to the spot next to her on the bed. "Talk to me." Eventually Marcelle says, "There's gossip among the servants that Lady Carnarvon is having an affair with a married man. She's in Paris with him most of the time now."

"Dear God." Eve frowns and crosses her arms across her chest. "Did you catch his name?"

"I don't know anything more, miss," the maid says.

Tiger, Eve thinks. What kind of a name is that?

After the maid leaves the room, Eve gives a long, low sigh. That day she cannot bring herself to ask her mother any questions. Lady Carnarvon appears the same as ever: furs and high heels; wavy, sandy hair; affectionate eyes; witty remarks; emerald and several diamonds on her ring finger. Christmas Eve arrives, and Eve's family exchanges presents before church. Then comes Christmas Day, and too soon, after a midday meal of roast pheasant, Porchey and Catherine say their goodbyes. They are leaving for London. From there they will travel on to India.

Eve tightens her grip on Porchey's hand, surprised at her reluctance to let him go. Despite their differences in personality and his aversion to writing letters, they share a closeness. Their mother sobs. Carnarvon gives Porchey his familiar British Army salute.

Afterward, Eve and Lady Carnarvon sit alone in front of the towering Christmas tree in the immense saloon, under a row of their family's heraldic shields. Carnarvon, whose familiarity with the servants swells at Christmas, entertains them in one of the cellar rooms with an Egyptian slideshow.

It isn't the time to talk over anything controversial with her mother. Still, Eve cannot stop herself when her mother says she will soon be going to Paris to do some shopping to spruce up the rooms that were occupied during the war.

"Tell me about your friend Tiger," Eve says to Lady Carnarvon. "He lives in Paris?"

With a gentle hand, Lady Carnarvon brushes Eve's hair away from her eyes. "Yes. He's a poor soul. He's Dorothy Dennistoun's husband— they're separated and are planning a divorce. About six months ago, Dorothy found out I was going to Paris, so she asked me to look in on Tiger to make sure he wasn't at death's door."

"What's the matter with him? Is he ill?"

"Moderately." Lady Carnarvon falters. "He's just poor. He was living in a flat with very little heat and couldn't get over a bad cough. I found him a better place to live."

Eve frowns. She's never known her mother to form an attachment to any man other than her father.

"I'm worried, Mother, that the friendship you've developed with this man is far too close. The servants say you're in Paris as often as you are here."

There is a long pause in which Eve can feel a headache coming on. Both her parents have surprised her for the worse lately.

"Baseless servants' gossip! I'm only helping a friend in need. That's all."

Is she lying? "I don't understand what this obligation is all about, Mother. This man isn't one of our relatives. Isn't there someone else who can help him?"

Lady Carnarvon's delicate cheeks are red as she turns her face to Eve. "Eve, *you* are the one who should stay home." Her tone is sharp. Her words are not a question. "Stop writing letters to Mr. Carter. Don't return to Egypt."

Eve bites her lower lip and slides down against the velvet of the sofa. How does her mother know about the exchange of letters? One of the servants must have told her. "I'm going to Egypt, and that's final," Eve says.

Lady Carnarvon sighs. "An intimate friendship with Mr. Carter could ruin your life."

"Oh, really, Mother," Eve says. "How could it possibly?"

"Your reputation, of course." Eve stiffens, knowing she will say more. "Your time for eligibility is closing in. This summer—I don't need to remind you—you'll be twenty-two. Once Porchey inherits the estate, you and I will have little of our own. Porchey would keep me on. Of course, he'd care for you, too, while you were unmarried. You might still live at Highclere for life. But think ahead, being an old maid, living with your brother and his family—"

"You've sidestepped the subject of why you regularly visit Paris," Eve says. "And you're talking as if Father were dead. How dare you!"

Eve crosses her arms and hugs herself. Lady Carnarvon gets up and pushes at a log in the fireplace with a poker. The fire crackles. Eve already felt out of sorts and headachy. Now this cold and calculating talk, on Christmas no less, makes her feel like something is pounding against her brain.

"I'm sorry, but I must remind you of what's at stake," Lady Carnarvon says, swinging around to face Eve. "You may find it very romantic to be 'in love' with Mr. Carter while you're comfortable at Highclere.

But marriage to him would not be so comfortable. Attend to your future and let Mr. Carter attend to his. While your father lives, he may continue to support Mr. Carter. But once your father is deceased, Mr. Carter will be penniless. And so might you be, if you're not careful."

Her mother's speech hits her like hot sand sweeping across her face. Eve draws in her breath sharply. "Howard Carter is quickly becoming the most famous archaeologist in the world. He could take a very prestigious position, even head of the British Museum."

"No." Lady Carnarvon straightens herself and fixes her eyes upon Eve. "Mr. Carter is not a man of privilege. He's never studied at a university, isn't accepted by scholars, and undermines every chance for advancement with his moody, caustic behavior."

Eve folds her arms again, trying to keep panic at bay. "I have faith in him, and that the world will recognize his genius," she says. "One day I'll marry Sir Howard Carter, a wealthy and revered gentleman."

Lady Carnarvon shakes her head and remains silent. She sits on the couch in a slumped position. Then, after a long while, as if talking to herself, she murmurs, "Eve, the world is a hard place. I don't want to see you hurt."

No, Mother, Eve thinks. I will follow my heart and return to Egypt, and you will cross the Channel to Paris to pursue the odd dream you are chasing.

I'll be the one who finds happiness.

12

Two weeks of train rides and pacing ships' decks have brought Eve to this moment. She stands alone at the rail of the *Nile Queen*, watching for Carter on the opposite shore as the ferry chugs along. With the sharp-edged clarity that Carter's nearness always brings, she senses the brown-green river, an egret alighting from the reeds, the smell of oil, and the vibrations under her feet. She feels the deliciously cool breeze on her face and clenches her hat.

There! She spots Carter's new Ford motorcar. On the embankment, its rubber tires hugging yellow spokes, the black car heads toward the landing. She calls to Carnarvon and Fearnside, seated under the awning and panting from the heat. Her father simply must see this miraculous sight.

Carter sits tall at the wheel. There he is, handsome as ever. Deep brown suntan. Muscular arms. Strong jaw. He's remarkably well dressed in a cotton shirt, linen trousers, a black bow tie, and a homburg. She waves. Ah, he sees her. He sounds the horn five times.

Carter slows to a stop and cuts the engine near the dock. Eve meets him at the end of the walkway. They embrace. Too quickly it is over, but he whispers to her, "Later, my darling, a real kiss." She cannot suppress her smile or her joy.

Followed by Fearnside, who is laden with bags, Carnarvon limps off the ferry with his cane. "By Jove, Carter!" he calls.

As Eve waits for her father, she touches the car. "What a wonderful new way to travel to the Valley."

"Isn't it? It's a Model T Ford Touring Edition," Carter says. "Your father had it shipped from Cairo in pieces, and I pushed to have it put together in time to surprise you."

Eve climbs into the passenger seat. Carnarvon inspects the car, bounces on its black-leather seats, presses against its retractable black canvas top, switches its headlights on and off, and tinkers with its gauge, throttle, and gear stick. "I'll drive us to the tomb," he says.

"No," Eve says. Oh Lord, the last thing they need is a motor accident. Forgetting herself, she adds, "Howard knows the road."

"So it's Howard now, is it?" Carnarvon says. Fortunately, all he does is laugh.

Before securing their bags on the trunk rack, Fearnside takes out three bottles of Dom Perignon and puts them on the back seat for safety.

"Carnarvon! You brought those all the way from Highclere?" Carter says.

"I certainly did," Carnarvon says, "to give our new excavation team a proper welcome."

Carnarvon relents by allowing Carter to drive them and settles in the back with Fearnside. Out of sight, Eve brushes her hand across Carter's as he holds the gear stick. Their eyes meet and he breaks into a smile. The Ford jolts into motion.

Though not as reckless as Carnarvon, Carter is a man of action and likes to travel fast. How different the trip is this time. They fly along the road of hardened mud, bordered by farmland that runs inland from the Nile. The Ford hits a bump, and the bottles of champagne rattle. Boys walking toward the road with their herds of goats stop to gape at Luxor's first automobile.

Beyond the farms, the road continues into the desert, offering views of the distant towering brown cliffs and the darker, rounded mountains beyond them. From nowhere, it seems, a cloud of dust arises and sweeps toward them. "Look out!" Carter says. He brakes to a stop and pulls Eve toward the floorboards. The Ford's windshield cannot block all the dust and sand. Eve hides in her hat, but dust still blows into her face and hair. Her eyes burn and smart. Carnarvon breaks into a fit of coughing. Then, just as quickly as it has rushed upon them, the storm dies down.

"Are you all right, Father?" Eve asks.

"Excellent," he says, his voice raspy.

"Dust storms become more frequent as February approaches," Carter says. "They come with the intense heat." Carter and Eve and Fearnside clear off the windshield, controls, and seats with spare cloths. "Before too long," Carter adds, "I'll have to close the tomb for the season."

"When?" Eve asks.

"Probably in March. I'll stay on to make sure that the first shipments of treasures arrive safely in Cairo."

Already she worries about having to say goodbye to Carter. Will her father want to leave for England in another month, or can they stay for two months? How will she and Carter find time alone? Eve is determined she will leave Egypt wearing an engagement ring.

The dust settles, Carter starts the car again, and they head west across the desert for another two miles, passing several donkey trains of tourists. Then they follow the curve of the road, southward and gradually upward, toward the ragged cliffs. The great triangular peak of el-Qurn looms the highest among them. The road forks, and they begin the dramatic crescendo, up and up into the Valley with its mysterious caves and pockets.

They draw closer to the official entrance to the Valley, then come to a standstill. A few hundred tourists jam the road. Eve clenches her jaw. She can hardly believe the crowd. Donkey trains, horses, and people walking under parasols. English and other Europeans, from the looks of it.

Four walls, all about three feet high, now enclose their Tutankhamun site. In front of and just to the side of Ramesses VI's tomb, tourists press all around the square. Others sit on the lumber pilings in front of a new storage shed and a half-completed guardhouse. Two Egyptian guards with the curved daggers Eve despises so much stand outside the opening of the new enclosure. Well, she thinks, we need these ruffians. Clearly.

Where is Carter's striped tent? Where is her pyramid-shaped rock, on which she painted the Carnarvon crest? Eve wonders who removed the rock without asking her.

Sightseers who recognize Carter and Carnarvon from news photos press into the Ford and ask for autographs. Cameras flash. Carnarvon grins his broad smile. He loves to be seen, recognized, and fawned over, while Carter mainly keeps his head down.

"I'm home again," Carnarvon says.

A grave, even a royal one, in the desert—home? As odd as the statement is, Eve can see his point. For her, as well, the place feels like an extension of herself. It is the place where her real life began.

Carter honks the horn to part the crowd and drives inside one of the empty Ramesses tombs across from their site. The Antiquities Service, it seems, has granted it to him for a parking space. He gestures uphill. "About ten sites up is the tomb of Pharaoh Sethos II, our laboratory, where we've already restored many artifacts." At the end of the archaeological season, these treasures, all from the Antechamber, will go to the Egyptian Museum in Cairo.

At last, free of the crowd, Eve and Carter trudge up a steep path, the one that branches out from the Ramesses tombs to the lab. Carnarvon, eager to sign autographs, tarries for a while near the Tutankhamun site with Fearnside. At the mouth of the giant Sethos II tomb, where the treasures that have been moved are now kept, a ten-foot gate made of crisscrossing steel bars protects the area like the portcullis of a castle. Outside it stands Pecky Callender. He nails long planks together as if he's building a coffin. "Lady Eve," he says, "welcome back."

Eve shakes his hand, then nearly gags from the acrid stench that comes wafting out of the tomb. "I'm glad to be back. Whew! What a stink!"

"It's the chemicals for preservation," Carter says.

Callender explains that he's building crates to hold the ceremonial beds. When Eve tells him that her father is signing autographs, Callender laughs. "Good for the lordy. I've missed you both." He puts down his hammer and unlocks four padlocks on the massive gate.

No sooner has Carter shut the gate behind them than a clean-shaven man in a seersucker suit hurries toward them: the pesky Arthur Weigall! Eve wishes he would disappear.

"Carter," Weigall says, "I see that Lord Carnarvon's arrived. I'd like to interview you both tonight."

"No, Weigall," Carter says. "Our policy is to talk only to the *Times.*" Carter reaches around and locks the padlocks one by one. "Carnarvon signed an exclusive contract."

They argue through the bars. "Damn you, Carter. You should cooperate a little. You'll be sorry if you don't," Weigall says. "Show me the laboratory and the tomb. No interviews, just a look. We can do it now and be finished in no time." Despite her dislike of him, Eve feels sorry for the poor reporter. Carter can be extremely unpleasant when angry.

Tight-lipped, Carter leads her into the Sethos II tomb and down a long, high passage. Tables line both sides. A string of electric lights both illuminates their way and adds to the heat around them. Eve stops to examine some of the tables. They hold rolls of wadding, tools, sealed boxes, and bottles of solutions—no doubt the odorous chemicals. Farther along are tables with large trays covered by linen cloths. She peeks underneath one to see ancient fiber baskets of coiled construction, some oval, some round.

Voices echo faintly through the corridor. Eve and Carter move toward them, past crates, then past more tables. A glow of gold indicates that items of higher value have been placed in this area. A few steps farther bring them to the golden throne with the panel of the queen anointing the pharaoh. Even in the low light Eve can see that the colors are more vibrant than she has remembered. But why does the throne look wet? She touches one of its arms and discovers it is coated with wax. Of course. The sheath of gold is very thin in places, and the wax will keep it from buckling until the chair can be fully restored.

Carter surveys all with a pleased expression.

"You're doing a splendid job, Howard," she says.

He gives a crisp nod. He is back to his confident self, thank goodness, she thinks. The anger has left him.

They continue down the passage, and the voices grow louder until they come upon three scholars engaged in their tasks. All have mustaches and wear suits, even in the heat. Carter introduces Eve to Arthur Mace, a white-haired gentleman whom she recognizes as a friend of her father's. He sprays a linen robe that is browned and stained. He shows Eve a child's glove—how marvelous! Carter says it is the oldest glove in recorded history.

Eve's gaze rests on three pairs of golden sandals. So beautiful! She could spend hours watching these restorations if she could put up with the smell. Will Carter give her jobs to do? Or will she be barred from helping with the artifacts now that the experts have arrived?

While Eve talks to the men, Carnarvon appears in the passageway, accompanied by Fearnside. Carnarvon erupts into a fit of coughing, then composes himself. "Good to see you all. Carter has many fine things to say about you. I've brought champagne to celebrate our venture."

This news is followed by cheers and good wishes. "After you and Carnarvon have a chance to see more of this laboratory," Carter tells Eve, "I'll round up the other scholars."

As soon as Eve coaxes him into a folding chair, Carnarvon begins another series of coughs. "Father," Eve says, taking his arm, "we need to get you into the fresh air. Now!"

Carnarvon's shoulders sag. Helping him out of his chair takes the combined strength of Carter and Fearnside. Once on his feet, Carnarvon sways. Carter catches him. Carnarvon grabs his cane and stands up straight. "I'm all right," he says unconvincingly.

Eve trembles. Her father isn't all right. He is exhausted. She faults herself for not paying closer attention to him, for allowing him to go into this hot, odorous cave in the first place.

He takes a step forward, then collapses face down on the stone floor.

Eve cries out. She and Fearnside both drop to their knees. Fearnside turns Carnarvon over. Eve leans in closer. He is breathing, thank God, but his eyes are shut. "He's fainted," Carter says.

Eve collects herself enough to think about what to do next. She's thankful her mother urged her to carry medical supplies in her bag. She takes out smelling salts and waves the vial under her father's nose. He breathes in, gasps, then opens his eyes. He looks at her directly, but he seems distant. Eve's mouth goes dry.

He's slowing down, she thinks. Their long journey to Egypt and its many transfers and sleep interruptions have been especially hard on him this time. And no doubt he also suffers from the heat and the chemicals. She leans over him and holds the smelling salts under his nose again.

Carnarvon blinks.

"Father. You're all right, thank the Lord," Eve says.

Eve squeezes his hand and puts her head on his chest. She feels so relieved, she could weep.

Carter and Fearnside help Carnarvon to his feet and support him step-by-step out of the laboratory. Eve is close behind, holding her breath against the fumes. Callender rushes forward and unlocks the gate.

It is hot in the sun, but the air is breathable. Holding her father's hand, Eve follows Carter down the slope to the Ramesses XI tomb, the place the scholars call the "dining hall." Miracle of miracles, fifteen minutes after his fall, her father sits at the head of a long table, just inside the entrance to the mouth of the large Ramesses tomb, casually chatting with the scholars as Fearnside pours him a glass of champagne. What a joyful sight! She stands outside the cave, holds her arms out wide as if to hug the world, then closes her eyes and thanks God. Her father is unstoppable.

Carnarvon makes light of the incident, saying, "It was the heat and the fumes." He coughs again, then takes a drink. Eve helps Fearnside serve Carter and the five team members present. Hoarsely, Carnarvon voices a toast. "To the gentleman scholars."

"To Carnarvon!" Carter says. Then he looks toward Eve, smiling in a playful way that she's never quite seen him do before, and he raises his glass again. To Eve it is as intimate as if they have embraced. She feels a flush of heat and, just for a moment, the certainty that she is part of his world.

"To Tutankhamun!" she chimes in.

Carnarvon drinks his champagne and lights a cigarette with his silver Fabergé lighter. "Don't!" Eve says, taking the cigarette holder from his hand. How could he? "You'll only start a coughing fit," she says, sounding like her mother despite herself.

"Eve," Carnarvon says, "give it to me."

She snuffs out the cigarette. Carnarvon accepts his defeat and turns to the table cheerfully. Drinking from glasses of various sizes, the group forms a makeshift, but still elegant, party in this unique setting. The champagne toast evolves into a series of briefings, each man as eager to please Carnarvon as if he were, himself, a pharaoh.

Eve's favorite of the group is the photographer Harry Burton, an energetic, friendly man with a clean-shaven face and jet-black hair. She sees on this day his images of Tutankhamun's Antechamber that she will treasure for the rest of her life. There it all is, just as she remembers it. A great jumble of things. Animal heads peering out. A widemouthed hippo laughing. Carnarvon grins as he studies the stack of glossy photographs. Burton glows with pride.

Eve notices from the easy way Carter talks to Burton that the two men get along well. It's clear that Burton admires Carter's brilliance for systems and organization. Carter has him photograph every article several times: in situ; separately with a placard; and then again after restoration. More than a thousand artifacts have already been accounted for in this way, Carter says, and not one has suffered a break. She glows with pride for him.

After a while, Arthur Merton from the *Times* of London arrives, and Carnarvon agrees to an interview. Carnarvon wants the scholars to stay and answer questions; Carter, who dislikes interviews, says he must return to his work. Eve sees her opportunity.

"Mr. Carter, will you take me inside Tutankhamun's tomb?" Eve asks.

"Yes," he says. "Certainly."

Will her father, the reporter, and the scholars try to join them? To Eve's relief, they remain in their folding chairs.

When Eve and Carter approach Tutankhamun's tomb, a pack of picture-taking British tourists surrounds them. "Back off," Carter says, his face reddening. He tightly holds Eve's arm until guards lead them into the walled enclosure. They start down the narrow stairway single file and stop at a high steel door. Carter opens a series of locks.

Inside the tunnel, Eve sighs. They are finally alone. Carter switches on the string of electric lights, and they make their way down the corridor. The stifling heat grows even hotter as they enter the Antechamber.

The room is half empty, though the mass of chariot parts and two ceremonial beds still fill one end. The north side is mostly cleared except for the two ka figures Eve remembers so well. With their obsidian-inlaid eyes, the figures still keep watch at the entrance to the Holy of Holies. The large basket lid, propped against the wall, still conceals the hole where she, her father, and Carter secretly entered. Carter has, no doubt, cautioned scholars not to shift any artifacts until photographed.

Eve takes Carter's hand as they stare at the figures. "Hello, guardians," Carter says.

"You talk to the ka figures?" Eve asks.

"All the time," Carter replies. "I promise them I'll keep them here as long as possible. They want to protect the king, you see."

"I understand," she says. How remarkable that Carter seems to share a camaraderie with them. It is as she always thought. He is, in his own way, magical. And she is, too, when she is with him.

From the silence there comes a ghostly whistling, like someone pumping the bellows of a fireplace. A faint snap follows, as if a twig is breaking from a tree. Then Eve hears a rustling, like leaves in the wind.

She swings around. "What was that? Did you hear it, Howard?"

"It's the tomb," he says. "The artifacts react to the air that's coming in from the outside world. Wood is expanding. I fear that they're going through many other physical and chemical changes. That's why I must clear this room as quickly as I can. But it also needs to be done with precise care and skill."

Eve looks at the nearest guardian statue as if he could listen to their conversation and advise them. He's been here for many centuries, grasping his staff, staring out at the dark, alert. The uraeus, the cobra springing from his forehead, also stares out as if alive. She gazes at the black-and-white eyes of the statue, and she could almost swear he winks at her. Yes, she is sure he winked. She touches Carter, feeling the perspiration on the back of his neck. "Howard," she says, "the eye of that statue moved."

"Yes, it did." Carter bends down in front of the guardian and studies his face. "This black resin is beginning to peel. We must have seen a bit flake off."

"That must be it." Eve eyes the statue, feeling foolish, then sad. She thinks about the two guardians leaving the tomb, which will be necessary for their preservation. She looks forward to having them at Highclere someday. Yet someone meant them to stay here for eternity.

Carter pulls her close to his side. He shuts off the lights in the Antechamber. Only the string of bulbs in the tunnel provides a tiny bit of illumination. Until her eyes adjust, the tomb seems bottomless, with no floor or walls. One of Carter's arms touches her shoulders, and the other reaches for her waist. She feels grounded again.

"There you are," she says, putting a hand to his face, which is hot. She touches his nose and traces his mouth with her finger.

"*Habibi*," he says. "That's Arabic for 'darling.'"

"*Habibi*," she echoes, enjoying this term of endearment. His lips and mustache taste of champagne and those Egyptian cigarettes he likes. Clove? She reaches up, on tiptoe, and closes his tired eyes with kisses. Then she kisses him above his nose. One of his hands strokes her cheek and the other strokes her hair. In the darkness of the tomb, time and place seem to pause in the hot air.

Now he presses his chest against hers and reaches around with both arms. With one hand, he lifts her dress, then caresses her bare leg. This is not how a gentleman behaves, she thinks, but she likes the feel of his hand so much that she doesn't stop him. She's shocked by his daring behavior, and even more shocked by her own.

Abruptly, as if sensing his mistake, he steps back. "We'll be missed," he says.

"Yes. We must go," she says. They cannot act this way at the excavation site ever again. Her father might send her back to England if he caught her. And, dear God, what a feast the reporters would have!

Eve smooths out her dress in an almost frantic effort. Then she combs her hair with her fingers. She takes a deep breath and composes herself. She must not let her face give her away.

13

In the coming days, Eve and her father escape from the crowds and sweltering heat to the Luxor Winter Palace Hotel. There, Eve issues the invitations for the opening of the burial chamber on February 16. Forty-one dignitaries, including some of the most prominent Egyptian officials, will attend. All the hotels in Luxor will host celebratory dinners and gala balls, so there's no need for her to cater a meal. Blessedly, Eve thinks, she's far away from the political demonstrations in Cairo. Although, it's possible that violence will spread. Mostly she worries about angry journalists.

January comes to a close. Eve wishes Carter would visit her. Though she understands that he must work with his team in the Valley, she feels excluded by him and all of them. Except for Sir Alan, newly arrived from London. Her father's chatty and portly friend, a connoisseur of fine foods and wines, regularly dines with Eve and Carnarvon at their hotel. Sir Alan tells them the news. And thanks to the telephone that her father has installed at Castle Carter, Eve and her father sometimes place calls from the Luxor Winter Palace.

One morning while Eve and Carnarvon enjoy tea and toast on their private balcony, a cool breeze blows up—a perfect accompaniment to a day in the Valley, Carnarvon says. Their secretarial work can wait. Carnarvon telephones Carter, who meets them at the ferry dock in the Ford. To Eve, the journey from the Nile, winding through the stark desert, and to the Valley's rock-cut tombs flies by. But once Carter parks the automobile, it seems that it takes just as long to push themselves through the crowds toward Tutankhamun's tomb.

The crowd cheers when Carter, escorted by a guard, shoves his way through the cordoned-off area. "Move aside!" he shouts.

Carter gives Eve an adoring look before he says, "See you soon," and disappears under the ground. Eve and Carnarvon remain at the tomb's retaining wall. There, along with a hundred or more tourists, they watch the workers and scholars carry artifacts from the Antechamber up the stone steps. The procession continues up a cordoned-off pathway past the Ramesses tombs to the restoration laboratory, the tomb of Sethos II.

What wonders there are to see. Dismantled parts of the golden chariots: Gold-sheathed wheels. Long golden poles. As each glistening part emerges into the sunlight, the crowd breaks into murmurs and shouts. Eve cheers with them. She thinks about how handsome the chariots must have been when they were pulled by horses. Axles follow, along with a chassis, and finally, brilliant with gold overlay and richly colored glass, the chariot body. Harry Burton hoists out his movie camera and tripod from the tomb and films the scene. All the while, with authority and ease, like the captain of a ship, Carter directs in Arabic and English from the base of the stairs.

Eve watches in fascination as blackened shapes, resembling the charred remains of a fire, come forth on stretchers. "Mummified parrots, cats, and crocodiles," Carnarvon says.

"No, Father! It's riding equipment." Eve recognizes the lumps as old leather tackle, saddles, and harnesses, melded together.

"This is as exciting as watching the Derby," Carnarvon says.

"I agree." She beams.

The spectators' exclamations grow loud again as another relic is revealed. From Eve's angle, it seems that young Tutankhamun, or at least his head and shoulders, rises toward her on a tray. It is a life-size wooden mannequin, the painted eyes opened large, its tall cap adorned with a cobra.

"A dress dummy," Eve says. "Maybe the king draped his jewelry on it."

A man behind nudges his way between Carnarvon and Eve. Who else but that cursed Arthur Weigall? "The lips are full," the reporter says. "This dummy must be of his queen."

Eve feels a sense of affront that the reporter has mistaken the young king for a woman. Forgetting herself, she blurts out, "It's Tutankhamun himself. There are similar images of him all over the tomb."

"It's the queen," says Weigall. "The king wanted her to keep him company in the afterlife."

"If that were the case," Carnarvon says, "she'd have arms and legs."

Weigall jots a note, then snaps a photograph of Carnarvon and Eve.

"Remember the exclusive," Eve whispers in her father's ear. She suspects his ribald joke will go right into print.

"If you would just cooperate with me, Lord Carnarvon," Weigall says. "Make Carter show me the inside of the tomb, and then I won't cause trouble for you. How badly do you want to keep your concession?"

Carnarvon casually removes his hat and fans his face with it. Eve wonders why he doesn't seem bothered by the threat. If it weren't for the *Times* exclusive, her father could give the journalist a private tour. Would that end the man's complaints?

"Please leave, sir," Eve says. But Weigall stays with Eve and Carnarvon, still attempting conversation. In another hour, Callender, speaking through a megaphone to the crowd, announces that the archaeological team has finished for the day. And only then, as the onlookers disperse, does Weigall leave Eve and her father alone.

So this is what it would be like to be married to Howard Carter, Eve thinks. She would spend her mornings and afternoons with reporters while he was busy with his work. She's waited for a week to see him, and so far today, they've barely talked. And yet it has been wonderful, magical, and a rare privilege to see those golden chariot parts sparkle in the sun.

The morning of the grand opening, the hottest of them all, Carter drives Eve and Carnarvon to the Valley from the ferry dock. Fearnside, suffering from a stomach ailment, stays behind at the hotel. Along the road, they pass by Egyptian *ghaffirs* in blue uniforms with brass buttons and red tarbooshes, and British and other European tourists with their donkeys and dragomen. All bodes well for a splendid day, Eve thinks. But beyond the ticket entrance, as they approach the enclosure of the Ramesses tombs, half a dozen robed men rush toward the roofless car. One shouts in English, "Independence from British meddling!"

Carter brakes, and the tires of the Ford spin in the sand and make a screeching sound. Eve's heart races. At any moment the protesters might reach the car. Eve has a parasol with her, something she doesn't usually carry, but it goes well with her lemon-colored frock. She waves it in the air, readying herself to use it.

Carnarvon's voice rises. "Where the devil is Mohammed Bey Fahmy and all the extra guards he is supposed to have hired?"

Guards and two *ghaffirs* on camels shout in Arabic and head the protesters off. Carter steers ahead.

"I don't like this," Eve says. She tries not to think about the news story she heard: more British tourists killed in Cairo. Despite strikes and protests, British troops remain in Egypt in order to protect the Crown's interests, including the Suez Canal. Egyptians want higher wages, trade unions, and the departure of foreigners, who control almost all business operations.

Carter sounds the car's horn. The protesters move as Carter, steering the automobile, forges through the crowd and past the checkpoint, where guards wave them in. He drives across the clearing and into the Ramesses tomb that serves as his garage.

"These nationalists want no British influence at all," Carter says. "And they are gaining the upper hand, I fear."

"They should be thrown into prison again," Carnarvon says.

Feeling dizzy and weak in the legs and knees, Eve steps out of the Ford. She holds her parasol out in front of her, just in case someone should break through the enclosure. Behind the checkpoint, the protesters shout in Arabic.

"Father, it's too late to cancel the event, isn't it?" she asks.

"Far too late," Carter says.

"We shall all be fine, my dear," Carnarvon says, his voice loud.

Eve doubts if he believes his own words. She pats the beads of sweat on her forehead with her handkerchief.

Carter mutters that it is Lacau's fault that protesters entered the Valley. As Eve well knows, Carter and her father wanted all the tombs to be closed to tourists for the day, not just the Ramesses tombs, and Lacau denied the request. It was folly on Lacau's part, Eve thinks, anger rising inside her.

The protesters continue to shout as they're led away by the Egyptian police. Eve holds her parasol in front of her with one hand and her father's arm in the other. Moving at Carnarvon's slow, hobbling pace, they cross the clearing of the Ramesses tombs. Carter rushes ahead. He and Callender, who has been waiting for Carter to unlock the tomb, disappear down the stone steps.

Eve has rented for the day a big white canopy for shade, which takes up nearly the whole of their enclosure. On two of its sides, it is held up by poles, and on the other two sides, it is attached by ropes to the boulders above the Ramesses VI hillock. The openness of the structure will allow for air to circulate, but there will be no hiding from the crowds today. Eve notices Arthur Weigall at the checkpoint where the road meets the Ramesses clearing. And he has the gall to be smiling at her.

"Look up, Lord Carnarvon," says Weigall, his camera outstretched over the roped barricade.

Carnarvon staggers, catching himself from falling with his cane.

"Father," Eve says, grasping his arm tighter. "Are you all right?"

"Quite fine. It's just the heat."

"Some of those protesters were Egyptian journalists," Weigall says. "They paid their entrance fees and have every right to be here." He pauses to take photographs. "You are not looking well, Carnarvon."

"Hush, Mr. Weigall!" Eve calls to him. How rude the man is. And it almost sounds as if he told the protesters to be there—did he? The worst of it is he is right about her father's health.

Carnarvon turns, his mouth open as if fixed in a shout. His hearing isn't as sharp as Eve's, and she hopes he hasn't heard the journalist's last remark.

Under the canopy, Carnarvon sits and stretches out his legs. His face is red, and he seems very tired. Feeling so tense that she is ready to cry, Eve remains above ground with her father so she can greet the guests as they arrive.

To Eve's relief, Mohammed Bey Fahmy, the chief of police, comes to the site by camel. Then by and by, four automobiles, a caravan of native dignitaries riding camels, and several donkey trains enter the cordoned-off area. Two Egyptian princesses in pink silk gowns, their scarves covering all but their eyes, join the group under the canopy along with Egyptian men in elegant Western dress and British gentlemen in their formal clothes and top hats. What a splendid sight, Eve thinks. She'd enjoy it if she weren't worried about a gun going off.

But at least her father is somehow taking the danger in stride. Refreshed by several glasses of water and a snack of figs, Carnarvon stands chatting, bowing, and making introductions. Eve looks about her, at Lord and Lady Allenby, the *mudir* of the city of Qena, and Pierre Lacau. The scholars gather toward one side of the tent, while the Egyptian officials—including the new Egyptian prime minister, Muhammad Tawfig Nasim Pasha—gravitate to the middle. She bows and smiles in turn to each.

Carter strides up the stairs from the tomb and says to Carnarvon, "It's time." Carnarvon and Eve lead the procession. Single file, they

pass through the open steel door and descend toward the Antechamber. Eve is impressed to see that Carter and Callender have set up the
room like a theater. Four rows of chairs face a stage, which conceals the
replastered hole. A green curtain hangs from the ceiling to the floor.
The ka figures frame the stage, intensifying the dramatic atmosphere.
But unfortunately, the crowd and the electric light bulbs overhead add
to the stifling heat.

Eve, Carnarvon, and Lady Allenby take seats in the front row. The
princesses and Pierre Lacau sit in the second row. There are only twenty
chairs for forty-one guests, so many of the gentlemen stand, pressed
together.

Carter steps up to the stage, looks down at his feet, and paces about.
Ready for the work at hand, he wears a simple white shirt with the top
button undone, suspenders, brown trousers, and sturdy shoes. Callender, in his red bow tie, stands to one side, with hammers and other
tools at his feet. Waiting on the other side of Carter is his foreman, Reis
Ahmed Gerigar, and three native workers with baskets.

Carter plants himself center stage, arms to his sides, woodenly, like a
shabti figure. He looks like he's in pain, Eve thinks. She catches his eye,
offers him an encouraging smile, then lifts her arm as if giving him a
toast. *Be steady. You're my hero*, she says silently.

His jaw is set, but for an instant, he smiles.

Carnarvon calls, "Carter, I think we should start. Are you ready?"

Carter unfolds a lengthy script and, after a painfully long pause,
speaks in a monotone. He's so wordy that he's nearly incomprehensible.
"Here in the Antechamber, I have seen an imperishable vision. At last,
a great civilization, in a land that was the earliest home of the most
refined culture ever brought forth by man, is adequately revealed to us
in supreme works of beauty."

Oh Lord, Eve thinks. Can't he talk more naturally? Where is that
dashing, self-assured, commanding archaeologist with whom she has
fallen in love? This is a disaster. Eve and Carnarvon exchange glances.
Carnarvon looks at Carter and cocks his head. Carter gets the hint. He
sums up his speech and Carnarvon, cane in hand, takes the stage.

Carnarvon can rise to any occasion, and he does so now. He looks
from one person to another, addresses some by name, and smiles. "I
welcome you to what is, for many of you, the site of your heritage. I'm
so glad you could be here. We're grateful to all who have helped bring

this about. Let's begin." Carnarvon gestures to Carter, then goes back to his seat.

Callender draws one side of the curtain, while Carter draws the other. Between the guardian statues, a wall comes into view. "Ladies and gentlemen," Carter says, "you see here a doorway that has been plastered over." He outlines the shape of the door with his hand.

Eve bites her lip. Is anyone noticing the slightly lighter gray, hump-shaped stain near the floor where she, Carter, and her father entered? Carter positions himself at the center of the wall, aims high, and taps the plaster. He narrates, rambles, and chisels enough plaster to reveal a lintel and regularly shaped blocks underneath it. She wishes he would stop talking and smash the wall into pieces.

Carter swings large and hammers the doorway with strong blows. The sound of the pounding provides Eve with a welcome distraction. Callender and Gerigar join in to help with the dismantling. Hammering the stones, loosening them with a crowbar, or simply lifting them out, Carter labors steadily from the lintel downward. He hefts the blocks to Callender, who passes them to Gerigar, and from him they go to workers who carry them out in baskets. The air grows heavy with dust. Carter's shirt quickly soaks up his sweat. His muscles strain with each blow. Eve shifts uncomfortably.

At eye level, Carter excavates a hole that is, by chance, shaped like a cat. Callender hands him a torch. The spectators fall silent. Carter thrusts the torch into the hole. "Ladies and gentlemen, I can see a gold and blue wall."

The group murmurs.

"Bravo, Carter!" Carnarvon calls.

Carter takes out more stones, lowering the opening until the light shines in and Eve can see the hues of gold and blue beyond. "It's a burial shrine," he announces.

"A royal tomb!" Carnarvon shouts. Eve worries that he has made the remark too soon. Carter continues to remove the stones. Nearly all the spectators rise to their feet.

"Give us room; soon everyone will be able to look," Carter says. With a large hole now exposed, Carter puts one leg into the chamber and then the other, disappearing. Carnarvon follows him, then narrates to the audience from the opening. "The shrine has two doors with bolts across them. Carter is drawing out the bolts."

The crowd is so still that Eve can hear the creaking of the ancient doors. The feeling of excitement is palpable.

Carter comes to the opening, eyes wide. "There is another compartment inside the first. It's another shrine. It's covered entirely with shining gilt."

The guests gather around the opening. Eve stands, too, craning her neck to see the patch of gold. Finally, unable to contain herself, she rushes inside the chamber to stand with her father.

"This second shrine has an unbroken seal. It seems to be intact," Carter calls, his voice rising. "There is a rope, also, knotted so perfectly that it cannot have been untied by a thief."

Carter slips out the bolt on the doors, then cuts the ends of the rope with a scalpel. The ancient doors creak open.

"A third gold shrine, bolted and sealed!" Carnarvon narrates. "Now he's opening it!"

Eve watches Carter slide another bolt and cut another braided rope. The third set of doors swings open to reveal the portals of yet another golden shrine. Eve wonders how many more layers there could possibly be.

Carter pauses. "I'd like to take a moment to translate the inscription on the doors of this fourth shrine. *I have seen yesterday, I know tomorrow*," he says. Then he severs the ropes and the seal of the fourth shrine.

The final set of doors slowly creaks open, and there stands the end of an immense yellow sandstone sarcophagus. Its corners are decorated in high relief with protective goddesses of the dead, their wings folding over each other in the rear section of the rectangular coffin. Eve feels tears forming in her eyes. Her father's decades of funding excavations have all been worth it for this moment. Carter turns to her and Carnarvon with misty eyes and a bright smile.

Carnarvon lets Carter have the honor of announcing the find. "Ladies and gentlemen, here filling the entire area within stands an immense yellow quartzite sarcophagus, intact, with the lid still firmly fixed in its place. Just as pious hands left it." Eve hears *oohs* and *aahs*.

An elegant cornice wraps around the top of the sarcophagus. It is beautiful, Eve thinks. It is so massive that surely it must contain more than one sarcophagus; in keeping with the way the ancient Egyptians did things, there will be several layers more before coming to the actual mummy.

It surprises her to see that the lid of the great tomb is red granite, mismatched with the rest of the coffin. As she stares at the winged goddess carved in low relief in the corner of the sarcophagus nearest to her, she thinks she feels the majesty of the dead pharaoh's actual presence—watching, hovering. Is he angry that he has been disturbed? Or is he simply confused?

Everyone talks at once.

One of the Englishmen in the audience yells, "Let me see!" Another joins him. Eve fears there might be a fight that could lead to damage inside the tomb. But spectators hush up the two.

Then all fall silent again when Carter moves around the side of the outside burial shrine and narrates from farther away. "There is another room in here. I can see golden objects. Many. A treasury!"

"Simply wonderful, wonderful," Carnarvon shouts. He grins widely as he and Eve step back into the Antechamber.

Carter joins them. "I'm overwhelmed by the beauty of it," he says. He wipes tears from his eyes. "You may all look inside now. Please be careful not to touch or fall against anything. Form a line: two at a time." He slips back through the mostly demolished wall.

Eve and Carnarvon tour first. Then they wait at their chairs as, two by two, the guests enter the burial chamber, then return, dazed and smiling. A few have tears in their eyes. After Lacau finishes his tour, he reappears in the Antechamber, fixes his clear blue eyes on Eve, raises his arms like a priest at mass, and says, *"Mon Dieu."*

Will Lacau and her father argue about the tomb being intact? Debate about Carnarvon's right to take his fifty percent of the treasures? Eve and Lacau speak in French about the exquisite gilt goddesses of the canopic shrine. She senses that he has the dignity to wait until a more appropriate time to have that conversation. There is something extraordinarily guileless about the man, she thinks. His integrity commands her respect and makes her feel all the more uncomfortable about her monetary thoughts.

Her father, Sir Alan, and Arthur Merton of the *Times* of London go above ground together; Carnarvon will grant one short interview. Eve lingers, waiting for Carter. The guests and the scholars gradually leave the tomb, several at a time. As rapt as they are, Eve sees, they're sweating and cannot stand the heat. After what must be at least two hours underground, she cannot stand it either. Leaving Carter, who inspects the sarcophagus, she makes her way out through the passageways and the tent and into the open. Cool air, at last!

The dignitaries, in their cars and on their camels and donkeys, depart through the picture-taking crowds. The azure sky will, in the next few hours, turn red behind the Theben hills. It will be a perfect evening, capping an unbelievable day. A day that, all things considered, despite terrors and aggravations, has turned out well. They know now, for sure, that they've found the untouched grave of King Tutankhamun. The body of the king, most certainly, must be nested inside that massive sarcophagus.

But when Eve goes to find Carter—looks down at the stairway at him and sees him locking and unlocking the padlocks of the steel door, again and again—she feels a pang of dread. He's held mostly steady all day, but now he acts very oddly. His hands tremble. The locks rattle against each other.

She rushes down the steps. "Howard!" she says. "What's the matter?"

Eve silently wills him to stop fumbling with those locks. "Howard," she says again. She puts her hand on his shoulder.

Carter stares back at her with so much fury, it seems he will explode. His eyes are so wide that Eve can see the whites all around his irises. His face twitches.

Eve cries out faintly and feels her chest tighten. This isn't his usual restlessness that manifests when he is angry or tired. He seems disoriented, hot and sweaty, as if feverish. Maybe he *does* have a fever. She has to get him away from the remaining crowd.

"Let's go back to your house now," Eve says. "Howard. Please."

Carter continues to test the locks. He shakes one of them. "Damn, damn, damn."

Eve tries to guide Carter away from the locks, but he will not budge. He talks to himself in a raised voice, muttering. His fingers quiver. He breathes irregularly, almost as if he were panting like an animal, Eve thinks. What on earth is happening to him?

"Howard, the locks are secure," Eve says, taking his arm. "We're going now."

Still fumbling with the locks, he tightens his face.

"Howard," she says gently. She stops short of saying the word *Habibi*. "Look at me."

He keeps on with the locks.

This is mad behavior, Eve thinks. Absolutely mad. Did she miss the signs of it before because she didn't want to see them? Or has his conduct changed? He is more than stressed; he is ill.

Eve rushes up the stairway and fetches her father and Callender. When Carnarvon sees Carter, he whispers to Eve, "I fear he's edging toward a mental breakdown."

By God, Eve thinks, it is true.

14

From the kitchen of Castle Carter come the sounds of dishes being stacked and the smells of onions, garlic, and coriander. Eve, her father, and Carter have each in turn bathed and changed clothes. They drink red wine and wait at Carter's square wooden table for Ahmed to serve them dinner. Seated across from her, Carter seems calm but removed, Eve thinks. He turns his head to one side, now and again, without making eye contact. He isn't making jerky movements, or raising his voice, as he was just hours earlier at the tomb. But he seems to be staring without seeing. He's not connecting with her, or indeed with anyone. She hopes, but feels no reassurance, that food and sleep will make Carter well again. What exactly prompted his odd behavior?

Keeping her voice low and steady for Carter, she uses all her strength not to break into tears. Eve tries to keep a conversation going. She is tired, she says, and is glad that the three of them aren't crossing the desert back to Luxor. Even if she's missing the gala at the Winter Palace Hotel.

The telephone rings in Carter's nearby office, a shrill-sounding double bell, and Carter jumps. Even Eve flinches; she has never heard the telephone in this house before. She answers the call and takes the message. The Queen of the Belgians, who missed the opening, requests a private tour with her entourage tomorrow. Oh Lord, what next? Eve supposes they will have to cater to her.

Back at the table, Ahmed brings the first plate of warm pita and bowls of a leafy green stew, *molokhia*.

"Carter," Carnarvon says, dipping bread into the green broth, "take some days. Eve and I can handle the Belgian queen's visit tomorrow. You're exhausted."

Carter's voice is steely. "Certainly not, Carnarvon."

"Howard should be present at the tomb, at least to meet the queen," Eve says, wishing she could talk to her father privately.

"Carnarvon, it's *you* who should take time off," Carter says. "It's *you* who seem especially tired." Carter knits his thick eyebrows. He squints for a moment as if they are still in the sun, and yet the room is dim.

"Please don't argue," Eve says, wishing Carter would look at her. My God, his mind stirs like a dust storm, she thinks. She fears he'll erupt at any moment.

"I'll have my rest when Eve and I get back to England," Carnarvon says. "For now, I must insist you take a holiday. If not tomorrow, then start the day after."

Carter's eyes flash. "Why? Are you planning to put Sir Alan in charge?"

"Nonsense," Carnarvon replies.

"Sir Alan?" Eve says. "What are you two talking about?"

Carnarvon calls to Ahmed, who is standing on call near the door to the kitchen, to pour them more wine. After taking a drink, he turns to Eve. "The other day at the hotel, Sir Alan confided in me that he wanted to leave our team. And he said that another of the scholars, Mr. Breasted, too, may go. But I told them to wait. I said that they—and Carter—should take a few days off."

Eve has been crossing her legs, dangling one sandal half off her foot. Now she sits bolt upright. She can hardly believe what she is hearing. How could any of the scholars think of walking away from the most phenomenal excavation ever? The excavation that will make all their careers?

Carter scowls. "I know the men say I'm difficult to work with. And I have been on edge as of late, I admit. But none of the scholars like me. They consider me coarse and uneducated and are looking for an excuse to get rid of me."

"Wait," Eve says, her voice rising. She looks toward her father, seated next to her, a chunk of flatbread in his hand. "Sir Alan says he's planning to leave the excavation? And no one has bothered to tell me?"

"Eve, there's nothing we can't make right," Carnarvon says, dismissing her. Ahmed fills his glass with wine. Carnarvon takes a sip and continues to talk as if Eve isn't there. "The men admire you, Carter. They know you as one of the foremost archaeologists in the world. But you must lead with dignity and an even temper."

Carter frowns. He drinks half a glass more wine.

Eve recalls a time when Sir Alan and her father had drinks at the hotel bar without her. She never thought they were discussing anything like this. "Father. You still haven't told me what occurred with the scholars."

Carnarvon pushes his bowl of stew and plate of pita away. "Sir Alan mentioned to me, just prior to the opening of the tomb, that he was unhappy. He says, my love, he doesn't like being bossed about. He told me Mr. Breasted feels the same."

Carter's nostrils flare. A deep vertical line creases the skin between his eyebrows. "Howard," Eve says, "the scholars are jealous of you."

"I doubt that, Lady Eve." He pulls out his cigarette case from his shirt pocket, finds it empty, and slams it shut. "Wealthy aristocrats like Sir Alan? Envious?"

"You know more than they do," Eve says, "for all their titles and advanced degrees."

"Try to get along with them, Carter. That's all I ask," Carnarvon says. "Let's talk again when we are fresh."

Carnarvon coughs into his handkerchief, and Eve remembers that too much wine makes his throat constrict. She shouldn't have allowed him to drink more than one glass. But on the positive side, he may fall asleep early tonight. Then she can soothe Carter in privacy.

Carter takes another drink from his glass, then leans back in his chair, his expression still fiery. Eve wishes she could put her arms around his shoulders. Once they are alone, she hopes he will unburden his feelings about the pressures of his work.

She knows she could help him to get along better with the archaeology team in time. She could host dinners for them all and instruct Carter how to behave during those occasions. If only he would allow her.

Carnarvon's head droops momentarily; then he wakes up again with a start.

"You're tired. You should turn in early tonight, Father," Eve says.

"No, darling," he says. "I'm going to use the darkroom first. I've left some films there, and I can hardly wait to see how they will develop."

Eve sighs quietly. She takes a few bites of the stew, and the sweet taste of coriander lingers in her mouth. She will go to Carter, she thinks. Offer herself. She will make him love her. Come what may, whatever the consequences are, they will do what lovers do. Then once he is completely hers, she will be able to help him even more.

By nine o'clock the house falls silent. Carnarvon has stopped going back and forth to Carter's makeshift photography lab, and Eve assumes her father has gone to bed. She puts on a simple cotton floral nightgown and paces about the courtyard, shivering a little. She looks toward the expanse of the Valley in the distance, but it is completely hidden in the moonless night.

When Carter doesn't come looking for her, as she has hoped, she goes inside. Her father's room is dark. The lights of the parlor, where Carter is temporarily making his bed on the sofa, shine under the door. She taps gently, then louder. "It's me."

"Come in, Lady Eve."

Eve opens the door, then closes it behind her. It's most unfortunate, she thinks, that none of the doors in the house have locks, not even the front door. Carter sits on the sofa, still fully dressed, surrounded by Egyptian newspapers. Chilly air comes in through the half-open window, and he has a ceiling fan on. A cotton blanket covers his lower legs. Carter looks at her questioningly, as if he doesn't know why she's come. How can he be so uncomprehending?

"After our talk at dinner, I wanted to see that you were all right," she says.

"Yes, thank you." His formal reply seems designed to push her away.

"I saw how agitated you were today," Eve says. "I wonder if you ought to continue your work as usual. Maybe, as Father says, you should take a holiday."

"My mood would be far worse if I *didn't* have my work," Carter says. "All my life I've struggled with moods. If I can manage a few good nights of sleep, I'll be fine."

To Eve's relief, he doesn't bring up Sir Alan or the other scholars. Afraid he'll try to brush her away, she steps slowly toward the sofa. Carter sets down his Arabic newspaper. "I was just reading the Arab commentary. They claim that if a mummy is found, Carnarvon will sell it to the British Museum. Total rubbish!"

"Yes, it is. Father already told the *Times* that if a mummy is found, he wants it to stay in the tomb. Why would anyone say otherwise?"

"It's Weigall and the anti-*Times* group spreading tales to turn the Egyptians against us. They're trying to pressure Lacau to cancel our concession."

"Those journalists are hateful. But Pierre Lacau won't be swayed by them," Eve says, glad that at least they are talking normally.

"He might if there's enough bad press," Carter says.

"Don't think about any of this now." Eve takes a seat on the sofa and smooths the blanket with her hand, wishing Carter were pursuing her and not the other way around. Why isn't he?

She gazes about the room. Books, newspapers, a projector, projector reels, and ashtrays full of cigarette butts clutter his low table. She notices the rock she had once decorated with the intertwining *C*s of the Carnarvon crest. Perhaps he took it for safekeeping. On another table near the window, she spots the lotus-shaped chalice that her father took from the tomb. Carter calls it the Wishing Cup. The sight of it gives her a start. How could Carter have it here in his house, out in the open, no less? She rises and takes the cup gently into her hands. It is very heavy and feels smooth and cool. It is exquisite.

"I'm putting it in the Annexe before I seal off the tomb for the summer," Carter says, a bit defensively.

"But Father found it in the Antechamber," Eve says.

"I know," Carter replies. "I can't bring it over there because the scholars have started photographing the area. They will notice if the chalice suddenly appears."

Her father was very wrong to have taken it, Eve thinks, but the deed is done. She fingers one of the tiny kneeling figures perched atop the vessel's handles. "Well, be careful, Howard. I'm surprised you left this just sitting out."

Carter's brow furrows. "None of the scholars has ever visited here. But you're right. There could be a first time."

The truth of his words stings. After working together all day, do the men never allow Carter to socialize with them? Even the Americans? She formed the opposite impression the day the group shared champagne.

"I can help you to get along with them," Eve says.

Carter sighs loudly. This is a sensitive topic, clearly. "Let me have the goblet, and I'll put it away right now." He holds out his hands for it, and she gives it to him.

Carter leaves the room and soon returns. Eve remains on his sofa and watches him stand near the door, hesitating. Then he takes a seat in his chair near the window. This awkwardness between them is painful.

"We haven't been so close to one another in the past few weeks," Eve ventures. "We've all been busy, and I know that you are preoccupied with the dig."

"It's true, my work is my life. But Lady Eve—"

"Call me Eve. Or *Habibi*," she says.

"There's no possible way we can be together. I can't stop thinking about the difference in our class. It's something the scholars throw in my face constantly."

"Class does not matter when people love and understand one another," Eve says. She tells him how her brother, Porchey, married an American who came to the family with little money. Carter has no reply to this.

After a long silence, Eve wraps her arms around her knees, showing Carter her bare legs. She sees that he is watching her intently.

She admires his glossy black hair, his dark suntanned skin, and the fullness of his lips beneath his mustache. "You've made your decision to separate from me, without talking to me first?" she says.

"Yes. It may not be what either of us wants, but it's for the best for now." He smooths his hair down with his hand.

The words "for now" give her hope. "Why for the best?" Eve asks. "And why for now?"

"You know why. My station in life, my lack of funds. And I need time for my scholarship. I've never had thoughts of love or marriage— until you."

"Oh," she says. It's a relief to hear him talk of marriage. She extends her legs to the floor.

To her surprise, Carter says, "I can think of marriage only when I can fund my own digs, or when a museum, hopefully, will fund me— and then, by some miracle, if you still want me."

She crosses her legs. "I'm pleased that you've been thinking about a future with me."

"But why do you want to marry me?" he asks.

"Because I love you," Eve says, "and I want to share your life of adventure. I love archaeology. I want to be an archaeologist with you, and live with you in London and in Egypt."

"You're confusing danger with excitement. The Wafdists could send us out of the country at gunpoint."

"If you no longer want me, I'll leave your room right now," she says, with no intention of doing so.

Eve rises from the sofa and moves slowly toward Carter. She knows he wants to touch her. She can see it in his expression. "Let me kiss you before I go."

She presses her lips to his. Then she wedges in beside him on the chair and puts her arms around him. He touches her face, and her neck, and runs his fingers through her hair. She wants more.

Eve puts her palms against his shoulders, feeling the cotton of his shirt, and unbuttons the top two buttons. She kisses the open triangle of his neck. Then she takes his strong calloused hands, hands that have unearthed the most fabulous treasures in the world, and touches her mouth to his fingers.

"You had better leave right now," he says hoarsely.

"And I thought you no longer wanted me," she says.

"You are everything a man could want."

They move from the chair to the sofa, where they sit for a long time with their arms around each other. Finally, Eve finds the courage to say, "I want you to—"

"Truly? Are you sure?"

"I'm yours," she says.

"You're a virgin?"

She nods and hugs her knees, not quite wanting to make eye contact.

"I shouldn't be the one. You'd regret it."

"No, I wouldn't."

There is another long pause. By the look in his eyes, she sees he is giving in. She strokes his thick hair; it is threaded with gray. He runs his hand down her back. They kiss. Then, with a strong hand, he pushes up her nightdress and runs his hand up her bare leg. As he continues to caress her legs, her nightdress folds up into her lap. She touches his thigh, thinking she'll move her hand upward when she feels brave enough. He guides it for her. Through the linen fabric, she feels him.

"Stop me now," Carter says, drawing in a breath. He gives her a pained look.

"It's what I want," she says.

"Truly?"

"Yes."

"We may both regret it," Carter says.

"I won't," Eve says.

"If you keep touching me like that, I will have to make love to you, even if it is the ruin of me," he says. "I've never wanted a woman so badly."

He moves his hand closer to her undergarments. She guides his hand inside and tells him what she wants without words.

Their lips meet. The only sounds are the ceiling fan and a breeze delicately lifting the curtain at the window. Slowly she unbuttons his trousers. Just as she bends toward him again to kiss him, there comes a knock on the door.

Eve spins out of the embrace. She and Carter sit up together on the sofa. As she pulls her nightdress down over her legs, she feels her heart pounding. Carter quickly moves to the other side of the room, his trousers falling to his feet.

The knock comes again, three times: *rap, rap, rap.*

Carnarvon calls out through the door. "Carter, are you awake?"

"I'll be there in a moment," Carter says, his voice strained.

"I saw the lights on. I have photographs to show you." Carnarvon pauses. "Is everything all right?"

Eve straightens her nightdress. Carter reaches to pull up his trousers.

The knob turns and the door swings open.

15

Eve tenses as her father stands in the doorway, his face folding into a frown.

"What's going on here?" Carnarvon asks.

Carter fastens his trousers and closes his eyes. He sighs loudly.

"I was just leaving," Eve says.

The lines on Carnarvon's forehead crease. He clutches his cane and his voice hardens. "Let's go into the dining area and talk there."

To Eve the short walk feels interminable. Carter leaves the room first, then Carnarvon, and Eve trails behind, her head down, looking at her bare feet. She clutches the edge of a chair and wishes she lay dead in a tomb.

The three of them sit around Carter's table, as they did several hours before. She smells onions and the rich scent of cumin from their earlier meal. But now, anger, guilt, and shame hang in the air. Outside the windows, the night appears black as kohl. Eve and Carter face Carnarvon as if on trial.

"Don't blame Mr. Carter," Eve begins. "It's all my fault, Father." Her mouth goes dry as she tells her father how she and Carter have been secretly courting each other since December.

Carter holds his head in his hands, then sits up again. "Carnarvon, I know it wasn't right to go behind your back," he says. "I'm sorry. I tried not to encourage it. I dared not hope it could be."

"You are my dear friend, Carter," Carnarvon says. "Now let us…let us all forget what has happened."

His words feel like painful stabs. "Father. How can I forget? I love Howard!"

"You may think you do, Eve. Girls your age have romantic fantasies. I ask you now to put such feelings aside." Carnarvon looks from Eve to Carter. "Eve, you are as precious to me as life. Carter, my regard for you has no bounds. I can only think of your future happiness. Some relations are not suitable in our world. There is nothing we can do about it."

Eve feels her cheeks burning. Surely this cannot be her kindly father talking. She rubs her eyes, trying to stop the tears from coming.

"Mixing classes, you mean," Carter says in a firm and altered voice. "You don't consider me your equal."

"I didn't say that," Carnarvon answers. "Some things just aren't done."

Carter turns to Eve with an expression of deep pain. "I didn't dare hope for your father's approval."

Eve breaks into a sob.

"Carnarvon, I love your daughter," Carter says. "I would not court her without your consent. But the world is changing. Please realize I am worthy and give your consent."

"No, Carter. It's nothing to do with 'worth.' You and Eve don't belong with each other." His tone, Eve finds, is surprisingly harsh.

Eve hates her father at that moment. He has let her down so desperately that she isn't sure she can ever care for him again. "Father! Don't say such a thing."

"I must."

She flinches at the uncharacteristic flash of anger in his eyes.

Carter jerks his head back; then he rises from his chair. "All right, Carnarvon," he says, his tone bitter. What he says next seems to come from some fiery place inside him. Yet to Eve's shock and sorrow, his words have nothing to do with her. "You're planning to put Sir Alan in charge of the tomb, aren't you?"

"This is all nonsense, Carter," Carnarvon says. "You know you're the man for the job. No other could ever replace you."

"In the morning, I want you both to leave this house," Carter shouts. "Carnarvon, you may communicate with me through Sir Alan."

"Howard, don't. Please talk sense," Eve urges.

Carter's irises appear to darken from brown to black. She feels frozen and powerless in the face of his intense anger.

Carter marches down the hall, his footsteps heavy on the tile floor. He heads for the living room, and Eve rushes after him. He slams the door shut. Before she can turn the knob, she hears him pushing something heavy against the door.

"Leave him alone," Carnarvon says.

Eve ignores him. "Howard, open up."

"Lady Eve, please let me alone," Carter says. Then, he chokes out, "I wish to God you'd never come to Egypt."

Carnarvon stands and lets his cane drop to the floor. He puts his arm around Eve and guides her away from the door. Crying, she returns to her room.

The walls of Carter's house are thin. Eve stays up late into the night listening for him, then dozes off. Early the next morning, she awakes with a start at the sound of footsteps and a door opening. She meets Carter just outside the threshold of the house, a leather bag over his shoulder. He strides toward the Ford, which he keeps parked in the shade of the acacia tree. He looks awful. Unshaven. The skin under his eyes is sunken and his hair isn't combed.

Eve grabs his arm. "Howard, talk to me," she says.

He averts his eyes. He may as well have stabbed her in the heart.

He gets into the car, puts his satchel on the passenger seat, and starts the engine. Eve's voice rises and hardens. She is shaking almost as much as the car. "Howard!"

He does not turn to look at her. Damn him and his moods.

"Remember the Belgian queen's visit! We need to plan it," Eve pleads. "Don't go!"

He is heading back to the tomb without her and her father. He drives off, leaving a trail of dust. Her eyes smart and her throat feels raw. Eve and her father must now travel to the site by donkey.

Eve aimlessly walks about the rooms of the house. She feels a pang when she notices the empty birdcage on the floor near Carter's desk. It is a symbol of all that has gone wrong.

Eventually, Carnarvon wakes. Eve determines that they will place calls to Luxor, organize themselves, and muster their way through their responsibilities. They must get themselves to the Tutankhamun site to meet Elisabeth, Queen of the Belgians. She doubts that Carter has the diplomatic skills to carry the meeting off.

Eve and Carnarvon put in their appearance at the tomb. Like an actor in a play, Eve walks through her part while the sun shines down on the sweltering Valley with its buzzing flies, camels, blue-uniformed *ghaffirs,* and foreign queen, who, against all reason, wears a mink coat and high-heeled shoes. Ordinarily, Eve would take more of an interest in her. But as it is, the day stretches on with an empty, washed-out feeling, like the desert itself. Carter remains sullen, but he manages, at least, to drive Eve and Carnarvon to the ferry dock. There, a barge ferries the limousine in which the queen of the Belgians travels.

Exhausted, Eve falls asleep at the Winter Palace Hotel and misses dinner. The next day she takes her meals in her room and naps in between them. Fearnside clears away the dishes. She doesn't see her father until he joins her on the balcony of their suite.

When he settles into a rattan chair that is too low for him, he swings his stiff legs and hips awkwardly. "Eve, darling," he says. He pours two glasses of sherry, his cue that he wants to talk. The Nile lies before them, a ribbon of blue in the glare of the sun.

Eve tenses, thinking of the blow that will fall. He'll tell her that he's disappointed in her. Perhaps he'll send her home to England. Instead, he says, "Let's go to Cairo soon to talk to Pierre Lacau. And afterward, I've booked a Nile cruise for us. We leave before the end of the month."

Eve sits up with a jolt. "You didn't ask me first!"

"A pity your mother isn't here to come with us. She always loved to see the ancient temples along the river," Carnarvon says. "But Sir Alan will probably join us."

"How can we possibly—"

"I'll leave Carter in charge, if he's up to it," Carnarvon says. He twirls one waxed end of his mustache. "I'll instruct the scholars not to make any major decisions until we return in a few weeks."

"*Weeks?*" Eve swallows hard. "I couldn't stand to be away for more than a few days."

The corners of Carnarvon's mouth turn down. "A fortnight, then. I can put us on one of the shorter cruises." He pauses. "The excursion is for you, darling. I want you to be happy."

"I would be happier if we could stay in Luxor."

Carnarvon pulls at his collar. "We must give Carter a chance to settle down and apologize to the scholars for the way he treated them."

Eve puts her chin on her knees and tries not to cry. Her father doesn't understand how much she loves Carter.

"Don't blame Mr. Carter," Eve says. "The night you found us, he said it was over between us. But I kept after him."

Carnarvon listens, scowling. All in one gulp, he drinks the sherry from his tiny crystal glass. Eve has not touched her own. "You've behaved very badly," he says. "I should tell your mother. What's more, I should send you back to England."

Eve sighs. She has seen this coming. "No! Please don't say anything to Mother. And I won't go home." Her voice sounds shrill.

A strained silence follows. "At least now I know that Carter did not try to take advantage of you, and nothing too improper happened. We can put it past us now."

"I can't," Eve says. "I love him."

Carnarvon's eyes widen. "It is incredible to me to hear you talk like this," he says. "In time you will forget him."

"No," Eve says. "Never. You cannot possibly know the depth of my feelings."

Does she dare talk about how her soul merged with Carter's? The truth sounds too fantastical to say aloud. Besides, it is sacred to her, private.

Carnarvon draws in a labored breath, then coughs. He looks thin and hunched.

"All along, I feared Howard and I would be found out," Eve says. "I didn't want to upset you. But I thought—I still think—you will come to accept him."

Carnarvon's voice is gentle. "Not as your suitor."

Eve bristles. "But Father...don't you realize you are being a hypocrite?" The words hang in the air. "You've never paid much attention to society before. Why start now? Porchey married an American who hardly came with a fortune."

"It's not just the money, or the lack of a title, or his age." Carnarvon slumps in his chair. "You deserve better. He could only ruin your life. He's not well, you know. His desperation is like a deep ocean. You could drown in it."

"No, I wouldn't. I'd help him," Eve says.

Her father shakes his head. He pours himself another tiny glass of sherry. "Carter sabotages himself. He might well be in Pierre Lacau's position by now if he hadn't turned his back on the Antiquities Service. He held chief inspector positions both in Upper and Lower Egypt. Heroically, he shored up collapsing sites. Rescued temples from the floodwaters. He enjoyed the work and excelled at it. But then—"

"What happened?" Eve asks. She can recall only a few details.

Carnarvon coughs, then closes his eyes for a moment and frowns. "One night at Saqqara, at a tomb complex under Carter's jurisdiction, a group of drunken Frenchmen broke into the site. There was a lot of violence that night in and around the tomb complex. Chairs and rocks were thrown. Eventually Carter arrived at the scene. He instructed his

native *ghaffirs*, tomb policemen, to defend themselves with truncheons."
Carnarvon pauses. "A number of the Frenchmen suffered injuries. As
the story goes, one of them had his head broken open."

Eve makes fidgety movements, curling and then flexing her fingers.
"Did he die? Become brain damaged?"

"I don't believe so, Eve. In any case, it wasn't Carter who hit him,
but ultimately Carter was responsible. Carter's supervisors asked him to
write a letter to the French government, issuing a formal apology. But
Carter refused."

"Oh." Her father has a point about Carter's mood swings.

Carnarvon finishes his second glass of sherry. "So Carter was de-
moted. Then he quit. Arthur Weigall took his position. And poor Carter
was selling his watercolors for tourists in a bazaar when I met him. He
was almost a beggar."

Eve leans forward toward her father, her elbows on her knees. "Father, you hired Howard because he didn't have a job. But he found
Tutankhamun's tomb for you. This story has a happy ending. Why do
you bring it up now?"

"You see, Eve," Carnarvon says, "he's been shutting doors for years
now. In his anger, he is convinced that the world is against him. And
that's part of his illness."

In the distance, gulls cry out as they circle over the Nile. Carnarvon
clears his throat.

"I was hoping for your blessing, Father," Eve says. "I was hoping we
could help Howard together."

He turns to her. "You have my love always, Eve. And Carter, that
brilliant but tormented soul, has my affection as well. I just cannot allow
him to drag you down."

Carnarvon draws in a wheezing breath. Then he lets out a low, re-
pulsive-sounding cough. His face turns red, and he spits into his mono-
grammed handkerchief.

The sounds jolt her. Eve can no longer focus on the conversation.

Oh, dear God. Her father is a sickly man. She thought she might
leave him and return to the Valley on her own. But she must stay with
him.

16

Carnarvon spends the next few days in long conversations with Sir Alan, and sometimes the other scholars, on one hotel balcony or another. As much as she wants to be apprised of the goings-on at the excavation, Eve cannot face her father. She takes her meals alone. But one small action of Carnarvon gives Eve a particle of hope. He shows her the letter he's written:

Luxor
19 February 1923
My dear Carter,
I have been feeling very unhappy today. I did not know what to think or do, and then I saw Eve and she told me everything. I have no doubt that I have done many foolish things and I am very sorry. I suppose the fuss and worry have affected me but there is only one thing I want to say to you which I hope you will always remember—whatever your feelings are or will be for me in the future my affection for you will never change.

I'm a man with few friends and whatever happens, nothing will ever alter my feelings for you. There is always so much noise and lack of quiet and privacy in the Valley that I felt I should never see you alone altho' I should like to very much and have a good talk. Because of that I could not rest until I had written you.
Yours,
Carnarvon

Eve pens her own letter, which she adds to her father's note:

19 February 1923
Howard, dear,
Father is no longer angry. Please, will you give up your angry feelings, too? He cares for you more than for any of his other friends.

He knows, as I do, how brilliant and capable you are, my love. He wants you in charge of the tomb, and I know that you wish the same.

Before Father and I leave on a Nile cruise, we will go to Cairo to try to get a settlement from Pierre Lacau and more freedom for you. I know how horrid it is for you to deal with endless visitors at the tomb.

I think of you every moment and hope to see you as soon as we return. Come to Luxor and we can plan our future together.
Yours with love,
Eve

One day passes, then another, and neither Eve nor Carnarvon receives a response.

Eve, her father, and Fearnside board a train to Cairo so Carnarvon can meet with Pierre Lacau. A settlement of the treasures might secure a future for her and Carter, Eve thinks. How could either of her parents say no to Carter after he brings them phenomenal riches when the artifacts are sold to museums? And won't these museums offer work to Carter? But when Eve and Carnarvon arrive at the Antiquities Service office at the Egyptian Museum, they learn that the Frenchman is home with the flu and will not be expected back for a fortnight.

So after only one night in Cairo, Eve and her father return to Luxor. A note from Carter awaits them. Carnarvon reads it, then leaves Eve alone to read it for herself.

22 February 1923
Carnarvon,
It's insufferably hot. We have had another dust storm here in the Valley. I must close the tomb for the season and begin crating the artifacts for their journey to Cairo. I wish I had more workers to help me, but at least there are no more crowds.
Yours,
Carter

Eve sighs. In the past few days she has done a lot of thinking. Her father's rejection of Carter as her suitor deeply humiliated him. The rejection exposed in Carter a carefully covered despair about his parentage. He longs to be an aristocrat—and she, by encouraging him to think he could be, only added to his misery.

She wants a title for him so badly that she still believes it is possible.

King George might well knight him one of these days. But would that make Carter feel strong and grounded? Help his moods? Probably not.

Another realization suddenly comes to Eve. *She* does not need her father's approval, as much as she loves him. But Carter does, and he isn't going to get it.

In the pharaoh's tomb, she and Carter experienced such wonders together. They shared a lightness of spirit, love, and magic. Their bond is lifelong and true. But it's clear to her now that he can no longer regard her romantically. They will never marry. She crumples the letter in her hand.

The most she can hope for, it seems, is that Carter will shake off his anger and depression, reconcile with her father, and stay in control of himself and the excavation.

Eve plans the Nile cruise with her father. It will take them only to the Aswan sites, not, as in previous years, to the more distant ruins. Fearnside and Carnarvon's three favorite Egyptian scholars will accompany them, all stodgy older gentlemen: Sir Alan, Sir Charles Cust, and Arthur Mace. Eve will tolerate their company for a few days.

So off they go in their own privately hired *dahabiya*, a barge-like vessel that can be either motored or sailed. My, but these scholars all have dry coughs! Eve thinks. They sound like her father. Perhaps it is their long years of breathing in dust from ancient tombs. Or is it disease from mummy wrappings? Or smoking too many cigarettes?

The horrid Nile mosquitoes arrive at dusk and descend from clouds above the deck. Until Eve can escape to her cabin below, she finds them everywhere: on her forehead, between her eyes, on her arms and legs. She covers her exposed skin with citronella and tries not to scratch her bites. Carnarvon doesn't bother to use the repellent half the time, and doesn't seem to care that his face looks patchy. His skin is aging far too rapidly, Eve thinks.

Their group tours the Princes' Tomb at Qubbet el-Hawa, the "Dome of the Wind," on the west side of the Nile, where a group of rock-cut tombs forms a dome on the peak of a hill. Eve charges up two long stairways from the riverbank to reach the tombs. They hold colorful wall paintings, but she is in no mood to appreciate them.

That night the boat docks in the shade of riverbank trees, and an exhausted Carnarvon retires to bed early. Finding her cabin too hot, Eve climbs back up to the deck. The night is moonless; there are only the distant lights of other small rivercraft. Fortunately, only one lantern illuminates the deck, and Eve creeps as far away from it as possible to avoid mosquitoes.

In the darkness, from some distance away, she overhears Sir Alan and Sir Charles talking.

"Lady Eve doesn't have a brain in her head," says Sir Charles. "When we're in the Valley, she has nothing better to do than chat about silly things, pester Carter, and interrupt his work. She and Carter seem awfully thick, have you noticed?"

How dare Charles Cust say such things!

"It's nothing. Talk about a May to December romance. How could there be anything between them?" says Sir Alan. "Don't be so hard on her. She's spoiled, but she has a lot of good in her. She's utterly devoted to her father."

"Yes, I'll give her that," says Sir Charles.

Do all the scholars talk about her in this manner? Even Sir Alan, a family friend she's known all her life? Pompous fools! How humiliating.

She slips out of the shadows into the lantern light, where the men sit on a bench. She knows better than to speak up, but she must. "Sirs, I caught a snatch of your conversation," she says, her voice cold. "Please forgive me for overhearing, but I feel you are entirely wrong in your views. I've not been chatting about 'silly things' with Mr. Carter; I've been making important contributions to our dig. I assisted Mr. Carter with note-taking in the early days before you arrived. Lately, I have served as a publicist, sent correspondence around the world, and overseen every event. The functions that I organized were essential for establishing the good relationships we have fostered with Egypt's elite. I know my father appreciates my help, if you do not. What would he say if he heard you now?"

That silences them. Sir Alan turns to her, the mouth in his portly round face wide open. Eventually, he says, "Apologies, Lady Eve. I should not have spoken as I did."

Eve inhales sharply. "I'm not silly. I'm not useless. When you insult me, you insult my father. Kindly remember who is in charge of the tomb."

In the dim light, Sir Charles meets her eyes. "I'm quite aware."

Eve storms to her cabin.

The next day, the *dahabiya* crosses to the opposite shore near Aswan, and Eve and the men see an impressive dam with many gates. Her father and his friends drone on about the engineering of the dam. Seeking solitude, Eve finds a spot in the shade. She thinks of Carter and, near tears, hugs her knees.

Later, their group visits an ancient quarry where an obelisk, believed to have been commissioned by Queen Hatshepsut, lies unfinished in its bedrock. It would have risen over a hundred feet if chiseled as intended, Eve learns, but it was never finished. The ancient craftsmen likely abandoned it because of a gigantic vertical crack that runs down one of its sides. Oh Lord, Eve thinks as she peers down into the pit of the quarry. She is in such a mood that even an ancient queen's broken wishes make her feel melancholy.

The next day, their group visits Philae, an island rich with temple compounds, which they approach through colonnades. On a side trip, Eve and her father share a rowboat that can accommodate only two people. Despite knowing better, Carnarvon stands up in the vessel to photograph Eve against the ruins.

A mosquito lands on his cheek. Swatting it, he loses his balance and falls backward into the rowboat. The small craft rocks and nearly overturns.

"Father!" Eve says.

Carnarvon edges himself up on the seat and laughs. Eve would laugh as well if, at that moment, two mosquitoes didn't land on her ankle. Without thinking, she says, "I hate this cruise."

"Sorry if it is dull for you, Eve," Carnarvon says.

Eve wishes she had not sounded so childish. It is rotten of her to complain when her father must be in far more discomfort than she. He might have hurt his back when he fell. And a large red welt has formed on his cheek. His face and arms already show numerous bites, but this one stands out dramatically.

"You have a bad bite on your cheek," Eve says.

He scratches the swollen bite. "It's nothing."

Poor Father, she thinks. He appears so scruffy and old. And she is sure she looks a sight as well. Despite her nightly washings in her cabin, she's collected rashes, sticky skin, and travel dust. Her hair, flattened down by her hat, is a mass of tangles.

But tomorrow the sightseeing part of their cruise will finish at last. Then they'll sail back down the river, toward Luxor. At the hotel, she will ask if there are any letters for her father or for herself, knowing what the answer is going to be.

Upon arrival at the Winter Palace Hotel, Eve finds there is no word from Carter. The next morning, Eve decides she'll take meals with Carnarvon again, and she joins him in his room for breakfast. She finds him in the bathroom seated next to the shaving bowl with Fearnside dabbing his face with a towel. Blood runs down his cheek.

"Father, what happened?"

"A shaving cut. No matter! I only nicked the scab of my mosquito bite," he says. But his voice is no louder than a whisper. He looks so tired he may drop.

"Where's the medical suitcase? I'll dab it with iodine," Eve says, remembering her days assisting her mother during wartime.

"I will do that, m'lady," says Fearnside. "Why don't you step out for now, and I will finish dressing his lordship."

Eve waits in the parlor of their suite and flicks away a fly that buzzes around her. How has a fly entered? The screens on the windows must not fit properly. She will tell Fearnside, who will discuss the matter with the hotel.

She wishes she had a swatter. But she doesn't even see a newspaper on hand to roll up. Who has thrown out all the copies of the *Times* without asking her? Small things are putting her on edge. With so much else out of her control, she wants to see that fly dead.

Fearnside opens the door to the parlor and approaches her, frowning. "M'lady, perhaps we should send for a doctor. I believe his lordship has a fever."

Eve's heart races. My God, she thinks. What next?

She crosses into the next room and finds her father in bed. He lies rigidly on his back, shivering, wincing.

Eve squeezes his clammy hand and cries out. Then she orders Fearnside to send for the doctor.

A young British doctor visits that morning and prescribes liquids and rest. Carnarvon turns away the tea and toast that she orders for him. She parts the curtains of the window so that he can look at the Nile and the cloudless sky, but he stares out blankly, his usual brightness and enthusiasm gone.

The concierge, a native man with a turban, places a telephone call to

Carter for Eve. Carter doesn't answer his phone. Eve jots him a quick letter. *Father is ill. He needs you,* she writes. *Put your argument aside, Howard. Please come to us. Eve.*

The day passes, and the next morning Carnarvon is no better. He isn't well enough to sit up and read the newspaper. She holds a cool cloth to his splotchy face, moving it around his bandaged cheek, and waits helplessly for the doctor. Perhaps she should send for her mother? Because of her father's weak lungs, he's prone to catching pneumonia and bronchitis. All fevers are potentially dangerous to him.

His mind wanders. Once, sitting upright in bed, he clutches the sheet with one hand and says, "Lacau, don't give me such a reproachful look. I take it you're suggesting I sneaked in." He pushes his chin out defiantly. "Go ahead, send me back, but keep Carter in charge."

Eve moves her hand onto his shoulder. "Father, it's me. Eve."

He blinks, still apparently unaware of where he is. "Eve. Darling. Bring me the pen." With his index finger, he makes loops in the air. "Lacau, I'm signing the papers... Fifty-fifty..."

Eve holds back a scream. Good God, she thinks. If he's hallucinating, he must be seriously ill. She wipes her father's forehead with a cool, wet cloth. Fearnside helps Carnarvon lower himself down into the bed again.

Another day passes. Eve will not allow any visitors besides the doctor, who calls both mornings and evenings now. He gives Carnarvon cherry cough drops and stinking cod-liver oil, remedies that are obviously inadequate. But perhaps the doctor is right: sleep is probably the best remedy.

Carnarvon's temperature remains high. His neck swells, and he loses one of his back teeth.

After Eve sends Carter three notes in three days, she finally receives one from him in return. *I will come as soon as possible,* he writes. *There is so much happening in the Valley, with journalists, visits from inspectors, and Egyptian officials; it is difficult to come away.*

Cannot he understand the state her father is in?

Eve instructs the concierge desk to keep calling Carter and to send for her when he answers. She finally speaks to Carter early the next morning. Unfortunately, the only telephone at the hotel is at the desk, where anyone passing by could hear their conversation.

She hears him clear his throat. "It's Carter," he says.

"It's me. Eve." The line hums. "Please come to Luxor. Father's temperature is still high. The doctor does not know why."

"I'm so sorry." Carter pauses. "We must be careful not to tell anyone he is ill. Not the scholars. Especially not the reporters."

Eve agrees to discretion. She hears herself prattling on. "The doctor says no alcohol, but Father says he wants you to bring him one of the bottles of wine he sent from Highclere."

"I suppose a sip won't hurt," Carter says. "I can't get away today. But I'll come tomorrow. With the wine."

"Thanks." Eve clutches the heavy black phone in her hand.

"Try not to worry. You know Carnarvon. He's a cat with nine lives. Think of all those car accidents he suffered."

At that moment Carter sounds so gentle that Eve begins to cry. The only reply is the sound of his even breathing.

"Come at once," she says, stifling the urge to keep the conversation going. "Goodbye, Howard."

17

A few days after the Nile cruise, and a month since Carter and Carnarvon's argument, Carter finally arrives at the Winter Palace Hotel. Despite her anger over the delay, Eve sees that his presence serves as a tonic for her father. For that morning, just after he sweeps into Carnarvon's room, bright yellow sunshine pours into the windows of the suite, and her father lifts himself up and props himself against the headboard. The wet cloth on his forehead makes him look, almost comically, like an old pharaoh, she thinks.

Carter kisses Eve on the cheek. The concerned look in his eyes comforts her.

Fearnside, inconspicuous as always, stands in a corner of the room, then slips out when Eve signals to him that she wants privacy. Eve and Carter pull up chairs beside the bed. Carnarvon cocks his head and smiles at them. Oh Lord! Her father's lost another tooth, just to the right of his center front teeth. And his breath is bad.

Carter takes out a cigarette and is about to light it, then apparently thinks better of it. After a long pause, he says, "I'm sorry about everything, Carnarvon. You know I have a temper."

Carnarvon extends his hand. Weakly, he leans toward Carter. They shake hands. "Now we are reconciled. Let's have no more talk of you leaving your post, or Sir Alan taking over. He won't be."

"Thank you," Carter says.

No one speaks for a long time. Then Carnarvon relates how he nicked a mosquito bite while shaving. "See," he says, touching his finger to the welt on his cheek. "An unspeakably filthy Egyptian fly alighted on it and gave me an infection."

"*Unspeakably filthy?*" Eve repeats. She laughs.

Carnarvon gives out a loud, hoarse cough that makes her flinch, then spits a chunk of yellowish phlegm into a handkerchief. She forces a smile as she hands him one of his cherry drops.

After Carnarvon clears his throat, he turns to Carter. "Did you close the tomb?"

"Yes. The tomb is sealed off," says Carter. "Next we need to move the contents of the laboratory to Cairo. Then we end the season."

"It's a pity we didn't see the mummy," Carnarvon says.

"We will, Carnarvon, in the fall."

"Yes, in the fall," Carnarvon repeats. His eyes cloud over. He's so tired, Eve thinks. It's good that he's planning another trip to Egypt—he certainly isn't expecting to die. But will he even have the strength to return to England for the summer, much less travel abroad again?

Carter talks of his system for moving the artifacts. "We'll set the rails—military-style, take up rails as we go along—to transport the treasures to the Nile for shipment to Cairo," he says. "The throne will be the first to go to the Egyptian Museum."

"I wish I could see it again." Carnarvon's voice is weak. "Carter, if you ever need it, the concession agreement's in my bank safe in Cairo. Mosseri's Bank. Do you have the combination?"

"Yes, you gave it to me."

Eve feels her heart skip a beat. Is her father preparing for his death? "Don't talk of such things, Father," she says.

"Carter. If I'm still laid up in a few days, you must meet Lacau on your own," Carnarvon says. "Firm up a settlement. Choose some of the best treasures for me."

"I will, as soon as the laboratory is cleared and the treasures are safely in Cairo," Carter replies.

Carnarvon has another fit of coughing. He reaches for his handkerchief and makes a horrid, guttural sound. When he spits into his handkerchief, Eve looks away, feeling both panic and disgust.

She pours him a glass of water. He gulps it down.

"Howard, tell us of any new discoveries," Eve says, feigning cheerfulness.

"We've opened up more boxes and found hundreds of garments in a sticky substance—balls of crumbled mud, feathers, and beetle wings. No one knows what purpose those things served."

"How odd," she says.

"Yes, yes? What else have you uncovered?" Carnarvon asks.

"We've found a marvelous swan made of wood, painted black," Carter says. "It's so lifelike, with its mouth open and tongue extended, you can almost hear it honk."

Carnarvon sits back and closes his eyes for a moment, looking serene and content, as if seeing and hearing the swan. Despite his cough, he's clearheaded today, she thinks. Once again, she allows herself to hope that her father will recover. "Mr. Carter's brought something for you," Eve says. "Your daily glass of wine," she adds, referring to his custom in England. In Egypt, he's not had wine in weeks.

"Bless you, Carter," Carnarvon says.

Carter and Eve both stand. From his leather carrying case, Carter shows her the bottle, then sets it down on the bedside table. She struggles to pronounce the German words. "Riesling, 1921. Scharzhofberger Spätlese."

"Ah, from the Mosel Valley. Excellent," Carnarvon says. Eve grasps his thin shoulders and helps him sit up straighter.

Carter takes out the elegant alabaster Wishing Cup and unwraps it from its cloth. He hands it to Carnarvon, who clasps the heavy, lotus-shaped chalice in his hands.

"Oh," Eve says, startled. "It's a lovely thought to have Father drink out of it." For the moment she puts aside her judgment that Carter shouldn't have risked bringing such a priceless artifact to the hotel.

Carnarvon gives Carter his widest grin. As he examines the cup in the lamplight, the golden stone becomes translucent and seems to glow from within.

"I chose a white wine so it wouldn't stain," Carter says. "Carnarvon, when I read the inscription, you'll know why I've named this chalice the Wishing Cup."

"We'll all drink from it. Drink to Father's health." Eve feels it is a prayer.

Carter opens the bottle with a corkscrew. Together, Eve and Carnarvon hold the alabaster cup while Carter slowly pours the wine. He fills it halfway. Eve wonders if King Tutankhamun was the last person to drink from it, three thousand years ago. The antiquity of the cup somehow adds to the power of the wish.

The cup is weighty; she grasps it firmly with two hands as she brings it to her father's lips. He takes one sip, then another. "Delicious. I can taste lime and wildflowers and wet stone, all at the same time."

"Here is what it says on the cup," Carter says. "*May your spirit live, may you spend millions of years, you who love Thebes, sitting with your face to the north wind, your eyes beholding happiness.*"

"Thank you, Carter. You are a true friend," Carnarvon replies.

Eve takes a drink of the wine, tasting roses and ancient limestone. Let this be a magic cup, she prays. Let Father recover from his illness.

Carter takes the cup in his hands, then drains it in one motion.

Carnarvon closes his eyes and dozes off, smiling contentedly. Bright sunlight glints on the window. There is a smell in the air of sickness, of astringents, of fear. But also, Eve thinks, there's a feeling of reconciliation. "Let's walk in the garden," she suggests, and he nods.

With its heady aromas, private sitting areas, and riotous plant life, the hotel garden seems made for romance. But all Eve seeks now is her own peace with Carter. The garden is empty, at least in the section away from the swimming pool, where she can hear laughter and splashing, and certain nooks are so overgrown that light barely penetrates into them.

Eve points ahead, and they walk down a path toward the aviary. The aroma of jasmine drifts through the warm air. They enter a tiny courtyard enshrouded by hedges and sit down on a stone bench. Before them, crow-like hob hob birds, with black and gray feathers, hunt for seeds on the watered grass.

He wipes away the sweat on his forehead with his handkerchief. "Lady Eve," he says, "you will always, always have my devoted and most heartfelt friendship. Remember that."

Even though she has been expecting and even wanting to hear these words, they are like a great weight pressing on her chest and squeezing all the air out of her lungs.

"What are you planning after the Tutankhamun excavation is over?" she asks.

He shifts his gaze toward her. "I expect I'll be in Egypt for years. But after that, if I can get funding, I'll search for Troy. Some ruins have already been discovered by the German archaeologist Schliemann. Those are of the wrong date. The lost city in Homer's *Iliad* may lie nearby."

"Move to Turkey?" she says, surprised. "It would be wonderful if you could discover Troy. You can do it, you can do anything."

"I appreciate your confidence in me," he says.

They sit in silence, and Eve watches the hob hob birds take flight. Suddenly this romantic little hideaway in the hedges feels quietly lonely. She thinks with longing about her mare, Lady Grey, and the thrill of cantering across the wet green hills of Highclere. Riding is her escape when the pressures of life weigh her down. As soon as her father is well enough to travel, it will be time for them to go home.

18

The next morning, Eve taps the door of her father's chamber and slowly opens it. He is snoring. She returns to her own room for a bath. By the time she checks on Carnarvon again, he's propped up against pillows, drinking coffee, and eating toast with marmalade. What a relief!

"I'm feeling excellent, Eve," he says. "It must have been the Wishing Cup."

"Father! You're looking well." She sits on his bed and puts her hand to his forehead. "No temperature." She feels so elated she could shout.

Standing in a corner of the room, awaiting instructions as always, Fearnside beams. "M'lady, his lordship is over the worst."

Thank you, God, Eve prays silently. Life is coming around, after all. Her father seems almost like his old self. Perhaps he'll gain back some of the weight he's lost.

"My appetite's returning, Eve." Carnarvon finishes half a slice of toast and starts on another. "I'd like scrambled eggs. Fearnside, please order a full breakfast for three and have Carter called. He and I and Eve can eat in the sitting room."

"Yes, m'lord," says Fearnside, grinning.

Eve leaves the bedroom while Fearnside dresses Carnarvon.

Carter walks into Carnarvon's room a while later, newspapers in hand. He meets her eyes, then, smiling broadly, strides over to her father. "Carnarvon, so glad to see you up and about."

"It was the wine and your ancient Egyptian incantation. I'm sure of it," Carnarvon says.

Eve half believes him. "I agree."

Over breakfast, Carter takes out his spectacles and reads aloud from his Egyptian newspaper. Meanwhile, Eve and Carnarvon scan the English and American papers. Thankfully, not one has reported Carnarvon's illness.

After some time, Carter says, "Carnarvon, seeing that you're all right, I must leave soon for the Valley. I need to help Callender crate the shipments for Cairo."

To Eve his words come like a slap. *Leave?* She feels a pang, though she knows that there is hardly a busier man on earth than Carter. Of course he has to return to the dig. It is unrealistic to expect him to stay on in Luxor.

"Please go, Carter, by all means," Carnarvon says. "Our work has to continue."

"Carnarvon." Carter pauses. His gaze grows intent. "If you feel up to traveling, you ought to go to Cairo as soon as possible. Today or tomorrow."

"Why?" Eve says, a flash of anger coming over her. "What business can be so important that Father can't take a few more days' rest?" she demands.

"Lady Eve," Carter says, "if the fever should return, Cairo is where Carnarvon should be. Egypt's best doctors are in Cairo." His measured tone chills her.

"Of course," she says. "Father and I will leave just as soon as we can."

Carnarvon gives Carter a clear, bright nod of the head. "Carter, the worry is over now. But I'm glad you are thinking in practical terms," he says. "And I ought to be in Cairo anyway. With some of the finest pieces shipping soon to the Egyptian Museum, I have to get to work and make our settlement with Lacau. Surely he's over the flu by now."

Carter paces. "Yes. It's time Lacau made us a definite offer," Carter says, his upper lip twitching. "If he won't go fifty-fifty, make a counteroffer. Ask for some of the greatest treasures, but insist we get all of the duplicates. Start with the alabasters and the shabti figures—so many of them look the same. The Egyptian Museum doesn't need them all."

"Duplicates, right," Carnarvon says.

Carter finally turns to meet Eve's eyes and smiles. "Lady Eve. Everything will be fine with your father," he says. "Write to me. Keep me informed."

"I will." He's slipped back into his own world again, to a life that does not include her.

Eve quickly sends off a telegram to the Grand Continental Hotel in Cairo. The answer comes just as fast: Yes, they can book a suite. Their group leaves right away for the train station, and she, Carnarvon, and Fearnside crowd into a first-class compartment. Carnarvon stretches out on a seat.

The train ride seems to sap whatever strength her father has regained from the alabaster cup. Within hours, he vomits and complains of dizziness, and his forehead is hot to the touch. Oh Lord, she thinks, he's lost another tooth!

In Cairo, a young, wiry, nervous, and clean-shaven Scotsman, Dr. Fletcher Barrett, comes to the Continental Hotel and gives Carnarvon a serum injection so he can sleep. The next morning, Carnarvon wakes up his old, cheerful self again, and Eve is so relieved that she hugs him. Carnarvon talks about making an appointment with Lacau for the next day. He goes to a men's club for dinner and a Charlie Chaplin film. But when he returns to the hotel, to Eve's great distress, Carnarvon collapses into bed, feverish once again.

Eve arranges for the doctor to come, then sends telegrams to Carter, her mother, and Porchey. Hours later, Streatfield, the steward at Highclere, replies. Lady Carnarvon is in Paris, he says. He will try to reach her. *Curse her and that lover of hers*, Eve thinks. Her brother is more responsive. He says he will set out from India as soon as he can.

Carnarvon, in between Dr. Barrett's milky injections, sleeps or talks gibberish. Once he turns to Eve and says, "Let me have a smoke!"

She wishes she could give him what he wants, but of course, smoking brings on coughing fits. The sweet smell of Egyptian clove cigarettes would be a welcome change, she thinks, from the odor that now pervades the room. It smells faintly of vomit, even though Fearnside instructs the maids to constantly change the sheets.

On their third day in Cairo, Eve can hardly believe how awful Carnarvon looks. His skin sometimes appears washed out, like mummy wrappings, and at other times it flushes red. The mosquito bite on his cheek stands out as a raised crimson welt.

A week goes by, and there is no word from Carter.

Dr. Barrett comes and goes, and he's as useless as anyone else in knowing what to do. Eve stays by her father's side nearly all the time, holding his hand and listening to his feverish ramblings. Though she has not been much of a churchgoer in recent years, she prays on her hands and knees, asking God, or any of the gods who might be listening, to restore her father's health.

19

Eve pulls the cord on the ceiling fan in her father's hotel room, and the wooden blades stir. The fan wobbles off-balance; it is a metaphor for the instability in their lives. It's now April. For over two weeks she's been turning the fan on and off as Carnarvon feels heat, then chills. His neck is swollen, his head seems too large because he's lost weight, and his skin looks red and splotchy. The big welt on his cheek now appears purplish.

To Eve, life feels interminable in that mostly lifeless room. But perhaps the goddess Isis is, at last, lifting her feather wings like a fan, stirring the stale air, and summoning the people who need to be there. On this day, Eve expects not only Carter to come to Cairo but also her mother. Lady Carnarvon has hired a biplane and a pilot to transport her and the Highclere family doctor, Marcus Johnson, referred to simply as "Dr. Johnnie," in a series of flights from England to Egypt.

That morning, Carter enters Carnarvon's room as he thrashes from side to side calling, "Water!"

"The water's right here," Eve says. Dr. Barrett brings the glass to his lips.

Carter removes his hat. He approaches Carnarvon and takes the chair Eve has just vacated. Carnarvon hurls his water glass against the far wall, where it shatters. Eve jumps.

"Are you angry with me, Carnarvon?" Carter's eyes open wide.

"He doesn't know it's you," Eve whispers. "His fever has gone up again."

Fearnside kneels to pick up the pieces of the broken glass.

Dr. Barrett's voice is grave. "I'll give him another shot." He goes to his medical bag on the desk at the corner of the room to prepare his syringe.

"Carnarvon, I met with Pierre Lacau yesterday," Carter says.

Oh? So Carter has already been in Cairo for a day and not contacted her?

"What did Mr. Lacau say, Howard?" Eve asks.

Carter does not reply.

Carnarvon tosses fitfully. "Sugar," he says. "I want sugar."

Eve wonders if the doctor should stop giving him laudanum. Half the time, her father makes no sense at all. And now that there might finally be some news worth hearing, Carter cannot communicate it to him.

Carnarvon swings his arms at Carter. Carter slides the chair back away from the bed.

The doctor injects the honey-colored serum into Carnarvon's skinny, bruised arm. Carnarvon moans.

Eve crowds in close to Carnarvon and takes his hand. "Rest, now, Father. Mr. Carter is here. Mother is coming. I've contacted Porchey and he'll be here soon. Everything will be well." She tries to believe her own words.

He smiles faintly and closes his eyes as the potent serum overtakes him. Just then, the bedroom door opens. It's Eve's tiny, impractically dressed mother, wearing an almost floor-length pink crêpe dress and high heels.

Lady Carnarvon parades in, her arms outstretched, and hugs Eve. Then she quickly moves to her husband's bed. Carter and Dr. Barrett make space for her. "George. I'm here, darling."

Carnarvon opens his eyes. "Almina." His voice is weak. But remarkably, he recognizes Lady Carnarvon, when today he has not acknowledged anyone else. He closes his eyelids again.

"The doctor gave him an injection, so he's groggy," Eve says.

"Move aside, Eve," her mother says. "I wish you had contacted me sooner. I am glad I am here now."

"I've sent you many—" Eve stops herself from talking about the numerous unanswered telegrams during her mother's Paris sojourn. Her mother puts her palm on her husband's forehead, turns his hand over, and moves his fingers one after the other, testing his pulse. Then she dips a washcloth in water and spreads the cloth across the top of Carnarvon's face and head.

Dr. Johnnie enters, and Eve feels herself soften. The old, balding doctor has been their physician for as long as she can remember. With his round spectacles and tweed suit, he has a studious, friendly air that has always put her at ease. "Thank you for coming," she says.

"Of course." He knits his eyebrows and frowns as he looks toward Carnarvon.

Carnarvon barely manages to stay awake during the examination. Then, as Dr. Johnnie holds a stethoscope to Carnarvon's chest, he has a fit of coughing. Together, Lady Carnarvon and Dr. Johnnie adjust Carnarvon's posture, and he falls asleep. Dr. Johnnie glances at Dr. Barrett and tilts his head toward Lady Carnarvon. "Let's have a word."

Everyone except Fearnside clears out of Carnarvon's room for the sitting room next door. Eve is glad to see that her mother is including Carter, who stands near the tall window, his arms crossed, moodily looking out toward El Opera Square.

Seated together on a white silk couch, across from Eve and her mother, Dr. Johnnie consults with Dr. Barrett: "Erysipelas—that bacterial infection on his face—has led to blood poisoning," Dr. Johnnie says. "On top of it, he's got lobular pneumonia in both lungs."

"Do you think we can get him to Highclere?" Lady Carnarvon asks.

"He's too weak to travel," Dr. Johnnie says. "As it is, we're losing him."

"No, dear God." Eve lets out a cry. This is the first time anyone has stated the facts so bluntly. She feels like she cannot breathe. The room suddenly seems to be closing in on her.

Lady Carnarvon leans toward Dr. Johnnie. "How long do we have?"

Dr. Johnnie frowns. "He could go at any time."

Lady Carnarvon gives a deep sigh. "I see."

Carter turns his head and gives Eve a look of anguish.

The doctors have failed. She has failed.

She does not know how she can go through her life without her father's grin, his witty remarks, and his exaggerated stories. Her eyes fill with tears.

Lady Carnarvon touches her shoulder. "Go and have a rest, Eve. I'll stay with him; the doctors and Fearnside will be here."

"Howard, will you accompany me to the gardens? I'll go to my room and get my hat, and I'll meet you in the lobby," Eve says.

Carter nods.

Eve watches her mother scan Eve's face and Carter's. Two pink circles appear on Lady Carnarvon's light skin; then she scowls. Of course, her mother's suspicions are now sadly misplaced. Eve's only dealings with Carter will be about her father's health and the treasures.

A short time later, as he waits in the Continental Hotel's huge lobby, Eve rejoins Carter. So far, reporters haven't discovered he's in Cairo, it seems. They will soon.

Eve and Carter venture out to El Opera Square among cars, carriages, and donkey carts toward the Ezbekiyah Gardens. Thank the Lord there are no demonstrators today. Not that she is overly concerned about her safety. They pass the statue of General Ibrahim Pasha on horseback. Her father always admired the impressive sculpture. Looking up at it, Eve thinks with dread that he may never see it again.

As always, the afternoon sun blazes. They stroll side by side without touching past a row of shops within orange and yellow buildings, then cross the broad boulevard. They pass through an archway into the gardens. Beyond lies a lake among wide-spaced palms and a pavilion, where tourists take tea.

Eve says, "Father is dying."

"Carnarvon has a way of defying the odds. He may rally yet," Carter says, but his voice lacks conviction.

They walk on the path that circles the lake. A veneer of light brown pollen dusts the paving stones. Dried banana and palm leaves crackle under their feet. The air is heavy with the smell of stagnant water and mud.

"How was your meeting with Mr. Lacau?" Eve asks.

"Not good. He won't decide about dividing the treasures now." Carter frowns. "He said we'll talk again when his people have studied and appraised everything from the Antechamber. That could take a year or more. I told him I cannot wait so long. I'm burdened by expenses."

"Which expenses? Isn't the Metropolitan Museum paying much of the costs?"

"Your father's concession will need to be renewed," Carter says, "and if we don't come up with the fee, the Egyptian government will take over the tomb and all its contents and send me packing to England. I feel sure Lacau's planning it."

"Howard," Eve says gently, "don't say that. Pierre Lacau admires your work."

Anger flashes in Carter's eyes. "Don't be taken in by him."

"Nothing can be solved today," she says.

They sit down on a park bench under a eucalyptus tree. Midway across the lake rises a lush island with stately palms. Just ahead of them, large dark rocks, streaked with white bird droppings, jut out from the brown water.

A middle-aged couple comes toward them—tourists from England, she supposes. Eve regains composure. The woman says, "Lady Evelyn, I'm so glad we've found you."

"My apologies. I don't recall meeting you," Eve replies.

"I'm Gertrude and this is my husband, Charles." The woman holds out her hand and Eve shakes it. "So sorry to hear that your father has been unwell. It's nothing serious—is it?"

"Who are you again?" Carter says.

"Friends of Carnarvon," the man says.

"I think not," Carter says. Turning to Eve, he adds, "Now I recognize him as a reporter who badgered me at the tomb. He's made up a patently false story."

The corners of the woman's mouth edge into a smile. How horrid she is, Eve thinks. "I ask you to please leave us alone," she tells the journalist.

"Ignore them," Carter warns. His sharp glare silences them.

The man struts off, with the woman behind him.

"They're vultures," Carter says, his eyes wide. His rage seems palpable, and his forehead is wet with sweat. "Damn vultures. Damn journalists. I wish I could kill them all. Damn—"

"You're not yourself," Eve says sharply. "We need to go back to the hotel."

"I am in a desolate place with myself." Carter kicks at the ground.

Eve lets her voice rise. "I'm talking to you. Listen. It's bad enough that Father is so ill. Pull yourself together now for the days ahead. Remember the Antiquities Service. Please don't allow your volatile behavior to ruin all of your good work. Father's work. *Our* work."

His eyes appear unfocused as he stares at the ground. Eve wonders if he has even heard her. He mutters and curses to himself. She shakes him, but still he won't look at her.

The realization comes to her that she must take on her father's responsibilities if Carter cannot. It's as if some invisible presence is putting a heavy gold headdress on her shoulders, a weight she accepts but does not want.

20

Late the next morning, Carnarvon lies still. Eve checks his breathing and finds it to be faint. He's unconscious, it seems. Panic fills her. She thinks he will die that day. And yet, in the week that passes, in which Eve and Lady Carnarvon are at his side, he occasionally opens his eyes, murmurs unintelligible words, and becomes aware enough to sip the water that is offered to him. He will not eat.

Lady Carnarvon dismisses Dr. Barrett. There is no point in having him there, doing nothing, she says.

Carter disappears for long stretches; he is no help, either, Eve thinks. She suspects he is sequestering in his room at the hotel.

Porchey is due to arrive on April 4, according to his latest telegram. The day finally arrives. Carnarvon, remarkably, remains alive, though he hasn't had any water in days.

Eve wishes her mother would stop blathering. "Darling, the Egypt Exploration Society has asked you to speak at a dinner. You must get well for it." Lady Carnarvon's voice is tremulous. "We are getting on at Highclere. Spring is coming. I've had five thousand daffodil bulbs planted and have ordered a reseeding of your golf course."

Eve combs Carnarvon's hair, and he remains eerily still. She notices that her mother's face has started to look older, more lined, with dark circles under her eyes.

Dr. Johnnie enlists Fearnside's help to turn Carnarvon from his side to his back to prevent bedsores. His back is wet with sweat, so the men stop, and Fearnside brings dry pajamas. When the men roll Carnarvon again, his eyes open unnaturally wide and he cries out. He gazes from Eve to Lady Carnarvon. The rolling seems to stir something in him, Eve thinks. He pulls himself up to a sitting position. Maybe he will recover after all? "Almina," Carnarvon says weakly. Then, "Eve."

"Yes, we're here, Father," Eve says.

"My girls. My sweethearts."

Lady Carnarvon kisses him; then Eve kisses him.

"I've heard the call," Carnarvon says. "They're coming for me."

His words give Eve a chill. "Who, Father?" Eve whispers.

Carnarvon slips away again. "Please, please, come back to us, Father," Eve wills him.

She strokes the top of his head, but he does not react.

For the next few hours, Eve and her mother sit with Carnarvon. Each takes one of his limp hands. "I love you, Pups," Eve says, using an old nickname. He gives no response.

She looks up and is shocked to see her brother, Porchey, come from India in his army uniform and standing in the doorway. He's slipped in so quietly, she didn't hear him.

"Porchey." Eve rushes to him. They embrace.

"Eve." His voice, as always, is low and strong. His skin is much darkened from the sun, but otherwise, he is his familiar self. What a comfort to see her brother!

Lady Carnarvon gives Porchey a brisk hug. "Your father isn't responding. But he may still hear you. Talk to him."

Porchey kneels lightly with one knee on the bed and reaches to tap Carnarvon on the shoulder. "Hello, Father." Then Porchey steps back and frowns, as if fully taking in his father's emaciated appearance. "Oh, dear God," he says. He leans closer. His voice louder this time, Porchey says, "It's Henry."

Eve eases her father's face toward them. "It's Porchey," she says loudly. "Come from India."

"He sat up and spoke to Eve and me not long ago," Lady Carnarvon whispers. "He said he'd 'heard the call.' Perhaps he's been holding on to see you again."

Her mother isn't quite telling the truth, Eve considers, though she is glad she said what she did.

"I want to be alone with him," Porchey says.

For the first time since she arrived, Lady Carnarvon agrees to leave her husband's side. Half an hour later, Eve, her mother, and Fearnside come back into the room and all, in various combinations, sit with Carnarvon throughout the day. Dread makes Eve's limbs feel heavy and listless.

Eve dines with Porchey. As much as she can enjoy anything at that moment, she is glad to be with her gregarious brother.

That night, Carnarvon's breathing has become so shallow, Eve can barely detect it. She traces his cheek with her fingers, avoiding the big welt. She strokes his hair. He does not react. He is like an empty vessel going deeper and deeper into the next world. Eve feels her heart breaking.

Lady Carnarvon continues by her husband's side. She insists that Eve go to her room and get some sleep. Though she doesn't want to leave her father, Eve can hardly keep herself awake, so she gives in to her mother's request.

In her dreams, Eve sees Carnarvon being rowed across a river against the current. She pictures Osiris, with his tall, ostrich-feathered crown of Upper Egypt. With a wave, Osiris greets Carnarvon. They pass from the riverbank along a corridor of ram-headed sphinxes and into a heavenly temple with golden walls.

Jackal-headed Anubis, hawk-faced Horus, and four robed goddesses surround Carnarvon. Osiris, taking the appearance of a mummified man, sits stiffly on his throne, his green-tinted face in profile. Motionless, and almost without expression, he grasps his crook and flail, the symbols of his power.

Against the temple walls, shadows move. The jackal-headed god, in a black cassock, looks exactly as Eve has always imagined him: sandy-colored fur, pointy ears, amber eyes, a dominating snout, and curved canine teeth. He sniffs as if scavenging for scraps. Her father watches, trembling, as Anubis places his heart on one side of a pair of golden scales twice her father's height. A pure white ostrich feather lies on the other side. The scales tilt back and forth, making a ticking sound. Anubis pivots toward Carnarvon and gives a low growl.

"I was a playboy. I was reckless." Carnarvon's voice cracks. "I crashed automobiles. I chased after women. I bet on horses and spent all of my wife's inheritance. But I never spoke ill of the deities."

The scales settle in perfect balance. The gods and goddesses whisper. Anubis's voice is low and gravelly, as if he has not spoken in a century. "Lord Carnarvon, you loved and were loved by a great many people. Your heart is as light as a feather."

Osiris rises from his throne and puts his greenish-brown hand firmly on Carnarvon's shoulder. "I deem you worthy to enter the land of the gods for all eternity."

The reply is as Eve expects. Her father has been a good man.

Carnarvon nods slowly. Then he turns to Eve for a moment. He looks wistful, and she senses he regrets leaving the world he has known behind. She meets his gaze. He beams one of his best, widest smiles.

Eve awakens with a start, remembering she is in the hotel. She feels for the chain of the bedside lamp. When the light does not go on, she gropes her way to the switch on the wall. Still no light. There must be a power outage, she concludes. They're common enough in Egypt. But it seems an ill omen. The hair on her arms stands on end.

In the darkness, she finds her robe, tiptoes to the sitting room, and pauses near the door of her father's room. She hears someone crying. She opens the door.

Dr. Johnnie stands in the dim light of a single candle. Her mother kneels at the side of her father, leaning over the bed, her head on his chest.

"Is he—?" Eve asks anxiously.

"He's breathed his last, Eve," Lady Carnarvon says. "He left us just when the power went out. One-fifty in the morning." Something inside Eve turns to ice. Her father's hands, too, are cold.

The electric lights go on and off, flickering, then stay off. Eve knows her father would have appreciated the odd, occult effect.

"Goodbye, Father," Eve whispers, but she knows her father is already on his way. Her dream has told her that. Tears form in her eyes.

She kisses her father's cheek, still a tiny bit warm to the touch. She does not like to see his face so still.

Lady Carnarvon rises, places her husband's hands at his sides, and closes his wide-open eyes.

Fearnside enters. "M'lady, the concierge has contacted an undertaker recommended by the British consulate," he says. "They'll be here soon."

"Let me be alone with him for a moment, please," Lady Carnarvon says.

Eve gives her father a final kiss on the forehead, then goes to the sitting room. She, the doctor, and Fearnside are soon joined by Porchey and Carter. Porchey must have gotten through to him, she thinks.

Carter sits down on the sofa, puts his head in his hands, and sobs. The only light is that of a candle. He stands, wipes away tears, walks over to Porchey, and shakes his hand. "I'm so sorry for your loss, Lord Carnarvon."

Porchey nods solemnly.

Hearing Carter address Porchey in this way gives Eve a start. She isn't ready to think of her twenty-four-year-old brother as the 6th Earl of Carnarvon. Nor can she think of Catherine, aged twenty-two, still in India and unaware of the late earl's death, as the new countess. On this day, April 5, 1923, all their lives will change. The realization comes to her that her brother will give up his army post. He and Catherine will move to Highclere now. The change in her brother's title comes with the responsibility of managing their large estate and all their servants, their land, their working farms, and the Highclere Stud.

Eve hugs Dr. Johnnie and Porchey, each in turn. Porchey opens the doors to the balcony, and he and Eve sit on wicker chairs. Even at this early hour, El Opera Square is filling with horse-drawn carriages and vendors calling to one another. Carter comes to sit with them, and they all stare out at the view, saying nothing.

The lights in the sitting room flicker on and off, then on again. The electricity has come back. It seems like a sign, but of what, Eve does not know.

Soon, the undertakers, Egyptian men in dark suits, arrive. They pass through the sitting room, pushing a wheeled stretcher. Eve gets up to her feet to watch what will happen next. She stands motionless as the undertakers reappear with her father lying on the stretcher, wrapped in a sheet. She follows the undertakers down the corridor to the service elevator, feeling her body grow heavier with every step. The undertakers wheel her father inside the elevator, and the doors close.

Eve bolts down the grand stairway and goes out to the front of the hotel. Facing the statue of Ibrahim Pasha, she watches and waits. As the stone of the Continental Hotel turns yellow in the sunlight, people have already begun to gather. Several of them say her father's name. How quickly news spreads. At no time is a place so full of life, excitement, and drama as when someone has died, Eve thinks. The crowd's energetic behavior feels wrong. Disrespectful.

A motorized hearse comes from the side of the hotel; it continues around El Opera Square and down Kamel Street. She gives a dull cry as the hearse disappears from sight.

Her father is gone, and though she has no heart for anything, she must take up his work.

21

The morning of Carnarvon's death, Porchey, assuming his new role as leader of the family, makes an announcement to the Cairo press and gives Arthur Merton of the *Times* an interview. It is only a matter of hours before telegrams of condolence arrive from all over the world.

That afternoon, Fearnside, now Porchey's valet, brings to the Carnarvon suite the first extra editions of Cairo newspapers with her father's photo, the long pages framed for the day in black borders. Arthur Weigall's sensational article in the *Daily Mail*, titled "The Pharaoh's Curse Claims the Life of Lord Carnarvon," begins the rumor that will forever circulate in connection with the earl's death.

Eve, Porchey, their mother, and Carter pore over the articles while having tea under an awning on their third-floor private balcony. The three Carnarvons sit at a round glass table, while apart from them, on a rattan chair near the wrought-iron railing, Carter stares moodily down at the newspaper on his lap. Below them, El Opera Square, lined with towering palms, is full of people, both tourists and natives, who apparently wait for Porchey to make an appearance. The smell of onions and lamb meat, sold from small cooking stoves of street vendors, rises in the hot air.

"The curse is bosh," Eve says, tossing down Weigall's paper.

"Of course it is," Porchey agrees. "Father was ill for most of his life. And it had nothing to do with an angry pharaoh."

"Not to mention that the tomb contained no written curses," Carter puts in. He lights yet another cigarette. His hair is greasy, his brow is covered in sweat, and his eyes are watery and sad. He's not holding up well. Eve wishes he'd refrain from smoking in front of her mother, as any gentleman would do.

"Let's attend to practical matters," says Lady Almina. Since her husband's death, she has already changed her title from Lady Carnarvon to Lady Almina, in deference to the new countess. And she already dons black silk, a black lace veil, and high-heeled black shoes, which Eve concludes that she carried in her luggage. Eve, less elegant but more in tune with the climate, wears a simple long-sleeved, white cotton flowered gown.

Feeling exhausted and overwhelmed, Eve listens distractedly as Lady Almina outlines a plan. Eve and Porchey are to leave immediately for Highclere, via the usual trains and ferry crossings. They will make preparations for multiple services: a funeral for family and the Highclere community, followed by a private burial; a service for the local townsfolk; and a large public service in London. Meanwhile, Lady Almina and Fearnside will travel to England by steamship with Carnarvon's body.

"I will organize the ceremonies," Eve says. "It is the least I can do." She tries to emulate her brother's outward calm.

"Lady Almina, I'll stay with you in Cairo until you can leave," Carter offers. Lady Almina and Porchey thank him.

Eve stiffens. "Howard, won't you come to England for the funeral?"

"No, I'm afraid it's impossible," he says. "I need to transport the Anteroom treasures to Cairo by rail. Finish up the season." He pauses, turning his gaze from Eve to Lady Almina. "This is what Carnarvon would have wished—for me to continue our work."

"I heartily agree," Lady Almina says.

"Can't you close down for the season?" Eve says. "The scholars have already left. It's too scorching to expect the workers to do anything for you. The Anteroom treasures are secure in your Sethos II laboratory, behind that steel door."

"What can be moved to the Egyptian Museum should be, before there's any further deterioration." Carter sighs. He rubs his unshaven chin. "And having the artifacts in Cairo will help me with my negotiations with Lacau. He'll see I'm keeping to my part of the bargain. One less reason for him to get rid of me."

"Explain the politics to me," Porchey says, leaning forward. "Do you feel our position with acquiring the treasures is in jeopardy?"

"Frankly, yes," Carter says. "Saad Zaghlul Pasha, who has been imprisoned in Gibraltar, has now been released. King Fouad is having to make concessions with the Wafdists to stay in power, and there are rumors that Zaghlul could be elected into office again. The nationalists want Prime Minister Nassim Pasha to step down." He takes a deep breath. "So it's far from certain what will happen if the government is overthrown."

"The Egyptian government has always been unstable. Maybe it always will be," Porchey says. "Those at the top of it have never been interested in archaeology. So we can hope that those in charge of it will remain in charge, and leave you be."

Carter grimaces. "We can hope."

He moves his chair closer to the family. "Lord Carnarvon. Lady Almina. I have enough funds to carry me only to the end of the month. Looking ahead, Carnarvon's concession for the Valley needs to be renewed by the end of August, for next season, and I would prefer you do so now—before anything more goes wrong."

"Mr. Carter, out of honor for my father," Porchey says, "I am taking your concerns seriously. But until my father's funeral is over, and I've had time to do a proper accounting, I cannot make any promises."

Carter curls his hand into a ball and holds it in front of his mouth. He looks toward El Opera Square with fiery eyes.

Lady Almina says she is tired and will go rest. No one sleeps in the chamber where Carnarvon just died; to Eve's consternation, her mother has taken the extra bed in Eve's room.

The plan is made. In two days, Eve will begin her journey home. She and Porchey will meet Catherine coming from India through the Suez Canal, at Port Said in northeastern Egypt. From there the three of them will travel to Alexandria, where they will board a ship to France. It's the beginning of a painful new life, the one she must live without her father.

22

Their uniforms pressed and clean, their backs straight, Highclere's household staff forms a military-style line on either side of the castle's front entrance to welcome Eve, Porchey, and Catherine. Seeing the servants in black armbands, mourning for her father, gives Eve a start. Many of the staff she has known all her life. She thought it would be a comfort to see them, but now she can hardly bear to look upon their stricken faces.

Eve takes in the familiar scene: the footmen and valets in black, the maids with white lace caps and aprons, the cedars of Lebanon along the castle drive. She loves Highclere and seeing the Carnarvon and British flags flying from the great central tower. She is home—and yet she feels it will never be truly home again, not with her father gone.

Streatfield, the household's steward, steps forward and bows to Porchey. Thin strands of gray hair are combed neatly across Streatfield's balding head. The old man's eyes show sadness, though he's attempting to conceal his emotions as his job demands. "Welcome home, your lordship. Your ladyships."

"Good to be home," Porchey says. "All looks well here."

"Thank you, my lord."

"I present to you all the new Countess of Carnarvon," Porchey says.

Eve thinks that Catherine, with her blond hair hanging loose on her shoulders, looks flustered and totally out of place. She wears a skirt that almost rises to her knees—how utterly inappropriate! Eve feels sorry for her. She's been introduced to the servants on previous visits, but now, as the new lady of the house, she's obviously uncertain about what is required of her. "Hello," she says, in her loud American way.

Streatfield lowers his eyes. "We are all so sorry to hear of his lordship's passing."

"Thank you," Porchey replies.

A respectful silence follows. Eve unclasps her hands, feeling tears come.

"Streatfield," Porchey says, "I'd like to meet with you and Mrs. Mc-

Lean in the library." His air of dignity and authority makes Eve proud. Though he's barely inherited his new title, he conducts himself with apparent ease.

"Very well, m'lord." The servants file around the corner of the castle toward their courtyard. Streatfield swings open the heavy oak door with its sculpted wolves' heads, and he and Mrs. McLean, Highclere's plump head housekeeper, whose set of keys jingles when she curtsies, enters with Porchey, Eve, and the others.

Eve loves their library, with its red furnishings and thousands of books shelved from the floor to the gold-paneled ceiling. Now the room seems empty without Carnarvon. She gazes at the small table-desk, which once belonged to Napoleon Bonaparte. Her father should be there, she thinks, writing instructions to the servants, with Susie at his feet on a certain threadbare spot of the red carpeting.

Porchey and beautiful Catherine settle on the couch near the fireplace. They sit close together, still acting, to Eve, like newlyweds, his hand in hers. She takes a chair across from them. The steward and housekeeper stand near, awaiting Porchey's discussion.

"Where's Susie?" Eve asks.

Mrs. McLean, who Eve suspects is a garrulous woman in her own milieu, belowstairs, erupts in a great flow of words in her Scottish brogue. "M'lady, Susie is dead. She died on the same day his lordship passed in Cairo, April fifth, though of course, we hadn't yet heard the news. I was in the servants' hall, waiting for the kettle to boil, when the electric lights flickered, then went down."

What a bizarre coincidence. Eve feels sadness pour over her for the loss of the dog, but she also feels jarred.

"What happened to poor old Susie?" Porchey asks. Beside him, Catherine shifts restlessly.

"Well, no sooner had the lights gone off than I heard a howl coming from the servants' parlor. After his lordship left for Egypt, Susie was in the habit of sleeping there in front of the fireplace. After I heard her, as soon as I could find a candle, I went to the parlor, and there she was, dead. She must have had a seizure, poor old girl."

Porchey and Catherine look at each other. "When I think of the pharaoh's curse, I have chills," says Catherine.

"Darling, no," Porchey says. "Susie was very old."

"But it may have had something to do with her love for my father,"

Eve says. "Animals know things. Mrs. McLean, what time did she die and the lights go out?"

"Just before midnight, m'lady."

Eve makes quick calculations. In Egypt, her father died at one-fifty a.m. With the time difference, Susie must have passed about five minutes after her father. Eve doubts that Mrs. McLean would have conjured such details as the power outage. She doesn't know what to make of the story. Things happen in life that cannot be explained.

Porchey clears his throat. "Streatfield, Mrs. McLean—we need to go over the names of the tenants and neighbors in the county. I'm having Eve extend invitations…"

Eve's mind wanders. She looks out the window and pictures her father strolling up the drive of cedars with Susie trotting at his side. Something about Susie seems different—the dog now has all four of her legs!

Porchey lightly strokes her forearm. Eve straightens up. "What were you saying, Porchey?"

He laughs. "Eve, you've gone foggy."

Two days later, Eve rides Lady Grey on a path through the woods of Highclere, passing by beech and oak trees, uphill to their Grecian-style rotunda, the Temple of Diana. Rain has washed over the estate in the night, and until late morning, a gray-white mist hangs over pastures of grazing sheep, filling the gullies of the downlands. She finds comfort in her horse's firm steps. Today she'll try to ride away her grief for her father, her loss of Carter, and the emptiness that flows through Highclere's many rooms.

Following the old path down again, continuing through the London Lodge gate, where the road heads south toward Winchester, Eve hears hooves trotting behind her on the gravel. Porchey. Her brother always has a sense of buoyancy about him. She feels especially glad to see him this day.

Holding his head and shoulders erect, he posts toward her on caramel-hued Romper. Despite his short, stout figure, Porchey is a commanding figure on horseback.

Porchey leans forward, pulling back on Romper's reins. "I'm joining you."

"Wonderful," Eve says.

Eve squeezes her legs against Lady Grey's sides. As she makes clicking sounds and Porchey whistles, they urge their horses forward. Without any need for conversation, they head to Beacon Hill. Though Eve's taken a meandering route around the parklands and he's come directly south from the stables, they both feel the need to look at Highclere from their father's favorite vantage point. Eve knows that she'll spend the rest of her life looking for Carnarvon in places that he loved.

Eve and Porchey veer off the road, gallop through fields, and take the upward path to the hilltop. There, on a dry, level stretch, they dismount and look across the sweeping park that is dotted with great cedars, across her father's golf course, and in the distance, to Highclere Castle, yellow in the sunlight.

Porchey has made an overnight trip to London, to hear their family's solicitor read Carnarvon's will and bring out other legal and financial documents. Eve is eager to know what her father's wishes were and how much money they've been allotted.

"What happened with Mr. Molony?" Eve asks.

"There is much to say." Porchey's voice is irritable. "I'll start with the burial. Father wants to be buried in a coffin of Highclere oak. Here, on Beacon Hill."

"Why am I not surprised? But all the Carnarvons are in the family plot."

"I know," Porchey says, "and we'll need to somehow haul the coffin up this rise. It's not as if we had a road, or tracks, for a hearse. But that's the least of our problems."

"What problems?" Eve gives Lady Grey a reassuring pat.

Porchey juts out his lower lip, in the way he used to pout as a boy. She's always found the expression endearing. Porchey has the sort of face that cannot hide what he is feeling. "I'll get to them. Firstly, we'll go ahead with the memorials you've been planning—both locally and in London. Whatever Mother wants, we'll do in style. But then we'll have to economize. We'll have to make some difficult decisions." At this, Porchey's shaven face flushes red.

Eve has been holding Lady Grey's reins loosely. She grips the reins harder. "Difficult decisions? What do you mean?"

"Father had a sizable overdraft at Lloyd's. We're not provided for. And we must pay his death duties. As you know, when an estate passes to an heir, the Crown is due more than sixty percent of all we've got—and they'll demand it any day."

A kind of sickness washes over Eve, a sensation of nausea mixed with tingling and faintness. It is just as if she's ridden to the edge of a cliff, one step away from dropping into a deep abyss.

Eve listens to Porchey's diatribe against Lloyd George for passing high taxes and then increasing the death duties many times over. These taxes, Eve knows, are meant to help rebuild Britain's economy after the war. Their father often grumbled about them, but until now she has not fully comprehended what they could mean for her family. How can Porchey come up with the money so quickly along with paying taxes on all the assets?

"Molony advised that I sell Highclere. And everything in it, and most of the land. Immediately," Porchey says.

"No." Heat rises to her head and she feels dizzy. At any moment she might retch.

Porchey gestures to the rolling hills. "Molony said, 'Find a corner of the land that you like and build yourself a small estate on it. You won't be the first aristocratic family to lose its house after the war. It may be the way all the great houses of England go in the end.'"

Lady Grey snorts and angrily tosses her head back and forth. Eve realizes she's given her reins a yank. "You wouldn't sell Highclere."

Porchey shakes his head defiantly. His voice rises. "Never."

She breathes in, trying to keep her nausea at bay, and settles herself deeper into the saddle. "But how will we pay the taxes?"

"I'll see to selling the automobiles. You make lists of all the jewelry, silver, china, paintings." He pauses. "And Father's Egyptian collection. I know Mother has always despised it."

"We can't sell Father's Egypt collection." My God, Eve thinks. Has it come to that?

Porchey sighs. "I'm sorry, for your sake. As for me, I say good riddance. I never liked those dreary things. Don't trouble yourself with the artifacts this week. Think of what else can go first."

She likes her family's oldest set of silverware; it has huge spoons and forks that are no longer in style. And she particularly likes the gold-rimmed set of dishes they use at Christmas. With a pang, she envisions these leaving the dining room cabinets and seeing blank spaces on the walls where paintings now hang. Her mother and Catherine might have to sell their diamond tiaras. Giving up such luxuries feels like too much to bear. But what choice is there?

Porchey points out the wide expanse of the Carnarvon lands. Before them, the holdings continue as far as their eyes can see. "There will be interested buyers in our property, but the selling process could take months or even years. I wonder when the money will—"

"I can't talk about this now." Eve strokes Lady Grey's mane and stifles a sob. Since 1769, when Highclere first came to Henry Herbert, who became the 1st Earl of Carnarvon, their family members have owned this expanse, revered it, grazed their sheep, laid out gardens, and ridden horses on wooded paths. The landscape is remarkable for its beauty. It's also rich in prehistoric remains. She loves its earthworks, carved out by Bronze Age farmers. Here on this very spot was an ancient hill fort. A place where the Celtic people lit roaring bonfires. She gazes out to the mostly wooded landscape, imagining how different it would look if divided into many more farms and dotted with houses.

Porchey clears his throat. "And you won't be surprised to hear that Father left you no dowry. Eve, you are going to have to rely on your looks to form a good match."

Eve almost feels like her heart has stopped beating. "Surely you aren't counting on me marrying so we can pay Father's death taxes?"

"Eve! Do you think so ill of me?" His eyes grow keen. "I have other ideas for income. I want to build up the Highclere Stud and make it profitable. From the stud, selling what we can, and the income from our farms, Highclere might just stay afloat. It has to."

"We will work together," Eve says, feeling a tiny bit relieved.

Porchey sits up higher on Romper and adjusts the reins. "I don't like to speak ill of the dead, but frankly, Father should have managed the estate much better. After he married Mother, he had an extremely sizable income. I thought they'd set enough aside to provide for the estate. I was wrong."

His words sting. Eve wants to defend Carnarvon, but Porchey speaks the truth. Their father let them down; he has left them in the cold.

"Does Mother know the extent of our debt?" Eve breathes in sharply.

"She must know," Porchey says. "I think she's known all along, but she couldn't stop herself from spending. Did she ever consider the ongoing expenses when she endowed her hospital?"

"You're being unfair. What Mother did was in response to a national emergency. Her hospital treated officers who had nowhere else to go," Eve says. "It's not her fault that there's been a war or a change to the tax system. And Father's Egyptian endeavors will pay off. The treasures will save Highclere in the end."

"Humph," Porchey says. "I'll believe that when I see the money."

"You will." She swallows hard. "I can assure it. If Howard Carter hasn't already made a good deal with the Antiquities Service, I'll take over the negotiations." She explains that she gets along better with Pierre Lacau than Carter does. "I must return to Egypt," she says. "Help me to persuade Mother. I'll need funds for my passage and hotel."

"Eve, think practically. You're as bad as Mother." Porchey's tone comes close to taunting. "Tea overlooking the Nile is lovely, but I know what those hotels charge."

"It would not be a pleasure trip."

"You know it would be." He rolls his eyes. "The balls, the gowns, the Nile cruises."

He can be so derisive at times, she thinks. Damn him.

"Listen, I'm serious," she says. "The Tutankhamun treasures will bring in more money than the Highclere heirlooms."

He glares at her. "Of course, I'll accept whatever the Egyptians give us. But I take Mother's side on this one. Father's digs have always lost us money. I won't put more into a losing business. Father squandered enough."

"You're not being fair. Our future depends on those treasures," Eve says. But Porchey rides off, entirely ignoring her.

She can hardly wait to prove him wrong.

23

Carnarvon's red-velvet robe, trimmed with ermine—the robe he wore at the coronations of King Edward VII and King George V—lies draped over his coffin carved from Highclere oak. His coronet sits atop the robe. To Eve, this sight is as exquisite as it is heartbreaking. It takes all her strength not to weep in front of the staff, who are gathered with her family at Highclere's mortuary chapel. With the title of Earl of Carnarvon comes pageantry, no more so than in death. The castle servants and those who work on the estate and grounds enjoy and expect such an aristocratic show. Her father, too, would have approved.

Eve finds herself somehow surviving this elaborate ordeal by orchestrating the details for the funeral and memorial services in one exhausting week. Porchey met their mother's ship in Plymouth only forty-eight hours before today's ceremonies.

Eve bows her head as the Reverend Best, of Highclere and Burghclere parish, offers a prayer. The small brick-and-flint mortuary chapel is full to overflowing, and many people wait outside to take their turns to come in. Some will also go to the memorial in the nearby town of Burghclere the following week.

After the service, Eve stands near the coffin and touches the soft ermine, then joins her mother, Porchey, and Catherine in greeting the household staff and outside workers. A heavy scent wafts from the enormous array of calla lilies and carnations. She notices the blooms of daffodils, tulips, and camellias in vases, and the lovely offerings of Queen Anne's lace and Canterbury bells that mourners have left on the coffin.

So beautiful, and so devastating. Eve lets out a sob.

Unlike some of his aristocratic friends, Carnarvon knew quite a few of his workers by name. In his will, he specified that eight retired servants, who lived on the grounds, each be given a "good, thick blue wool coat lined with red cotton." Porchey has ordered the coats. Following Carnarvon's instructions, he's given a hundred pounds each to Highclere's steward, valets, and head gamekeeper. With the cost of shipping the body from Egypt, the funeral arrangements only add to the family's mounting debts.

Irrationally, Eve looks for Carnarvon to make an appearance as the line of the mourners, wearing black armbands, approaches through the high-arched door past the carved-oak pews. The line extends out the chapel door, past the family and servants' cemetery, and partway down the lane of Highclere Village—the cottages and houses in which the gamekeepers, groundskeepers, farmers, and dairy workers live. It is a gathering of the entire Highclere community.

When most of the mourners leave, workers prepare the casket and flowers for transfer to an army field ambulance. It is the end of April and still chilly enough for a coat. Eve changes into her flat-soled shoes to prepare to hike up Beacon Hill. Gleaming black automobiles pull up to the chapel. Peering out the first car's window is Granny Elsie—Elizabeth Herbert, Dowager Countess of Carnarvon, her father's stepmother—a handsome woman dressed entirely in black velvet.

Automobiles will transport the family to the golf course, and from there the youngest of them will go on foot. The older passengers will take their luck in cars, though the motors might not make it up the rugged hill.

Carnarvon's friend Major Rutherford has lent the family the ambulance to transport the coffin and a soldier to drive it. The major directs the traffic of people and cars. Porchey, in his black formal wear and felt top hat, stands beside him guiding their mother, Granny Elsie, and Uncle Mervyn, Carnarvon's half brother, into an automobile.

Castle footmen shoulder the coffin and slide it into the ambulance, along with the lilies, red-velvet robe, and coronet. Eve, Porchey, and Catherine ride with their father's sisters, Winifred, Margaret, and Vera.

Moving at a slow pace, the line of seven cars follows the ambulance past the cottages, out of the village, up and down the winding drive, and through the pastureland. It is ten o'clock by now, and the sun shines brightly. Even in her sadness, Eve appreciates the beauty of the day. Life is all around her: lambs resting in the shade of spreading cedars, pheasants darting out of the way of the cars and into the thickets bordering the drive. The car reaches a patch of woods, then curves around to the golf course, where Eve and all who can handle the walk get out. She watches the spectacle of the ambulance and three of the other automobiles tackling a route never before attempted by a motorcar.

What a sight! Her father would have reveled in it. Even under the circumstances, Eve enjoys the adventure of cars attempting to reach the top of Beacon Hill. The Rolls that carries her three aunts backs up on the golf course and then, with a roaring engine, takes the hill at high speed. With engines revving and sputtering, filling the air with the smell of exhaust, and wheels spinning, the cars and ambulance labor upward. Almost at the summit, the ambulance becomes stuck in the mud, precariously angled. Fearnside and two other men come forward and shove the ambulance to the crest of the hill.

At the very top, a priest has consecrated the burial site, and workers have prepared the earth. Porchey, Major Rutherford, Fearnside, Streat-field, a valet, and the head gamekeeper carry the coffin. Lady Almina takes the arm of Granny Elsie. The deep blue sky stretches above them all. A cluster of blackbirds takes flight, and a cool wind lifts Eve's hat and blows away lingering car exhaust. Once again, the air is "clear as champagne," as her father always said.

The Reverends Mr. Jephson and Mr. Best, elderly gentlemen wearing white vestments, take their places at the coffin, and the twenty or so mourners assemble around the grave. Porchey rearranges the ermine-trimmed robe over the coffin covering the bronze plaque with Carnarvon's full name—George Edward Stanhope Molyneux Herbert, 5th Earl of Carnarvon—followed by "26 June 1866–5 April 1923." Fearnside places the coronet on top of the robe for the ceremony.

Eve hears a roaring and looks up to see a biplane. It is a pleasant surprise, at first. Her father loved airplanes. His aviator friends test flew planes from Beacon Hill. But now Eve is irritated to see, in this craft, a man leaning out with a camera. "Those horrid journalists!" she says.

"Can't we be private even here?" Porchey says.

The plane of journalists circles, then heads away. Eve sighs with relief.

In the warming sun, her mother takes off her coat, kneels on it, and puts her hands on the coffin. Seeing Lady Almina cry makes Eve cry as well. Despite their bickering and arguments, her mother loved her father. For a second that seems like forever, Eve is shocked to see her mother put her head on the casket.

The rectors take turns reading from the prayer book. "O God, whose mercies cannot be numbered: Accept our prayers on behalf of thy servant George Edward Stanhope Molyneux Herbert, and grant him an entrance into the land of light and joy…"

Gazing beyond the people, at the edge of the hill, with Highclere in the distance, Eve believes she sees Carnarvon as a hazy spirit, wearing his tweed jacket and canvas hat, smiling his broad, slightly crooked smile. Eve wonders: Does he know her thoughts now? Does he realize how much she loves him and wants to continue his work in Egypt? Her yearning for him, she knows, will never heal.

Eve and the spirit of her father make eye contact, and then he waves his hand at her. She does not know if the gesture is a greeting or a farewell.

Five days later, another service follows in the town of Burghclere, and a week after that, the service at St. Margaret's at Westminster Abbey, for Carnarvon was a London gentleman as well as a country lord. After the memorial, Eve feels her heart bursting as Handel's "Water Music" opens grandly on the organ. It is time to process out of the old church and, once again, to stand in a queue and greet fellow mourners. She longs to be alone, to cry without anyone watching her.

Eve buttons her coat and tries to summon the will to continue her social obligations. Her longtime friend Anne joins her in the empty pew. "I'm sorry I have to return home. My daughter has a fever today. Visit me soon," Anne says. She hugs Eve. Eve feels a pang when Anne leaves, though she understands her friend's obligations.

Bracing herself to greet a hundred or more people, Eve pauses in a side pew, near a column of the nave, before heading down the narthex and going out through the massive double doors toward the receiving line. Porchey waves her toward him, their mother, and Catherine, to stand in front of the church.

Here in the queue, on the stone steps worn by age, is Brograve. She watches him button up his overcoat and wrap an Eton blue-and-black scarf around his neck. Black trilby hat in hand, he looks downward. He has not noticed her yet.

Eve is glad to see Brograve, yet she's not sure she wants to talk to him. She remembers the embarrassing encounter with her father's spiritualist friend and the awkward goodbye at the opera.

Finally, Brograve turns his dark eyes toward her. Kind eyes, she thinks. He is even more distinguished looking than she remembered.

He has good cheekbones, a straight nose, and clear skin. His auburn hair has a luster to it. She likes his trilby hat with its white silk band. Wearing a top hat and tails, as many men are doing today, seems overly staid. She likes his informality.

Eve must shake the hands of at least forty people before Brograve reaches her. He says, "I'm so sorry about Lord Carnarvon. I thought the world of him. I know you will miss him greatly."

"Thank you." Eve's voice is hoarse from talking. And she has no idea what to say.

Brograve isn't accompanied by any young woman. But why would he be, at a memorial service?

Brograve holds out both his hands, and she takes them in her gloved ones. Their eyes meet briefly. Turning to a middle-aged couple behind him in line, he says, "Let me introduce my parents: Baronet and Lady Beauchamp."

The baronet, like his son, is tall. Brograve's mother seems plain, perhaps a bit old-fashioned with her small hat and black veil. One would hardly notice her. Her face is serene. She's just the opposite of Eve's mother.

"Your father was a remarkable man," says Baronet Beauchamp.

"You knew him?" Eve asks.

"Everyone knew Carnarvon," the baronet answers, "and loved him."

It is true: simple folk, royalty, and everyone in between adored her father. The compliment lifts Eve a little.

Hesitating for a moment, Brograve repeats, "Again, I'm very sorry about your father."

"Thank you for coming." Is this pat phrase the best she can manage? Then again, Brograve's remarks have been stilted as well.

"Others are waiting. So I'll say goodbye, and hope to see you again soon," Brograve says.

Not knowing what else to do, Eve nods. Does he hope to see her *soon*? What could he have meant by that? Her requisite year of mourning means she won't be attending social functions.

The Beauchamps offer condolences to her mother. Then Brograve chats with Porchey. Eve remembers Porchey saying that the baronet has recently stepped down from a post in Parliament; St. Margaret's, the parish church of the House of Commons, is probably his family's church as well as her own. Perhaps this is what Brograve meant when he said he hoped to see her. But he must know that she isn't often in London.

She watches Brograve and his parents stroll across the strip of church lawn toward the exit, where a crowd of onlookers presses behind a high wrought-iron fence. Those people remind Eve of the tourists at Tutankhamun's tomb—eager for a show, aggressively waiting for a sight to capture on their cameras. It seems she can never escape such crowds. Hopefully, the Met Police will keep them at bay.

Eve scans the trimmed lawn and the drooping tulips within the enclosure. A gentle breeze showers pink petals from a cherry tree. The choirboys, who have changed out of their red cassocks and frilly white ruffs, now run boisterously, tagging one another. How could anyone be so carefree on such a day?

Organ music continues to pour from the church doors as Eve greets what seems like an endless line of mourners. She shakes the hands of the Duke of Marlborough and her grace. "So nice of you to come." She does not know who most of the guests are. About now, if Carnarvon were here, he'd be receiving them himself and launching into some story she's heard many times before, like his anecdote about Queen Hatshepsut. She misses her father with her whole heart.

Out of the corner of her eye, Eve notices movement. It is a group of about fifteen men darting across the lawn. Why are they running? They wear dark suits and hats, but they didn't attend the service. One is very tall with red hair and a beard. Most are young. All too soon the steps swarm with more people, and the unnerving realization comes to her that they are reporters. They have somehow gotten past the Met Police. Eve goes rigid. Photographers vie for places around her mother. In her black felt hat—wide brimmed, draped with black chiffon and trimmed with ostrich feathers—Lady Almina certainly stands out in the crowd.

Reporters shoot questions at her mother. "Do you believe in the pharaoh's curse?" Eve hears one ask. At first, Lady Almina smiles at the cameras. But then, as the reporters surround her, she shakes and cries. She hides behind her hat and looks as though she might faint.

"Mother!" Eve calls.

Porchey bounds out from the place where he was standing just inside the church. He steps forward into the crowd. "Please, privacy now." He pulls one of the newsmen away from Lady Almina.

The reporter grabs Porchey, looking ready for a fight, then apparently thinks the better of it and lets him go. Catherine cries out as Porchey loses his balance and falls backward. Porchey takes his time getting up. He wraps his arm around his mother, whom everyone is watching.

Gentlemen from the crowd begin to loudly confront the reporters. Where are the Met Police? Finally, Eve sees two of them, dressed in blue uniforms, racing up with clubs in hand.

Some of the newsmen have packed in close to Eve. She's been identified. A man with a camera takes a step toward her. Eve puts her gloved hands over her face. She can feel the reporters gathered around her, watching her. She is afraid they will trample her.

During this chaos, the orderly melody of "Westminster Chimes" plays from the nearby tower of Big Ben. Then the big bell loudly tolls. Eve can hardly stand its loudness. Like a child, she moves her hands from over her eyes to over her ears. Her heart pounds.

Pushing through the people on the steps, Brograve catches his breath. His voice is gentle. "Eve. Are you all right?" He puts his hands on her shoulders.

No, she is not all right, she thinks. She may never be.

24

Reading the *Times* of London becomes an obsession. When the family returns to Highclere from London, Eve studies the articles about Egypt that she did not have the time to read earlier. The demonstrations in Cairo grow increasingly violent. The Wafd party does not accept the new constitution, which British politicians drafted without consulting them. There is rapid changeover in the government. Prime Minister Nassim Pasha only ruled for a hundred and five days before stepping down in March. The new prime minister, Yahya Ibrahim Pasha, is not expected to last long—the masses want an election, and they want to vote in Saad Zaghlul.

Early one morning, in her father's terra-cotta-colored smoking room, Eve pores over the latest paper. The world news has now shifted. The lead articles feature the journey of the Tutankhamun treasures from the tomb to the banks of the Nile. Eve is so proud of Carter that she cannot stop smiling. She clasps the newspaper to her chest. He is like a master engineer of three thousand years ago; the feat of moving those massive crates across the desert is nothing short of incredible.

She stares at the photos of Carter, imagining the scenes, and wishes she were in Egypt. Carter's men place rails over the tomb's steep stairway for flat railway cars to take the heavy crates to the surface. Even at five in the morning, it is so hot that the laborers pour water over the tracks to keep themselves from being burned. The rails sizzle and steam. Sweat runs down the backs of Carter, Pecky Callender, Gerigar the foreman, and the workers as they push the coffinlike box holding the ceremonial beds up the forty-five-degree incline. The men pant and groan.

The workers bring up eighty-nine crates from the tomb. Carter has ten straight and three curved sections of rails that need to be pried up and laid out over and over across the scorching desert to the Nile. It's five and a half miles of Herculean labor and agony from the tomb to the river. Windstorms blow hot dust into the men's faces.

They arrive within sight of the river as the orange sun disappears beyond the pyramid-shaped peak of el-Qurn. Carter and his men camp for the night in a dried-up canal. Armed Cairo police, who have accompanied the barge and tugboat that awaits on the Nile, guard the treasures with pistols and curving knives.

The next morning, again at five, the men begin moving the crates toward the river. They go down a steep riverbank and come to an area of low water. On this terrain, the rails are of no use, so they must carry the crates. A photo shows Carter and a worker, shoulders straining under a great weight, sloshing through the water. Hours later, the men, numb but joyous, finish loading the barge. They collapse in exhaustion on the bank, then bathe in the Nile, splashing each other with warm water and laughing. Eve stares at a picture of Carter, his face wet with the Nile's water and his own tears. Surely Carnarvon must be looking on from heaven.

"*The Tutankhamun treasures begin their journey four hundred miles up the Nile to Cairo*," Eve reads aloud, though there is no one to hear her. "What a story!"

Time has passed since Harry Burton's photographs in the paper were taken. Eve wonders if by now the Anteroom treasures have reached Cairo. She uses her father's gold-plated scissors with Moorish geometrical designs to cut out the articles from the paper. Next, she will paste them into the atlas-sized, gold-tooled leather scrapbook her father started to hold Tutankhamun keepsakes. She hears a gentle knock on the door. "Come in," she says. It's her mother.

Lady Almina's long, full black taffeta gown rustles as she enters. "I thought you were still in the dining room inventorying the silverware, but Fearnside told me you were here," she says. "Come sit with me."

Eve thinks her mother looks pale. Her voice is soft and tremulous. These days she is always nervous. They sit together on Carnarvon's worn leather sofa that faces the small marble fireplace under a Baroque Dutch painting, a still life including a dead swan, an artwork that Eve despises. On the carved, dark wooden mantel—between two black Chinese urns and bronze figurines of a quail and rabbit—a clock with two round faces for the sun and moon, one atop the other, chimes the hour of nine in the morning.

Lady Almina hands Eve a telegram. "This is from Mr. Carter. The treasures are in Cairo," she says, but her voice sounds flat.

Eve sits up, straight and alert. So the artifacts survived their voyage! This is cause for celebration.

15 May 1923

To Lady Almina Herbert, Highclere Castle

The treasures arrived in Cairo in perfect condition. Lacau is very pleased with my work. Despite the chaos here in the city, all goes well at the Egyptian Museum. I will do my best to ensure that your family receives your rightful portion of the treasures before any further political events unfold.

Carter

Eve rereads the telegram and feels her good mood deflate. The message seems to contain a veiled warning, one she's heard before, that when Saad Zaghlul becomes prime minister, the Wafdists will take control of Egypt and Carter will be replaced by an Egyptian. And yet, on the other hand, nearly four thousand artifacts are safely in the hands of Pierre Lacau at the Egyptian Museum. Lacau and his staff are certainly aware of Carter's expert handling and conservation work. So, surely, negotiations with Lacau will be favorable. Won't they?

"Howard doesn't say when he'll be in England," Eve says. "I'm guessing he'll be able to leave Egypt in a fortnight. Arrive at Highclere in a month."

Her mother's voice is brittle. "Call him Mr. Carter." She clears her throat. "Why must he come here at all? Don't you see, Eve? Here's the opportunity for our family to break with Howard Carter and Egypt, once and for all." Her mother's clear blue eyes look hopeful. "Mr. Carter's taken what's worthwhile out of that godforsaken Valley. Either the Egyptian government gives us what's owed us or they don't."

"No, Mother! You don't understand at all!" How could her mother not have paid better attention to what nearly all the world knows? "Only the treasures from the Antechamber have gone to Cairo. The artifacts in the Annexe, Treasury, and burial chamber have been sealed off, in their rooms, in the tomb. In future archaeological seasons, these artifacts will be carefully restored, cataloged, and moved out of the tomb as well." Eve pauses. "When Howard comes, we'll all talk things over. We must give him a chance to negotiate with Lacau for the treasures, and then we can sell our portion to the museums of the world."

Frowning, Lady Almina fingers her emerald. She's taken to wearing her jewels even during the day. It's as if her mother thinks Porchey will sell them out from under her.

Eve wonders once again how she might raise the funds to go to Cairo to meet with Pierre Lacau.

An hour later, Eve joins Porchey for a ride over the parkland and a visit to the stud farm. Mornings with Porchey have become respites from the bitter chore of inventorying silver and china. Neither her mother nor Catherine has any interest in visiting the stud farm, and at no other time of day will her amorous brother part company with his wife. Consequently, Eve takes advantage of her mornings alone with Porchey to talk over important matters with him.

They meet with their breeder to discuss Highclere's mares and the stallions to which they will send them. Then, leaving the horses at the stable, Porchey and Eve walk over the south lawns, back toward the castle. Eve brings up Egypt.

"It would be a smart business move for me to go in the fall," she says. "Someone needs to act in Father's stead."

"You saw the articles in the newspaper about the riots and Saad Zaghlul Pasha. You are a silly fool for thinking it safe for you to be in Egypt. The topic of Egypt is off-limits today," he says.

She admits to herself that Porchey has a point.

At their mother's wildflower meadow, Eve mentions the other matter on her mind. "Mother plans a trip to Paris next week. It's to see that man Ian Dennistoun—so soon after Father's death. It's unseemly."

"I couldn't agree more," Porchey says. "I've thought about whether we should step in. I need to go to Paris, too, to see Jacques Cartier. I want to meet this man Dennistoun."

Porchey's mentioning of the famed jeweler, a family friend, puts Eve on edge. She will mourn the loss of the family jewels.

"By the way, Eve, how are the pearls looking?"

Days earlier, Porchey took an antique double-strand necklace of large pearls from the family safe. They were dull from being stored for so long. Eve agreed to wear them so that the oils from her skin will polish them up.

Touching her neck, Eve recalls the weight of the precious strands. She wore them all yesterday. "They're gleaming beautifully now. But I'm getting attached to them."

"Don't. Cartier wrote that he has a client willing to buy them for fifty-five thousand pounds. A maharaja in one of India's princely states wants them for his turban."

Here is another bizarre episode in her life. Eve sighs.

They approach the walls and arches of the formal gardens, and Eve spots a sports car driving around the bend of their long driveway.

"That must be Beauchamp," Porchey says. "He's early."

"Brograve?" Her voice rises. "He's coming today?"

"I asked him for the weekend. I thought we might have a game of golf." Porchey's grin reminds her of her father's.

Eve hears the wheels of the car crunching on the pebbles of the drive, but she does not see it. The castle and cypress trees block out much of the view in that direction.

"How dare you invite Brograve without asking me," she says.

Porchey chuckles. "I didn't know he was coming for certain until this morning. But why not surprise you now and then?"

Eve holds back angry tears she does not want him to see. His meddling makes her boil.

Eve dashes toward the servants' entrance to avoid the front door. Then she notices the driver and stops. At the wheel of the navy-blue Bentley is a middle-aged man in tweeds, a striped tie, and a bowler hat. He has a small mustache. It isn't Brograve after all. She cannot place the man.

"It's Joe Duveen," Porchey says, "the art dealer. But *he* isn't supposed to come until Monday. Or did I forget it was today? Dealers are like that, always eager for the hunt."

"He's that man who tried to make Father sell Napoleon's table-desk," Eve says, remembering with a pang. "He'll be after our best paintings. Don't give him any portraits of the Carnarvons."

"Agreed," Porchey says.

"Did you tell Mother that you'd called him?"

"No," Porchey says, "I know she won't like it."

That is an understatement, Eve thinks. Her mother will be heartbroken to see the artwork leave the castle. And she'll never forgive Porchey.

The man gets out of his car, smiling. "Lord Carnarvon, it's good to see you."

Porchey makes the introductions. "Eve, this is Sir Joseph. Joe, this is my sister, Lady Evelyn Herbert."

Eve greets the art dealer, then goes off to change her clothes. A short time later, she finds her mother and Porchey in the green drawing room with Duveen. He balances on a stepstool, magnifying lens in hand, examining their 1693 childhood portrait of the Duke of Gloucester by Sir Godfrey Kneller. Lady Almina sits, teary-eyed, on the orange silk couch, and Porchey, standing with his arms crossed, eyes the dealer. Eve sits beside her mother and puts her arm around her. Though she wasn't very sympathetic toward her mother earlier that day, she feels for her now.

High up, and on the very far side of the room, the art dealer cannot hear the family's whispering.

"I never thought I'd see this day," Lady Almina says. "Our walls will be stripped bare. Porchey, you're too cruel."

"Mother, as a man of the army, I must be direct. A few of our paintings must go. Today. Be thankful we don't yet have to sell Seymour Place."

The mention of the family's London house leaves Lady Almina quivering. She wipes her eyes as Duveen, still oblivious, moves about the room. Eve herself is too riled up to cry. Her gaze goes to Anthony Van Dyck's portrait of the 1st Countess of Carnarvon. She wears the same double strand of pearls that is destined for the maharaja.

"This is excellent, too," says Duveen, pointing at Sir Joshua Reynolds's *The Infant Bacchus*. The painting features a plump baby and two reclining lions. "The plaque says the model is the 2nd Earl of Carnarvon, 1776."

Porchey sends the dealer a fierce look. "That one is not for sale. None of the paintings of the Carnarvons are for sale. I told you that."

One up for Porchey, Eve thinks.

Sir Joseph nods but then moves the stepstool to a portrait of the 1st Earl's children, pictured with his small growling dog, Pincher.

"Follow me, Joe," says Porchey, as casually as if he were speaking to a family member. "We're expecting another visitor soon and must hasten to conclude our tour."

"I'll stay with Mother," Eve says. She doesn't think she can stand another minute with the dealer. "Show Sir Joseph that painting of the dead swan."

"I've seen it, and I doubt if we'd have any high offers for it," Sir Joseph says. "But if I'm remembering correctly, your husband showed me Napoleon's table-desk."

Eve and Porchey speak up in unison. "It's not for sale."

"All right. And the Van Dyck?" Duveen adds in a cautious lower tone, "Charles I on horseback?"

"No," Porchey says. He takes the art dealer's arm and guides him out of the room.

Lady Almina dabs her eyes with a handkerchief. "Eve, you are going to have to marry someone with wealth and a title, that's all there is to it," she says.

Eve raises her hand in warning. "Mother, don't start," she says hotly.

"We wouldn't be in this predicament if Porchey had married a wealthier heiress," Lady Almina says. "I thought all Americans were rich."

"They're not." Eve can hardly believe they are having this conversation. She knows her mother isn't overly fond of Catherine, but this is a mean-spirited remark. "Speaking of Catherine, where *is* she today?"

"In her room," Lady Almina says. "She's wise to stay out of this."

Eve and her mother sit in silence. Outside, the gardeners roll their new handheld cutting machines across the wide lawns. Whatever else is happening, the grass continues to grow and needs cutting.

Porchey returns to the drawing room about twenty minutes later. He announces that he's accepted the dealer's bids for eight paintings, including Joshua Reynolds's *The Wood Gatherers* and Thomas Gainsborough's two portraits of Carnarvon's late relations, the Earl and Countess of Chesterfield.

"Duveen will pay twenty-five thousand pounds for the lady but only seventeen thousand for her husband," Porchey relates. "Duveen says everyone enjoys seeing beautiful women more than handsome men."

Eve rolls her eyes upward. "Oh, Porchey! Couldn't you have held out for more? He should at least pay equally for the paintings. Especially since Sir Joseph purports to be a friend of Father's."

Porchey bends his head. "As Father always said, 'There are no friends in business.'"

"Ha!" Eve says. Her family has sunk to a new, sordid level, both in their finances and in the company they are keeping. She doesn't know whether to laugh or cry.

25

As Sir Joseph rides off in his Bentley, damp winds blow across High-clere's great lawns. Eve is more than ready to see Duveen go. But she feels completely unprepared to meet her next guest: Brograve. The two men probably pass each other on the castle driveway, because shortly after Duveen leaves, she sees Brograve approaching in his red, open-topped Baby Austin.

Arguing, Eve and Porchey wait outside the front door of the castle to greet Brograve. "You shouldn't have set me up like this," Eve says in a low voice. She's still glowering at Porchey when Brograve parks his car.

Minutes later, there he is, tall, clean-cut, cheerful, stepping out from his tiny car. His tweed suit and fawn-colored trilby hat give him a dapper appearance. Eve cannot help but notice again how his dark eyes and long face resemble Carter's, though he doesn't have Carter's "fret" lines across his forehead. Truthfully, Brograve is even more handsome. He is younger. Not that he is anywhere near as brilliant, accomplished, or interesting. But he is knowledgeable and thoughtful. Eve appreciates his cheerfulness.

Over lunch, Porchey smiles to himself more than usual as he makes Brograve promise to visit Highclere frequently. Lady Almina and Catherine exchange gossipy looks, and Eve makes a face at her brother. Lady Almina asks Brograve about his family's country home and whether they keep any horses. (They do not.) Eve is glad for the diversion when Porchey suggests that their group practice hitting golf balls.

On Highclere's driving range, overlooking the ornamental Dunsmere Lake, Porchey swings smoothly, sending a ball far down the range. To Eve's irritation, Catherine blows him a kiss and claps, and Porchey beams back. Soon, however, Porchey starts an argument with Brograve. It is over Lloyd George, who stepped down from office the previous year, and it involves his betting taxes, which Porchey feels harm the sport of horse racing. Eve senses Porchey is in the wrong but isn't sure.

"I wish there were one royal bureau controlling all the bookies," Porchey says.

"That wouldn't be just," Brograve says. "We'd throw half a million people out of work."

"If it makes so many men lose their jobs, it's a bad idea," Eve adds.

"Humph. Brograve takes a liberal stance in every discussion," Porchey says.

"He knows more than you do. And I mostly agree with him," Eve tells Porchey. Then she turns to Brograve and, as if he were the cause of her family's financial problems, says, "Still, if women under thirty get the right to vote, I'd take Porchey's side to reduce death taxes."

Eve does not wait for a response. With a whoosh of her driver, she whacks a ball and then hears a thud as it lands in a muddy area near the lake. Today, out of sorts and unable to focus, she slices more balls than drives them straight. But at least she has more skill than Brograve, whose wild swings and errant shanks are comical.

Brograve glances at Eve with a relaxed smile, as if he's already forgotten the heated remarks she and Porchey made earlier about Lloyd George. He takes a ball from the basket and tees it up. "Everyone stand back," he says.

Giving Brograve plenty of space, she goes down to the lake to pick up balls. Then she hears Brograve back at the tee yelling, "Fore!" His drive comes farther than usual. There is silence as the four of them wait for the ball to hit the ground and bounce. Eve sees it coming toward her and tries, too late, to jump out of the way. It hits her on the shoulder, hard enough to hurt, but mostly it is the shock that makes her cry out.

Brograve drops the club and stumbles toward her. "I'm so sorry, Eve," he says.

Eve looks up at Brograve's startled face. "It's all right." She rubs her shoulder. She's not in much pain. But suddenly she feels her eyes well up. Like the unexpected force of the ball against her shoulder, all the losses in her life suddenly hit her. She wishes for the hundredth time this day that her father were alive. She wouldn't mind selling all Highclere's jewels and paintings if only he could come back to them.

How pathetic, that a silly golf ball puts her over the edge. She bites her lip, willing herself not to cry, and tries to save face.

Wiping away tears, Eve turns away from Porchey and Catherine as they approach the lake. She looks back at the silhouette of Highclere in the distance until she composes herself. Only Brograve has seen her break down.

"Good shot, Brograve. But bad luck with your direction," Porchey says.

"I know it." Brograve puts his hand on Eve's arm. "So sorry. Are you sure you're all right?"

"I'm fine," Eve says.

"I'll take you to the castle," Brograve says.

"Thanks," she says. "I've had enough of golf for one day."

"We'll all go," Catherine says.

"No, please. You and Porchey stay. Play a round," Eve says, more abruptly than she intends. She needs to get away from Porchey and Catherine as well as the golf game.

To Eve's surprise, she hears herself blurt out, "Brograve, would you like to see Father's cars?"

"Why not?" he says. "I am quite interested in cars, and I've heard your father's collection is one of the finest in England."

All Porchey says is "Right, enjoy yourselves." Society dictates that Eve and Brograve need a chaperone, but clearly her brother and sister-in-law fly in the face of convention. Even Lady Almina, lately, seems to be just barely playing by the rules at home and by no rules at all in Paris.

So the day begins again, and Eve and Brograve, side by side yet keeping some distance between them, start the long walk back to the castle by way of the south lawns. The grass is mostly dried out by the sun, though the rain from the evening before has left puddles in shaded areas. They near the gardens, where the head gardener and assistants tidy the litter of fallen flowers and leaves.

The stables near the servants' courtyard serve as Highclere's garage for the larger and more frequently driven automobiles. After a brief tour of these, she takes Brograve to see her father's sports cars, kept some distance from the castle, in an old carriage house.

Eve's heart feels heavy when they walk by the polished motorcars of different colors and makes: the Mercer Raceabout, the Stutz Bearcat, the Mercedes Rennwagen, and the Rolls-Royce Springfield Silver Ghost. Her father will never drive them again. She folds her arms across her chest, feeling the pain of his loss once again.

Brograve's eyes open wide. "My word, what a collection."

"Yes, Father loved it." She does not add that Porchey will sell them soon.

"Did he drive all of them?"

"Yes. Some more than others. But my parents always had lots of guests during race season." It is sad to talk in the past tense. "We drove *en masse* to the tracks, to Ascot and Windsor. And, of course, to Newbury, right here."

"Your family is so involved in horse racing," Brograve observes. "One of the most active I know."

"Well, you saw that Porchey is concerned about the betting tax. He's going to make the stud farm his livelihood. He has to find a way to keep Highclere." She doesn't care if she is blunt. She adds, "Thanks to your Lloyd George."

"You mean because of the death taxes?"

"That," she says, "among other things."

Eve normally wouldn't have spoken so honestly with an outsider, but something about Brograve makes her feel safe. He stares, no doubt surprised at her spilling private concerns. She feels embarrassed.

"At risk of selling Highclere! That's terrible," he says. "I had no idea."

Eve looks away. He tilts his head politely toward her. "I'm so sorry."

She steps back. There is an uneasy silence. "It's all right." But of course, it isn't. These days, it seems that nothing will ever be all right again.

"I hope you don't mind my saying this. But I would be happy to advise your brother. I know about finance."

"Thank you. Porchey can use the help," Eve says. More at ease now, she starts walking around the automobiles with him again.

Brograve pauses near a yellow-and-black racing car, a two-seater with a long hood. "A fine Bugatti," he says.

"One Father liked best. He saw it at an auto show in Milan and had it shipped."

"It has only four cylinders," Brograve says. "But it's faster than cars with larger, more powerful engines."

Brograve's enthusiasm for cars reminds her of her father. "Well," Eve says, "to be frank, it's probably yours if you want to buy it. Or any of the others."

"No. I won't buy it, but it would certainly be fun to ride in it sometime."

Eve has a dizzying idea about the sort of adventure she is used to having in Egypt. "Why don't you try it? You can take us for a drive."

Brograve hesitates. "Are you sure? I mean, just us—"

"A short drive." She catches herself. One reason young women aren't supposed to be alone with bachelors is for safety, but Brograve is a reliable sort. As for guarding her reputation, who would notice or care? "Mother won't mind," she adds, though she isn't sure. Truthfully, she should at least ask her.

"I've never driven a race car before," Brograve says, clearly tempted.

"This one, I think, was in the Grand Prix."

Eve rings a bell for a chauffeur, who comes with the key to the Bugatti. The chauffeur helps her into the passenger seat. Eve ignores his scandalized look. Brograve takes his place behind the wheel and starts the engine. Grinning, he slowly drives out of the carriage house, then shifts and accelerates, and they are off.

They motor out beyond the castle along the drive, and out through the great iron gate with the Carnarvon coat of arms. Brograve turns onto the post road. They pass Beacon Hill, where her father is buried. Eve pictures him coming down the hill and standing by the side of the road. Have fun with that Beauchamp; show him how to have a good time, Carnarvon seems to say. He's a worthy candidate for your affection. Tell Porchey *not* to sell the Bugatti!

Brograve shifts into the fourth and highest gear as the road flattens, and the car speeds past sheep, cows, and here or there a low stone farmhouse. What fun it is to drive so fast! Eve smiles. Brograve has something of her father's joy, his fearlessness. They've left Highclere Park but are still on Carnarvon land.

Eve holds on to the side of the seat as the car moves faster. The engine is at a fine-tuned roar. Her heart races. Does Brograve know what he is doing? "Slow down!" she says.

He slows and loops back toward the castle, and they travel at what feels like a good pace to her, exciting but not reckless. Over the wind, over the sound of the engine, Brograve breaks into song. "God save great George our gracious king! Long live our noble king, God save the king!" he sings, off-key.

"You're too funny. Keep singing. I like it."

With a little laughter and coaxing from her, he goes on. "Send him victorious, happy and glorious, long to reign over us, God save the king!"

Eve joins in. As they sing "scatter his enemies," the car enters the gate and the castle boundaries. He shifts down through the winding drive.

At the carriage house there is no one in sight. The servants must be having their tea break. Brograve turns off the ignition. He exits the car and comes around to open the door for her.

Eve's low mood has lifted. "The ride was lovely," she says. "Thank you."

"I enjoyed it, too. Greatly."

He seems amused. But then he adds, his pretense of lightness sounding forced, "And I'm glad I could entertain you with my singing." He clears his throat. She begins striding toward the castle and he keeps to her pace.

"Eve, families in mourning don't always have the same customs. I'm wondering how yours is observing it. How long will it be until you can go out—I mean, receive callers?"

His question is a silly one, she thinks, considering she has already received Brograve himself. Porchey obviously wanted his friend to court her. Their mother has not stopped him.

"Anytime, I suppose," she says. "Father didn't always stand on ceremony. He would have observed mourning for others but wouldn't have cared a whit what we did."

"Would you like me to call upon you?" Brograve says.

There it is, a direct inquiry, summoning her to be direct in return. She can feel herself reddening. Words form in her mind about telling him she plans to return to Egypt. Yet when she opens her mouth, the words do not come out.

Brograve picks up her hand, urging her to look at him. "Do you want me to call?" he repeats.

He calms her and entertains her. She has fun with him. And he is handsome and charming.

"Yes." How firmly that reply comes out!

Brograve's face seems to soften. She relaxes, too.

They come to the great oak door of the castle.

"God knows what you think of my family," she says. "You're aware of Father's consulting with spiritualists. My passion for Egypt. Porchey and his politics. I'm surprised you want anything to do with me."

He looks at her with a gleam in his eye. "I feel as if I've gone down Alice's rabbit hole, but I don't want to come out of it."

Eve realizes she is far more interested in Brograve than she ever thought she could be.

26

It is a dark day in Highclere's history when half of its servants leave the castle. The twenty-five domestics whom Porchey has dismissed exit through the courtyard, where cars wait to take them to Newbury. From there, they will go by train to London and elsewhere to seek new employment. Seeing the men and women queue to shake hands with Porchey reminds Eve of her father's memorials; only in this case, they are receiving their final payments—another kind of death. It is heart-breaking, dreadful, as though an earthquake were shaking the founda-tions of Highclere itself.

Stoic as ever, Streatfield the steward and Mrs. McLean the house-keeper stand with Porchey to say goodbye to the departing staff. With words of praise, and hugs and kisses from Mrs. McLean, the servants take their leave. The cars exit the courtyard, and Porchey releases Streatfield and Mrs. McLean, wiping her tears, to go back to work in an emptier house.

"Well, Eve, it's over and done," Porchey says, his face somber.

"That was awful," she says. "I wish we could have kept them on."

He nods and puts his arm around her. "Come with me to meet with the breeder. There's time to exercise our horses first."

"I'll change my clothes and meet you at the stables," she says, though Eve wonders if it's right to enjoy a ride when so many others are suf-fering. But she badly needs a respite from the task of cataloging her father's antiquities collection.

Ironically, some of its proceeds could finance her trip to Egypt, if Eve can handle the sales on her own. Neither Porchey nor their mother cares enough about those artifacts to closely monitor what Eve is doing with them. In fact, both her mother and brother have been away from Highclere quite a lot recently. Porchey joined Lady Almina in Paris for two days in order to sell jewels to Cartier, and he might well return there.

Eve lingers outside the castle, listening to the pigeons cooing from the rooftop and the puttering of the cars on the drive as she thinks about the situation in Egypt.

What she reads in the papers concerns her. Saad Zaghlul Pasha has been nominated for prime minister and will likely win the election. Eve thinks of a photo she saw, published in the *Times*, of bearded Zaghlul, robed and wearing a tasseled tarboosh as always, speaking near the mosque in Cairo's Ismailia Square. Eve recalls the place because it is very near the Egyptian Museum. A busy neighborhood. Government buildings, banks, and apartments. Tourists and natives, talking, eating melons and fried bread. But now it is a place where masses gather and shout, "Long live Zaghlul!" and "Freedom for Egypt!" and "Down with the British!"

Does she truly want to return to Egypt? Yes, she thinks. Her father's work there remains unfinished.

By the time Eve meets Porchey at the stables, two of the grooms have bridled Lady Grey and Romper. Porchey and Eve mount the horses and set off on a path that leads across the east lawns, the pace easy enough for conversation.

"Porchey, I still think you should have waited for Mother to come back before you let go half the servants."

"It's kinder that she didn't see them go. You write to her. Stress the positive. We still have the core staff, and over a dozen others. It's more than enough, really. I didn't keep the pastry chef, even though I very much wanted to."

Eve bemoans the fact that her maid, Marcelle, will have the additional burden of serving her mother and Catherine. "Mother's had her own lady's maid her whole life," Eve says. She tries not to sound accusatory. "She still wears gowns that require lacing and her hair needs to be put up. Will she understand that she must give up her maid while you still have Fearnside to yourself?"

"Eve. Listen to me. She doesn't need her own maid here because she's hired one in Paris. She's spending away while we're trying to economize. She's set up a household of sorts at the Ritz Hotel with Dennistoun. He's divorced now."

"How awful, with Father so recently in the grave." Eve pats Lady Grey and takes comfort in her gentle presence as she turns off the lawns onto a wooded path. "Do you think Mother will marry Mr. Dennistoun?"

"I hope not. You should see him! He's an asthmatic old rascal. He's got sunken eyes and drawn cheeks. He may have been a lieutenant colonel in the Grenadier Guards, but now he's in a wheelchair, recovering from a broken hip, and he wheezes through a breathing apparatus. I could see her wanting him if he had money. But he doesn't."

"I don't know what she sees in him, either. Though she says he's funny and clever, and good company. He appreciates her, I suppose."

"She's playing Florence Nightingale." Porchey's remark stings like nettles. "But real nurses don't spend like she does. Her way of living only sinks us deeper into debt."

"Don't disrespect Mother," Eve says. "I'm angry with her, too, but I don't like the words you use."

They ride up the crest of a hill, and on, without speaking. From Jackdaw's Castle, a Grecian-style folly, Eve brings Lady Grey to a stop. Her brother comes up beside her. A breeze touches her face.

"Brograve's visiting this Saturday," Porchey says.

Eve sits up straighter. "You should have asked me."

"What with dismissing the servants, I forgot. Sorry. Brograve wanted to know whether I would be here, or Mother, so he could properly visit you. I thought you wouldn't mind." Porchey gives her his smug little smile. "Has he kissed you yet?"

"You *forgot*? You think I *wouldn't mind*? Stop meddling!" She narrows her eyes at Porchey. Saying each word slowly and distinctly, she adds, "And if you must know, we just went for a drive that one time, and talked."

"I see," he says. "Not yet."

But thinking of Brograve singing to her in the Bugatti, Eve is not altogether sorry for Porchey's interference.

In the next few days, Eve awaits word from curators at the Metropolitan Museum about purchasing the whole of her father's antiquities collection. She'll bypass the British Museum because, in her father's correspondence, she discovered that he himself had already begun a dialogue with the venerable New York institution about selling his collection to them.

On the Saturday morning that Brograve is due, in a spare room on the third floor, Eve continues cataloging and sketching her father's Egyptian artifacts. She has written to her mother in Paris to say she'll be moving the collection out of the first-floor parlor. Unsuspecting of Eve's true motive to conduct her business privately, Lady Almina has embraced the change, as has Porchey. The new arrangement, to turn the

Egyptian room back into the morning room where breakfast is served, is better for the smaller group of servants. If all meals aren't served in the dining room, the staff has more time to clear the dishes.

As Eve sketches a limestone statuette of a pharaoh with crossed arms, she hears steps and looks up to see Porchey come in. Brograve stands shyly behind him. Eve wishes she had been downstairs to greet him. She stands and says, "Hello."

"Cheers," he returns. He walks over and studies her sketch. "You draw well, Eve."

"That's kind," she says.

Porchey speaks up. "Eve, Brograve, if you'll excuse me, I have a bundle of letters to finish. Catherine and I will see you at luncheon in an hour."

She is glad that in their mother's absence, Porchey lets social customs lapse.

Eve and Brograve stand facing each other at a respectful distance. He's so handsome! Strong. Very tall. Glowing with health. She likes the way he looks in his tweeds, so much newer than her father's. Today he wears a smart-looking blue-and-black Eton tie. He glances around with curious eyes.

"Over time, Father excavated or bought around fourteen hundred pieces," Eve says. "I'm cataloging the collection in a way that I've learned from…an archaeologist in Egypt." The phrase catches in her throat. "After I number these objects, and draw some of the others, I'm going to have them photographed."

"An ambitious project," Brograve says.

"All of this is going to be sold," Eve says, trying to hide the sadness she feels. "This cataloging and Mr. Carter's notes"—she pauses—"will help the sale. And I'll make sketches of the pieces I love best to remember them by."

Brograve looks blankly at her for a moment, as if he is about to ask a question, but says nothing. Eve leads him on a mazelike course around the boxes and cases. "They're arranged by excavation sites," she explains. And silently, she thinks about how each site represents a chapter in Carter's life during his long association with Carnarvon.

Brograve examines artifacts that Carter dug up from trenches around Deir el-Bahri at Queen Hatshepsut's temple: mud bricks, papyri, mysterious wooden knots, workers' tools. "It's like being inside a diorama in the British Museum," Brograve says. "May I?" He hefts a hatchet, then puts it down.

She moves on to items from her father's and Carter's explorations at the Nile Delta sites. At first shy to talk to Brograve, she finds herself now heady with excitement. There is so much to show: figures of a bull and an ibis, a tiny gaming board, and silver bracelets shaped like bending snakes.

"This is the piece I love most." She puts the blue faience hippopotamus Carter gave her into his hand. "Now, look at *this*." She brings him to a low case that holds a coffin. They shift boxes so Brograve can see the woman painted on the coffin lid. The portrait has wide eyes with dark irises gazing upward. A striped headdress frames her face, and the wings of Isis spread across her chest. "This is Irtyru. She lived three thousand years ago."

Eve opens the case, lifts the coffin lid, and sets it on the floor. Inside there is linen, browned with age. "She's not in there. That's her shroud," Eve says.

"There isn't a body?" Brograve asks.

"It had disintegrated. Or maybe there were just a few bones. I was a little girl when Father told me about it." Eve pauses.

Brograve fixes his eyes on the shroud. His face clouds. Eve tries to understand what he could be thinking. There is no decaying mummy, no leathery skin tight over a skull. There is only a dead spider and its web in the corner of the coffin.

"What's wrong?" she asks.

"Oh. I suppose it's the idea of displaying a coffin in one's home," he answers.

"I would find it creepy myself if a mummy were in here. But don't you think it's an interesting portrait?" She puts the painted lid back and shuts the case. "After all, it was meant to celebrate her. Isn't it wondrous that after so long it can still bring her to life?"

He only frowns. "I know it's an avid pursuit for archaeologists. But I don't see why the dead or their burial relics have to be removed. It seems just about everything here was dug up from tombs."

She stands absolutely still, aware that her mood is quite abruptly going sour. "It's far better that archaeologists take it for study than vandals, or those who sell to private collections where the world will never know of it."

To explain, she tells him how her father and other collectors have opened their homes to scholars.

"I suppose that's true," Brograve says. "But why should British gentlemen be taking it? Egyptians are starting to think the same."

Eve frowns.

"Egyptians are resenting Britain for all sorts of things now," he says. "There could be ramifications from our taking their antiquities."

So Brograve is rallying for Egypt. She cannot help but see his words as slighting her father. She doesn't know if she is more angry or devastated.

She steps away from Brograve to the other side of the coffin. "Father paid Egypt dearly for the right to explore and acquire artifacts from specific places. He's preserved and cared for them." Her voice rises a bit. "Now, when his efforts have led to a major find—which has brought the family near financial ruin—the head of the Antiquities Service may be casting doubt on the legal contract, which would allow Mother to recover the costs of excavating over many years."

"I see. That's a compelling point of view. May I ask—the agreement was…?"

"Father, now his estate, was awarded fifty percent of any antiquities found in the area where Tutankhamun's tomb was discovered. But my family may receive nothing." She tells him about the clause that specifies that if a tomb is intact, Egypt takes all. "That's the catch. Still, there's proof that the tomb was broken into in ancient times. Goods were stolen."

Brograve nods, obviously weighing what Eve has said. "By all means, the Egyptian government should compensate your family for the expenses."

Eve finds Brograve's sense of authority, of his own rightness, more than a little irritating. In a low, measured voice she says, "You think the Tutankhamun treasures belong in Egypt."

"Didn't you ever ask yourself about that?" Brograve says. "Didn't your father?"

Eve has questioned it, yes. Mostly, she has wondered if her father had a right to spirit artifacts away from the tomb before its official opening. But on the whole, he behaved honorably toward Egypt—didn't he?

"As soon as I can," Eve says, "I'll likely return to Cairo. If Mr. Carter has not already done so, it will be up to me to negotiate a settlement with Pierre Lacau, the director-general of the Antiquities Service. Or, if need be, his superiors in the new government."

Brograve's wide eyes show his shock. He gives her a long look. "I'm concerned for your safety, Eve. I don't want you to go, I admit. But just out of common sense, I have to tell you it would be foolhardy—and dangerous. You wouldn't get very far with the Wafdists. Zaghlul Pasha may have noble aims, but his group is discontented. Our army might make a counteraction. Please stay in England, out of harm's way. This is a matter for the Crown."

"Oh." The back of her neck starts to sweat. She is flattered that he's concerned for her safety, but it's vexing that he thinks she is naïve. Maybe she is. Still, she is prepared to make the trip to protect her family's interests.

Brograve's thick eyebrows furrow. Eve feels his gaze probing. "Tell me this: Are you certain you want to defend your father's position? *Was* he in the right?"

"Yes," she says, though nothing feels clear at this moment. She should have asked Brograve where he got his information about the Egyptian government, but she is finished listening. She frowns and makes for the door. "Now, if you'll excuse me, I need a few moments to myself before luncheon."

"I didn't say your father was a bad person."

Will Brograve never stop talking?

"But some of the laws here and abroad have to change as Britain's colonies take their freedom," he continues. "It's right that Egypt be in charge of its canals, roads, tourist attractions, and all its resources. Our Crown can't go on viewing other lands as rich layer cakes ready to be cut. It has caused violent problems." He pauses. "Say something. I'm very worried about you."

Ignoring him, she slips down the hallway and dashes up the nearest staircase. She hears Brograve coming after her, following her past the guest bedrooms, even into the family wing.

Eve reaches her bedroom just moments before he does. Brograve speaks to her through the closed door. "Eve, let me apologize. I'm sorry for being so blunt. I shouldn't have spouted off. Please, talk to me."

She opens the door a crack. They eye each other. His face is flushed.

"Eve, I shouldn't have questioned your father's position. You're still in mourning for him, for God's sake. I don't know what got into my head."

She looks down at her feet.

"I should go home," Brograve says.

"You'd better. I'm sorry things worked out so badly," she says.

She closes the door, stretches out on her bed, and studies the cracks on the ceiling. But Brograve continues to talk to her on the other side of the door. What a muddle she's made of things! Feelings flood through her. Brograve has been arrogant and rude, she thinks, but she has treated him arrogantly and rudely in return. Why is she being so defensive? She cannot, or will not, consider that her beloved father was in the wrong.

Brograve gently knocks again. "Please, Eve. Come out!"

Eve remembers knocking on Carter's door in just this way and thinks she can finally understand him.

She feels quite certain now that she has made a mistake in encouraging Brograve's attention. She does not want him as a suitor. So after letting him knock and plead for a while longer, she says the words that will rid him of her. "Please leave and do not return. We have fundamentally different views. We are incompatible."

Half an hour later, by the time Eve composes herself and goes down to the dining room, she finds to her astonishment that he is still there, chatting with Porchey and Catherine. She makes sure that she and Brograve do not have another chance to talk alone.

27

Another week passes and Lady Almina returns from Paris. Her mother's life is in limbo like her own, Eve realizes, torn between her love of Highclere and her desire to be somewhere else. They do not talk about this. Instead, Eve argues with her mother over which family heirlooms they might still sell.

She has not heard from Brograve. She hasn't apologized for her behavior toward him and she is sure she does not want to see him again. Even so, she feels ashamed of the way she acted toward him. At a distance, she can admire the way he speaks up for his beliefs and appears to live by his values.

In the smoking room, searching for news about Egypt, Eve sits at her father's big oak desk with the *Times* spread before her, just as he used to. Prime Minister Zaghlul has made Morcos Bey Hanna, a leader striving to end Britain's protectorate of Egypt, his minister of public works. So Pierre Lacau has a new supervisor. What will that mean for Egypt's Antiquities Service? At least it seems that Lacau is still in his job. Eve wonders if Arthur Weigall and his group of journalists are still complaining to him about her family's *Times* exclusive.

Hearing her mother's familiar quick steps in high heels, Eve looks up to see a letter in her hand. Even at a glance, Eve recognizes its meticulous penmanship. Startled, she turns to Lady Almina. "It's from Howard Carter."

"Yes. I invited him to visit, to discuss mutual business that concerns us."

With trembling hands, Eve reads his letter.

17 June 1923
Dear Lady Almina,
My respectful greetings to you and your family. When I spoke to his lordship on the telephone upon my arrival on June 5, I learned that you were in Paris. I trust that, by now, you've returned to Highclere, and I would like to meet with you at your earliest convenience.
Yours sincerely,
Howard Carter

"Mother, I'm disappointed to hear that Howard's been in London for ten days without anyone telling me." Eve feels suddenly queasy. She and her brother are not as close as she thought they were. "Why didn't he pay us a call immediately?"

Lady Almina frowns. "Of course Mr. Carter would be very busy. And clearly, he's been waiting for my invitation."

"Porchey still could have invited him. Or he and I could have gone to London," Eve says.

"I told Porchey that if he should hear from Mr. Carter, he should refer him to me," Lady Almina says, her voice curt.

Eve looks past her mother, at the series of small Dutch and Italian paintings of Venice and pastoral scenes that one Carnarvon or another picked up in the 1700s and 1800s as mementos of their grand tours. She's surprised there's anything left of value on the room's dark orange walls.

Lady Almina's voice is steady. "He's likely coming to ask for more money."

Eve draws a deep breath. Maybe Pierre Lacau has released the Carnarvon share of the Tutankhamun finds. But then, why wouldn't Carter have written to them with that news?

Lady Almina opens a hidden compartment in the desk and draws out a carved ivory box with a colorful inlaid bird on top of it. Inside is a key. "This is to your father's financial cabinet. Please acquaint yourself with our family's expenditures for Mr. Carter's digs. Ledgers of invoices aren't romantic."

Of course, Eve goes ahead and finds the file container tucked in her father's desk. Ledgers show his expenses in Egypt from 1907 to the present. She pulls out the 1922–1923 account book and places it on top of the dark green blotter with leather edges.

Lady Almina leaves the room, and Eve studies each page in the ledger: packing crates, lumber, supplies and wines from Fortnum & Mason, Carter's automobile, his telephone, and shipments of materials. Ten thousand pounds here and twenty thousand pounds there. Good God, her father spent a lot.

Her mother was right: though Carter and her father were visionaries, many people might say that if expenses drained a large fortune without repayment, there wasn't much romance about them. Feeling a headache coming on, Eve looks through other years of ledgers. An hour later, she stops totaling money spent and puts the records away. Her family supported Carter's digs for well more than a decade, to the tune of half a million pounds. It is far more than she imagined. She wants to jam all the papers into a crackling fire.

This knowledge of the finances, which, in a general sense, she's always known, rattles her to the core. Eve realizes with a twinge of guilt that she has been a fool in thinking she had so much freedom and independence in Egypt. The daring life she shared with Carter in those months wasn't so "free" after all. Her father was paying for it, and now the future of Highclere is at stake.

A long week goes by until the day of Carter's arrival. Eve does her best to compose herself as she and her mother, Porchey, and Catherine wait in the saloon.

"Mr. Carter is here," Streatfield says. Ignoring decorum, Eve dashes into the entrance hall. Porchey follows.

Carter stands motionless at first, frowning. His expression does not change when he sees her, Eve notices.

He kisses her on the cheek. Eve grips her elbows and goes quiet. As they and Porchey walk on the soft Persian carpets to the saloon, Carter looks about sadly. "I keep expecting Carnarvon to walk down the stairs."

"I feel the same," Eve says.

For the Carnarvons, conversations on challenging topics have their time and place. A walk outdoors will be followed by refreshments and dinner, all occasions for a frustrating amount of small talk. After greetings are made, Lady Almina uses her powers of persuasion to corral everyone outside to see her roses. "It will take a few minutes of your time, Mr. Carter," Lady Almina says. She inspects Carter up and down as if he were a mummy to be stared at in the Egyptian Museum.

Carter is strangely quiet as Lady Almina shows him cherry, quince, and crabapple trees on the way to the flower beds. The path with the arches leads to a huge circular bed of many varieties of roses, and while the family congregates there, Eve manages to have a conversation with Carter, some distance away from the others. She comes up behind him as he bends forward, examining a pink-and-gold rose. "Howard," she whispers, "is something the matter?"

"Yes." He steps back and their eyes meet. "While I was still in Cairo, a week after delivering the artifacts, Lacau requested a meeting with me. We met at his office at the Egyptian Museum. The moment I entered and saw the life-size head of the child Tutankhamun on Lacau's desk, I knew trouble was coming."

Eve remembers the gentle-faced wooden bust with almost cinematic clarity. Even then, she wished Carter had not stashed it with his supplies. "I'm guessing that the head never got put back into the tomb."

"Yes. It was in the supplies we kept in the shelter of the tent, and then briefly housed in the Sethos II tomb, then moved to the new storage building near the tomb. I confess that I forgot all about it."

Eve feels a constriction in her chest. "Who brought it to him?"

"Lacau would not tell me," Carter says. "He only said he'd gone through my inventory and found the bust was not recorded there. And in the same detailed inventory, he found mention of a large alabaster goblet that was not among the items supplied to the museum."

Eve gasps.

"Lady Eve," Carter says, "please believe me that I intended to add the Wishing Cup to the shipment of artifacts slated for Cairo. I couldn't because the crates were already labeled and packed."

Silently, Eve blames Carter for not being more careful.

Just then, Lady Almina, with small clippers in her hand, comes up and takes a yellow rose, ending their discussion. On the walk back to the castle, Carter only agrees, cryptically, that he will continue his story later.

At dinner, with Porchey at the head of the table, Carter, as the honored guest, sits at Porchey's right, across from Catherine. Eve and her mother face each other. "We shall enjoy a peaceful dinner," Lady Almina proclaims, which to Eve means that her mother will feel free to change the subject of the conversation at any time.

Carter eats heartily, but when the elegantly dressed footmen take the roast lamb and potatoes away, Eve has barely touched her plate. Then, as the next course is served, Carter announces, "I've been invited to give a talk at Buckingham Palace."

"Good man," Porchey says.

Eve feels a tiny flame of hope that Carter has not gotten himself into trouble with the Egyptian government, after all.

"When will this be?" Lady Almina asks.

"During the Royal Scottish Geographical Society meeting on July 26."

"I'm so pleased to hear it," Eve says, wondering if Carter will be knighted. A meeting with King George V is an extraordinary sign.

Porchey, despite his mother's disapproval of talking about business or politics at dinner, says, "Carter, what's the picture now in Egypt? The papers say that the Antechamber artifacts arrived all right at the Egyptian Museum."

"Yes…" Carter's face falls. "When the treasures were uncrated and accessioned, they had made the trip across the desert and down the Nile with no harm. The golden throne is displayed now, along with the painted chest." Carter looks down at the table toward Eve. "And I believe—the latest I've heard—the Wishing Cup. A long story, but it's found its way to the Egyptian Museum."

Eve flashes Carter a look. Brograve's words about the Egyptians reclaiming their rights tug at her.

Porchey, his eyes keenly attentive, says, "So how do you think the artifacts on display will be divided with us? Is a settlement close?"

"Lacau hasn't come clean yet," Carter says. "And to be honest, he may never do so. Lady Almina, we will talk about it when we meet together. My position has… Well, you know that the Egyptian government has changed hands."

More bad news on that score, Eve thinks. What did Carter mean about his position? That crack of hope, which opened a few minutes earlier like a shutter, now closes again. Even if Carter were to win the admiration of King George, his situation in Egypt has changed. She senses there is much more that he's not telling them. Her stomach knots.

"I'm aware of the persistence of nationalists like Zaghlul Pasha," Porchey says, "despite his prison sentence years ago. Or because of it. I dealt with the same thing, you know, in India."

Eve still wonders what the changing politics in Egypt have to do with Lacau obtaining the bust of the boy king.

Porchey, as if deep in thought, motions to Streatfield, and the footmen set out fruits and cheeses. Eve touches her wine glass to her lips, trying to keep her hand steady. She waits for her mother to introduce the topic of the family's share of the artifacts.

"Mr. Carter," says Lady Almina calmly, "we will meet tomorrow morning in the library. What time suits you?"

Eve sets the glass down with a thump. More waiting. What does Carter have to tell them?

28

Highclere is a vast place if someone wants to hide. On the evening of Carter's first day at the castle, Eve cannot find him. His guest room is empty. He is walking the grounds, she supposes.

The next morning, at Eve's insistence, her mother allows her to be present at the meeting she's set up with Carter in the library. Carter takes a single chair near the fireplace, while Eve, Porchey, and Lady Almina, all wearing black, sit on two red-velvet couches. Outside the tall windows that look out to the green lawn and gardens on one side, the front driveway on the other, rain comes down in long horizontal streaks. Electric lights in small lamps throughout the vast oak-paneled room glow warmly in the semidarkness. Carter's eyes look haggard, Eve thinks. Perhaps he's been awake all night, as has she.

"Lady Almina," Carter begins. His tone is somber. "By now, you know of the tumultuous events in Egypt and a little of why my return was delayed. There is much to tell you."

"Go on," Lady Almina says. The Carnarvons are quiet.

"Several days after the artifacts of the Antechamber came to Cairo by barge," Carter says, "I spoke to Pierre Lacau of the Antiquities Service. Lacau said he'd never met a more exacting archaeologist than me. He said he thinks I am still the best choice of anyone he knows to head the Tutankhamun excavation."

"Of course you are," Eve puts in. She takes a breath.

Carter sits with his arms crossed, frowning. "Lacau said he trusts me just as much as anyone in his museum. But that he cannot trust me, or the late Lord Carnarvon, completely. He said he'd been wondering whether we'd entered the tomb before an inspector was present and taken some artifacts."

At hearing the words "entered the tomb," Eve's holds back a cry. Porchey puts a hand over his mouth. Their mother looks at Carter blankly, as if she does not care about such details.

"On Lacau's desk," Carter continues, "he had a wooden bust of the pharaoh as a child—Lady Eve knows the one. Someone searched through my supplies at the tomb."

Eve swallows hard. "Who do you think—?"

"Whoever it was—how dare they?" Porchey says.

Eve explains to Porchey that Carter, with their father's sanction, hid the bust in a wine crate. Neither Porchey nor Lady Almina seems taken aback. The part of the story that interests them more, Eve sees, involves the family's stake in the treasures.

Carter's eyes take on the fiery expression that always makes Eve fearful. "I don't know who broke into my storage boxes, but I can guess the journalists were behind it." Carter turns toward Porchey, who has his hands up in the air in a questioning gesture. "Since last winter, as soon as your father gave the *Times* of London exclusive rights to cover the dig, there has been a group of them against me. Those men have, several times I think, met with Lacau and urged him to get rid of me. And lately—Lacau told me this—they've gone above Lacau's head to Morcos Bey Hanna, the new minister of public works. One of Saad Zaghlul Pasha's men. A nationalist who wants to rid Egypt of the British."

"Good Lord," Lady Almina says.

"I don't like the sound of this," Porchey says. "So are you about to tell us, Mr. Carter, that you are no longer in charge of the excavation?"

Carter rubs his hands over his cheeks and pulls at his mustache. Eve knows him well enough to see that when he's not smoking cigarettes, he falls into other, more awkward nervous habits.

"Lord Carnarvon, I'm getting to that point," Carter says. "First, I need to tell you about something Carnarvon took from the collection." He explains about the chalice. "Your father and I named it the Wishing Cup. Lacau read about it in my inventory and could not find it in the shipment. He read to me my exact description: *Large alabaster chalice created in the form of a lotus flower. On handles are kneeling figures, each holding an ankh. Hieroglyphs indicate prayer to the deceased king Tutankhamun. Exquisite craftsmanship.* Lacau said if I or someone else were to bring him the chalice, he'd drop the matter since I'd done such a remarkable job handling and inventorying the many hundreds of treasures delivered to him—all without breakage."

"We read about your railway, and the heroic way you got the artifacts to the barge," Eve says, feeling a bit of hope again. "And one of the more recent articles said the Wishing Cup was on display. So you returned it to Pierre Lacau?"

Carter sighs. "Believe me, I would have. I wanted to. In that meeting with Lacau, he concluded by scolding me about my treatment of the world's journalists. He said I must convince your family to give up the *Times* exclusive. And we set up a meeting to continue talking the next day. But then, Zaghlul was speaking that day in Cairo. Cairo's masses gathered at bazaars, parks, and government buildings. Hundreds of demonstrators—students and others—thronged into the park in front of the museum. I found the museum locked, and hence, Lacau's office closed. Not even a secretary answered the door."

"And then?" Eve asks. Her head throbs. All eyes are upon Carter.

"I took the train to Luxor, to wait out the political uncertainty at my home. But I opened the door to my house to find papers strewn all over the floor. In my office, I found file drawers open and my chair over-turned. In my bedroom, boxes had been carried out and emptied. The drawers of my bureau were left open, and my clothes were flung across the floor. And I saw the undershirt that had been wrapped around the Wishing Cup, flat on the floor."

"I'm horrified," Eve stammers.

"You poor man," Lady Almina says.

Porchey bites his lower lip, and Carter takes a handkerchief from his pocket and wipes his brow. Not one of them comments on Carnarvon's and Carter's retention of the chalice in the first place, Eve notices. It is just this type of attitude that has put the British in a bad position with Egypt.

"I spent some days inside my house, feverish, in the wretched heat. And I was alone, my servant gone. My mind was playing tricks." Eve knows he must have been in one of his depressive episodes. "Finally, I had the presence of mind to go outside and check on the tomb. Some-one had slashed the tires of my Ford. So I saddled one of the donkeys. When I came to the tomb of Ramesses VI, then Tutankhamun's tomb, I was startled to see red-hatted, armed Egyptian police with camels and horses. Most alarming of all, a new hill of debris rose near the entrance, and I saw that the stairway had been dug out. Another shock met me. There was a sign affixed to the door, worded in both English and Arabic. *The tomb of Tutankhamun is closed until further notice. No person is permitted to enter. This applies in particular to Mr. Howard Carter and his collaborators. By order of the Government.* One by one, I tested my keys and found that the padlocks had all been changed."

"No!" Eve says. "You, the discoverer of the tomb! The Egyptian government had no right."

Carter gives a long sigh. "I agree. With lightning speed, and without due process of law, the government took over the tomb. Before I left Egypt for England, Lacau confirmed to me that your family's concession in the Valley has been canceled. And Egypt will be keeping all the treasures."

Eve bites down on her bottom lip. She thought this news might be coming, and yet hearing the words makes her whole body go rigid. "Why hasn't Pierre Lacau written to me or Porchey or Mother?" she demands.

"Shhh, Eve. Let Mr. Carter talk," Porchey says.

For most of his speech, Carter has averted his eyes from Eve, as if he cannot bear to look at her. He addresses her now. "Lady Eve, things are in a confused state in Egypt, much more than even the newspapers indicate," he says. He turns to her mother. "Lady Almina, I did not think about sending you a telegram. Some things are best said in person."

Lady Almina looks at Porchey, then at Carter. Even in the light of the small lamp beside her, her face, all at once, seems very pale and stricken.

"What is to be done now?" Eve asks.

Porchey curls his lip. "Quiet, Eve. Questions later," he says.

Carter seems rooted to his seat, frozen. Eve resists the urge to chastise him in front of her mother and brother. He should have communicated this urgent news to her family right away.

Porchey rises, goes to a small table at the corner of the room, and in the absence of a footman, pours himself some sherry. Eve has never seen him drink in the morning before. This is what the day has come to. She hears a clink of the bottle and the liquid flowing into the sherry glass. When Porchey finishes his drink, he resumes his place on the sofa.

"Howard, I still don't see how the Egyptian government can break the agreement," she says. "Isn't the concession up for renewal on August 31?"

Carter bites his lip and dabs a spot of blood with his handkerchief. He explains how Lacau has dissolved the contract on the pretense of thievery, because of the wooden bust first and then the Wishing Cup. "But I believe my dismissal has everything to do with the new order of Egyptian officials coming into power."

Eve remembers her painful conversation with Brograve and takes a deep breath. "How foolish Father was to remove those treasures." Then she blurts out, "You, too, Howard."

"Mr. Carter, is there no recourse?" Lady Almina asks.

"I'm afraid not." Carter sits on the edge of his chair, turns, and faces Lady Almina. The panic he must be feeling seems about to choke him. "While I was still in Egypt," Carter says, "I consulted your husband's lawyer in Cairo, Sir John Maxwell. He has political sway. But he reviewed the concession. He says it is in the Egyptian government's legal right to break the agreement and to take everything in the tomb."

"We must talk to Lord Allenby then," Eve says.

"I've already done so. He says it's better that our government not become involved." Carter reaches for his cigarette case in his pocket, pulls it out, then apparently thinks better of it.

"I'll personally talk to Mr. Lacau. And if need be, the king," Eve says. "And take Sir Alan with me."

"Lady Eve," Carter says hotly, "please understand that your efforts would not do any good, considering the political situation in Egypt."

"Don't dismiss all my ideas," Eve answers, her voice firm.

Carter clears his throat. Facing Lady Almina, he says, "I must bring up another matter. In closing the tomb, transporting the artifacts to Cairo, and paying the workers, I have exhausted all the funds Lord Carnarvon gave me. Now, in resettling in London, I find myself ten thousand pounds in debt and need money immediately," he says. "I will support myself, in the future, through lectures and a book I've already begun."

Eve flashes Carter a look to show him how thoroughly disgusted she is with him. Porchey and her mother are also scowling at Carter. The moment feels tawdry, awful. Eve watches her mother's eyebrows go up. Porchey rises from his seat again to pace the room. He seems about to explode.

"Wait," Eve says, her voice rising. "Won't the Metropolitan Museum remain involved?"

Carter's back straightens. "No. The director of the museum provided me with the services of those great scholars in hopes of receiving a large portion of the treasures. If they can't have any of the treasures, the museum is out."

Eve turns to her mother and holds out both her arms. "Mother," she says, "Father would have wanted to settle Mr. Carter's debts."

"He would have *wanted* it, yes, Eve," she says. "He did not leave us the means."

"We simply cannot support you, Mr. Carter. I'm sorry," Porchey says. "Pardon me, but I was counting on you to help us, and not the other way around. Whatever we can do to pressure the Egyptians to make good on our half of the treasures should be done."

"I'm powerless with this government," Carter says, his voice breaking.

"Perhaps you have not tried hard enough," Eve says.

"Shush, Eve," Porchey tells her.

Lady Almina's expression goes sour. "I need to rest," she says. "Porchey, I leave you in charge."

"Yes, of course, Mother," Porchey says.

Soon after Lady Almina leaves the library, Fearnside comes to tell him that Catherine is asking after him. Eve notices that for several mornings in a row Catherine has sequestered herself. She's been putting on weight; though no one has mentioned it, her sister-in-law surely must be pregnant. Porchey, distracted, departs and leaves Eve unchaperoned with Carter.

"Howard," Eve says, "let me show you the new Egyptian room. It's upstairs now."

"Yes. Please, Lady Eve."

She leads Carter out of the library and into the great saloon, where the dark portraits of the Carnarvons, who seem to be observing them from the balcony and stairway, cast her a disdainful look. The ancestors don't seem to approve of her. Damn them, Eve thinks. She will no longer act in a way to please anyone—not her mother, Porchey, Howard Carter, or even her beloved late father. Everyone has let her down.

29

In a hall of mostly empty rooms vacated since the war, Eve pushes open a door, revealing her father's Egyptian artifacts, now packed or neatly assembled and labeled on tables.

From a glass case, she hands him the tiny striding horse, gazelle, and puppy figures, all from Tutankhamun's tomb. He lovingly picks up each one in turn before replacing it. Then, from a velvet-lined box that she put in her skirt this morning, she takes out the tiny gold ring Carter gave her. His face reddens. "Remember that evening when we danced at Shepheard's?"

He seems unable to look at her; his eyes are locked on the statuettes in the case.

She breathes deeply and holds out the ring. "Here," she says.

"Yours to remember me by. Please," he says.

"Thank you, but no," she says. "I don't want to be reminded of your broken promises to me. Nor your theft from the tomb." She pauses. "Someday I hope you will return it to Egypt."

Despite all that has happened between them, she feels a pang when he takes the ring from her.

With a sigh, he makes his way around the room, stepping over some boxes and peering into others. He heads to the coffin of Irtyru against a wall and gazes at her painted face wistfully, as if greeting an old friend. "It was so strange not to see these in their old parlor downstairs."

"It's easier for me to work with them here. Besides, Mother does not want to be reminded of Egypt."

Carter gently brings his hand near Irtyru's painted cheek. "Being here makes me miss your father more than ever. Highclere seems hollow without him."

"I know exactly what you mean," she says.

She shows him the notebook in which she has cataloged the artifacts as he would have done. He takes it into his hands and leans against the wall. "Your work is so good. It will expedite selling these pieces if you ever have to."

"I'm afraid I must. Immediately," she says. "I have in mind to sell almost the entire collection to the Metropolitan Museum."

"Oh?" he says.

She fetches a paper from her files and reads aloud a brief paragraph of references in her father's scrawl. Certain pieces Carnarvon wished to give as bequests to the British Museum, the Ashmolean at Oxford University, and the Metropolitan Museum. She points at a paragraph and reads it aloud, "*Statue of Tothmes III—bequest to M.M. Winlock says he'd purchase rest of the collection in its entirety.*"

"I see," Carter says.

"Do you think I could finalize the sale by the end of the summer, before Porchey needs to pay more taxes?" she asks.

"I doubt it." Carter looks at the notebook, then at Eve. "Even with this documentation and a single buyer, someone will still need to pull together the provenances. There could be a lot of back-and-forth."

"Handle it all for my family," she says impulsively, "and we'll give you a commission. I know Porchey would agree, if you told him how much money we seek to gain."

"I've placed myself with a booking agent to give lectures," Carter says, at last making eye contact. "And I must attend to a book I'm writing with Arthur Mace. My literary agent, Curtis Brown, is waiting for a draft."

Every detail he gives her is like oil dripped on a fire. "The book is your priority, then."

He talks on, and she only halfway hears him. It is so painful to listen, she can hardly stand it. He is not just self-centered; he is selfish.

"Publicity for the book will help me gain a world presence as an archaeologist. It may assist me in taking charge of the tomb again—that is, if politics in Egypt ever change." He moves to the doorway. "But of course, I want to help your family as much as I can. I owe you so much."

"Owe me? Or my family?" she says.

"Both," he says, his voice strained. His eyes look wistful and deeply sad. "On some level we are joined. I don't deny it. You shared the most important time of my life with me. I will always be grateful." He takes a deep breath. "But I must grapple with the day-to-day business of life." His voice is firm.

"The book, more lectures—do they make you happy?" She regrets the words as soon as she has said them.

She walks toward him and takes his large, rough hand. Carter squeezes her own hand, then eases his grip and pulls away. "Yes. I'm going to America for a while. Start fresh. Earn money speaking and writing."

With the mention of America, Eve feels herself growing angry again. He should not be abandoning her family by going to America on a speaking tour. He should be fighting for their portion of the treasures and their concession in the Valley.

"Will you first speak with Mr. Lacau about recovering our investments?"

He shakes his head. "I'm afraid I won't have the time, but I'm sure he'll come around."

Eve is irate. "Then I'll go to Cairo and talk to Pierre Lacau on my own," she says coldly. "At the least, I can insist he repay the money Father invested."

"I can hardly believe you'd suggest such a thing." He strokes his mustache and frowns. "Egypt is in chaos. You know it as well as I do."

Eve will step up to the challenge. Carter's argument sounds a lot like her mother's old complaint that Egypt is destitute, dirty, and full of snakes.

"I'm serious," she says. "You underestimate me."

"You can't. You're a woman—"

She quells him with a glance. "There is no point in continuing the conversation. I'll see you at dinner," she says, rising.

"I'd like to spend more time with Carnarvon's Egyptian collection before I return to London tomorrow."

"Fine. I trust you not to take anything," she says, an edge to her voice. Then Eve leaves him alone with the artifacts, most of which he discovered himself, and with his memories.

Eve puts in an appearance at dinner and finds Carter absent.

Hours later, when the household has turned in for the night, she walks by the room where she's storing her father's Egyptian collection. She is not surprised to find Carter still sitting at the table, leaning his elbow on the only available space on the crowded surface, making notes in a notebook. He rises when he sees her. His eyes are red rimmed.

Eve feels a bittersweet sort of intimacy as they handle the artifacts on the table. He focuses on them with greater intensity than ever, as if he is afraid to look at her.

"I'm sure Carnarvon would have wanted you to set aside some special items for yourself—and the same goes for me," Carter says.

She is not surprised he intends to take some of the artifacts. She is only surprised that he is asking.

"Maybe none of this should have left Egypt in the first place," Eve says.

He looks straight at her. "No. Carnarvon paid for the concession."

He shifts from one foot to the other. "I know you must sell to the Metropolitan," he says, "and they will appreciate the collection. But there are many lesser artifacts here. Let me know what you want. I could tell you whether the museum is likely to know of them and whether they'd be missed."

It will be safest, Carter says, to keep the selected artifacts at Highclere. He is as cagey as ever.

She clears a corner of the room for the items to be saved. For herself, she chooses a pair of little leather balls, the turquoise-blue hippopotamus, scarabs, a writing tablet, and a small turquoise-colored figure of a lion-headed goddess. Carter sets aside, among many other pieces, ancient tools he found near Queen Hatshepsut's temple, kohl makeup pots, a statuette of a sphinx, and a calcite shabti head of Amenhotep III.

"All these things are of little value," he says, as if justifying himself. She does not believe him. "Perhaps someday I'll need these items for research purposes, to compare them to the Tutankhamun treasures. If I write another book after the one Mace and I are working on."

Eve decides that Irtyru's coffin will go on loan to a local museum so that she can see it when she likes; it isn't valuable, Carter says.

They put off the most important decisions until last. Eve joins Carter at the display case that holds the bronze-and-gilt puppy, the gazelle, and the leaping horse of painted ivory. These things, more than any of the others, tempt her.

Carter says that though the artifacts do not have seals, their style could still be recognized, and a handful of scholars would certainly be able to tell that they came from Tutankhamun's tomb. He refutes Eve's idea of returning them to the Egyptian government as too risky. Lacau might press charges, he says.

"These tiny, hugely valuable artifacts will raise the overall selling price of the collection, and you don't want your family to be caught with them. Besides, the Metropolitan will do a good job caring for them and displaying them."

Eve hesitates. Then with a sigh, she says, "Agreed."

Carter asks her to find him some of her father's cigar tins. He spends the next hour packaging the antiquities to be concealed. Meanwhile, at Carter's request (according to some devious plan he will not divulge), Eve moves the items to the smoking room. Cradling a few pieces at a time, she creeps down the hallways and flights of stairs, barefoot. Her heart races. She flinches at the sight of her own shadow. But by sheer luck, she manages a dozen trips without awakening the household.

It is very early in the morning when Carter shuts the door to the smoking room. The antiquities they have set aside are now in tins and boxes, or neatly wrapped in tissue paper, labeled in Mr. Carter's hand.

"Where will we store them?" Eve asks.

"Follow me." At Carter's prompting, Eve fixes her eyes on the wall that divides the smoking room from her mother's green drawing room. A worn, dark tapestry of a hunting scene takes up most of the terra-cotta-colored wall. In front of that, near the leather couch, stands a folding screen on which are painted farmyard animals in a romantic Arcadian setting.

Carter flips back a portion of the tapestry and keeps it open by sliding the leather couch in front of it. He reveals an alcove that would have led into the drawing room if it were not blocked by the back of a giant bureau. In the area between the two rooms, on either side of the doorway, the woodwork is decorated with simple panels.

Carter stands beside the middle panel, which rises from waist level to the top of his head. To Eve's amazement, he turns a tiny key in the middle panel, and it opens. Eve steps forward to get a closer look. The same key opens the middle panel on the other side of the doorway. Secret cabinets on both sides of the doorway, each containing five tiers of mostly empty shelves, extend several feet into the walls.

"My God! I knew nothing about this," Eve says.

"Your father showed me." Carter pulls out some large envelopes. "He kept some of his photographs here, which he'd share with his gentlemen friends."

Eve takes the envelopes from Carter and begins to open one. "Wait," Carter says.

"Why?" She pulls out the photographs. Some are shots of Highclere from the air; others are of ladies very scantily dressed. She is shocked.

"Try not to let it upset you. Your father photographed many subjects."

Eve *is* bothered. Next, she finds a leather camera case; in it are bills that she counts out to one hundred thirty pounds. The only other contents of the cabinets are bottles of sherry.

"Do you think your brother knows of these compartments?" Carter asks.

"I doubt it. Porchey and Father weren't close."

"How about Streatfield? Or Fearnside?"

"Maybe," Eve says. "But if they do, they'd probably leave it alone and not ask questions."

"Let's get started, then." Carter packs the cabinets on the right side of the doorway, while Eve takes one shelf on the left. Reaching in, she places tins and boxes, and wrapped statuettes and pottery vessels on the shelves. She holds the blue hippopotamus and presses it to her cheek before she gives it a place of honor next to the figure of the lion-headed goddess.

The ten shelves fill. For a fleeting moment, Eve relives the magic of what it was like for her to be with Carter at the tomb. She loves Egyptian artifacts as much as he does. Perhaps this is what gives her the determination to plead her case.

Eve closes her panel door, and Carter closes his. He moves the tapestry back into place, along with the folding screen and heavy leather sofa.

Carter gives her a conspiratorial look. "This will be our secret."

"Yes." She puts her finger to her lips, but she frowns. She's not happy with herself for deceiving her family. Still, her father would certainly have approved.

She looks through the window of the smoking room and sees the sky beginning to lighten. It's morning now. She can hardly wait until Carter leaves for London. Her dealings with him in the past few days have utterly exhausted her.

Eve has lost faith in Carter, but not in her ability to deal with Pierre Lacau.

30

Six weeks after Carter's visit, Eve takes the boldest action of her life by traveling to Cairo on her own. She's gotten all the way to Shepheard's Hotel by bravery, determination, and sheer good luck, she considers. Also deceit. She shouldn't have told her family she was visiting Anne in London. And she shouldn't have taken the money Herbert Winlock of the Metropolitan Museum gave her mother as a guarantee that they'd sell Carnarvon's Egyptian collection to him.

But she had to do it, she thinks. There is no other way to meet with Pierre Lacau, who does not answer her letters.

Now, finally, on this sweltering August morning, Eve will go to the Egyptian Museum to talk to the Antiquities Service's director-general. The comic sight of pelicans, flopping about like drunkards on their large, webbed feet at the back of the hotel, calms her. It's time to find herself a carriage. Evading peddlers with fragrant sandalwood boxes and bales of silk, who have somehow gotten into the hotel and roam the corridors, Eve rushes toward the entranceway. Trying not to think of Carter and their night of dancing, she passes under striped Moorish arches and between ancient Egyptian-style pillars. Soon she's in the parching heat again, under the awnings of the hotel shops that face the street. She spots a couple stepping out of a *hantoor* pulled by a gray Baladi and waves her arm. In another minute, she's inside the carriage. There! For once, the interaction was easy.

Feeling heady with independence, Eve takes the carriage to Ismailia Square, in the heart of the city, and strides toward the colossal dark pink two-story building that is the Egyptian Museum. She imagines herself entering the grand, arched, pillared hall, proudly gazing at the Tutankhamun artifacts displayed among the rows of seated stone pharaohs and mounted glass cases. Then she'll climb the wide corner stairway to Pierre Lacau's office, one of the rooms edging the interior balcony, talk about the dig, and request that he pay her family the half million pounds he owes them.

But outside the museum, Eve cannot turn the brass knob of the mighty front door. It's locked! She holds back a cry. She knocks loudly. No one answers.

A heavyset adolescent guard carrying a pistol on his belt meets her at the top of the steps. "Closed!" he says in accented English, pointing to a sign that is printed in both English and Arabic. His large, robed body blocks the sun. Eve asks him when the museum will open again. He doesn't appear to understand her. To every question, his reply remains the same—"Closed!"

Hot and already exhausted by the morning's efforts, Eve rests on a stone bench in the shade of a palm tree. She looks out to the long, rectangular water pool and the statuary surrounding it, including a weathered red-stone sphinx, just a bit larger than one of Highclere's hunting dogs. This is what she likes best about Egypt—its beauty, its unique character.

Seven raggedy, barefoot children of various ages appear as if from nowhere and cry out, "Madam! Coins! We're hungry!" The smallest, a girl of about four years who has flies buzzing about her watery eyes, clutches Eve's long white skirt. From her satchel, Eve takes out a bag of peppermints. The children grab the red pinwheel sweets and the coins Eve offers. Then a tattered-robed man, likely a parent to some of these children, appears and begs for money. His breath is bad; he has a missing tooth and dark spots on his existing teeth. After giving him a bill, Eve bolts away from the museum with the group trailing after her. This is what Eve dislikes most about Egypt—its ugliness, its poverty. She can hardly wait to return to the shelter of the hotel.

She loses the beggars at the circle within Ismailia Square, where horse-drawn carriages, donkey carts, and the occasional automobile circle around an obelisk. "*Hantoor!*" Eve calls with the raise of her arm. Three carriage drivers argue in angry Arabic as to who will take her. Eve chooses a *hantoor* pulled by a surprisingly well-fed chestnut Baladi and driven by an older, robed man with a long beard. Soon she relaxes into the horse's clomping rhythm. But when they arrive at Shepheard's Hotel, Eve realizes she has given away all her Egyptian coins and asks the driver to change an English bill that is worth ten rides. The driver spews a stream of incomprehensible words. Why isn't there a porter to help her? With a clenched jaw, Eve watches as the driver gallops off with her money.

In the next few days, in the safety of the hotel's arched, Moorish-style meeting rooms, Eve writes and places calls to English and Egyptian government officials. They deny her requests for meetings to talk about payment for the Tutankhamun artifacts. Almost none of her father's friends hold positions under Zaghlul's new regime.

Eve wishes that while she was in England, she had tried harder to make an appointment for her and her mother with Lord Curzon, King George's foreign secretary. She should have at least waited for a response from Pierre Lacau.

Now it is Eve's biggest fear that her mother will discover she's in Egypt and send Porchey to escort her home. This must not happen before Eve has a chance to meet with Lacau. How humiliating it would be to return to England a failure. Carter would be the first to say she should never have gone.

So, determined as ever to find Lacau, Eve invites Arthur Merton of the *Times* to dine with her at Shepheard's one evening. It comforts her to see his slim, tidy self; his balding head, small mustache, and cheerful eyes. He tells her the Egyptian Museum has temporarily closed because of the demonstrations in Ismailia Square. "I don't know where our director-general is," he says. "If I were him, I'd go to the Valley of the Kings to make sure Tutankhamun's tomb is being protected."

"You mean it isn't?" Eve says.

"As you may know," Merton says with a frown, "Morcos Bey Hanna, Egypt's new minister of culture, now holds the keys to it. He brings his cronies there."

Eve tenses. "Accompany me to Luxor. Please."

"I cannot," he says. "I return to Istanbul tomorrow. I'm writing a story on the new Turkish Independence."

Eve nods, feeling very alone.

The next day, Eve goes to the train station to find that the trains are not running. It's the holiday of Ashura. She waits until the following afternoon to board the new Sapphire Luxury sleeper. Standing in a queue to enter the dining car, she hears an unmistakable French accent. Though she can only see a suited man, wearing a fedora, from the back, she knows with a feeling of breathlessness who it must be. "Director-General?" Eve says, stepping carefully between cars.

"Lady Evelyn!" Elegant as always, Pierre Lacau takes off his hat and bows.

Eve considers it must be her father in spirit form who orchestrated this incredible happenstance. She feels hope for the first time in what feels like weeks. Lacau invites Eve to dine with him. They sit at the far end of the car, as far away as possible from the other first-class passengers, who are mostly English and German.

Over fish and vegetables, at the table set in green and gold-rimmed china plates, with silver and heavy crystal, and a purple orchid in a vase between them, Lacau says in French, "It is a great pleasure to see you." He raises an eyebrow when she tells him she's traveling alone. "You should not have come to Egypt without an escort."

Eve crosses her arms and gazes out at the canals and brown-stubble fields of the Nile's East Bank. She turns back to Lacau and continues to speak in French. "May I ask why you didn't answer my letters?"

He taps his silver spoon on the linen tablecloth.

Eve fills the silence. "I suppose you're afraid Prime Minister Zaghlul will—"

"Stop." Lacau lowers his voice and pinches his thick eyebrows together. "It's better you do not say that name."

A waiter brings a pot of strong English tea. Lacau takes his cup with three teaspoons of sugar. The nervous way he keeps stirring his tea and clinking the spoon makes Eve want to reach out and stop him. She clenches her napkin under the tablecloth.

"Arthur Merton told me that Inspector El Mofty Effendi has been promoted," she says.

Lacau strokes his trim, white beard and pushes up his round spectacles. "He's a man of integrity—"

"But he doesn't stand up to bureaucrats, does he?" Eve says. "He's let high-ranking officials into the tomb. And they invite their friends—"

"I'm on my way to Luxor to put a stop to such gatherings," Lacau whispers. "My sources hint at vandalism."

Eve sets down her cup quickly. "In what way?"

"I don't have particulars," Lacau says. "But I've brought armed police with me."

Eve closes her eyes for a moment in an attempt to stay calm. She draws in a long breath. Has the situation in Egypt gotten as bad as all that, for one government branch to police another? Outside the window, the sky has turned from blue to a startling eerie pink.

Lacau slumps slightly forward. "I know from your letter how strongly you feel, that I unfairly dismissed Mr. Carter and unjustly canceled your mother's concession." He taps his spoon again. "But the days of letting foreign excavators take priceless cultural objects out of Egypt are over."

The rattling of the china plates seems to Eve to be like her own shaky feelings. Her voice breaks. His words, though not a complete surprise, sink into her body with a terrible feeling of heaviness. "I am coming around to this realization as well. But my father paid for fifteen years of excavation work in Egypt. Because of his half-million-pound investment, Egypt now has Tutankhamun's tomb. Doesn't the Antiquities Service owe my mother that half million?"

Lacau's voice is steady and firm. "I intend to reimburse your family for at least *some* of your father's expenses."

"Some, not all? My father kept receipts—"

The Frenchman furrows his brow. "The Service is lacking in funds. It is not easy for me to bring up the matter with my colleagues. I will keep pushing for you."

"But how soon can we expect—"

"I do not know," Lacau says.

Has my trip been a waste? Eve thinks. Lacau is not being fair to her family. But there's one matter that's far more pressing now. The safety of the tomb's remaining artifacts, including Tutankhamun's giant sarcophagus, is at stake. Despite everything that has happened between her and Howard Carter, he needs to be in charge of the excavation again. Her trip will not be a complete failure if she can convince Lacau to reinstate him.

Eve follows his hand circling the table as if the dishes were the artworks. "The tomb's precious, fragile artifacts need meticulous attention—and we both know the man who will give them that attention." She ventures, "I have a proposal. Could you create a new concession if my mother gives up her interest in the artifacts? Will you let Mr. Carter back at the tomb if she does—and have the Antiquities Service pay him a salary to finish the work there?"

Lacau picks up his tea, takes a sip, and puts it quickly down again as if it's gone cold. "I cannot. But I do admit that no one has Mr. Carter's skill in properly handling an excavation. I was highly impressed with what his team did to conserve, pack, and have the pieces transported so expertly, under such difficulty, from the Antechamber to Cairo. Remarkably, they suffered *no* damage." He sits back with puckered lips, looking thoughtful.

Lacau seems suddenly too eager to show his goodwill toward Carter, Eve thinks. Could Lacau possibly be saying yes, when he just refused the suggestion to rehire him?

"I'm glad you see the tomb was in the hands of the best man," Eve says. Then she forgets herself by speaking so boldly. "How could you have taken Mr. Carter off the work?"

Lacau looks at her with sadness. "I had no choice."

"Didn't you?" Eve stops herself. Her tone has been too accusatory. "Excuse me. I have spoken out of turn."

Lacau reddens, whether from embarrassment or anger, Eve cannot tell. Her voice rises. "Couldn't you see that Mr. Weigall's group set out to defame Mr. Carter? Breaking into his house and turning it upside down. They should not have done it."

"What Mr. Weigall's men did to find the alabaster chalice was a trap, yes. I could easily have let that go if Mr. Carter had been less hotheaded and more helpful." Lacau scowls. "All along, he felt it was his right to tell reporters to stay away from the tomb. Instead of talking things over with me, he would treat them angrily—and rudely." He pauses. "Did Mr. Carter ever consider how his stubbornness got in the way of my own, dedicated work to preserve the treasures for Egypt?"

Eve takes a long breath and says nothing. Lacau speaks the truth.

Lacau takes off his small round spectacles and rubs his eyes. "With all due respect, Lady Evelyn, Mr. Carter and your dear late father made the mistake of believing the tomb to be theirs."

Eve stiffens. She remembers her conversation with Brograve about the arrogance, the ethical wrongfulness of one country assuming the ownership of another country's treasures. She feels very close to admitting that Lacau is right. And yet her father's longtime funding and Carter's many years of excavating deserve proper compensation. "Again, I have to remind you. My father spent a fortune on the Tutankhamun excavation."

"Lady Evelyn." Lacau's elegant smile collapses. "You have come a long way here. As I have said, I will try to persuade my supervisors to allot your family some recompense." He dismisses further conversation with a wave of his hand.

Eve sighs. She wonders if she has made any progress at all. In the darkness of the night, the train rattles on.

Even before the Luxor sky turns red at dawn, Eve finds Lacau in the lobby of the Luxor Hotel, where they have both taken rooms. She wants to accompany him to the Valley, and as she has anticipated, his party is ready to set out very early; that is the only way that travelers can go to the Valley and return to Luxor on the same day. Lacau gives instructions in Arabic to two Egyptian policemen dressed in khaki drill cotton with black tarbooshes as Eve strides toward them.

"Director-General, I would like to go with you to the tomb," Eve says.

Lacau hesitates. "But Lady Evelyn—"

They argue in French. The policemen, one young and clean-shaven and the other of middle age with a scraggly beard, look on curiously.

Lacau finally agrees to have Eve join his party, and together Eve and the Frenchman proceed to the ferry dock, the orange sun still low on the horizon. After they've made it across the Nile, Eve hires a donkey for herself. As she has done many times before, Eve rides along the green river plains, bumps over desert hills and a sandy, boulder-strewn expanse, and ascends toward the brown cliffs of the Valley. As ever, el-Qurn rises above the gullies and rock-cut tombs. Encountering no other travelers, the party angles up the trail toward the Ramesses clearing.

At the Tutankhamun site, two Antiquities Service guards in white uniforms with red caps sit in the shade with their backs against the storage shed, talking and chewing on flatbread. When they stand up to give Lacau a salute, Eve sees the pistols and knives that they carry on their belts.

On the ground, near the retaining wall of the stairway, Eve spies a carpet-like, rolled-up mass. In her sun-seared eyes, it shimmers brown and gold. At first, she thinks it is Egyptian women's dress clothes on the ground. Then in the heat, her body goes cold with a realization. She's seeing the gilt framework of the pall and the red gossamer curtain that once hung between the outermost and next inner burial shrines. She is glad that Carter is not here to witness the damage. Flashing through her brain is the night she and her father and Carter entered the burial chamber. Carter drew the delicate curtain aside and pocketed several golden rosettes that had fallen to the floor. Carter's indiscretion was nothing compared to this. These men have left a precious treasure to rot!

Pointing, Eve says to Lacau, "Look there!"

"I can see," Lacau answers, his voice gruff.

They dismount and go closer. Lacau reprimands the guards in Arabic, and Eve guesses his words: "What is the pall doing out here? You were supposed to be guarding this tomb and its contents. You understand me?"

A guard answers, and Lacau summarizes for Eve: "I'm the one who contacted you." The guard gestures vigorously. "Some of Mr. Morcos Bey Hanna's associates became disorderly after he left. We drove them away."

Lacau mutters under his breath as he leans down to inspect the items. He shakes his head, frowning.

"Is there anyone inside now?" Eve asks the guard in English.

"I'm not sure," the guard replies.

"You're not sure?" Lacau glares.

One of the policemen draws his pistol and leads the way down the stairs. Eve follows Lacau and the police. Her heart beating rapidly, she pulls the gate aside, its open padlocks hanging, makes her way down, and steps into the tunnel. The electric lights have been left on.

The tomb has the familiar smell of dust and chemicals for restoration mixed with cigarettes. In the Antechamber, three men lie on the floor in their robes, next to ashtrays, bottles, glasses, and pieces of cake. What a sight! Not only have these men been disrespectful to the tomb, but they have violated their religion, which prohibits alcohol.

Lacau shakes the men. One rolls over and opens his eyes. Eve recognizes him as El Mofty Effendi. Lacau grabs him by the sleeves. "Sit up. What are you doing here? Why is there this mess?"

El Mofty rubs his face to wake up. He says, his voice hoarse, "It was Morcos Bey Hanna's orders. He entertained his guests here."

Lacau scowls. "I entrusted you with the keys. You were to bring nobody in here without my permission. You're a disgrace to Egypt."

Eve steps by the men on the floor. She peers into the burial chamber; its lights are also on. The golden shrines are completely dismantled and lie in sections against the walls. And there, bare, with no shrines around it, stands the magnificent sarcophagus of lemony yellow stone. In a corner lie three crowbars and a heap of blankets and ropes. Someone has tried to pry the lid open.

Lacau, coming behind Eve, says in French, "This is a great shock!" She hears his uneven breathing as well as her own.

Eve leans her hand against the wall to steady herself. Heat rushes to her head. She thinks she might faint. "I'm horrified," she says, noticing flakes of gilding on the floor. The gold must have come from the shrines.

"*Mon Dieu*," Lacau says. "This is a tragedy. This damage could have been avoided."

El Mofty follows them into the burial chamber. Lacau turns and demands to know who got inside here. "It's an outrage!" he roars.

El Mofty hangs his head. "Some of the guests of Morcos Bey Hanna snuck by us." He stands straighter. "But we heard them and fought with them."

"Where are they?"

"They ran out. They disappeared up top into the hills, past the guards. We tried to follow them and apprehend them, but it was hopeless."

Lacau shakes his head. "Get the guards. Clear this out. And clean up your rubbish."

Eve looks over the boarded-up entrance to the Treasury. "At least this door hasn't been broken into," she says. The small magical statues in recesses of the burial chamber's painted walls look out with haunting eyes, as ever. It would have been easy for the men to pocket them. Yet nothing from the tomb appears to have been stolen.

She walks around the sarcophagus, taking in its monumental mystery. She runs her eyes over its smoothness. The ancients chose beautiful red granite for the lid only. She looks up toward the high edge of the rounded lid, red granite flecked with white and black, down to the side, milky yellow also flecked with dark and light. How well-proportioned this outer coffin is. Its cornice edges the top and lends formal dignity and grace. The lovely goddesses of protection—Isis, Nephthys, Neith, and Selket, each on a corner in raised relief—spread their wings in graceful overlapping symmetry. Eve pauses at one end of the sarcophagus, where an incised *wedjat* eye—the pharaoh's sight to the outside world—seems to peer out at her.

In the mind of the pharaoh, seeing out through the *wedjat* eye, is she, too, an interloper? Even so, one form of intruder is not the same as another, Eve considers. She takes in the wall paintings around her, vignettes of Tutankhamun's mummy delivered by barge, of meeting deities, and of the Opening of the Mouth Ceremony. She loves these observances and ancient high arts, just as Carter does. Her heart aches over the level of disrespect that she has seen today. Her allegiance is to these lovely, ancient things: not to their monetary value, but to their beauty and meaning.

Eve turns to the Frenchman, who has his hand over his mouth, staring at the sarcophagus. She goes to him and rests her hand on his shoulder. "Director-General," she says. Now is the time to remind him of the proposal she made to him on the train. "I know you want to preserve the tomb as it should be. Mr. Carter will help you, if you will only let him."

31

Back in London, Eve endures the awkwardness of explaining her trip to her mother and brother. Porchey and Lady Almina accept the fact that all they can expect now is reimbursement for Carnarvon's investment, but they are still angry when they return to Highclere. Eve decides to stay on at Seymour Place for a few days while emotions settle. She writes to Carter and asks him to visit her.

When he comes to the door, she steps outside. A light early-September rain mists down on them; it has been several months since the day he last left Highclere, but she can still barely coax herself to look into his eyes.

"Hello, Howard. Please come in out of the wet."

She offers her hand. It's her hope now that he will return to Egypt to finish the job of cataloging, restoring, and moving the Tutankhamun treasures to the Egyptian Museum. Carter, not anyone else, must be the one to lift the lid of that heavy sarcophagus. Lacau would agree. But is Carter capable of approaching Lacau with humility? And will he agree to cancel his upcoming tour of America?

The footman takes Carter's umbrella, coat, and homburg. "Lady Eve. I'm glad you asked me to come now."

Because he's about to leave for New York? "And it's good to see you, Howard. I hope you are well."

Oh Lord, they are being so polite. This genius of a man is pitifully lacking in social skills. She leads him to the parlor. Carter takes a chair across from her, near the window that looks out to the rainy street. He has lost weight. His bow tie is neat, his collar clean and white against his deeply suntanned face. His pinched frown shows how much his spirit is cast down.

"I trust that you are well," Carter says. "And your family?"

"We're all fine. Porchey and Catherine have a son they've named Henry. A healthy, strong little lad."

"Yes, I heard," Carter says. "Your mother wrote to me."

"Did she tell you she's marrying again?" Eve tries not to sound disapproving.

"Yes," he says, his voice flat.

"Mother seems very happy with Lieutenant Colonel Dennistoun."

Carter nods, his dark eyes dim. After the footman serves tea, Carter slowly lifts his cup to his lips. "Lady Eve, your letter concerned me greatly. That fragile gossamer pall lying on the ground, the shrines crudely dismantled. Barbaric."

She recounts the shock and dismay at what she has seen. "I emphatically said to Lacau you needed to be brought back, Howard, to handle everything professionally. Especially the sarcophagus. Who will protect Tutankhamun properly if you're not there?"

Carter's face reddens. He looks as though he might get up and pound the wall.

"Who is there now?" Carter asks.

"When I left two weeks ago, Mr. Lacau had closed the tomb again. He put new locks on the steel door, and only he has the keys."

"I fear those inept officials at the Egyptian Museum will try to haul out the sarcophagus. They may break it."

"That's my main concern, too. That's why you're so right for the position. You have to leave for Egypt at once and stop them," Eve says.

"What can I do? The government has canceled the concession." Carter's tone is harsh. "I'm sorry I didn't make more of an effort to get on with Lacau."

Carter's admission surprises Eve. It is a good sign.

"Pierre Lacau would likely reinstate you if you went to him now. No one can oversee the tomb as you can. He knows that." She looks into Carter's dark eyes. "If Mother signs a new contract agreeing that the artifacts stay in Egypt, and giving all journalists equal coverage, there's a good chance Mr. Lacau would hire you. I put it to him directly. He didn't say yes, but he didn't say no. And at this point, Mother doesn't expect to see any money from the sale of the treasures. I've already spoken to her about it. She would cooperate."

He says, "Egypt signed an agreement with Carnarvon. They should have kept to it." Carter stares at the bright chandelier, then takes out his cigarettes. After Eve frowns, he puts the case away. She wonders if he will ever learn propriety.

Eve calls the footman for brandy. She hopes it will calm him.

"Of course, I hope to work there again, that there might be some way." Carter scowls.

"Against all odds, no one has fired Pierre Lacau," Eve says. "The Egyptian government reveres him, even though he's French. They'd go along with his decision to reappoint you and show you the respect you deserve as an archaeologist."

Carter says, "I don't know if that's possible."

Eve leans toward him. "Put aside your pride. Apologies can be made on both sides," she says. "My father is to blame, in part, for giving the *Times* exclusive rights. I'm afraid we acted as if the tomb were ours."

"Of course the tomb is ours. I found it." There is an edge to Carter's voice. "Your father paid for the concession and the excavation. Your mother is due fifty percent."

"I do have doubts now about who owns that tomb," Eve says, "but I have no doubt that you're the best caretaker for it. You must go back, Howard. What's stopping you?"

"I simply can't go back." He says again that he needs the income that his lecture tour will provide. He will not hear her, she realizes, even if some of the world's greatest treasures are at risk of being destroyed.

"Your pride is getting in your way," Eve says. "Same as when you lost your job with the Antiquities Service so many years ago."

"There's nothing left to discuss," he says.

She walks with him down the corridor, and he says a curt goodbye.

Through a window, Eve watches him march down the steps of the townhouse in the thin rain and disappear into the mist.

A few weeks later, Porchey hosts his first large event as the Earl of Carnarvon. It is still the racing season, and at Eve's request, he invites Brograve. Whatever his feelings for her might be, she is ready to admit that he was right about Egypt's claim to the golden treasures.

For the occasion, she chooses a pink silk dress, sleeveless and bare at the back, and a light string of pearls. Her hair, grown out of its bob, is shoulder length and curled. She hasn't paid much attention to her appearance for months. Today is a start.

Through a library window, she sees Brograve arrive in his open-topped Baby Austin. She meets him at the front door, and they stand between the wrought-iron Carnarvon wyverns. His smile is reassuring; perhaps he isn't still angry with her. "It's good of you to join us," she says.

"I was pleased by the invitation," he says.

"Surprised?"

"Yes. Very."

Can he truly be pleased to see her after the way she behaved?

He pauses. "Your eyes are sparkling."

"Are they?" Unsure how to greet him, she finds herself clutching her hands. Stop being so nervous, she tells herself.

"I was wondering if you would drive us to the races in the Bugatti."

"That would add to the adventure," he says.

A footman takes Brograve's suitcase to one of the second-floor guest bedrooms off the gallery. Eve and Brograve go to the old carriage house to look at the now much smaller collection of cars. Soon they take off for the Newbury tracks in the race car.

Fast open-air cars are not the best for conversation, Eve realizes. But it's a relief to take a rest from small talk.

Everything is green—the late-summer rushes and brambles have grown in profusion. After parking, they follow a fence that encloses the wide infield and the grandstand.

"I don't make wagers," Brograve says.

"That's all for the best!" Eve hesitates. "Watching horses Porchey has bet on isn't as fun as it used to be." She does not say they can't afford to lose.

Brograve senses her meaning. "Has Porchey paid off the death duties?" Then, as if realizing his mistake, he says, "Sorry, I don't mean to pry."

However politely, he is prying. "Porchey's halfway there. He's paid enough to hold on to Highclere—at least for now."

"I'm glad to hear it."

They make their way to the grandstand, to Porchey and beautiful Catherine, to their friends, to the crowd, and to a view of the pageantry. Lady Almina, back from Paris for a time, stays at Highclere today with baby Henry and the nurse.

The gun sounds and the first race begins. Through it and the ones that follow, Eve finds that Brograve glances at her almost as much as he follows the races. The drama unfolds around them. As always, the jockeys hold off until the final furlong if they know their horses can close in fast. Hooves pound like thunder. There is the laughter of the men whose horses win them earnings, and the grimaces of those who absorb their losses. Porchey's features are easy to read. When Porchey screws up his face after a Highclere horse has failed to place, Eve and Brograve exchange glances.

Brograve says in a low voice that only she can hear, "With a debt to the Crown, doesn't he think twice about betting?"

"It's part of the fun. Like Father, he's fearless. But unlike my father, he better calculates his risks. And these days his bets are quite small."

"I talked to Porchey once about finances, about going to the right advisers and investing in safer long-term markets," Brograve says. "He gave me half an ear. He's open to suggestions, I think."

"Please do talk to him again. Porchey trusts you and will listen to you." She is touched by Brograve's concern for her family and calmed by his cautious approach.

"For a liberal in politics, you're more conservative, personally, than I'm used to in my family," Eve says.

He frowns, then touches her arm lightly as if he might say something.

"I didn't mean it as a criticism." Her words come out quavering. In her low-heeled shoes, she scrunches up her toes. It seems both she and Brograve are at a loss for conversation.

After the end of the races, Brograve drives them back to Highclere. They take a long walk on the castle grounds.

"The last time you were here, I behaved badly," Eve says finally.

"You had every right—" he starts.

"I was upset, and I was rude," she says. "Please accept my apology."

"I apologize, too, for what I said. I can be quite outspoken." He stops, turns, and looks at her. He rests his hand on her forearm, and she lets him keep it there. Feeling excited but suddenly shy, she tilts her chin down, then looks up again. She takes in his large, dark eyes, high cheekbones, and full mustache. What is it that makes him so attractive? It's his candor and sincerity, as well as his obvious intelligence.

"I like your honesty. Since my father died, I've been reading the newspapers quite a lot and thinking. You're right—Britain should stop taking antiquities. Too little will be left for Egypt, for its people's heritage." Eve pauses. "All we are owed is compensation for my father's expenditures."

As they walk forward Brograve says, "I had no right to single out your family for their actions in the colonies. Most English estates have done business this way. And your father did help give something great to Egypt."

The conversation becomes easier, even more comfortable, as they climb the rise to the Temple of Diana, Highclere's domed rotunda. As Eve has done so often, she looks out to the far castle's yellowish-gold aura in the late-afternoon sunlight. She climbs up two more steps and draws level with his height. She feels heady, almost dizzy, as she studies his lips and dark eyes.

Maybe she should act more like the lady she has been taught to be. But why start now?

Eve moves closer.

"You're lovely," he breathes. Then he leans near and kisses her lightly on the forehead. His lips linger.

Eve rests her hands on his shoulders and waits. She nuzzles her cheek against his, and he lets her, but he does not kiss her. Is he too shy, or does he feel it's too soon, or both? How embarrassing! She has behaved far too forwardly! He's acting as a gentleman ought to when a couple has not agreed upon an engagement.

"Let's return to the castle," she says, taking a step back from him. She walks to the bottom of the stairs, where he meets her.

He stops her from taking the path from the rotunda that leads to the main drive. "Wait," he says. When next Eve looks, his face is flushed. She feels foolish. He puts a hand up as if to tell her not to apologize or feel bad.

"Eve," Brograve says. "I wanted to…"

She waits.

Usually so articulate, Brograve seems tongue-tied. Then he says directly, "I would like to court you. But there is so much we have not discussed. Porchey told me you'd gone to Egypt. Are you planning to return there?"

"No, but—" She can feel her heart beating. She scrunches her toes in her shoes again. Now is the time to be honest with him and with herself. She has no right to lead him on if she isn't willing to commit to him. Eve's mind floods with thoughts of her past and of the years to come. She will never abandon her passion for ancient Egypt. That passion runs deep in her, and any man who does not understand that cannot be an important part of her life.

"I'll never give up Egyptology. I've been raised on the Egyptian antiquities in the British Museum, even the mummies." Eve purses her lips. She pauses, looking at the blue sky between the columns of the rotunda, then glances again at Brograve. "But I doubt that I'll return to Egypt. Certainly I'll never go alone again. That was foolhardy."

He stares at her, his eyes serious. Perhaps he is grappling with her words.

"We do not have to agree on everything," Eve continues, "but I'd like us to respect each other's opinions."

"Of course." Brograve nods. He lays a hand over his heart. Again she senses his sincerity.

She waits for him to make the next move.

"Shall we try once again? May I court you?" Brograve asks.

"Yes, I would like that very much. Except I have one more request," Eve says, her tone lightening. "I want you to sing 'God Save the King' to me whenever I need cheering up."

He laughs. "Then 'God Save the King' it is."

They leave the rotunda and begin the long trek back to the castle, leaving a bit of distance between them. Eve does not look at him much, and it seems right to allow him that privacy, though with every step she is aware of him. She feels changed. She knows she wants him in her life, and not only as someone who would make a good husband. He's someone she can talk to, be playful with, have fun with—and with whom she can be herself.

By the time they arrive at the castle, it is nearly time for dinner.

At the meal, when Porchey, Catherine, and Lady Almina are gathered, Brograve says, "If it's acceptable to all of you, and if Eve's no longer in mourning. I'll be calling on her regularly now."

Eve looks from one face to another, checking her family members' reactions. Lady Almina makes no effort to hide tears, and Catherine smiles gracefully. Porchey appears downright gleeful.

Porchey stands and says, "Well, my man." He chuckles. "I couldn't be more pleased. And look how you have made her blush!"

Porchey is impossible. Today, she'll forgive his teasing. Eve feels aglow, as if soaking in beams of hot sunlight. She did not think she could ever be this happy again.

Brograve gives her a wide smile and holds out his hand. She grins, then takes his hand in return.

Epilogue

Forty-Eight Years Later

London
March 30, 1972

On the opening day of the Tutankhamun exhibit at the British Museum, Eve reads one of the letters from Howard Carter that she has kept in her father's Egyptian cigar box all these years. It is hard to believe nearly half a century has gone by. She received the letter in 1925, when she was just twenty-three. In several months she will turn seventy-one. And this letter on yellowed stationery, its black ink faded, still brings tears of joy to her eyes.

1 February 1925
Luxor
Dear Lady Eve,
Congratulations on your marriage. Already it is a year and a half after our meeting in London, and by now, you must know from the newspapers that I am back in Egypt. I wanted to tell you myself how things are and thank you for your part in the joyous events of this year and week.

As you know, when I was in America, terrorists in Cairo shot and killed a British commander of the Egyptian army. Then Britain sent troops to reclaim Egypt. Prime Minister Zaghlul and his cabinet resigned, and a pro-British regime under Ahmad Ziwar Pasha came into power.

So it is partly because of this changing of the guards that I find myself in charge of Tutankhamun's tomb again. But it is also, in large part, due to you that I have mended my relationship with Lacau. Thanks to you, he led me back into a position with the Antiquities Service. Thanks to you, Lacau accepted your mother's renunciation of her claim to the Tutankhamun's treasures, the *Times* exclusive was canceled, and I and my team of scholars reentered the Valley of the Kings.

I write you now about yesterday's opening of the stone sarcophagus in the tomb. During the weeks since my colleagues and I started work again, Callender had rigged sturdy scaffolds and pulleys. At long last, at the appointed time, scholars and dignitaries circled King Tutankhamun's sarcophagus, now bare without its shrines.

I tugged the ropes carefully. Lacau and onlookers gasped as the lid loosened, inched upward, then hovered above the sarcophagus at last. I cinched the ropes and peered inside the blackness. While the lid gently swayed above my head, I rolled out the linen shroud and found a second one. My heart pounding, I pulled back the second shroud to reveal a face, haunting in the eerie light, and shimmering in gold.

The handsome gold effigy of the boy king in low relief is finer than anything I could have imagined. How magnificent he is. How captivating are his eyes of aragonite and obsidian, his arching eyebrows of lapis lazuli. The gold of his face and hands has a darker tinge than the rest. And crafted out of a different alloy, these portions, used in the flesh skin tones, seemed especially real and, even in the death chamber, lifelike.

The entire figure, rising to a blue-striped headdress, is inlaid with lapis lazuli and other stones. His arms, crossed over his breast, hold a crook and flail, the twin symbols of royal power. A vulture and a cobra, emblems of Upper and Lower Egypt, stand watch from the king's forehead.

Since this tomb was built, great empires have risen and disappeared, wars and catastrophes have changed the face of the land. And here the pharaoh lies in the peace and grandeur that only death and the grave can give. In awe and reverence, aware of my own small place in the cosmic order, I reached out to touch the golden face.

All my labors in the Valley culminated at that moment. I waited a long time for this event and wished you and Carnarvon had been with me.

Yours sincerely,

Howard Carter

Eve refolds the letter and holds it to her heart before she carefully places it back in its box. Then, just several hours later, she and Brograve; their daughter, Patricia; and Patricia's husband and two grown sons drive to the British Museum. In the company of Queen Elizabeth and the other honored guests, Eve supports herself with her cane as she slowly but steadily thumps forward to the center of the main gallery, where a large gold object, mounted upright in a glass cube, dazzles her with its golden luster.

Tutankhamun's death mask. The pharaoh's youthful face is framed by his striped *nemes* of blue glass and gold, and by his collar, banded by precious stones. On his brow, the vulture and cobra keep watch, protecting him. The design is marvelous, and the sensitivity of the features is extraordinary. Leaning on her cane, Eve steps on tiptoe. In the white quartz of those haunting almond-shaped eyes, she can see touches of a red pigment.

Eve's heart feels full. She has been waiting for this moment for nearly fifty years. Of course, she has seen Tutankhamun's sensuous young face in magazines and books, but nothing—in those photographs or in her imagination—has prepared her for the mask's lifelike image and brilliant radiance. No wonder ancient people associated this shining material with the gods, with magical properties, with agelessness and timelessness.

"Mother, how you smile," says Patricia. "I wondered how it would be for you."

"That part of my life is finally complete now." Eve is so mesmerized by the gold, she wonders if she might faint. "I only wish that my father could have seen this sculptured mask," she says. She has mourned Carnarvon for all her adult years; never has a day passed when she did not think of him.

She fondly remembers her mother as well. Three years ago, Lady Almina passed on at age ninety-two. Eve wonders if her mother would have come to this exhibition if she'd had the chance. Perhaps not. In 1930, seven years after Carnarvon's death, the Egyptian government paid Lady Almina £36,000 for her husband's efforts in the Valley. Lady Almina continued to feel cheated. Eve's brother, Porchey, still earl and still living at Highclere, remains resentful, as well.

Her back to the crowd of guests, Eve stands at the front and center of the display case. Her nose almost touches the glass. Staring at the gold mask, and imagining herself once again as a young woman in the pharaoh's burial chamber, she is startled out of her reverie by a voice saying her name. A long-haired young man, wearing a suit and holding a camera, stands before her.

"Lady Evelyn Beauchamp, is it? May I photograph you here?"

"Certainly." When she accepted the museum's invitation, she agreed to be photographed. Let the world see me with all my wrinkles, she thinks. She stands next to the glass container with the mask. The photographer takes shots from different angles as Eve admires her old acquaintance, the boy pharaoh. Today, on the opening day of an international exhibit that will go on to the USSR, the United States, Canada, and West Germany, Tutankhamun is once again a celebrity, and so, by association, is Eve.

Queen Elizabeth, who has opened the exhibit and had her walk-around, slips out with her bodyguards. Now, with the major celebrity of the day gone, a crowd of other guests gathers around Eve. Somehow word has leaked out that she, this hunched old woman, is the glamorous young lady in some of the exhibit's photographs. Being the object of captivated stares is a sensation that she has almost forgotten. Eve feels shy, even lost for a moment, until she spots Brograve again and waves to him.

Decades have gone by since Eve's photo was last taken for a public purpose. Brograve has kept their family life private for their safety, especially during the years he served in Parliament. But now, Eve concludes, such a small intrusion no longer bothers him. They have lived through huge events in history; they have seen the results of the Second World War's devastation and the map reconfigured to a new Europe.

Now she is taken back to the years 1922 and 1923 as she walks about the exhibit with Patricia. There is the glossy wooden box with painted battle scenes. There one of the shrines from the Treasury. Ah, the golden throne. She stares in rapture at the blue-nosed lion goddess from one of the ritual beds—oh, how Eve adores her. Eve marvels at a walking stick decorated with beetles' wings, a stool with duck-headed legs, and then an ivory headrest decorated with lions. For many years, she has yearned to see the treasures once more. And, to her delight, standing here in this exhibit is one of the guardian ka figures, his skin a dark black resin, his garments glowing with precious metals. He seems to look at her with his gold-rimmed eyes. She imagines that he says:

We meet again. To me, not much time has gone by. Even centuries pass in the blink of an eye. Do you remember when I winked at you?

How could she ever forget?

His eyes have been fully restored. There will be no more blinking and peeling. Delighted by his company, Eve takes a seat on a marble bench near the ka figure. Patricia joins her.

"Mother," Patricia asks, "why, after all those years since you married, didn't you ever go back to Egypt?"

Lost in her memories, Eve doesn't immediately respond. Patricia touches her shoulder. She repeats the question, her voice softer this time. "Why didn't you go back?"

"Well, I did return after my father died. Only once. Alone," she says. Eve doesn't want to talk about that trip. "It is odd, isn't it, that I could have let almost fifty years go by? I do so love Egypt."

Eve can think of many answers to why she never traveled there again. She isn't sure, though, which is the real one. "Egypt was always changing governments—administrations that didn't think kindly about the earlier British control," she says. "Then, of course, there was the war in Europe." She pauses. "And your father didn't want us to go. But most of all," she says, grasping Patricia's hand, "was my sadness over my father's death. The Valley of the Kings could never be the same without him. Nor Howard Carter."

Eve alternately gazes at her friend the ka figure and Patricia; she is glad the two have met.

"I was in love with Mr. Carter once," she confides.

"I thought so, because of the way you talk about him," her daughter says. "Mother, there's a flush across your cheeks!"

Eve glances at the life-size guardian statue. How calm he looks, foot forward, gently clasping his staff. You saw everything, she thinks. You know my secrets.

"I often wonder why I was so captivated by him," Eve says. "He was volatile. Difficult. And more than a little mentally unstable." He was not a good match for her; she admits this now. "But I've sorely missed him over the years. I wanted to go on knowing him my whole life."

Eve pauses, then continues. "You see, we experienced something extraordinary together. He and Father and I." Without them she was, in a way, alone.

Patricia lightly strokes Eve's forearm. "When did Mr. Carter die?"

"Oh, it was over thirty years ago." Eve touches a hand to her lips. "It was 1939. Lymphoma took him. He was sixty-four." She pauses. "After spending a decade clearing King Tutankhamun's tomb, he died shortly afterward. He did not live long enough to enjoy the advantages of his fame. Who knows what he could have gone on to do?"

"That's so sad," Patricia says, her voice soft.

Eve pushes away a memory of standing near Carter's glossy coffin with her mother and brother at Putney Vale Cemetery in London. Hardly anyone attended the funeral. What a contrast his memorial service was to her father's crowd-filled gatherings. Poor Howard!

"Things did not go well for Mr. Carter after my father died," Eve says. She tells Patricia how Carter was temporarily ousted from the tomb by the Egyptian government. "Fortunately, he returned to Egypt the same year you were born," she says. That was 1925.

The following year, in the summer of 1926, Eve and Lady Almina completed the sale of Carnarvon's collection of Egyptian artifacts to the Metropolitan Museum. Eve remembers the melancholy day when the tiny gilt puppy, the African gazelle, and the leaping horse left for America.

"We still have—" Eve begins.

"What, Mother?" Patricia says.

Eve stops herself from telling Patricia about the Egyptian artifacts that remain in Highclere's walls. The knowledge would be a burden to her. How could she ask Patricia to keep the secret from her uncle and cousins?

When the time is right, someone will find them, Eve says to herself. She doesn't want to be the center of sensational news for tabloids. Nor does she wish that for Porchey.

"What do we still have?" Patricia asks again.

"We still have each other!" Eve says.

Patricia glances over her shoulder, then squeezes Eve's hand. "Daddy's trying to get your attention," she says.

Eve looks up. Brograve strides toward them with a grin. "This is all jolly terrific," he says. "These treasures are spectacular."

Eve struggles to get up from the bench and follows Brograve to the silver-and-copper-alloy trumpets he wants to show her. She doesn't recall ever seeing them before. After a while, with a mischievous look in his eye, he says, "I'll be in the gift shop. Take your time."

Eve nods. "Right." She suspects he is going to buy her a gift and wants to surprise her. Bless him, he has been a good husband, father, and grandfather. He has upheld her all these years with his steadiness. In every kind of hardship, he manages to say something that gives her a glimmer of hope. They love each other in an easygoing, forgiving way that makes for an enduring marriage. She wishes she'd been able to conceive again after Patricia's very difficult birth. Still, she and Brograve are grateful for their beloved daughter.

A silver rod, capped by something shaped like a flat seashell, catches Eve's attention. A fan. When she last saw it, it held two ostrich quills, which must have disintegrated long ago. Sometimes alone, sometimes with her daughter, son-in-law, and grandsons, she walks and pores over baskets and boomerangs, walking sticks and staves. She wishes she could use one of those animal-headed walking sticks now as she hobbles through London parks.

Eve's decades of reading books and articles about Tutankhamun tell her exactly what she is seeing. Sir Alan wrote scholarly books that some thought dull but Eve found fascinating. Arthur Weigall, the most annoying of all journalists, turned out to be a magnificent writer. Though most of the people she knew in Egypt during that time are dead, Eve is still learning from them.

At last, Eve spots the lotus-shaped Wishing Cup. By now people have begun clearing out of the exhibit. The private opening is over. Patricia finds her looking at the translation of the hieroglyphic inscription, which she knows by heart, and moving her lips. Carter read it to her father during his illness. Many years later, consulting with Carter's favorite niece, Eve arranged for it to be carved onto Carter's gravestone.

May your spirit live, may you spend millions of years, you who love Thebes, sitting with your face to the north wind, your eyes beholding happiness.

Eve will always love Carter. She loves Carter for himself, and she loves him for bringing excitement, adventure, and magic into her life. Their intimate time together had its season. Her time in Egypt, which was far from idyllic, also needed to come to an end. But in some respects, she has carried the passion of her young years with her. In her rounds of daily activities, she has learned to pause and appreciate the beauty around her, like the shape of a tree or the flight of a bird. Her ability to give wonderful things her meticulous attention she owes to Howard Carter.

Now, somewhere in the distance of a hallway, Eve hears a guard announcing that the building is about to close. She's glad she has purchased tickets to visit the exhibit four more times in the next few months. Allowing herself to be waved out of the gallery, she pauses at the door to gaze over her shoulder for one last look at the golden mask.

HISTORICAL NOTES

In the following letter, Lady Evelyn Herbert, daughter of George Herbert, the 5th Earl of Carnarvon, writes to archaeologist Howard Carter on December 26, 1922.[1] She is home in England for the Christmas holiday with her father, who is Carter's patron. Eve is twenty-one and Carter is forty-eight. The world is just learning of Carter's recent colossal find: two small storerooms of dazzling artifacts that appear to be part of King Tutankhamun's nearly intact tomb. Carter has not yet announced his discovery of the tomb's two other small rooms: Tutankhamun's burial chamber and its adjoining Treasury, which he, Eve, and Lord Carnarvon secretly entered during Eve's last visit to Egypt. These rooms would be officially opened in the presence of Pierre Lacau, director-general of the Egyptian Antiquities Service, on February 14, 1923.

Dearest Howard,

I would like to think this letter would reach you on New Year's Day, but alas it won't though it will get to you quicker than if I posted it [letter is perhaps carried by a London friend going to Egypt]. My dear I wish you just the very best of <u>everything</u>. May you be as happy as you are successful and for many, many years—bless you—you deserve it. By now you are world-renowned and your name dear will be added to the famous men in the annals of history. It is wonderful and I wish you could have flown to England if only for a few hours, for the genuine, universal interest and excitement that your Discovery has created would have thrilled you with pleasure and would have justly rewarded the many years of labour and disappointment that you have had.

Of course one is pestered, morning, noon and night, and I know you are too. There was no place or hour that one was not met by a 'reporter' when we first returned. Pups [her father, Lord Carnarvon] really has had a lot of work to do and was somewhat fatigued when we came down here Sat. However, he revels in it all, and when

---

[1] *The Path to Tutankhamun* by T.G.H. James, 464.

slightly weary calls me in to tell him again and again of the 'Holy of Holies,' which always acts like a magnum of champagne! I can never thank you sufficiently for allowing me to enter its precincts. It was the Great Moment of my life. More I cannot say, except that I am panting to return to you.
Bless you. My best love
Yrs truly grateful and affect.[affectionate]
Eve

Here we see a passionate young woman who'd recently journeyed from her opulent home in the English countryside to the Valley of the Kings to partake in a great adventure. Her father's longtime dream of finding an intact royal tomb had been realized. In the Valley's underground, Eve, Carter, and her father had shared a breathtaking moment as they peered through a hole in an ancient wall and discovered the lavish riches of King Tut's golden hoard. At the time she wrote the letter, Eve considered Carter, the discoverer of the fantastic golden treasures, to be her hero.

Was there a romance between Lady Eve and Carter? If so, it was brief. Carter discovered the tomb in November 1922. After her father, Lord Carnarvon, died in April 1923, Eve never again returned to Egypt. She announced her engagement to Sir Brograve Beauchamp in July 1923 and married him in early October.

This passionate letter, found among Carter's possessions after his death and eventually acquired by the Metropolitan Museum of Art in New York, poses a mystery in terms of Carter's relationship with Lady Eve. As many scholars have pointed out, the way letters were worded over a century ago, and the values ascribed to these phrases, have changed over time. Another note, which Eve wrote Carter in Egypt on February 22, 1923[2], also shows Eve's affection:

I am so terribly sorry to hear that you have been taken seedy with your tummy out of order. I wish I had been with you to look after you dear—for you know how I fancy myself at nursing!

Anyhow I am popping over tomorrow just to have a glimpse of you and shall come very early so as to avoid all the 'ducks' [reporters or tourists?] and shall call at your house lest you shouldn't have already gone up [to the excavation].

[2] James, 294.

Poor Marcelle [Eve's maid] has been very seedy but I pray the worst is over now,

Bless you dearest Howard

Eve

Arthur Mace, a member of Carter's scholarly team, records the following in his diary:[3]

[3 February 1923] The Carnarvons are rather a nuisance. He potters about all day, and will talk and ask questions and waste one's time. Lady Carnarvon is not coming out. Lady Evelyn is rather an empty-headed little thing I should think. She and Carter seem very thick.

Note the cryptic last phrase—unfortunately, it is not explained.

Carter's diaries mention Eve only in passing. Whatever letters he may have sent to Eve have never publicly surfaced and were probably lost or destroyed.

On February 23, 1923, a few weeks after the above entry was written, Lord Carnarvon and Carter engaged in a short-lived argument, the subject matter unknown. Two days later, Lord Carnarvon penned the following apology note:[4]

Friday evening

My dear Carter,

I have been feeling very unhappy today, and I did not know what to think or do, and then I saw Eve and she told me everything. I have no doubt that I have done many foolish things and I am very sorry. I suppose the fuss and worry have affected me but there is only one thing I want to say to you which I hope you will always remember—whatever your feelings are or will be for me in the future my affection for you will never change.

I'm a man with few friends and whatever happens nothing will ever alter my feelings for you. There is always so much noise and lack of quiet and privacy in the Valley that I felt I should never see you alone altho' I should like to very much and have a good talk because of that I could not rest until I had written you.

Yours,

Carnarvon

---

[3] James, 283.

[4] James, 293-294. *Tutankhamun: The Untold Story* by Thomas Hoving, 222-223. Hoving's view of argument, 221-222.

Several scholars who participated in the Tutankhamun excavation commented on the intensity of the disagreement. James Breasted noted that Carter, in a rage, ordered Lord Carnarvon to leave Carter's house and never return. Herbert Winlock speculated whether Lord Carnarvon and Carter would ever repair their friendship. Could the argument have been over Eve?

The late Thomas Hoving, past president of the Metropolitan Museum of Art, speculated that Eve was infatuated with Carter and had told her father of her feelings for him, and that subsequently, Lord Carnarvon expressed his disapproval of Carter as her suitor. Later, according to Hoving, Eve may have admitted to her father that Carter had done nothing to encourage her flirtations and was not to blame. In apology, Lord Carnarvon sent Carter the letter.

In any case, archaeologist and patron soon reconciled; then Lord Carnarvon and Eve took a Nile cruise. Soon after, Carnarvon became ill with erysipelas and pneumonia. On March 18, 1923, Eve wrote to Carter from Cairo:[5]

> Pups asked me to write you to say that Lacau is laid up with influenza so is hors de combat and what is much more important is the old Man [Lord Carnarvon] is very very seedy himself and incapable of doing anything. You know that mosquito bite on his cheek that was worrying him at Luxor, well yesterday quite suddenly all the glands in his neck started swelling and last night he had a high temperature and still has today. He feels just too rotten for words. I have Fletcher Barrett looking after him and I think he is very competent, but oh! the worry of it all and I just can't bear seeing him really seedy. However there it is... We miss you and I wish Dear you were here. I will let you know how he goes on
> with our fond love
> Eve

At the time of Lord Carnarvon's death, April 5, 1923, at the Continental Hotel in Cairo, Carter was staying at the hotel with the Carnarvon family.

I have taken some liberties with the facts, but my novel in the broadest sense is true. Eve, swept up in the excitement of the Tutankhamun

[5] James, 297-298.

excavation, gushingly acknowledged Carter's talent, great knowledge, determination, perseverance, and accomplishments. Carter, who was painfully insecure about his humble upbringing, must have delighted in Eve's praise. It's fair to say she loved, or at least had great affection for, Carter, both for himself and for bringing excitement, adventure, and mystery into her life. Though she seldom saw him after her marriage, when Carter died in London on March 2, 1939, newspapers reported that Lady Evelyn Beauchamp was one of the few mourners at his funeral.[6]

In March of 1972, when an exhibition of Tut's golden treasures toured the world, Eve, in her early seventies, was among the first to visit the British Museum to see them. She returned to the exhibit numerous times.[7] Clearly, the dazzling experience she had as a young woman in Egypt stayed with her for the rest of her life.

Eve's true passion for Egyptology probably did not extend to her wanting to be an archaeologist herself; and the opinions about the politics of Egypt, imperialism, and archaeology of her husband, Brograve Beauchamp, are purely guesswork on my part. Likewise, whatever Eve did or didn't say to Pierre Lacau has been imagined.

Howard Carter was likely bipolar; he certainly suffered from extreme mood swings. He admitted to having an explosive temper. According to one biographer, Carter's writings indicate that late in life he regretted his behavior regarding an incident in 1905 involving drunken French tourists at Saqqara. Apparently Carter came to realize that his reactiveness to authorities in the aftermath of the episode cost him his stellar career with Egypt's Antiquities Service.[8]

I've fictionalized a few details involving Carter for the sake of creating dramatic scenes. He did not carry a gun (because he once regretted shooting a bird and watching it suffer).[9] He never learned to drive a car, though he owned one in Egypt and another in England. Of greater significance, exactly which uncatalogued items were taken from the Tutankhamun tomb and by whom cannot be proven absolutely. Carter probably pocketed a gold ring, which he gave to his dentist in London,

---

[6] Hoving, 366.

[7] Eve's daughter, Patricia Leatham, phone calls with author 2011-2014, and personal visit April 15, 2014.

[8] Winstone, 88-93.

[9] Winstone, 47.

not to Eve. I've taken the most artistic liberty with the Wishing Cup, which was never used in modern times for drinking wine. For a detailed discussion of the tomb's uncatalogued artifacts, see *Tutankhamun: The Untold Story*.

The following superb nonfiction books (full bibliographical information can be found in the Select Bibliography on page 239) provide full, accurate, detailed accounts of the Tutankhamun excavation and its personalities: *The Tomb of Tutankhamen* by Howard Carter; *Howard Carter and the Discovery of the Tomb of Tutankhamun* by H.V.F. Winstone; *Howard Carter: The Path to Tutankhamun* by T.G.H. James; *Howard Carter: Before Tutankhamun* by Nicholas Reeves, *The Complete Tutankhamun: The King, The Tomb, The Royal Treasure* by Reeves and *The Complete Valley of the Kings* by Reeves and Richard H. Wilkinson; and *Tutankhamun: The Untold Story* by Thomas Hoving.

For more information on the Egyptian artifacts from Carnarvon's private collection, which Carter on his own likely sequestered in hidden cabinets at Highclere Castle in 1925, see *Ancient Egypt at Highclere Castle: Lord Carnarvon and the Search for Tutankhamun* by Nicholas Reeves. These artifacts resurfaced in 1987 after a retired butler pointed them out to the 7th Earl of Carnarvon. They are now on display in Highclere's Egyptian exhibit.

Lady Almina Carnarvon, a colorful and dynamic personality as well as a generous benefactress to charities, was beloved by Eve and all the Carnarvon family. Though she did not share the passion of her husband and daughter for archaeology, she probably did not try to stop Eve from going to Egypt. She was likely grateful to Eve for serving as her father's travel companion.

For more information about Lady Almina and Lady Catherine, I refer the reader to two excellently researched and written books by Fiona, Countess of Carnarvon: *Lady Almina and the Real Downton Abbey: The Lost Legacy of Highclere Castle* and *Lady Catherine, the Earl, and the Real Downton Abbey*. Several other family accounts also include details of Carnarvon family history during the early 1920s: *The Short Story of a Long Life* by P. E. Leatham (Eve's daughter, Patricia); *No Regrets: Memoirs of the Earl of Carnarvon* and *Ermine Tales: More Memoirs of the Earl of Carnarvon* by the 6th Earl of Carnarvon (Eve's brother). Such anecdotes as Brograve Beauchamp singing "God Save the King" while driving Carnarvon's Bugatti and Porchey selling heirlooms to art dealer Joseph Duveen, as well as Eve shining up pearls destined for a maharaja's turban, come from these accounts.

To cut back on the number of minor characters in the novel, I've combined the dialogues and actions of several anti-*Times* journalists into the personality of Arthur Weigall. To read about this fascinating, multitalented man, see *A Passion for Egypt: A Biography of Arthur Weigall* by Julie Hankey.

Two letters and telegrams in the book are recounted verbatim (pages 1[10], 125[11]); several others have been slightly modified from the original (pages 50, middle[12], 77[13], 78[14]). The rest were imagined, but tell of actual events.

Finally, "truth is stranger than fiction." Some of the more seemingly bizarre episodes in the novel come from historical accounts: Carter's canary swallowed by a cobra; Carnarvon's involvement with the spiritualists Velma and Cheiro, and their warnings that he should not return to Egypt; Susie the fox terrier dropping dead on the same day as her master; and the power outages at Highclere and Cairo during Lord Carnarvon's passing.

The novelist, to create a stirring story, must always blend fact with fiction. I hope that readers will not be stopped by fictional constructs and, instead, will join in Eve's feelings of magic, enchantment, and excitement over the most fantastic archaeological discovery of all time. Eve was there. It's my hope that you have enjoyed watching over Eve's shoulder.

---

[10] James, 252.

[11] James, 293-294.

[12] Hoving, 117.

[13] Collins and Ogilvie-Herald, 95.

[14] James, 464.

SELECT BIBLIOGRAPHY

Carnarvon, Fiona, The Eighth Countess. *Carnarvon and Carter: The Story of the Two Englishmen Who Discovered the Tomb of Tutankhamun.* Newbury: Highclere Enterprises, 2007.

———. *Egypt at Highclere: The Discovery of Tutankhamun.* Newbury: Highclere Enterprises, 2009.

———. *Highclere Castle: The Home of the 8th Earl & Countess of Carnarvon.* Newbury: Highclere Enterprises, 2011.

———. *Lady Almina and the Real Downton Abbey: The Lost Legacy of Highclere Castle.* London: Hodder & Stoughton, 2011.

———. *Lady Catherine, the Earl, and the Real Downton Abbey.* London: Hodder & Stoughton, 2013.

Carnarvon, Earl of, *Ermine Tales: More Memoirs of the Earl of Carnarvon.* London: Weidenfeld and Nicolson, 1980.

———. *No Regrets: Memoirs of the Earl of Carnarvon.* London: Weidenfeld & Nicolson, 1976.

Carter, Howard. *The Tomb of Tutankhamen.* New York: E. P. Dutton, 1972.

Collins, Andrew, and Chris Ogilvie-Herald. *Tutankhamun: The Exodus Conspiracy: The Truth Behind Archaeology's Greatest Mystery.* London: Virgin Books, 2003.

Fellowes, Jessica. *The Chronicles of Downton Abbey.* New York: St. Martin's Press, 2012.

———. *The World of Downton Abbey.* New York: St. Martin's Press, 2011.

———. *A Year in the Life of Downton Abbey.* New York: St. Martin's Press, 2014.

Hankey, Julie. *A Passion for Egypt: A Biography of Arthur Weigall.* London and New York: I. B. Tauris Publishers, 2001.

Hoving, Thomas. *Tutankhamun, The Untold Story.* New York: Simon and Schuster, 1978.

Humphreys, Andrew. *Grand Hotels of Egypt in the Golden Age of Travel.* Cairo and New York: The American University in Cairo Press, 2011.

James. T.G.H. *Howard Carter: The Path to Tutankhamun.* London and

New York: Taurus Parke Paperbacks, 2008.

Leatham, P. E. *The Short Story of a Long Life.* Hernes Keep, Winkfield, Windsor, Berkshire: Wilton 65, 2009.

Reeves, Nicholas. *Ancient Egypt at Highclere Castle: Lord Carnarvon and the Search for Tutankhamun.* Newbury, Berkshire, Highclere Castle, 1989.

————. *The Complete Tutankhamun: The King, The Tomb, The Royal Treasure.* London: Thames & Hudson, 1990.

——————. *Howard Carter: Before Tutankhamun.* New York: Harry N Abrams, 1993.

————, and Richard H. Wilkinson. *The Complete Valley of the Kings: Tombs and Treasures of Egypt's Greatest Pharaohs.* London: Thames & Hudson, 1996.

Thompson, Jason. *A History of Egypt: From Earliest Times to the Present.* New York: Anchor Books, 2008.

Winstone, H.V.F. *Howard Carter and the Discovery of the Tomb of Tutankhamun.* Manchester and Beirut: Barzan Publishing, 2007.

ACKNOWLEDGMENTS

Thank you to so many people for making my longtime dream of publishing *To Chase the Glowing Hours* a reality.

Jaynie Royal, Founder, Publisher, and Editor-in-Chief of Regal House, you are my happy ending. I'm thrilled to have found an editor who has a graduate degree in archaeology. Jaynie, Pam Van Dyk, Elizabeth Lowenstein, the Regal Team, and fellow Regal authors, my thoughts are always with you as we forge ahead in the challenging environment of book publishing today.

For editorial assistance, I thank Cindy Kane, line editor, Renée Cafiero, copy editor, and Diane Amison-Loring, proofreader. I remember with fondness the late Peter Nelson, who edited an early draft, and I thank Greta Nelson for her friendship and belief.

I'm indebted to University of Washington professor Scott Driscoll, and to all in our circle, especially: Dave Brewer, Danny Glasser, Mira Martinovic, Janet O'Leary, Elizabeth Sharpe, Rishabhkumar Shukla, Ember Sol, Rasa Tautvydas (The Write Tribe); Pamela Harlow, Karen Landen, Amy Muia, Dean Stahl, Ron Swanson; and workshop teachers Jennifer McCord and Roberta Trahan. I've relied heavily on your suggestions and insights.

I acknowledge the generous support of longtime writer friends, who happily came into my life through Madeleine L'Engle: Patricia Barry, Dana Catherine, Stephanie Cowell, Jane Mylum Gardner, Casey Kelly, Pamela Leggett, Judith Lindbergh, Andrea Simon, and Sanna Stanley; and to Amy Baruch, Stephanie Cowell, Linda Aronovsky Cox, Jane Mylum Gardner, Karen Finch, Rhonda Hunt-Del Bene, Kathleen M. Rodgers, and Andrea Simon (The Lady Bunch).

I appreciate my SCBWI friends Donna Bergman and Suzanne Williams. Mary Elizabeth Cresse, Cheryl Chapman, Carol Sue Janes, Vickie Johnson, Susan Swanson, Elizabeth Wein, and Karen Wennerstrom, you inspire me. Nancy Garrett, Nancy O'Leary Pew, and all Seattle Public Librarians past and present at the Lake City Branch, I'm your fan. Cheers to you, Shirley Litwak, for being an expert listener and insightful book critic.

Thanks to Jennifer Kirkpatrick, Eric Zicht, and Alice Zicht for accompanying me to Egypt; and thanks to Sidney Kirkpatrick and Nancy Webster Kirkpatrick for listening to me read the entire novel aloud and providing helpful insights.

To my own family, John, Alex, and Gwen, who put up with me for twelve years while I researched and wrote this book, you're the best.

Heartfelt gratitude to all.